MARTÍN RIVAS

LIBRARY OF LATIN AMERICA

OXFORD

MARTÍN RIVAS

A Novel by

ALBERTO BLEST GANA

Translated from the Spanish by

TESS O'DWYER

With an Introduction by

JAIME CONCHA

2000

OXFORD
UNIVERSITY PRESS

Oxford New York
Athens Auckland Bangkok Bogotá Bombay
Buenos Aires Calcutta Cape Town Dar es Salaam Delhi
Florence Hong Kong Istanbul Karachi
Kuala Lumpur Madras Madrid Melbourne
Mexico City Nairobi Paris Singapore
Taipei Tokyo Toronto Warsaw

and associated companies in
Berlin Ibadan

Published by Oxford University Press, Inc.
198 Madison Avenue, New York, New York 10016

Copyright Data on file

1 3 5 7 9 8 6 4 2

Printed in the United States of America
on acid free paper

To my mother and father
Chung Soon and Jack O'Dwyer

Contents

Series Editors' General Introduction

The Library of Latin America series makes available in translation major nineteenth-century authors whose work has been neglected in the English-speaking world. The titles for the translations from the Spanish and Portuguese were suggested by an editorial committee that included Jean Franco (general editor responsible for works in Spanish), Richard Graham (series editor responsible for works in Portuguese), Tulio Halperín Donghi (at the University of California, Berkeley), Iván Jaksić (at the University of Notre Dame), Naomi Lindstrom (at the University of Texas at Austin), Francine Masiello (at the University of California, Berkeley), and Eduardo Lozano of the Library at the University of Pittsburgh. The late Antonio Cornejo Polar of the University of California, Berkeley, was also one of the founding members of the committee. The translations have been funded thanks to the generosity of the Lampadia Foundation and the Andrew W. Mellon Foundation.

During the period of national formation between 1810 and into the early years of the twentieth century, the new nations of Latin America fashioned their identities, drew up constitutions, engaged in bitter struggles over territory, and debated questions of education, government, ethnicity, and culture. This was a unique period unlike the process of nation formation in Europe and one which should be more familiar than it is to students of comparative politics, history, and literature.

The image of the nation was envisioned by the lettered classes —a minority in countries in which indigenous, mestizo, black, or mulatto peasants and slaves predominated—although there were also alternative nationalisms at the grassroots level. The cultural elite were well educated in European thought and letters, but as statesmen, journalists, poets, and academics, they confronted the problem of the racial and linguistic heterogeneity of the continent and the difficulties of integrating the population into a modern nation-state. Some of the writers whose works will be translated in the Library of Latin America series played leading roles in politics. Fray Servando Teresa de Mier, a friar who translated Rousseau's *The Social Contract* and was one of the most colorful characters of the independence period, was faced with imprisonment and expulsion from Mexico for his heterodox beliefs; on his return, after independence, he was elected to the congress. Domingo Faustino Sarmiento, exiled from his native Argentina under the presidency of Rosas, wrote *Facundo: Civilización y barbarie,* a stinging denunciation of that government. He returned after Rosas' overthrow and was elected president in 1868. Andrés Bello was born in Venezuela, lived in London where he published poetry during the independence period, settled in Chile where he founded the University, wrote his grammar of the Spanish language, and drew up the country's legal code.

These post-independence intelligentsia were not simply dreaming castles in the air, but vitally contributed to the founding of nations and the shaping of culture. The advantage of hindsight may make us aware of problems they themselves did not foresee, but this should not affect our assessment of their truly astonishing energies and achievements. It is still surprising that the writing of Andrés Bello, who contributed fundamental works to so many different fields, has never been translated into English. Although there is a recent translation of Sarmiento's celebrated *Facundo,* there is no translation of his memoirs, *Recuerdos de provincia (Provincial Recollections).* The predominance of memoirs in the Library of Latin America series is no accident—

many of these offer entertaining insights into a vast and complex continent.

Nor have we neglected the novel. The series includes new translations of the outstanding Brazilian writer Joaquim Maria Machado de Assis' work, including *Dom Casmurro* and *The Posthumous Memoirs of Brás Cubas.* There is no reason why other novels and writers who are not so well known outside Latin America—the Peruvian novelist Clorinda Matto de Turner's *Aves sin nido,* Nataniel Aguirre's *Juan de la Rosa,* José de Alencar's *Iracema,* Juana Manuela Gorriti's short stories—should not be read with as much interest as the political novels of Anthony Trollope.

A series on nineteenth-century Latin America cannot, however, be limited to literary genres such as the novel, the poem, and the short story. The literature of independent Latin America was eclectic and strongly influenced by the periodical press newly liberated from scrutiny by colonial authorities and the Inquisition. Newspapers were miscellanies of fiction, essays, poems, and translations from all manner of European writing. The novels written on the eve of Mexican Independence by José Joaquín Fernández de Lizardi included disquisitions on secular education and law, and denunciations of the evils of gaming and idleness. Other works, such as a well-known poem by Andrés Bello, "Ode to Tropical Agriculture," and novels such as *Amalia* by José Mármol and the Bolivian Nataniel Aguirre's *Juan de la Rosa,* were openly partisan. By the end of the century, sophisticated scholars were beginning to address the history of their countries, as did João Capistrano de Abreu in his *Capítulos de história colonial.*

It is often in memoirs such as those by Fray Servando Teresa de Mier or Sarmiento that we find the descriptions of everyday life that in Europe were incorporated into the realist novel. Latin American literature at this time was seen largely as a pedagogical tool, a "light" alternative to speeches, sermons, and philosophical tracts—though, in fact, especially in the early part of the century, even the readership for novels was quite small because of the high rate of illiteracy. Nevertheless, the vigorous orally transmitted culture of the gaucho and the urban underclasses became the linguistic repertoire of some of the most interesting nineteenth-century writers—most notably José Hernández, author of the "gauchesque" poem "Martín Fierro," which enjoyed an unparalleled popularity. But for many writers the task was not to appropriate popular language but to civilize, and their literary works were strongly influenced by the high style of political oratory.

The editorial committee has not attempted to limit its selection to the better-known writers such as Machado de Assis; it has also selected many works that have never appeared in translation or writers whose work has not been translated recently. The series now makes these works available to the English-speaking public.

Because of the preferences of funding organizations, the series initially focuses on writing from Brazil, the Southern Cone, the Andean region, and Mexico. Each of our editions will have an introduction that places the work in its appropriate context and includes explanatory notes.

We owe special thanks to Robert Glynn of the Lampadia Foundation, whose initiative gave the project a jump start, and to Richard Ekman of the Andrew W. Mellon Foundation, which also generously supported the project. We also thank the Rockefeller Foundation for funding the 1996 symposium "Culture and Nation in Iberoamerica," organized by the editorial board of the Library of Latin America. We received substantial institutional support and personal encouragement from the Institute of Latin American Studies of the University of Texas at Austin. The support of Edward Barry of Oxford University Press has been crucial, as has the advice and help of Ellen Chodosh of Oxford University Press. The first volumes of the series were published after the untimely death, on July 3, 1997, of Maria C. Bulle, who, as an associate of the Lampadia Foundation, supported the idea from its beginning.

—Jean Franco
—Richard Graham

Introduction

JAIME CONCHA

I

The work of the Chilean novelist Alberto Blest Gana (1830–1920) has secured an unquestioned place among nineteenth-century Spanish-American writers of note. While lacking in the ideological complexity expressed in the work of the Argentine Domingo F. Sarmiento (1811–88) and surely very distant from the intellectual and political scope evident in Cuba's José Martí's work (1853–95), Blest Gana stands, nevertheless, as the author of a significant literary corpus, consisting principally of novels, which has across the years reached a wide audience, especially within Chile. Requisite reading in the education of Chileans as Chileans, his works have become key components of the national imagination. Admittedly, Blest Gana by no means possesses the esthetic sensibility of Jorge Isaacs, the Colombian author of *María* (1867), nor does he share the colonial background that provides breadth and richness to the works of Ricardo Palma (1833–1919), his Peruvian contemporary. And yet, fully understanding Chilean literature is inconceivable without accounting for Blest Gana's narrative project to tell the story—and the history—of the new South American republic from the early years of the struggles for independence on through to the gray, even obscure climate at the close of the nineteenth century.

One of the best, and clearly the most popular, of his novels is *Martín Rivas* (1863), a work that English-speaking readers can now read translated into the language of one of Blest Gana's forebears.

II

Blest Gana's family background would seem to provide many keys to understanding the future writer's political and literary propensities. Alberto Blest Gana was born June 16, 1830, into the household of Guillermo Cunninghan Blest and María de la Luz Gana, who had married in 1827. Born in Ireland, Guillermo Cunninghan Blest had arrived in Chile in the early 1820s. Prospects in Chile were bright: Independence was secured and O'Higgins's government welcomed British immigration. Studying in Edinburgh and Dublin, where he trained as a physician, Blest Gana's father, with the support offered first by Minister Portales and later by Andrés Bello, would be instrumental in the development of the study and teaching of medicine in Chile. These political connections might suggest Cunninghan Blest's Liberalism to be of a rather moderate character, akin to an English Liberalism linked to the 1688 revolution. His political stance and especially his participation in the university student-led condemnation of the government's banning of Bilbao's *Sociabilidad chilena/Chilean Society* in 1844 suggest that this was not, however, the case. What is clear is that both the father's Liberal political leanings and medical profession had a decisive influence on the young Blest Gana. The works of Walter Scott and Charles Dickens undoubtedly figured among his earliest readings. And while critics have tended to focus on the impact of French writers in his work (Balzac, Stendhal, Sue, and even Hugo),[1] it is obvious that narrative and compositional techniques, and even moral stances, in his first works point to an early formative influence of Dickens. While perhaps out of synch with the Chilean historical and literary milieu of the times, it should be noted that Blest Gana's father's profession probably led to his developing an analytical bent that contributed to the development of his observational and critical faculties.

Blest Gana's mother's family—of Basque origins—on the other hand, had already been in Chile for many years. Arriving in the mid-eighteenth century, they belonged to the landholding class and several family members had pursued military careers; some of Blest Gana's maternal relatives were officials in the Chilean Independence struggles. This military background would have a formative role in Blest Gana's early education, as we see him enrolled in the National Institute in 1841 and later, in 1843, on the rolls of the Chilean Military Academy.

Cunninghan Blest fathered several illegitimate children—not an uncommon occurrence in the Chile of the period, and elsewhere for that matter. The three "legitimate" male Blest Gana offspring, however, followed family tradition and pursued intellectual or literary careers. Alberto, of course, was to become a writer, but Guillermo, the eldest, and Joaquín, the youngest, would also both write and see their works published. Guillermo Blest Gana, best known as poet and historical playwright and writer of nationalist and intimist poetry, left three volumes of solid work. Despite the questionable overall caliber of Chilean romantic poetry when compared to that of other countries, Guillermo Blest Gana is without a doubt Chile's chief nineteenth-century romantic poet. When Rubén Darío visited Valparaíso at century's end, his appreciation for Guillermo Blest Gana's poetry appears genuine and not merely the perfunctory praises of a guest visiting Chile for the first time. Aside from Guillermo Blest Gana's poetry, we should also note his place in the political events that shaped Chile; in 1858 he took part in a revolt against the Montt government—for which activity he was sentenced to death and was saved only by his father's political connections and after agreeing to leave Chile. After living in exile in Perú for several years, Guillermo Blest Gana would be granted amnesty by the incoming president and return to Chile in 1862 to serve long and faithfully under Balmaceda.

Joaquín, the youngest Blest Gana brother, on the other hand, presents us with a much less likable figure. According to most versions, he was at best accommodating and at worst opportunistic in his dealings. A journalist and politician, he made it a point to curry favor with whatever party held power at a given time, a tactic that allowed him to benefit from his ties to the Ministries and Parliament.

What is striking in all of this is the fact that political behaviors exhibited by the Blest Gana family are in direct correspondence to the various options characterized by "political agreement" of the ruling Chilean clans of the period. We have the meshing of the father's professional bourgeoisie with the landed oligarchy represented by the mother's side of the family; the former's moderate and occasional strident Liberalism is taken to its extreme political limits by Guillermo but is blunted in the case of Joaquín. Alberto Blest Gana's political stance, evidenced in *Martín Rivas* and his other works, assumes an intermediate, if contradictory, political positioning that allows for an exaltation of political action tempered by moderation. It is in this fashion that Blest Gana manages to inscribe the operating social and political reality of the period, evidenced as well within his own family: both moderate and radical versions of Liberalism were contemporaneous, mutually determined rather than mutually exclusive. In light of this, it is likely that Blest Gana's playing out of these two political tracks derives less from the novelist's attempt at providing an objective "take" on Chile's political arena and more from Blest Gana's well-honed practice of political prudence and equilibrium, traits that seem perhaps more in keeping with the tactics of a diplomat than those of a writer!

Despite inhabiting the always hazy and contradictory world of the diplomatic corps, Blest Gana was not marginal to the key political events that shaped both Chilean and world history. He was, in fact, an eyewitness to two of the pivotal events in the class-based struggles developing in Europe at the time: the June insurrection of 1848 and the Paris Commune in 1871. He is an 18-year-old military engineering student on a government scholarship in Versailles when the first great proletarian revolution erupts. When the *communards* take over Paris in 1871, Blest Gana, the diplomat, is in Paris once again, dealing principally with matters having to do with the recent Franco-Prussian War. And as far as events in Chile are concerned, Blest Gana would, upon his return from studying in Europe, witness the final moments of the 1851 Liberal uprising. His positioning as an eyewitness to these crucial Chilean and international nineteenth-century events could not have other than impacted Blest Gana and left its mark on his writings, especially since his works are profoundly invested in portraying both Chilean history and the avatars of Liberal ideology. In light of this, to say that Blest Gana "was not drawn to politics. Social issues left him cold. The tumult of 1848 left no mark on him"[2] would seem, at best, unfounded.

There is, in fact, clear proof of the keen interest with which the young novelist observed the events that brought about the fall of France's July Monarchy (1830–48). We find it in a brief novel entitled *Los desposados/The Newlyweds,* published in Santiago's *Revista de Santiago* soon after Blest Gana's return to Chile. While the narrative is primarily a romantic melodrama, it does offer a vivid portrayal of political events in Paris.

> On June 23rd, 1848, the city of Paris was the scene of one of the bloodiest combats ever seen in this bristling center: the canon and gunshots echoed everywhere, all the streets were taken over by military forces and one could see the terror in the faces of the few who ventured out of their homes. It was a terrible battle to the death; the different factions waged an unbridled combat in the great capital city. There was talk of Legitimists allying with Bonapartists against the power of the National Assembly; it was said that both parties had roused tensions in the city and among workers on leave, which ultimately led to the rioting later to be known as the Revolution of June; these were days of great desolation and bloodshed, during which more than ten thousand citizens fell victim—either dead or wounded—in the course of that useless—even if valiant and stubborn—sacrifice.[3]

The melodrama's key players stand for specific and identifiable social actors. The novel's antagonist, Alphonse Dunoye, who stands as the chief obstacle to the lovers' happiness, is described in clearly defined social terms:

> A member of the French bourgeoisie class, this merchant, had by virtue of doing well in commerce and more notably by his holding a seat in the National Assembly, managed to surround himself with an aura of importance and intransigence that enabled him to exert a good measure of influence in government circles and absolute dominance in all matters relating to home.[4]

Later in the novel, drawing out this same description, Blest Gana terms Dunoye "a domestic tyrant"; this stands in marked contrast to the portrayal of Luis d'Orville as "a poor student, without means or mentors" who is in love with Dunoye's daughter. The most the young hero can attain to is a position in the Ministry of Public Works, a post from which he is fired thanks to Dunoye's machinations in the Assembly. If in *The Newlyweds* we have the oppositional pair Dunoye versus d'Orville, in *Martín Rivas* a similar antagonistic relationship exists between Dámaso and Martín; moreover, d'Orville's character anticipates both *Martín Rivas*'s Rafael San Luis—in his battle in defense of Liberal ideology—as well as Martín Rivas, insofar as his social background and class status are concerned. This emphasis on the characters' social origins and location, as well as *The Newlyweds*' representation of the populace in arms as an "undisciplined and rabid mob," will foreshadow the portrayal of the masses in the 1862 novel.

III

The Newlyweds, published in 1855, belongs to what we could designate the first phase of Blest Gana's work. Having left the armed forces in 1853, the fledgling author secures a position in the civil service. Foremost in his mind, however, is becoming a writer; part of that project involves establishing the groundwork for a national Chilean literature. We can, in part, follow Blest Gana's project and his determination to focus on his literary undertaking in his correspondence with fellow Chilean José Antonio Donoso, who had been to Europe with Blest Gana. Even during these early years in which Blest Gana is still developing as a writer and delineating what will be his overarching literary project, he already has a clear vision of the primacy and urgency of "setting down the foundations of the literary edifice that the nation needs,"[5] as he stresses to Donoso in an 1856 letter.

Later, in a highly expressive letter written to Vicuña Mackenna, we find Blest Gana explaining how "after reading Balzac,"[6] and thanks to the master's example and inspiration, he moved away from his initial interest in writing lyric poetry—traces of which are especially evident in his early narratives. In breaking with poetry Blest Gana defines himself as a novelist and at the same time sets a separate literary course from that of his brother. Still, this poetic prehistory, even if soon set aside, will leave marked traces in his earliest works, particularly in one of his key characters, often cast as a hero-poet or figured as a young and sensitive dreamer.

Blest Gana's turn toward narrative as a result of his reading the work of the principal European novelist of the first half of the nineteenth century is neither insignificant nor coincidental. The connection is revealing in several respects. First, there is a clear link between Balzac's *Human Comedy* and the history of revolutionary and postrevolutionary France (1789–1848) with Blest Gana's idea of a series of historical novels on Chile, a project that as early as 1860 is the driving force behind his work. Second, one can also see a correlation between this initial decade of novelistic trials and narrative experimentation that characterizes Blest Gana's work in the 1850s and 1860s and the early Balzac, say from his schematized play *Cromwell* in 1819 to his unsigned serialized novels. What we could term the apogee of Balzac's art has its seed in these early works. His *Human Comedy* is, as is well known, born in that little gem of a work, *Les chouans* (1829), which narrates the counterrevolutionary activities of the *Vendée* in France's western provinces. Third, like Balzac's narrative project for a series of historical novels, Blest Gana's, too, is conceived in a postrevolutionary period. Just as Balzac writes between 1830 and 1848, after the French July Revolution, and just as Zola, for his part, conceives of his tableau on the Second Empire after the events of the Paris Commune, so too Blest Gana, even if considered to be working in a minor scale, will take on the most representative part of his work once Chile's *Girondin* uprisings of 1851 and 1859 have taken place. Thus we encounter the bourgeois novel as—almost always—an attempt to carry out a retrieval of lost ideals, something patently evident in the very titles of Blest Gana's novels.

Aside from an isolated early attempt at writing a dramatic piece *(El jefe de la familia/Head of the Household,* 1858) Blest Gana writes seven short novels during this period. The events narrated take place as follows: two are set in Paris (the already mentioned *The Newlyweds,* 1855; and *La fascinación/Fascination,* 1858, the latter set in the world of *elegantes* and *artistes)*; four, by contrast, have settings that are both Chilean and urban: *Una escena social/A Social Scene,* 1853; *Engaños y desengaños/Deceptions and Disillusionments,*

1855; *El primer amor/First Love,* 1858; and *Juan de Aria,* 1859; only one novel during this period presents a rural setting, *Un drama en el campo/A Drama in the Countryside,* 1859. The novel's denouements abound in suicides, deaths, and cases of madness, fixing the truculent and melodramatic tone of a good many scenes and episodes.[7] Their national specificity aside, Eugène Sue's and Charles Dickens's influence converge here to provide us with strongly sentimentalized characters and a highly dramatic and rhetorical dialogue. At bottom, the problem Blest Gana faces in these narratives is the impossibility of reconciling feeling and reality, soul and society, love and money. There will be vestiges of this dilemma in the next phase of his work, in tales such as *El pago de las deudas/The Repayment of Debts* (1861) and *Venganza/Revenge* and *Marilúan,* the latter two appearing in 1864. It is evident that, at this stage in the novelist's development, Blest Gana has not yet come upon the appropriate formula for dealing with what he terms "the conditions of life" and "its everyday incidents."[8] His perspective is wholly idealist at this stage. In order to more fully capture the nature of Chilean social life Blest Gana will not only have to work out his narratives further, but also work on his dialogue, descriptions, and character development, grounding these elements in solid national soil, that is, the historical humus that the Chile of the period provides him.

IV

In a letter dated December 7, 1863, addressed to the newspaper correspondent mentioned above, Blest Gana writes: "I need not tell you, I suppose, that the greater part of the scenes and characters in *El Ideal* are taken from reality. You know, of course, or I'll tell you in case you don't, that since I wrote *La aritmética del amor/The Arithmetic of Love,* that is, since I wrote the first novel which I consider Chilean literature, my artistic principle has been to copy the everyday accidents of life to the degree that Art can. I have been especially painstaking in applying this principle in *El ideal de un calavera/An Ideal Rogue.*"[9]

Blest Gana had published three of his most important novels—

The Arithmetic of Love, (1860), *Martín Rivas* (1862), and *An Ideal Rogue* (1863)—by the time he wrote this letter. Thereafter, there is a marked hiatus in his literary production, principally due to his administrative duties as Governor in Colchagua, and later, his diplomatic postings to Washington, London, and Paris. Under President Balmaceda's administration he resigns from his post as Chilean representative, ending his long life in Paris, in 1920. Some of Blest Gana's most important novels belong to his later years, including *Durante la Reconquista/During the Reconquest* (1897), *The Uprooted* (1904), and *El loco Estero/The Madman Estero* (1909). These works reveal an entirely different problematic which goes beyond the scope of this introduction. They will be mentioned only tangentially insofar as they relate to *Martín Rivas.*

The three most important works of what we have termed Blest Gana's second phase are closely bound together. Their very interrelatedness, in turn, sheds special light on each of the novels in question. *Martín Rivas* marks a decisive moment in Blest Gana's development as a writer, and assumes an intermediate point between *The Arithmetic of Love* and *An Ideal Rogue.* In *The Arithmetic of Love* the dominant tone is that of conciliation, while in *An Ideal Rogue,* we can see how the sociohistorical matrix provides the work with greater density and depth. Fortunato Esperanzado is linked to Martín in terms of his upward social mobility; for his part, Abelardo Manrique, *An Ideal Rogue*'s hero, operates as Rafael San Luis's correlate. In this fashion, the increasingly historical specificity gives rise to our having the key bourgeois protagonist presented as a seemingly complementary double figure, although in the end the two ultimately develop as necessarily antithetical. This bourgeois Janus has Jacobin and Liberal faces, but they are body and soul of the selfsame historical reality that provides for the death of one and the triumph—however accommodating and prosaic—of the other. The anti-Portales rebel of 1837 and the *Girondin* hero of 1851 are vanquished in Blest Gana's novels, enabling the prototypical bourgeois figure to move forward and upward socially, as is the case with Martín Rivas, who emerges unscathed from the political battles and is newly positioned to be the ultimate winner. The particulars of this process is what will interest us next.

V

Blest Gana provides precise historical dates for the events narrated in *Martín Rivas.* The novel's plot begins in July 1850 and culminates in October 1851, not coincidentally framing a crucial moment in Chile's political history. It is during these years that Chile's first major Liberal revolution is shaped; starting with street riots and barracks uprisings, the revolt attains a national scope with events such as the rebellions in the northern provinces, the Army revolt in the south, and the bloody events led by Cambiaso in Punta Arenas, standing out as watershed moments of this major collective phenomenon.

There are incontrovertible links between these episodes in Chile and the events taking place in 1848 in France. Historians dealing with this period, including Vicuña Mackenna and Francisco Antonio Encina, are in agreement with respect to this connection. Speaking of the set of historical factors that led to the Chilean Liberal revolution, Encina remarks on "the powerful influence of the 1848 Revolution and the fall of the French monarchy."[10] The key proponents of this version of history are none other than the so-called Chilean Girondins, expatriates living in France, like Francisco Bilbao or Santiago Arcos, who within the *Sociedad de la Igualdad* provide the movement with its driving force and radical Liberal ferment.

The weight and impact of French events in 1848 on Chile's national life is best seen in Blest Gana's writings, especially in his characters' dialogues. In the following exchange Don Dámaso's son refers to these events with his characteristic frivolity:

> "In Paris there are many political parties," said Agustín. "The Orleanists, the Bourbon *brancha,* and the Republicans."
>
> "The *brancha?*" asked Don Dámaso.
>
> "The Bourbon line, in other words," replied Agustín.
>
> "They say everyone up north belongs to the Opposition," said Don Dámaso, addressing Martín again.
>
> "I think that is the generalization," he responded.[11]

We should recall that Blest Gana comments on these events from a distance of ten years. From the onset, we should be aware that it is not, however, a purely formal device alone that is at work here, separating the historical events from their literary representation. The interim period is in no way homogeneous, but rather defined by the vicissitudes of Chilean political life. The ten years or so from 1851 to 1862 cannot be taken as a simple temporal demarcation, but rather as an experience; they not only demarcate a temporal distance, but also what we might term an ethical distance. They signal, above and beyond all else, a rejection of a previous moment. Therein lies the real objective of the operation carried out by the novel upon its historical material.

In fact, Martín Rivas entirely omits mentioning the 1859 revolution and gives relative short shrift to the events of 1851. No mention is made of the key uprisings in the country's north, and the novel's plot deals exclusively with events in the capital, focusing only on Urriola's revolt and ending precisely prior to the spreading of the revolt throughout the country. Blest Gana's bracketing of the revolt—halting the narrative precisely prior to its taking on a national character—cannot but have a special significance, as it reveals to us Blest Gana's system of exclusions and preferences as he looks back on these events from a distance of ten years. Blest Gana's selection allows him, on the one hand, to avoid dealing with his own family's involvement in the revolution (i.e., his brother's role in the revolt) while, simultaneously, and more importantly, privileging and giving special weight to one particular event within a complex historical process. In order to understand better Blest Gana's political positioning we need to consider carefully the whys and wherefores of these series of choices.

To understand what is at stake it is worthwhile to look for a moment at what takes place in *The Arithmetic of Love,* as it is highly revealing. Critics have commented in detail on the novel's Part II, arguing that it lacks cohesion and that it fails to follow through on its premise of fully portraying the world it seeks to represent. One crucial issue, however, has gone curiously unnoticed: the novel's plot and intrigues—all taking place in some unnamed provincial town—can, in a sense, be seen as a grotesque parody of the confusing and highly contested state of national politics of the period in question. The struggles and antipathies portrayed, the backroom pacts between the novel's Selgas and Ruiplán factions, for example, are but thinly veiled transpositions of the divisions, most more apparent than real, which characterized the Chilean political scene of the period. Despite its being granted a prize by the Universidad de Chile, there is a way in which we can speak, then, of *The Arithmetic of Love* as a failed attempt; but it is precisely where it fails that is of interest to us since it reveals what will be increasingly evident in Blest Gana's novels: his inability or unwillingness to deal with historical material that he finds ever more unpalatable, leading him to focus his next novel, *Martín Rivas,* on the events of 1851.

We should recall that it is precisely during this period in Chile that the political parties standing in opposition to Manuel Montt's government undergo a major reshuffling. At the beginning of Montt's second term, the majority of the Liberal Party makes an alliance (some have termed it a fusion) with an important segment of the Conservative Party, a coalition that had perhaps more to do with common interests and less to do with what some have posited as a shared hate for Montt. Be that as it may, this union of parties had the effect of blurring the lines between Liberals and Conservatives. Organized by Manuel Antonio Tocornal and Domingo Santa María, that unseemly coalition of political enemies would seem untenable to a whole set of Liberals who upheld the hardline Pipiolist principles and who considered it ideologically unthinkable to amalgamate proclergy precepts with rationalist notions. This 1857 alliance, deemed unacceptable by many Liberals, is at the very core of Blest Gana's critique.

In his *The Arithmetic of Love* Blest Gana takes on his own party members' political opportunism and ideological vagaries, making them the object of a sardonic comical representation. His portrayal of these meandering Liberals dovetails with that made by a contemporary historian who states:

> In order to please the few survivors—headed by don Benjamín Vicuña Mackenna—who were in an uproar, as well as to appease the future Radicals, the owners of Copiapó and of the greatest fortunes of the period poised to be invested in Chile's regeneration, a farce was agreed upon. Tocornal would open the door to a formal agreement between parties, by asking the Liberals how they saw matters, and Domingo Santa María would, in turn, consent to the

> alliance with the stipulation that the 1833 Constitution be amended to provide for freedom of religion.[12]

It is apparent that *The Arithmetic of Love* reenacts this same "farce," the same lack of ideological coherence and conviction that Blest Gana detected and critiqued in the bourgeoisie of the period. Even so, his bracketing of the events of 1851, along with his blindness in regard to the events of 1859, obliges us to see that Blest Gana's highly selective thematic choices in *Martín Rivas* are in no way arbitrary. On the contrary, the justification must be sought out in the novel's implicit rejection of the political deal-making between Liberals and Conservatives in the year 1857, a highly significant date, moreover, in Blest Gana's literary production. It is in this polemical political light that we can better understand why subsequent editions of *Martín Rivas* dispensed with the Blest Gana's original subtitle: *A Novel of Politico-Social Customs.*

Among the many novels subsequently written by Blest Gana, none hereafter deal with national events after that crucial 1857 date. In fact, his most important works (excepting *The Uprooted,* 1904, dealing with the lives of Chilean expatriate bourgeoisie—which either remains outside these considerations or ratifies them decisively) present us with settings that recede in Chile's historical time. *An Ideal Rogue* narrates the assassination of Minister Portales in 1837; *The Madman Estero* is set at the end of the Chilean war against the Peruvian-Bolivian Confederation; and most patently, *During the Reconquest* pretends to seek out something akin to the roots of Chile's nationhood in the bygone days of the struggles for Independence. The particular circumstances surrounding this last novel are especially revealing. *During the Reconquest* appeared in 1897, some years after the events of the civil war of 1891, which although Blest Gana followed from abroad undoubtedly had a profound impact on him. In this novel Blest Gana carefully scrutinizes and selects from the complex process of Chilean Independence the phase that reveals the greatest display of patriotic energies and involvement of popular forces, that is, the guerrillas and the peasant uprisings of Manuel Rodríguez. Interestingly, Blest Gana's rendering of this period contrasts sharply with, for example, that of Luis Orrego Luco, whose novel, *1810. Memorias de un voluntario de la Patria Vieja/Memoirs of a Volunteer of the Early Independence,* focuses on the initial stages of the struggle for Independence, centering on the political intrigue and legalistic debates of the period and necessarily highlighting the role played by the lawyer Juan Martínez de Rozas.

Thus, if we follow the trajectory of his works, there is for Blest Gana one watershed period in Chile's history: the middle decade of the century, and more concretely, the year 1857. This year stands out as the moment of crisis and insuperable horizon for Blest Gana's Liberal ideology. Later, as the century winds down and the twentieth begins, Blest Gana will increasingly focus on the early years of the Chilean nation. His 1897 novel, *During the Reconquest,* deals, as we have already seen, with events of the year 1814; these dates give us two historical poles between which lies a great chasm, precisely the one produced by the ideological crisis that arises and that underpins the historical events narrated in *Martín Rivas.* This goes far in explaining why the Urriola revolt is placed at center stage in the narrative and is the focal point around which the novel's events revolve. Involving as it did large sectors of the population, Blest Gana selects this turbulent historical scenario for underscoring the heroic agency of the bourgeoisie. Only there, within Chile's national boundaries, do we find an instance in which personal élan, the crowning superiority of the leader, is coupled with the fighting zeal of the anonymous popular masses. We thus find these masses—portrayed picturesquely elsewhere in the novel via quaint *costumbrista* sketches of manners, as in the section dealing with the national patriotic celebrations—take on, in the key Plaza de Armas scene, an entirely different role: they are now the substrate, both collective and popular, which buttresses and gives impetus to the acts of Chile's Liberal and progressive political forces.[13]

As so it is that in *Martín Rivas,* Rafael San Luis's sacrifice, along with Martín's wounding during the key battle, enables the investiture of a heroic scope for the events of April 1851 for Chile's history. Henceforth, precisely after *Martín Rivas,* the confluence of the hero and the popular masses in Blest Gana's novels will no longer be the motor force of historical events; rather the contrary will be the case, with the notion that such a shared vision is something only to be reminisced about and realized only through a process of novelistic reconstruction. How, then, are we to understand the exaltation and centrality given to the popular masses in *During the Reconquest?* Here we must observe with care that this exalted representation is depicted as belonging to a glorious but entirely bygone era, a glorious but closed chapter in the nation's past. So it is that *During the Reconquest,* despite its popular, Liberal, and even revolutionary subject matter, represents in reality the death knell of Blest Gana's Liberal political ideals. With the turn of events at mid-century, the actualization of a Liberal politics in Chile lies henceforth for Blest Gana outside the realm of possibility.

It is precisely this temporal and historical demarcation that enables positing as a valid hypothesis what we might term an ulterior ideological motivation underpinning *Martín Rivas.* The fact that the novel is dedicated to Manuel Antonio Matta, among the most stalwart defenders of the anticlerical wing of Chile's Liberals, is not without relevance. Matta, as is well known, would soon become the driving force behind the creation of Chile's Radical party. The publishing house that prints *Martín Rivas* also publishes the newspaper *La Voz de Chile,* which will enable the voice of disenchanted Chilean Liberals to coalesce until they break off to form a new political party. In fact, *Martín Rivas* first appears in serialized form in this same evening paper, which also published essays written by Isidoro Errázuriz, the Gallos, and Matta himself. Among the many telling articles published in *La Voz* we find, for example, that Matta penned numerous opinion pieces; in *Política,* for example, the writer moves away from issues of individual will, the cornerstone of early Liberal thought, calling instead for a series of laws to monitor the arbitrariness of behaviors. We are here obviously faced with a different phase of Chilean Liberalism, a different sense of an organization with its attendant class ideology. Matta's article, *Proposal for a Law Exempting Taxation on Copper Smelted with Native Fuels,*[14] for example, advocates waiving tariffs for copper export across the board and not on a case by case basis—in keeping with Courcelle-Seneuil principles—and strictly in line with the financial interests of Chile's mining bourgeoisie; so too in another piece, *Chile's Coal,*[15] we find Matta espousing a clear sense of shared goals when he states: "We do not wish to see the creation of antagonisms between the mining interests of the northern and southern sectors of the Republic."

We need to keep this particular context in mind as we consider the portrayal of the novel's hero, Martín Rivas, as representative of the northern mining provinces; more specifically, we need to see him as a prototype of the sector of mining bourgeoisie which would be the motor force behind the emergence of the new political party. Thus Martín Rivas is not to be taken so much as an exemplar of a compromised Chilean Liberalism but rather more as a prototype of a new—still at this stage inchoate—political entity. Moreover, it would be conceivable to suggest that the novel *Martín Rivas,* in fact, becomes the ideological vehicle by which this emergent mentality, and therefore ideology, is expressed and disseminated. As was the case with Lastarria in the 1840s, once again we find Chile's literature paralleling or even anticipating mind-sets that will afterward manifest themselves in the political sphere.

This observation allows for a point of clarification on a common misreading of Blest Gana's *Martín Rivas.* Melfi, for example, terms Martín Rivas *a hero of the middle class,* and, in a suspect and anachronistic move, links Blest Gana's mid-nineteenth-century protagonist to Chile's emergent middle class in the twentieth.[16] For his part, Alone exults on *Martín Rivas,* proposing that the novel reveals "the triumph of the poor, yet intelligent and hard-working middle class, over the pompous—although not entirely without merit—upper class."[17] Accounting for this assessment—this mirage, really—is only possible if we trace the class composition of adherents of Chile's Radical party, whose bourgeois nucleus managed to attain the consensus of other, less wealthy, sectors of the populace, also in search of political representation.

In sum, what we have in Martín Rivas is a character ostensibly born during the burgeoning of Pipiolismo, that is, before the Battle of Lircay (1830). We can infer this from the fact that in 1850, as the narrator states, Martín is *22* or *23*. We know, too, that he arrives in the capital from the northern mining districts of Coquimbo and Copiapó, unquestioned strongholds of the new bourgeoisie; his shaky financial situation notwithstanding, Martín Rivas pursues a career that during the period was the purview of only the wealthiest sectors of society.[18] All these features point to Martín Rivas as a clear stand-in for the national bourgeoisie; but we need to be clear on one point: he is an exemplar of this class not at its stage of full economic consolidation, but rather at its ideological moment of inception.

VI

The years covered in *Martín Rivas* coincide with a period of formidable capitalist development in Chile. We need only consider the following: national income grows fourfold in the space of sixteen years, derived principally from agricultural and mining exports (silver and copper).[19] Twice Blest Gana's novel makes mention of the importance that exports of grain to California have had for the Chilean economy. It is worth recalling that the market created as a result of California's Gold Rush firmly consolidated the export-oriented character of Chile's economy while at the same time set in motion a set of circumstances in which the interests of the ascendant Chilean industrial bourgeoisie would also be tied to investments in land and agriculture. This in turn led to a fusion between the traditional landed *hacendado* class and Chile's new capitalist sectors.[20] Against this historical and economic backdrop, *Martín Rivas* focuses on two perfectly identifiable moments—discrete and yet interrelated—in the constitution of Chile's bourgeoisie. These are given to us in the novel on two chronological planes, which allows for differences and nuance in the representation.

The character of Don Dámaso emblematizes the origins of the class in question; his ascendancy and shady dealings result in greater wealth and influence via the route made available then by Chile's capitalist development. Blest Gana 's position is absolutely clear and in a few brief lines he summarizes for us the benchmarks of this class's ascendancy:

> At the age of 24, Don Dámaso had married Doña Engracia Núñez, more for social advancement than for love. Back then, Doña Engracia's want of beauty was compensated by an inheritance of 30,000 pesos, which so incited the passions of the young Encina that he asked for her hand in marriage. Don Dámaso was employed

> by a commercial lending house in Valparaíso, and his meagre salary was all that lined his purse. However, the day after his wedding he had at his disposal 30,000 pesos with which to paint the town, and since then his ambitions knew no limit.[21]

In describing Don Dámaso's association with the father of Martín Rivas, Blest Gana provides us with information on Don Dámaso's mining investments, his financial speculation—still termed by the narrator "usury on a grand scale"—the purchase of a ranch near Santiago and a mansion in the Capital. We are also given Don Dámaso's ultimate ambition: his aspirations to secure a senator's seat in the nation's Parliament, the crowning touch of his bourgeois aspirations. Fostered by the heated economic environment generated by British commerce and investments, which were centered particularly in the city of Valparaíso, Blest Gana has us follow the course of Don Dámaso's social ascendancy: originally a simple employee he becomes rich with the boom in the silver market (these are the years of the Chañarcillo boom in the early 1830s) and soon thereafter we find him in the role of agricultural entrepreneur, rubbing shoulders with the old landed aristocracy and seeking to consolidate his economic position by means of access to political and legislative power. What in fact Blest Gana lays out before us is Martín Rivas's class apprenticeship and an itinerary for social ascendancy. It is worth remarking, for example, that as the novel opens we have Don Dámaso asking for the day's newspapers. As he does his daily reading, Don Dámaso is, in effect, reading himself and his social class. His reading of Government and Opposition viewpoints contained in the newspapers can be taken, moreover, as the height of class introspection!

Don Dámaso's social and financial ascent is launched at the age of 24. Martín Rivas, the text indicates, is—tellingly—"22 or 23" in the year 1850. Martín will marry at exactly the same age as his mentor. That the two coincide in this regard signals the contiguity that is established in the text between the bourgeois exemplar at the height of power and the young man who, poised to initiate his ascent, does so with a markedly higher degree of awareness of his social location and class agenda. Martín Rivas's narrative projection will be played out on three levels: his background and social origins, the friendships he establishes, and, finally, the object of his amorous affections.

Martín's Background

Martín is the son of José Rivas, who is described as an adventurer, a prospector in Chile's mining country, "a madman" who had lost his fortunes searching for an imaginary mother lode. In this sense, we can take Martín's father to stand for the epitome of individualist élan, the vitality of individual will and effort that corresponds to the earliest forms of capitalist development. In Chile, it has its correlate in the fabled figure of the prospector Juan Godoy, whose legend was picked up and later monopolized by men such as the Cousiños, the Gallos, and the Urmenetas. Within Blest Gana's narrative, the story of the intrepid miner José Rivas and his ultimate economic downfall offers a moving prehistory that stands in contrast to the cold and calculating prose of the consolidated bourgeoisie whose fortunes are diversified and secure. Foregrounding the values of unyielding tenacity and self-sacrifice that ostensibly characterized the beginnings of the bourgeois class, the figure of José Rivas provides Martín with a link to a more "heroic" class ancestry, that of its initial stages.

Martín's Friendships

If in the novel José Rivas is meant to be emblematic of a certain type of economic activity, Rafael San Luis carries out a similar role with respect to the realm of ideas and political action. This is precisely what makes the pairing of the two young friends especially noteworthy. *Martín Rivas* is very much about the "heroic dreams" of the bourgeosie. Martín will be wounded in the same battle in which his friend Rafael will perish; as a survivor of that combat in which Rafael gives up his life, Martín is cast as actively participating and sharing in these "heroic illusions." Rafael San Luis's passion and piercing gaze is manifest in Martín Rivas not outwardly, but by an invisible burning within, as evident in eyes that gaze out darkly, and Rafael's vigor and commitment are forever fixed in his friend's heart. Thus the portrayal of Martín Rivas, this meditative, somewhat austere, even cold exemplar of the new class, is—curiously and significantly—anchored, on the one hand, by a father's Quixotic economic background and, on the other, with the pathos of his best friend's sacrifice to Liberal ideals. The figure of Martín Rivas stands before us as the spawn of his own class, of its avatars and struggles, the product of individual wanderings in the desert and of bloody collective combats: the measured and well-groomed bourgeois man, full of talent and potential.

Martín's Loves

It should be clear by now that Blest Gana's *Martín Rivas* is about much more than affairs of the heart and romantic liaisons. The nature of the relationship that develops between Martín and Leonor, wherein the social coefficient is so pronounced, has the effect of catalyzing the expression of a class ideology. Thus, where José Rivas sublimates material practices and Rafael San Luis highlights political ideals, the figure of Leonor invests the class with spirit or soul—particularly in regard to its cultural endowment. The depiction of the novel's heroine bears this out:

> Their luxury served as a magnificent frame around the beautiful Leonor. Had anyone seen this 19-year-old girl in a shabby setting, he would have accused Fortune of being capricious for not creating an ambiance befitting her beauty. Thus, to behold her reclining upon a majestic sofa lined with celestial brocatelle, to catch her image reflected in a gothic mirror, to see her petite foot grazing free and easy over a Persian rug, anyone would have to admire the lavishness of Nature in blissful accord with the favors of Destiny. Leonor sparkled like a diamond surrounded by gold and precious gems.[22]

One cannot but remark on the fact that we are first given this portrait and the material splendor surrounding her in a description that resembles a finely inlaid piece of marquetry all prior to the description of Leonor's face. She is presented as yet another beautiful objet d'art among the ubiquitous markers of class, wealth, and refinement in the Encina household. This stands in stark contrast to how the novel brings Martín into focus; we see him first outside the house and progressively he is placed within it. The opposite is the case with Leonor; she first appears depicted in the interior scene mentioned above with all the trappings of her class; later, we see her again at her toilette when her brother Agustín pays her a visit; later still we come upon her as she looks at herself in the vestibule mirror as she is about to leave the house. In each case her portrait is accompanied by concrete references to various cultural registers, especially the arts. We find her continually and in various ways linked to different artistic forms; playing the piano she demonstrates the artistic education befitting her class; the *pose nonchalante* in which she is given to us as she reclines on the sofa is meant to invoke sculptural forms; painting is also clearly summoned when Blest Gana gives us Leonor as reflected in mirrors. More subtly perhaps, in the description of her graceful and lithesome movements is there not an allusion to the gestures of dance? Always appearing as an icon of bourgeois refinement, Leonor's beauty is continually tied to her elegance and cultivation of the arts. In the novel, Beauty and Elegance are taken as synonymous; conjoined as they are in Leonor, it is precisely that subtle halo of elegance, in combination with her physical beauty, which first impresses Martín and draws him to her.

Drawing prestige from the figure of the lone adventurer of his father; sharing in, but surviving, the battle for the "heroic ideals" that claim his friend San Luis; and finally, in marrying Leonor, Martín Rivas stands before us as the quintessential expression of ascendant bourgeois manhood. He stands for and upholds the constitutive characteristics and values of the class: first, although initially economically disadvantaged, he is financially savvy; second, in standing with San Luis he is brave and can lay claim to political righteousness; and third, from his association with Leonor, Martín derives cultural capital from her elegance and spirituality.

If, then, this constellation of traits makes Martín Rivas a full-fledged ideological bourgeois being, why, one might ask, does the novel insist upon the need to draw out for us his entry into this same class? What appears in the novel as an ambiguous and at times difficult-to-understand issue brings us back to the matter of the mistaken view of Martín as "a hero of the middle class," to which we referred above. We must perhaps look at the matter from a different perspective. As a representative of the mining bourgeoisie of the north, Martín Rivas comes to be incorporated into the national bourgeoisie which is, in the Chilean context, by definition based in agriculture, commerce, and finance. It is in this sense that we must read the novel's need for Martín's trip, arrival, and adaptation to the culture of the capital city of Santiago; Martín represents the incorporation of a sector—a new and emergent sector—into a constituted and already considered traditional bourgeois class; it is therefore entirely a matter of nineteenth-century intraclass dynamics.

Running parallel to the novel's representation of hegemonic class dynamics, however, there is also clearly an abstract and ideal operation at work in *Martín Rivas.* While possessing the requisite traits and clearly standing as an archetype of his class, Martín Rivas is, curiously, lacking in one key area: capital and private property. It is as if Blest Gana were tracing out for us what could be termed the ontological proof of the Chilean bourgeoisie. In an operation in line with that of many Christian philosophers, like Saint Anselm, who deduced the existence of God from the attributes implicit in his perfect essence, so too in *Martín Rivas* we have first the image of the ideal bourgeois, awaiting its materialization, its investiture as it were; the realization will be enabled by accessing Leonor's wealth.

The above is suggested to us particularly in the details of the portraits drawn for us of Martín Rivas. The image of Martín that first springs to mind is that of the provincial newcomer to the city who dresses anachronistically and knows nothing of cosmopolitan elegance. While noting his unfashionable attire, the novel immediately goes on to emphasize Martín's certain air of distinction; again his physical presence is what stands out: his eyes that gaze out darkly; his commanding stance, the absence of a too-perfect set of features, culminating in the following revealing portrait:

> Martín looked mechanically at the mirror over the mahogany sink and found himself pale and homely; but the voice of reason persuaded him to abandon his childish discouragement before it dampened his spirits.[23]

The novel offers up to us that truth resides neither in dress nor physical attributes; it is to be found within the individual and consists precisely of those traits of determination, willpower, and rational thought with which Martín Rivas is fully endowed. While seemingly simple and unimportant, we must view these representations of Martín in their dialectical relationship to the character's overall portrayal; his dress contrasts with his "air of distinction"; his awareness of his lack of comeliness strengthens his determination all the more. Insofar as portrayals of Martín are concerned, the "negatives" attributed to him in the novel's early pages ultimately add dimension and personality to his character. Afterward, in an inverse process, Martín fits in seamlessly as he takes on the trappings of dress, manners, speech, and taste of the class whose essence he ostensibly carries within him. This process starts early on in the novel, precisely in the Plaza de Armas scene where Martín comes off rather badly, as much due to his own lack of savoir faire as to his interaction with his "compatriot worker comrades" in the city:

> A peddler approached him, saying, "Patent leather boots, Señor?"
>
> These words brought to mind Agustín's shiny footwear and the reason Martín had left the house. He thought that with a swank pair of leather boots he would fare better with the stylish family who had opened their doors to him. Inexperienced and unintimidated, Martín hesitantly looked at the peddler, who had already begun to walk off, and the man returned immediately.
>
> "Let's see the boots," said Martín.
>
> "Here ya go, buddy," replied the man, luring the newcomer with the glassy reflection of his goods.[24]

Here again, we have Martín viewing all to which he aspires in the reflection of the shiny surface; the scene militates against the idea of his lack of comeliness. Thus, despite the derision he suffers, despite the comical jailing he undergoes—anticipating his later, more dramatic, jail stay—Martín, starting at his feet, initiates the material realization his nature requires in order to rise slowly and stand firmly upon the ground. His meditative qualities ensure that he is up to the task. Going far beyond any romantic melancholia, Martín's pensiveness and reflective nature are everywhere stressed in the novel; he thinks, he ponders, he extracts lessons from what he sees and develops maxims from these lived experiences: "Having run all of his errands, he returned to Don Dámaso's studio and sat down to work at his des, saying to himself, 'She doesn't disdain me.'"[25]

There is a way, too, in which the moral development of the character of Martín Rivas brings to mind the work of Blest Gana's contemporary, Samuel Smiles, apologist of the English middle class and author of such prosaic works as *Character* (1871), *Thrift* (1875), *Duty* (1880), and, particularly, *Self-Help* (1859), books that undoubtedly served as models for all subsequent self-help manuals published in the United States for a successful and prosperous life.

Again we must bear all this in mind to fully understand Martín Rivas's place in the novel's dynamics. Taken by the character's presence and its social connotations, criticism on the novel has made much about the differences between Martín Rivas and Don Dámaso or his son Agustín. But in fact the bourgeois world of *Martín Rivas* is a unitary whole, with a panoply of characters serving as variations of the same human type. The notion of "situational analogies" is useful in this instance to talk about the novel's plots and subplots, and productive as well in viewing the work's many structured and intentional contiguities and congruencies. The preponderance of these is such that they merit listing: the nearness in ages (the young Dámaso, Martín, Rafael, and Agustín are all 23 or 24 years old); the amount of Don Dámaso's 30,000 peso dowry is picked up again in the 30,000 peso purse Agustín travels to France with; Clemente Valencia has a 300,000 peso capital at his disposal; Leonor's other suitor, Emilio Mendoza's salary is 3,000 pesos; and finally, Martín Rivas earns a very modest 30 pesos for his services as Don Dámaso's secretary. These numbers mark clear distinctions, but they are somehow also meant to ally the different characters and circumstances. Martín can be taken as a morally superior, evolved rendering of Don Dámaso and, likewise, an intellectually superior version of Agustín. He is their ideological complement, seeking to find in them, as we noted earlier, his societal grounding. Martín is distilled moral virtue, distilled talent, and this is his only capital. His capital—and the zeros that go with it—will increase later, but his essential "worth" is given at the onset.

About the novel's ending it has rightfully been said that "Blest Gana here applies the notion of commutative justice: Dámaso Encina has become wealthy at the expense of his former partner; these men's daughter and son fall in love and the better part of Encina's fortune is to ultimately to be passed on to the former partner's son via marriage, when Martín conquers Santiago as well as the heart of the haughty heiress."[26]

Two key letters frame the novel's beginning and end and allow us to situate Martín Rivas further. Early in the novel we find the letter written by his father which introduces Martín to the man who will be his mentor in Santiago. As the novel draws to a close, we have the letter in which Martín informs his mother and sister that he is to marry Leonor. The two halves of the narrative romance are thus joined, giving us a perfect sphere. It is interesting to note how Blest Gana's novel's resolution stands in marked contrast with other nineteenth-century Latin American works; without intimating incest, as is the case in Juan León Mera's Ecuadorian novel *Cumandá,* or suggesting the semi-incestuous situation we find between Efraín and his cousin in Jorge Isaac's *María,* and refusing the close-knit family scenario typical of so many romantic idylls, Blest Gana's *Martín Rivas* sketches out a different problematic, an economic incest of sorts, in that Martín and Leonor are rooted, that is, they are the offspring of the same capitalist entity. Thus, in effect, Martín inherits the business from Don Dámaso, as would a son:

> Don Dámaso Encina turned all of his business affairs over to Martín Rivas in order to devote himself more freely to the political fluctuations which he hoped would one day land him in the House of Senate. Don Dámaso was one of many master-weavers who disguised his lack of conviction by acting in the name of Moderation.[27]

VII

At first glance, nothing could be more simple or direct than the narrative emplotment of Blest Gana's *Martín Rivas.* The narrative movement advances and rests upon a series of successive and interconnected mistaken identities and entanglements. Each link in this series of chains is made up by a pair of lovers: Leonor–Rafael; Matilde–Rafael; Rafael–Adelaida; Adelaida–Agustín; Agustín–Matilde; Ricardo–Edelmira; Edelmira–Martín; Martín–Leonor. The entire set of circles links up and fits in perfectly in line with the conventions of the *comedia de enredos* or those of the serialized melodrama. Let the following serve as one of the more noteworthy examples of these entanglements: at the novel's start Martín believes Leonor to be in love with Rafael. It is under the shadow of this belief that the youth's love grows. And farther down the line we also see Leonor's love for Martín grow when she believes him to be smitten by Edelmira. Three points stand out when considering the string of these narrative complications in the novel:

1. These entanglements are generally established between members of different social groups, more precisely, between a member of the upper class and one from the lower middle class.
2. The development and denouement of these situations—be they sentimental, comical, or dramatic in nature—are parallel with and correlated to shifts in Martín's social and sentimental situation.
3. Specifically, in the case of the novel's hero, his personality is in fact defined by the two poles of his sentimental attraction: Leonor and Edelmira.

As to the first point, it is clear that Martín moves not only up socially as Don Dámaso's secretary and advisor. The benefits his mentor derives from Martín's counsel are not limited to the business realm exclusively, but involve another more problematic domain that casts Martín in the role of intermediary or facilitator in matters of love. In this odd alchemy, Martín is always the agent of amorous affinities that ultimately belie clear class-based filters. His intervention manages to bring together those that are socially homogenous while driving apart those that are not. He is, for example, the go-between for linking Matilde and Rafael, but at the same time is responsible for separating Rafael from Adelaida. As for Martín himself, we see that he is drawn closer to Leonor but cut off from Edelmira, who, readers of *Martín Rivas* undoubtedly recall, selflessly sacrifices herself for him. In an odd fashion then, Martín operates as a go-between in reverse in this and in other places in the narrative. It is curious indeed that critics have for the most part neglected this negative agency, this double directionality in the novel's love emplotments which is signaled positively with respect to Leonor and, (sadly,) negatively in regard to Edelmira. Martin's talent rests then on his savvy application of the laws of class valences to ensure socially "legitimate" amorous associations. Indeed, it is on these grounds that Martín can make the following highly revealing comments in a letter to his sister:

> I went to Alameda my second day back, which was Sunday. I was walking arm in arm with Leonor (you can imagine my pride) when we came upon a couple coming toward us from the opposite direction. I recognized it was Ricardo Castaños, who with a triumphant air, offered his arm to Edelmira. We spoke with them a while. Later I asked myself whether this poor girl, born into a social class inferior to her noble sentiments, was happy. I really couldn't say because the serenity and joy of her words seemed to contradict the melancholic expression in her eyes.[28]

Surely the image of the "opposite directions" in which the two couples move in this scene speaks to much more than a simple spatial orientation!

It is thus that, despite the sympathetic eye with which the narrator views Martín Rivas's moral physiognomy, there are in the novel fuzzier zones that reveal the degree to which the actual social conditions determine behaviors. Above all an ethical subject, Martín Rivas is bound to the rules of his own class, to its prejudices and constraints. It is also to Blest Gana's artistic credit that the novel's complexity and stress-points reveal themselves in the narrative interstices. While the work is above all else an unabashed apologia for the personality, both ethical and social, of Martín Rivas, the novel also brings to bear upon him an underlying ironic critique. Like other great works of the period, even if in a more modest key, *Martín Rivas*'s narrative richness allows for the potential double reading requisite of all significant works. The interplay of greatness and madness in *Don Quixote,* the ascent and decline of Julien Sorel, the splendor and misery of Emma Bovary, the rebelliousness and pettiness of Mathieu Delarue—to this incomplete list of contrasting narrative representations the addition of Martín Rivas's conjoined honesty and scheming seems plausible.

If we pursue this notion of narrative duplicity, we become aware that it is a fundamental thread in the narrative. The novel's narrator, for example, goes on at length—giving it nearly a full page—to explain what Santiago's society understands by the phrase *servir mucho*/to render great service, saying:

> "The expression 'he'll be very useful to me' must be clarified within its social context.
>
> Love, the guiding star of youth, leads a young man into a salon where the stillness in the air prevents him from voicing the adoration in his eyes, for fear of being overheard. However, the knot in his throat dissolves when *Simple Admiration* evolves into *Tender Admiration*—to quote Stendhal—because glances no longer satisfy the demands of the heart. It becomes necessary to hear the lady's voice and to confess to her all the sweet afflictions of his lovesick soul. In order to steal an intimate moment to elaborate his choppy, suspenseful phrases, the young man engages an accomplice to entertain her mother or her sisters, who are always quicker to lend an ear to the banalities of a young bachelor.
>
> It is in this context that Agustín thought Rivas could be very useful to him at the home of Doña Bernarda, whose vigilance was all the sharper because the stakes were all the higher, granted that the suitor was the son of a very well-to-do family."[29]

If we look only at this passage dealing with the intervention and aid provided by someone in advancing a lover's courting, we can understand the way in which the phrase *servir mucho* applies perfectly to Martín's role as a go-between in amorous affairs. It is precisely here, however, that through the author's explicit intervention, the expression takes on its fuller meaning in the novel, as it foregrounds Martín Rivas's location and agency in the narrative. The narrator's deliberate emphasis on this point is in this way explained. We can also more fully understand in this light the elder Encina's use of *servirme mucho* as he considers taking on Martín as his secretary:

> "I've been thinking," said Don Dámaso to his wife, "that Martín may be able to assist me in keeping my books."
>
> "He seems like a nice young man, and I appreciate the fact that he doesn't smoke," said Doña Engracia.[30]

It is important here to draw attention to how the expression *servir mucho* is used in the novel both in regard to the official and publicly recognized tasks tied to Martín's bourgeois apprenticeship under Encina, as to the more secretive dealings and clandestine arrangements in the social realm. We are likewise made to see the continual linkages established between Don Dámaso and Martín in the novel. For Leonor, for example, her main underlying concern in arranging Matilde's and Rafael's happiness is undoing the harm done by her father: "Yes, another reason. I want to make amends for my father's actions. As we both know, he was largely responsible for throwing Rafael out of your house."[31]

For his part, in aiding Leonor, Martín repairs the wrongs committed by Don Dámaso. In doing so, however, he simultaneously creates a situation that, while perhaps not as self-serving, is not entirely unlike that unleashed by Don Dámaso's meddling. To be sure, interfering in the marriage of Adelaida and Agustín is justified, in part, in view of the trickery involved; nevertheless, Martín's advice is nothing short of brutal. We can likewise find echoed traits or gestures among the key characters as when we see Martín employing a Gallicism (*Usted hiere la dificultad*)—likening him to the Frenchified Agustín—as he speaks to Adelaida: "You miss the point, Señorita," Martín replied. "What we are talking about here is buying."

But what are we to make of the relationship between Adelaida and Rafael? Here our attention is diverted to the greed of her wastrel brother, Amador. Our doubts remain, however, unresolved and Martín acts unwillingly and ill-humored; if there is any remorse, it is meager.

It would be surprising if in *Martín Rivas* Blest Gana were not sometimes to toy with his characters' names as he does in *The Arithmetic of Love.* Here he baptizes some characters with comical names that border on the Rabelaisian, as is the case of Fortunato Esperanzano, whose every hope is set on his exceedingly slim chances of coming upon a fortune, or the caricaturesque name of Ciriaco Ayunales, given to a monk who has little to do with candles and even less with fasting. Earlier, in *The Newlyweds,* characters' names have to do with making a different kind of point. Blest Gana perhaps drew on Eugène Sue's serialized novel *Thérèse Dunoyer*—published in Copiapó's newspaper *El Pueblo* at about the time when Blest Gana was returning from Europe[32]—when it came to choosing a name for his novel's antagonist. For a French speaker, the association of the word with the image of drowning has been, in all probability, lost; not so, however, for a non-native speaker. Thus it is that just as the lovers in Sue's novel find their death in the Seine River, so too in *The Newlyweds* the name Dunoye foreshadows the death by suicide of the young lovers. It is worth remarking as well that if one were to trace back the history of Blest Gana's selection of character names, one would note a marked shift from his earlier novels. *A Social Scene* (1853), for example, both opens and closes with the figure of the servant Martín, whose time upon the novel's stage is longer even than of the main protagonist Alfredo. The latter describes his servant as follows:

> "Martín was my servant and confidant, he was 45 years old and had a great deal of experience of the world; he was French by birth and was bound to me by ties of great affection; his countenance was as grave as one of La Rouchefoucauld's maxims; his hair, at most two centimeters long, gave him a certain Puritan air (. . .) Martín was one of that sort of men that, though born into the lower orders, upon close observation revealed themselves to be most interesting (. . .) He had a curious way of expressing himself; by drawing on his native tongue he would somehow give each phrase a certain French twist."[33]

The ironic relationship between the servant Martín in Blest Gana's 1853 novel and *Martín Rivas*'s titular hero had to have been clear in the author's mind as he chose to give the same name to both characters. The broad experience and severe countenance ascribed to the one correlate with the moral attributes associated with the other. Taken further, the first Martín's "Puritan" qualities might also explain the almost Lutheran sense of Rivas's first name, which stands in marked contrast to the patently Catholic names of

Rivas's friend Rafael San Luis. The Frenchified speech and manners of *Martín Rivas*'s Agustín Encina are likewise also anticipated in "the French-born" servant Martín of *A Social Scene.* There is then a way in which the early figure of Martín the servant holds possibilities that are later drawn upon and developed in several of Blest Gana's subsequent characters.

But that the figure of Martín is not the only one to reveal this curious inversion must respond in some way to Blest Gana's overarching project for a series of novels on Chilean society. Adelaida de Farcy, the heroine of Blest Gana's 1858 novel *Fascination,* for example, is a lady of the aristocracy who carries the same name as Doña Bernarda Cordero's meretricious and ambitious daughter. In Blest Gana's 1862 *Martín Rivas* Adelaida is downgraded and Martín's homologue is ennobled. One can trace these curious reversals of fortune among namesake characters in other Blest Gana novels, but even within *Martín Rivas* fortuitous ironies of this sort are suggested as we can see in the following scene: "Her daughters are Adelaida and Edelmira. The elder was named by her godfather, and the younger by her mother who came up with a theatrical name because she was with child when she saw *Othello.*"[34]

Are we to think Doña Bernarda mistook Edelmira for Emilia, Desdemona's servant? Might it be an oblique reference to some diva of the period? Neither guess can be substantiated, but in any case the semantic connection is made to some staged event, seen and admired. One also might consider the correspondences and phonetic links between other characters' names in the narrative. Dámaso-Diamela-Damián; here two fathers, one from the bourgeoisie and one from the lower orders, not only share the same first three letters of their respective names but resemble all too closely that of Doña Engracia's pet lap dog, Diamela. Rafael's and Fidel's names are also worth mentioning in regard to Matilde: both the zealous father's and the dismissed suitor's names rhyme. We also find a phonetic pairing in the surnames Elías-Rivas: the first, the prototype of political inconstancy and the latter, the hero of the April Liberal uprising. And just as there is an absolute consonant rhyme between Martín-Agustín, yoking the homegrown *criollo* with the Francophile, the novel also asks us to note how, in the pairing of the surnames of the two central families in the novel,

Encina-Molina, their names belie a certain kinship, despite belonging to entirely different social spheres.[35]

It is in this sense that the above-mentioned "rhyme structure," these fragmentary superpositions as it were, allow us to see in the character's names in *Martín Rivas* a crossword puzzle of sorts that, at one basic level at least, points to a number of meaningful analogies in the text. When taken with the novel's already mentioned reiterative use of certain numbers, names, and ages, these correspondences underscore a particular set of relationships within the text.

Special mention needs to be made of Martín Rivas's name; standing opposite Rafael San Luis's, linked to Fidel Elías's, jingling like Agustín's, summoning up that of an old French servant, Martín's name is charged with a series of connotations. These various social resonances, coupled with Martín's surname, Rivas, suggest a possible link with Balzac's emplotment of the arriviste.[36]

VIII

Martín Rivas takes place in a distinctly urban environment. This narrative space is that of Chile's capital city, Santiago. This itself marks a point of divergence when we consider *Martín Rivas* vis-à-vis other key nineteenth-century Latin American novels. This fact is attributable, at least in part, to Chile's relative higher degree of economic and political development and the attainment of greater centralization of social life within the nation-state. Politics is a topic under constant discussion by the majority of the novel's characters; they live and breathe it daily. The interrelatedness of the public and the private is foregrounded, culminating in the April rebellion that, for a short while at least, throws bourgeois family life into turmoil. When men gather at Don Dámaso's tertulia, talk centers openly and unabashed on the political news of the day and national affairs. It is especially worth remarking that even women characters in *Martín Rivas* interest themselves in political matters. Don Fidel's wife, for example, manifests a clear interest in social and cultural issues and even considers herself to be a follower of George Sand's brand of feminism. This representation stands in sharp contrast to that of women in novels like *Cumandá* or *María*, where they are at best only symbolically connected to the political and concerned with history.

In this regard the novel's discussion of discourses related to national holidays and public celebrations is especially telling. Chile's Independence Day celebration on September 18[37] is specifically highlighted in *Martín Rivas;* its representation and the multiple dimensions and implications within the narrative can be schematized as follows:

1. The depiction of the national celebration given in the course of the narration's lineal development underscores the existence of an already consolidated sense of national unity and identity. If Santiago is given as Chile's spatial core, the temporal plane is represented by these collective patriotic festivities, rendered in *Martín Rivas* as the nucleus of the entire nation's social life. The novel (simultaneously) points to and applauds this national unity, claimed by the Chilean bourgeoisie as a key outcome of its efforts in the political sphere.
2. Seen from a more strictly ideological vantage point, the bourgeoisie is very much interested in offering up the image of a unified and united society; as represented in the novel's civic festivities all, masters and servants, upper and lower classes, come together in perfect harmony—achieved by a combination of drink and the effervescence of celebration, as prescribed by the nation's leaders.
3. That Chilean political unity had been attained is not at issue; by 1862 it is a historical reality, notwithstanding continued conflicts with the Araucanian Indians—but then these ancestors were not "Chileans" but rather "barbarians" in the Liberal parlance of the period. What was, however, clearly at the forefront of the bourgeois agenda was promoting the illusion of social unity. This notion of a popular base—as much an illusion in 1862 as today—was an inherent and pressing necessity for a hegemony of the ruling class. Thus, if the novel's hero is to be bourgeois, he will require, minimally at least, a backdrop that includes the common people and against which he stands out; the

statesman's statue is to rise on the pedestal—that is, on the shoulders or backs—of the people. We find then in *Martín Rivas* a certain "reaching down" to the common people as part of the objectives of bourgeois hegemony, a practice evident as well in another classic nineteenth-century Liberal text, Sarmiento's *Facundo* (1845). Even if we admit that Sarmiento's representation of the common people is ambivalent at best, autochtonous Argentine "types" such as the trail-scout or the gaucho are, in fact, considered seminal figures without which the representation of the "nation" would be incomplete. And while often cast as obstacles to national progress, they nonetheless "authenticate" claims to nationhood.

4. Noël Salomon's[38] work has beautifully demonstrated how the validation of these social "types," as well as their *costumbrista* representation, fits in with the overall Liberal project in Latin America. What results from this project is the overbearing patriotism of the bourgeoisie, never without a certain disdain and condescension toward the lower orders which, although acknowledged as part of the nation, are, under the aegis of "scientific observation" considered to be less evolved members of the national collectivity. For these nineteenth-century Liberal "patriots," social "classes" are akin to zoological species which are to be set in hierarchical order. From their vantage point, the lower orders have at least the merit—and the advantage—of belonging to them, of being claimed by them.

IX

Martín Rivas stands as a benchmark of the Chilean novel. Standing alongside Alonso de Ercilla's epic and the works of our more contemporary poets, Blest Gana's novel is a classic text with an assured place in Chilean literature. As in the case of Ercilla and Neruda, Blest Gana's narratives again underscore the fact that an author's transcendence does not rely exclusively on his work's formal merits, but on the intensity and richness with which sociohistorical relations are represented. Running counter to Valery's esthetic, in the best novels the celebrated Marquise goes out at five

P.M.—and at whatever other time it suits her. What matters is the author's skill, the density and internal dynamism of the world represented. In *Martín Rivas,* each detail has its place and reason for being, from the author's rendering of Don Dámaso's tics to the minute description of a particular daguerreotype—the latter invented during the French July monarchy and quickly transported to Chile, which interestingly, according to Freund,[39] would prove indispensable to the Chilean bourgeoisie's development of a sense of self.

Artistic practices can better be understood when taken as teleologically conceived activities with historic-social aims. Assuredly then, following the novel's program Martín Rivas, the character, stands tall, head and shoulders above the rest in the Blest Gana's novel, but we need also to recall that we are dealing with a work that the author himself made it a point to qualify as *a novel of sociopolitical customs,* a narrative whose driving strategy of scrutiny can serve both to exalt and to expose its heroes.

X

With the critical distance afforded by one hundred years of history, *Martín Rivas*'s author ultimately stands before us as a somewhat skeptical Liberal, a skepticism born of that deep disenchantment suffered by Liberals upon seeing that by the nineteenth century's close *Droits de l'Homme* was not the timeless and unequivocal Gospel for progress. Some, like President Balmaceda, for example, critiqued the depth of Blest Gana's ties to Chile, terming him a *desnacionalizado.* Blest Gana did, after all, live out his nostalgia for his faraway country among the hotels and elegant avenues of Paris for over fifty years.

Yet for all of this, despite, or even perhaps because of his rootedness in a bourgeois worldview, Blest Gana did, in fact, manage to envision what would be one of the core problems facing Chile, both in his own time and in the future. His acute sense of the key issues at stake can be seen in the following excerpt from a letter to Aníbal Pinto. On May 3, 1878, just as Chile was about to declare war on its neighbors to the north, Blest Gana wrote of his satisfaction in learning that the Courcelle-Seneuil proposal on taxation on mining revenues was to go forward:

> It is true that under this new tax code, if implemented along the lines M. Courcelle-Senueil suggests, both banks and the monopolist will suffer losses; it is true as well that the capitalists will see a drop in their profits, which until now have been safeguarded more than Sacred Cows among the Hindu who believe in reincarnation. The Nation will benefit, however, and stand on stronger financial ground, conditions necessary to undertake a radical reform of our public treasury.[40]

It is striking indeed, particularly given Blest Gana's undeniable bourgeois credentials and ideology, to look back over one hundred years later to find this Chilean Liberal taking the position that unfettered capitalism and the state's role in safeguarding profits were ultimately objectionable and short-sighted, and part of a most unhealthy and barbaric doctrine.

NOTES

1 Balzac and Stendhal are often mentioned in studies on Blest Gana. We shall return to this later. Sue is referenced less frequently, perhaps fearing to diminish Blest Gana's literary heritage. Sue's works were, nonetheless, widely read in Chilean newspapers at mid-century (see note 32, below). Hugo's influence has been addressed in Guillemo Araya's worthwhile essay, "El amor y la revolución en *Martín Rivas,*" *Bulletin Hispanique* (Bordeaux: Janvier-Juin, 1975), 5–33.

2 Alone, *Don Alberto Blest Gana. Biografía y crítica* (Santiago: Nascimiento, 1940), 38–39.

3 See *Los desposados. Novela Original,* dated October 1985, which appeared in serialized form consisting of twelve chapters in *Revista de Santiago,* directed by Diego Barros Arana (Santiago: Imprenta Chilena, 1855), 659–68, 726–37, and 777–800.

4 Ibid., 665.

5 The letter in question is dated June 24, 1856. It is cited in Ricardo Donoso's "Un amigo de Blest Gana: José Antonio Donoso," 190, in *Homenaje de la Universidad de Chile a su ex-Rector: don Domingo Amunátegui Solar* (Santiago: Imprenta Universitaria, 1935), vol. II, 177–200.

6 Blest Gana's letter to Vicuña Mackenna is dated 1864. It reads: "You are right. One day, after reading Balzac, I enacted an *auto de fe* before the chimney and condemned into the flames of the fireplace all the rhymed

impressions I had written in my youth; it was then that I swore to become a novelist."

7 At times, very much in a Dickensian fashion, Blest Gana establishes a conscious correspondence between the world of his most truculent characters and a feverish childhood bestiary. The following passage from *Juan de Aria* is revealing in this regard: "A singular individual, no doubt, exclaimed Juan to himself. What is there in common between us? Certainly nothing, and yet seeing him fills me with foreboding of what lies ahead. There is something fateful in his eyes that brings back to me the monsters that filled my boyish nightmares, or reminds me of the grotesque figure of a Satan escaped from some old convent painting." *Juan de Aria* (Santiago: Librería Mirand, 1904), 15.

8 See the previously cited Ricardo Donoso article, xvi, n. 13.

9 Idem, 199.

10 *Historia de Chile* (Santiago: Nascimento, 1949), vol. 13, 139.

11 *Martín Rivas,* 18.

12 See F. A. Encina, *Historia de Chile,* vol. 13, 258–59. See also René León Echais, *Evolución histórica de los partidos políticos chilenos* (Buenos Aires: Francisco de Aguirre, 1971), 35 and following.

13 Further elaboration on this point can be found in Guillermo Araya's previously cited article (supra, note 1). Similarly, the Enzo Faletto and Julieta Kirkwood monograph, *Sociedad burguesa y liberalismo romántico en el siglo XIX* (mimeograph copy), provides insights into the events and issues in question.

14 Idem, July 24, 1862.

15 Idem, August 30, 1862.

16 See Domingo Melfi, *Estudios de la literatura chilena* (Santiago: Nascimiento, 1938), 9.

17 Alone, *Don Alberto Blest Gana,* 163.

18 César A. de León provides the following information: *During that period the social status of doctors and lawyers was not entirely based on the practice of their respective professions. A list of these professionals during the period exists and from it one can confirm that the great majority of them belonged to aristocratic ranks.* See César A. de León, "Las capas medias en la sociedad chilena del siglo XIX," *Anales de la Universidad de Chile* 132 (October–December 1964).

19 In 1844 exports represented 6 million pesos of the GNP; in 1860 this had risen to 24 million pesos. See Aníbal Pinto Santa Cruz, *Chile, un caso de desarrollo frustrado* (Santiago: Editorial Universitaria, 1957).

20 *Martín Rivas,* 13 and 22.

21 Ibid., 5.

22 Ibid., 7.

23 Ibid., 15.

24 Ibid., 22.

25 Ibid., 28.

26 See Hernán Poblete, *Genio y figura de Alberto Blest Gana* (Buenos Aires: Eudeba, 1968), 111.

27 *Martín Rivas,* 387.

28 Ibid., 385–86.

29 Ibid., 117. See also 68, 76–77, 94.

30 Ibid., 25.

31 Ibid., 107.

32 December and January 1851–52.

33 See *Una escena social* (Santiago: Editorial Zig-Zag, n.d.), 51–52.

34 *Martín Rivas,* 34.

35 Intentional parallelisms of this sort abound in the novel. It is obvious, for example, that the representation of the tertulias, or gatherings of the elite class, is structurally identical to the description of the *picholeo* in the home of Doña Bernarda. The groupings, games, entertainments, drinks, topics of conversation, and musical instruments may vary slightly in manner or content, but they evidently are made to be correlates. The point Blest Gana makes here is not to be underestimated, for it goes far in undermining the notion of a distinct hierarchy of social practices.

36 Naturally, the term *arriviste* did not originally have the negative petty bourgeois associations it now carries. Uttered initially by the aristocracy and taken up by the younger and newer strata of the bourgeoisie, the term clearly represents the parvenu, but highlights his effort and audacity. Even the Spanish spelling of the term vacillated historically between *arrivismo* and *arribismo,* underscoring the term's social ambivalence. The nineteenth-century bourgeoisie attributed it to the verb *arriver;* the twentieth-century petty bourgeoisie take it (or imagined it) to mean *hacia arriba* (upward).

37 These take place between Chapters XXXVI and XXXVII in the novel.

38 Noël Salomon's works are indispensable resources for understanding Sarmiento, expecially his *Apropos de quelques aspects 'costumbristas' dans le* Facundo *de D. F. Sarmiento* (*Bulletin Hispanique,* 1968).

39 See Giselle Freund, *La fotografía y las clases medias en Francia durante el siglo XIX* (Buenos Aires: Editorial Losada, 1946).

40 See Raúl Silva Castro, *Alberto Blest Gana* (Santiago: Imprenta Universitaria, 1941), 161–62.

MARTÍN RIVAS

I

In early July 1850, a young man, 23 or 24 years old, crossed the front gate of a stately manor in Santiago.

His old-fashioned clothing and manners made him the classic example of the poor provincial who visits our elegant capital for the first time. He was sporting a pair of black trousers, tucked into lambskin gaiters, in the style of 1842 and 1843; a narrow, short-sleeved frockcoat; a black satin vest with wide open flaps, forming a sharp angle against his waistline; an odd-shaped hat; and a pair of leather boots, fastened at the ankles by black shoelaces. His entire outfit had an outdated look which only rustics revive from time to time in our city streets. And the way that he approached a servant of the house, who was leaning against the front door, revealed the shyness of someone who enters an unfamiliar place wary of the reception that awaits him. When they were within speaking range of each other, the provincial stopped to greet the servant, whose eyes were riveted upon him. The servant responded with curt reservation, inspired perhaps by the stranger's rueful countenance.

"Would this be the home of Don Dámaso Encina?" the young man asked, hardly able to hide the chagrin that the discourtesy had apparently caused him.

"This is it," answered the servant.

"Would you advise him that a gentleman wishes to speak with him?"

Upon hearing the word *gentleman,* the servant endeavored to restrain a derisive grin that twisted his lips.

"And whom shall I say is calling?" he asked dryly.

"Martín Rivas," he replied, attempting to control his impatience, which nevertheless glimmered in his eyes.

"Well, wait here," said the servant, as he slowly withdrew into the inner quarters.

It had just struck high noon.

Let us seize this moment, while the servant is away, to better acquaint ourselves with the man who has just introduced himself as Martín Rivas. He was a well-built young man of average size who walked with his head held high. Judging by what could be seen from under the brim of his hat, he had a full crop of chestnut hair. His black eyes, although not large, were nonetheless striking because of the melancholy air they gave his face. He possessed a pensive, sullen look, shaded by bags under his eyes which offset his pallid cheeks. A trim black mustache, covering his upper lip and the tips of his lower lip, gave him an aura of resolution. His overall appearance had a certain air of distinction that clashed with the poverty of his attire and led one to conclude that had this youth been elegantly dressed, he might have passed as a good-looking man to those who do not judge physical beauty solely on the basis of a rosy complexion and classic features.

Martín did not move from the spot where he had stopped to address the servant. For the first few minutes he studied the frescos on the patio walls and the gilded moldings on the window frames. As time went on, he seemed to grow impatient with the delay, and his eyes wandered aimlessly until the door finally opened.

"Please, come in," said the servant, leading Martín to a chamber door. "Here you'll find the master of the house."

The youth stepped inside and found a man who was, as the French would say, *caught between two ages*—which is to say, he stood on the brink of old age without actually stepping into it. His black suit, starched collars, and the luster of his leather boots showed him to be a methodical man who subjects his person, as he does his life, to invariable rules. His expression bared nothing. He possessed none of those characteristic traits, so prominent in some people from which an observer may surmise a great deal about one's disposition. Perfectly shaven and meticulously groomed, his face and hair revealed only that cleanliness was one of his rules of conduct.

On seeing Martín, he removed a cap from his head and approached with an inquisitive look. At least that is how the young man interpreted it, and so he quickly greeted him, saying, "Señor Dámaso Encina?"

"I am at your service," he answered.

Martín handed Don Dámaso a letter from his coat pocket, saying, "Would you be so kind as to read this letter?"

After taking his time to unseal the letter, Señor Encina read the signature and said, "Oh, it's you, Martín. And how is your father?"

"He passed away," Martín answered sadly.

"Passed away!" the gentleman repeated, taken aback. Then, as if he were distracted by a sudden idea, he added, "Have a seat, Martín. Excuse me for not having offered you a seat. And what is this letter about?"

"Would you be so kind as to read it?"

Don Dámaso walked to a writing desk, set the letter down, and picked up a pair of spectacles, which he carefully cleaned with a silk handkerchief, before placing them on his nose. As he sat down, he set his eyes upon the youth.

"I can't read a thing without my spectacles," he stated, somewhat satisfied with the time he spent preparing himself. Then he began to read the following letter.

My Dear Sir,

I am gravely ill, and I wish, before God calls me to His divine judgment, to introduce my son, who will be the head of my unfortunate family before long. I have made my final arrangements so that upon my death my wife and children can make the best of my limited resources. However, with the interest of their meager inheritance, they will live very poorly if Martín is to finish his legal studies in Santiago. According to my calculations, his monthly allowance, a modest sum of 20 pesos, will not cover the basic necessities; and, therefore, I have thought of you and I pray that you will take my son into your home until he is able to support himself. This boy is my only hope, and if you grant him this kindness, which I humbly ask on his behalf, you will receive the blessings of his good mother on the earth and mine in Heaven, if God grants me eternal glory upon my death.

I remain most sincerely and faithfully yours,

José Rivas

Don Dámaso removed his spectacles as carefully as he had put them on and placed them back where he had found them. Rising from his seat, he inquired, "Do you know what your father asks of me in this letter?"

"Yes, sir," replied Martín.

"And how did you come here from Copiapó?"

"In a freight coach," he answered proudly.

"My friend," said Señor Encina, "your father was a good man, and I'm indebted to him for some services that I am glad to repay to his son. Upstairs there are two unoccupied chambers at your disposal. Did you bring any luggage?"

"Yes, sir."

"Where is it?"

"At the inn in Santo Domingo."

"The valet will fetch them. Show him the way."

Martín stood up from his seat, and Don Dámaso called for the valet.

"Go with this gentleman, and bring back whatever he gives you."

"Sir," said Martín, "I don't know how to thank you."

"Well, well, Martín," said Don Dámaso, "you're at home now. Bring your luggage and make yourself comfortable upstairs. Dinner is at five. Come early so that I may introduce you to the lady of the house."

Martín expressed a few words of appreciation and withdrew.

"Juana! Juana!" called Don Dámaso, raising his voice so that he could be heard in the next chamber. "Bring me the newspapers!"

II

The stately manor where we have just seen Martín Rivas introduce himself was the home of Don Dámaso Encina, his wife, their 19-year-old daughter, 23-year-old son, and three small children who were away at a French boarding school.

At the age of 24, Don Dámaso had married Doña Engracia Nuñez, more for social advancement than for love. Back then, Doña Engracia's want of beauty was compensated by an inheritance of 30,000 pesos, which so incited the passions of the young Encina that he asked for her hand in marriage. Don Dámaso was employed by a commercial lending house in Valparaíso, and his meagre salary was all that lined his purse. However, the day after his wedding he had at his disposal 30,000 pesos with which to paint the town, and since then his ambitions knew no limit. Sent away on business by his employer, Don Dámaso arrived at Copiapó a month into his marriage. Good fortune allowed Encina, who was sent to collect on a rather small note, to meet an honest man who told him the following.

"You could shut me down because I have nothing to pay you. But if you'd like to gamble, I'll double this note and make you my equal partner in a silver mine that I'm sure will strike rich within a month."

Don Dámaso, a man of repose, returned home without any hint of his own intentions. He consulted many sources, all of whom warned him that his debtor, Don José Rivas, was a madman who had lost his entire fortune pursuing an imaginary vein. Encina weighed their advice against Rivas's good faith, which had left him with a favorable impression.

"Let's take a look at the mine," he told Rivas the next day.

They set out together, talking so much about mining along the way that Don Dámaso Encina saw mineral beds, veins, layers, lodes, and other deposits of inexhaustible wealth drifting before his very eyes, without understanding the differences among them. Don José Rivas possessed all the eloquence of the miner whose faith lives on long after his money gives out, and as Encina listened to his voice, he began to see silver shining in the rocks along the road.

In spite of his fascination, Don Dámaso thought of a business proposal that he would offer to Rivas if he liked what he found at the site. Encina was inspired by what he saw, and this is what he said: "I don't understand a word of this, but I wouldn't mind having a piece of it. Give me twelve bars of silver, and I'll have my boss agree to new terms and reduce some of the interest. We'll work the mine by halves, and we'll make a deal. You'll pay me one and a half percent on the capital I invest in the mining and grant me first option to purchase your share or any part of it."

Don José found himself under threat of debtor's prison, which would leave his wife and one-year-old son, Martín, in dire straits. Before reluctantly agreeing to this proposal, Rivas voiced some futile objections, but Encina held firm to his terms and compelled him to sign the contract.

Don Dámaso moved to Copiapó, where he represented his employer and managed some of his own business on the side. During the course of a year the mine paid for itself, and Don Dámaso purchased his partner's shares little by little until Rivas was left as the administrator. Six months after acquiring the last share, the mine suddenly struck rich, and a few years later, Don Dámaso purchased a splendid country estate near Santiago and the manor where we have seen him receive the son of the man to whom he owed his great wealth. Thanks to Don José Rivas, the Encina family was counted among the most aristocratic families of Santiago.

In Chile money dispels family disrepute more readily than in old European societies. Over there they have what is called nouveau riche, who, in spite of all their pomp and luxury, never manage to crawl completely out of the obscurity of their cribs. But in Chile nowadays, all that matters is all that glitters. This is hardly a step toward democracy, however, because those who base their vanity upon blind favors of fortune usually adopt an insufferable insolence. They try to deny their obscure past and disdain those who, unlike themselves, cannot afford to purchase respectability.

The Encina family was noble in Santiago by pecuniary right and as such enjoyed the social courtesy extended them for the reasons we have just noted. They were notorious for their luxurious tastes and their prestige was enhanced by Don Dámaso's solid credit, due to his main line of business—namely: that of grand scale usury so common among Chilean capitalists.

Their luxury served as a magnificent frame around the beautiful Leonor. Had anyone seen this 19-year-old girl in a shabby setting, he would have accused Fortune of being capricious for not creating an ambiance befitting her beauty. Thus, to behold her reclining upon a majestic sofa lined with celestial brocatelle, to catch her image reflected in a gothic mirror, to see her petite foot grazing free and easy over a Persian rug, anyone would have to admire the lavishness of Nature in blissful accord with the favors of Destiny. Leonor sparkled like a diamond surrounded by gold and precious gems. Her expressive green eyes and long lashes; her olive complexion and soft, rosy lips; her small forehead, partially covered by neatly combed, black tresses; the arch of her eyebrows; and her smile for which the tired comparison of teeth to pearls seemed to have been invented—in essence, all of her features and delicate oval face, composed an ideal beauty, the kind that makes young men seethe and old men dream of happier times.

Leonor was the apple of her parents' eyes because she was the best-looking child (the criteria used by most parents), and they spoiled her from the start. She had long grown accustomed to viewing her splendor as a weapon of absolute dominion over those around her, including her own mother.

Doña Engracia, also born willful and headstrong, took great pride in the 30,000 pesos she had brought into the marriage, the origin of the wealth the family now enjoyed. However, now that she was gradually being eclipsed by her daughter's ascent, she began to treat the rest of the family with indifference and spared no one from her "cool treatment" except her darling, little lap dog.

At the time this story began, the Encina family had just hosted a grand ball to welcome home Agustín, who had brought back hoards of clothes and jewels from the Old World (instead of knowledge, which he had not bothered to acquire during his trip abroad). His curly hair, charming grace, and perfect elegance could almost make up for the emptiness of his brain and the 30,000 pesos that he spent roaming the cobblestones of the major European cities.

Aside from this young man and Leonor, Don Dámaso had other children whom we will not describe as they have little relevance to this story.

Agustín's return and some good business deals had predisposed Don Dámaso toward the benevolence with which he had welcomed Martín Rivas into his home. These circumstances had also distracted him from his preoccupation with hygiene, which he swore maintained his good health. He surrendered himself wholly to Politics, which incited his capitalist patriotism and fueled his vehement desire to hold a seat in the House of Senate.

That is why he called for the newspapers after welcoming the young provincial into his home.

III

Martín Rivas had left home at a time of pain and sorrow for his family. His sister, Mercedes, and his mother, Doña Catalina Salazar, were his only loved ones on earth, now that his father had died. Together they had kept a steady vigil at Don José's deathbed for fifteen days. During this mournful time when grief seemed to tighten the familial bonds, the threesome had been equally courageous and supportive of each other, concealing their anguish behind feigned strength.

The day that Don José realized that the end was near, he called his wife and children.

"This is my will," he told them, showing them what he had drawn up the previous day, "and here is a letter that Martín will personally deliver to Don Dámaso Encina, who lives in Santiago."

Then he took his son's hand and said, "From now on, the fate of your mother and your sister will depend on you. Go to Santiago and study hard. God will reward your perseverance and hard work."

Eight days after Don José's death, Martín's departure renewed his family's sorrow, just as they were beginning to accept their loss. Martín caught a freight coach to Valparaíso, and arrived there, eager to begin his studies. Nothing in the station or the town caught his eye. He thought only of his mother and sister and seemed to hear his father's last words in the air. Intensely imaginative and dignified, Martín had grown up in Coquimbo (away from his family due to their poverty) with an elderly uncle who supported his education. The only days of happiness were holidays, when he was able to visit his family. In his loneliness, all of his thoughts were with them, and when he arrived in Santiago, he vowed to return to Copiapó as a lawyer so that he could improve the lot of those who placed their hopes in him.

"God will reward my perseverance and hard work," he said to himself, faithfully reciting his father's last words, while arranging his modest belongings upstairs in Don Dámaso's stately mansion.

At four o'clock that afternoon, Don Dámaso's eldest son knocked on Leonor's chamber door. He donned a blue frockcoat and light trousers, the hem of which touched his patent leather boots, decked with little gold spurs on their heels. In his left hand, he held a riding whip with an ivory handle; in his right, a fat Havana cigar, half-smoked.

He knocked at the door, as we have said, and heard his sister ask, "Who is it?"

"May I come in?" asked Agustín.

Opening the door without waiting for an answer, he entered with an air of pure elegance. Leonor, combing her hair in front of a mirror, turned to her brother, smiling.

"Oh, how dare you bring that cigar in here!"

"Don't make me put it out, little sister," pleaded the dandy. "It's an Imperial. A box goes for 200."

"You could've finished it before you dropped by."

"That's what I had intended. First I went to talk to Mama, but she threw me out claiming that the smoke suffocated her."

"Have you been out riding?"

"*Oui, ma cherie,* and if you would be so gracious as to allow me to finish this Imperial, I'll tell you something you'll appreciate."

"What is it?"

"I went riding with Clemente Valencia."

"And so?"

"He was singing your praises!"

Leonor turned her nose up, and Agustín retorted, "Come now, don't be a hypocrite. You don't dislike Clemente."

"As well as many others."

"Perhaps, but there aren't many others like him."

"Why?"

"Because he is worth 300,000 pesos."

"But he isn't very handsome."

"Nobody with money is ugly, little sister."

A smile brightened Leonor's face, but it would be impossible to say whether its source was the maxim uttered by her brother or the satisfaction for the artful way she had arranged her hair.

"Nowadays, my girl," he continued, reclining in an armchair, "cold, hard cash is your best mate."

"Or beauty," replied Leonor.

"Which is to say that you prefer Emilio Mendoza because he is handsome. *Fi, ma toute belle!*"

"I said no such thing."

"Come now, open up to your big brother. You know I adore you."

"What would be the point, if I love no one?"

"You're incurable. Let's talk about something else. Did you know that we have a houseguest?"

"That's what I heard—a young man from Copiapó. What is he like?"

"Dirt poor."

"I mean, what does he look like?"

"I haven't seen him yet. Probably a ruddy country bumpkin."

Leonor finished touching up her coiffure and turned to face her brother.

"You're simply *charmante,*" observed Agustín who, unable to master French during his trip to Europe, adopted a great profusion of Gallicisms and Frenchisms to create the impression that he was fluent.

"I need to freshen up," said Leonor.

"You mean you're throwing me out too? Well then, I'm off! *Un baiser, ma cherie,*" he added, kissing his sister on the forehead. Then, as he was about to leave, he turned around to say, "How you despise that poor Clemente."

"And what of it?" the girl replied, pretending to feel pity.

"300,000 pesos, mind you. You could go to Paris and return as the queen of fashion. I give you *ma parole d'honneur* that you'll make Clemente *cire et pabile,*" he said, adding a French flair to the vulgar expression, "he'll be putty in your hands."

Leonor, who spoke French better than her brother, burst into laughter at her brother's fatuity and returned to her dressing table.

The two young men whom Agustín had named were known to be the most viable candidates for the hand of Don Dámaso's daughter, but Society had not yet predicted which of the two would win Leonor's favor. As we have heard, each suitor held opposing titles in the arena of gallantry.

Clemente Valencia was 28 years old, average-looking but remarkably stylish (thanks to the 300,000 pesos which Agustín so strongly recommended to his sister). In those days, which is to say 1850, genteel bachelors had not yet adopted the trend of driving to Alameda in coupés or calèches as they do today. Those who aspired to be lions were content with more or less elegant cabriolets driven by postilions to Daumont for the grand celebrations and festivities of the 18th. Clemente Valencia had imported one from Europe to serve as a platform to show the commoners his great opulence. His cabriolet drew adulation from young ladies and criticism from old men who, sitting in judgment at El Paseo de las Delicias, condemned all signs of superfluity. However, Clemente paid little heed to their criticism and succeeded in attracting women, who, contrary to respectable gentlemen, rarely consider excessive ostentation as useless. Thus, the young capitalist was welcomed everywhere and revered for his money, the idol of the day. Mothers offered him the best seat in their salons; daughters flashed their pearly whites and batted their lashes at him; and fathers consulted him deferentially on business matters as though he were a potential benefactor for an important investment.

Emilio Mendoza, the other suitor, possessed the good looks Clemente lacked, but in turn lacked his rival's passport to the most aristocratic chambers of the Capital. He was handsome, but poor. Yet his poverty did not preclude him from mingling among the lions even though he had no cabriolet at his disposal to rouse the kind of sensation at Alameda that his rival did. Emilio belonged to one of those families that had discovered a lucrative speculation in Politics and had always enjoyed good salaries in various public offices. In those days, he held a position paying 3,000 pesos, half of which he spent on shirts, jewels, and expensive stitching that nearly eclipsed those of his powerful adversary.

Both, aside from their attraction to Don Dámaso's daughter, were driven by similar ambitions to marry the girl. Clemente Valencia hoped to fill his pockets with Leonor's likely inheritance, while Emilio Mendoza sought, aside from the money which would come later, a priceless immediate asset: Don Dámaso's political influence. There were two important points of rivalry: the girl's heart and her father's esteem. There were also two serious obstacles: Leonor's feisty disposition and Don Dámaso's lack of character. He fluctuated between the Ministry and the Opposition, depending on the opinions of his friends and the latest newspaper editorials; and she, according to popular opinion, held her beauty in such high esteem that she found no man worthy of her heart or her hand. While Don Dámaso would lean to whichever party he believed would triumph, his daughter would also give and take from each rival whatever hopes he had lulled himself to sleep with the night before.

Thus it was that Clemente Valencia (who belonged to the Opposition due to familial relationships rather than convictions, which he altogether lacked) would find Don Dámaso, in the evening, agreeing with him about the faults of the Government and the necessity to denounce it, and then, the very next morning, pledging his allegiance to the Conservative party. Likewise, he would find a smile upon Leonor's lips as he approached her, just when he was almost convinced that Emilio Mendoza had already won her heart.

The same was true of his rival, who was devising a plan to put Don Dámaso in the Senate out of blind allegiance to Authority; Emilio Mendoza would also suffer Leonor's reproach just when he was convinced of her love.

IV

Martín Rivas was lost in deep thought after arranging his personal effects in the upper floor of Don Dámaso's mansion. His mind was a whirlwind—seeing himself alone in the big city that he had heard so much about in Copiapó; worrying about his family, whom he pictured in mourning and poverty; and wondering about the wealthy strangers who had taken him in so suddenly. His heart ached at the thought of leaving his poor family behind while he was living among the well-to-do with his humble clothing and unrefined manners. He had learned from a servant that Don Dámaso's house was the crown jewel of Santiago estates and that his children were the beau ideal of high style. The thought that he would have to sit beside these people, who were so accustomed to all the refinements of wealth, wounded his pride and distracted him from the ambitious vows that had brought him to Santiago.

At half-past four o'clock in the afternoon, a servant informed Martín that his host wished to speak with him. Martín looked mechanically at the mirror over the mahogany sink and found himself pale and homely; but the voice of reason persuaded him to abandon his childish discouragement before it dampened his spirits.

His gloomy disposition vanished under a healthy flush the moment he entered the chamber where the family waited. Don Dámaso introduced Martín to his wife and to Leonor, who acknowledged him rather impassively. Agustín then entered and extended Rivas a slight nod of the head upon mutual introduction by his father. This icy reception was enough to disconcert the provincial, who stood there without knowing where to put his arms or how to pose as gracefully as Agustín, who ran his fingers through his perfumed curly hair. The voice of Don Dámaso, offering him a seat, filled the awkward silence. Avoiding any eye contact, Martín selected a chair away from the rest of the group, while Agustín bragged about his wonderful ride through the countryside and the superb qualities of the horse that he had ridden.

Martín was envious of Agustín's idle chatter and his affected French accent. And he was dazzled by the wealth of furnishings unknown to him until now: the profusion of gold, the majestic curtains draping from the windows, and the medley of ornaments decorating the side tables. From his perspective of inexperience, these discoveries were attributes of true greatness and superiority, and they instantly inspired in his enthusiastic nature that yearning for luxury which seems to be the legacy of youth.

At first, he was timidly stealing glances and seemed unaware of this self-effacing behavior. However, when the loquacious Don Dámaso inquired about the mines in Copiapó, all eyes turned to Martín, and this sudden attention, oddly enough, brought him a sense of confidence and poise. He answered loudly and clearly, and calmly looked back at those who found him rather quaint. Serenity returned to his naturally energetic spirit as he spoke, and only then could he mindfully observe his captive audience.

In the dimmest corner of the room he noticed Doña Engracia, who always lingered in the least light to avoid suffocation. The good lady had upon her lap a little white pooch with long curly hair, which must have just been combed, so fluffy were its curls. Every now and then, the pooch would lift her tiny head, rivet her bright eyes on Martín, and growl. Doña Engracia would then affectionately spank her, as if it were a spoiled tot who had done something naughty, and she would gently say, "Diamela! Stop that!" Martín paid little mind to the discontent of the pooch and its mistress, and also ceased to admire the dandy's pretentious manners in order to feast his eyes upon Leonor, whose beauty inspired in him unspeakable awe. To comprehend the sensations surging through Martín's veins in Leonor's presence, one would have to imagine what a traveler feels standing before Niagara Falls or what an artist feels standing before Raphael's masterpiece *The Transfiguration.* Over an embroidered pinafore, exposing the Valenciennes ruffle of an exquisite petticoat, she wore a white gown with a loosely draped sash around her waist like an elegant Roman statue. The bodice had a low neckline that revealed the pure contours of her throat and suggested the divine perfection of her bosom. This simple yet precious dress seemed to achieve an impossible: the embellishment of Leonor's splendor, which drew Martín's eyes with such persistence that the girl looked away, mildly impatient.

The butler entered, announcing that dinner was served, while Agustín was describing the Parisian Boulevards to his mother, and Don Dámaso, who was leaning toward the Opposition that day, was setting his Republican beliefs into practice by treating Martín with courtesy and kindness.

Agustín offered one arm to his mother, while trying to scoop Diamela up with the other hand.

"Careful, careful, boy!" exclaimed the lady of the house. "You'll upset her!"

"Never!" replied the dandy. "I wouldn't dream of harming Mama's *charmante* little baby."

Following his wife and son, Don Dámaso offered his arm to Leonor, then turned to Martín, saying, "Let's dine, my friend."

Martín heard the word *friend* as an indication of the vast distance between him and the family with whom he found lodging. As he humbly followed them to the dining room, he felt renewed discouragement at the sight of Agustín's shiny boots striding across the carpet with such arrogant sally and Leonor's high-held face radiating with all the pride of beauty and wealth.

"In *Frères provençaux* I had a delectable turtle soup every day," Agustín commented after tasting the soup and patting the corner of his lips with a napkin. "Oh, the bread in Paris is *divin,*" he added, breaking a piece of what we call French bread. "It's simply *mirobolante.*"

"How long did it take you to learn French?" inquired Doña Engracia, feeding Diamela a spoonful of soup, while looking at Martín as if to boast of her son's superiority.

Whether the spoon missed Diamela's little snout or whether the high temperature of the soup burned her delicate lips, the pooch let out a yowl that made Doña Engracia jump in her seat, causing the bowl and its contents to spill across the tablecloth.

"What have I been telling you? That's what happens when you bring animals to the table!" shouted Don Dámaso.

"My poor little baby," said Doña Engracia, ignoring her husband to comfort her howling baby.

"Come now, hush up, *polissonne,*" Agustín told Diamela, who, wrestling to escape from the arms of her mistress, suddenly stopped howling.

Doña Engracia lifted her eyes to Heaven as if to admire the power of the Creator, and then looked at her husband, cooing, "Look dearest, Mama's little gem understands French!"

"Oh, the dog is a positively intelligent creature," remarked Agustín. "In Paris I called to them in Spanish and they followed whenever I showed them a piece of bread."

A new bowl of soup appeased Diamela and restored order to the table.

"And what do they say of Politics up north?" the master of the house asked Martín, who replied, "I have lived an isolated life since my father's illness. I know very little about public opinion there."

"In Paris there are many political parties," said Agustín. "The Orleanists, the Bourbon *brancha,* and the Republicans."

"The *brancha?*" asked Don Dámaso.

"The Bourbon line, in other words," replied Agustín.

"They say everyone up north belongs to the Opposition," said Don Dámaso, addressing Martín again.

"I think that is the generalization," he responded.

"Politics *gâta* the spirit," observed the young Encina.

"Got what spirit?" asked his father, puzzled.

"*C'est-à-dire* it spoils everything," answered his firstborn.

"Nonetheless, every citizen ought to be concerned with public affairs, and the rights of the people are sacred," said Don Dámaso, who, belonging to the Opposition that day, emphasized this phrase which he had just read in a Liberal newspaper.

"Mama, what kind of *confiture* is this?" asked Agustín, pointing to a compotier to turn the disagreeable topic of Politics to something more palatable.

"And the rights of the people," repeated Don Dámaso, ignoring his son's dissatisfaction, "are as sacred as the Gospels."

"Apricot," said Doña Engracia.

"Apricot what?" asked Don Dámaso, mistaking his wife's remark as an opinion on the rights of the people.

"No, darling, I was talking about the marmalade," answered Doña Engracia.

"*Confiture d'abricots,*" corrected Agustín, as if he were a preacher quoting from Latin scriptures.

During this dialogue, Martín watched Leonor, who refrained from the family discussion out of apparent apathy.

After dinner they all filed out of the dining room in the order they had walked in and resumed their favorite topics in the main salon. Agustín described to his mother the aroma of the after-dinner coffee he enjoyed in Tortoni; Don Dámaso paraphrased Liberal phrases that he had picked up in the morning newspaper; and Leonor leafed distractedly through a book of English prints. By seven o'clock, Martín was able to free himself from the Republican discourses of his host and retire to his room.

V

Martín sat down at a table like a weary traveler after a long sojourn. His feelings about moving to Santiago and living with a prosperous family, and his humbling impressions of Agustín's social graces and Leonor's ravishing beauty—all whirling through his mind like fantastic illusions—left him exhausted.

The contemptuous belle, who did not deign to speak with her own family at the dinner table, humiliated him with her wealth and beauty. Could it be that she had nothing to say because she was as vapid as the rest of them? Martín asked himself this question defensively, as if to console himself over the impossibility of attracting the attention of a woman like Leonor. As he thought about her, he caught his first glimpse of Love as one would see it at his age: as blissful as Paradise; as ardent as the hopes of Youth; as golden as the dreams of Poetry, that inseparable companion of the heart that loves or longs for love.

A sudden memory of his family lifted his sullen spirit from the circle of fire threatening to consume it. He took his hat and went down to the street, wanting to acquaint himself with the area and the people who lived there. He also wanted to buy some books, and asked the first person he encountered in the street for directions to the nearest bookstore. On the way, he stopped at Plaza de Armas.

In 1850 the Plaza fountain was not surrounded by a pretty garden like it is today, nor were there benches where strollers could sit down and enjoy the view. Back then people would sit on the stone rim, especially the locals, who would hang around the Plaza at night. There were always plenty of peddlers among them, offering a pair or boots or shoes to whomever passed by at these hours.

Martín cut through the Plaza from the corner of Calle de las Monjitas and walked to the fountain, where he stopped to admire the two marble figures that crowned it. A peddler approached him, saying, "Patent leather boots, Señor?"

These words brought to mind Agustín's shiny footwear and the reason Martín had left the house. He thought that with a swank pair of patent leather boots he would fare better with the stylish family who had opened their doors to him. Inexperienced and unintimidated, Martín hesitantly looked at the peddler, who had already begun to walk off, and the man returned immediately.

"Let's see the boots," said Martín.

"Here ya go, buddy," replied the man, luring the newcomer with the glassy reflection of his goods. The peddler placed a kerchief on the stone rim of the fountain, saying, "Sit down and try 'em on."

Rivas sat down, pulled off his old, rugged boot, and tried on a shiny, new one, when—to his complete surprise—six individuals surrounded him, offering him a different pair of boots all at the same time. While trying to shove his foot into the shoe, Martín felt more bewildered than the Captain of the Guard in *The Barber of Seville* when he found himself surrounded during the scene at Don Bartolo's house.

"See, these are much better," one was alleging, while another dangled a pair of boots under Martín's nose, insisting, "Try these on, Señor. See this workmanship? It doesn't come any better."

"But *deeze* are gonna last a lifetime," a third murmured in his ear.

And others were hawking their goods in equally aggressive ways, thereby unnerving the poor chap, who rejected the first pair because they were too tight, the second pair because they were too wide, and the third because they were too expensive. The number of salesmen accosting the youth multiplied until Martín grew tired of their persistence. He put on his old boot, stood up, and said that he would buy on another occasion. At that instant, he witnessed a drastic change in their attitudes and heard the first peddler say, "If ya ain't gonna buy, don't waste our time, pal!"

And another added, as though he were an apprentice to the

first, "Maybe he's broke."

Then a third chimed in, "Aye, whatta poor lookin' bugger!"

Martín, a newcomer to the capital, tried to ignore the insolence of his working-class compatriots, but felt his patience wearing thin. He announced to the crowd, "I have insulted no one, and I will allow no one to insult me."

"What's wrong with bein' poor? We're poor too."

"So, let's just say he's rich, okay," said another, crowding closer to the youth.

"Yeah, well if he's so rich, then why ain't he buyin' nottin'?" jeered the first peddler, crowding even closer than the other fellow.

Rivas lost his temper at this point and pushed the man back, causing him to fall at the feet of his cronies.

"Ya gonna let some hick deck ya?" someone sneered.

"Get up, man. Don't be a sissy," taunted another.

The peddler stood up and charged at Martín. A fistfight broke out, much to the delight of the others, who applauded and cheered the punches that each man happily landed into his opponent.

"Smack him in the honker," incited one.

"Knock his lights out!" shouted another.

"Hit him hard and low," exclaimed yet another.

A voice out of nowhere made the crowd magically disperse, leaving the fighters to themselves.

"Here come the cops!" some of them yelled as they ran off, with the rest of the crowd trailing behind them.

A policeman seized Martín by one arm and the peddler by the other, saying, "You boys are coming with me."

Startled by the sight of the uniform, Martín pleaded, "Please release me. None of this was my fault."

"Com'on, boys, let's get a move on it," answered the policeman, who started to blow his whistle.

It was useless for Martín to explain how it all began. The policeman refused to listen and continued to blow his whistle until another policeman appeared. With him, Martín's eloquence failed the same way. Unmoved by Martín's story, he also repeated the stock phrase of Santiago's police force: "Com'on, boys, let's get a move on it."

Before such a uniform mode of speech, Rivas knew that it was better to resign himself and go peacefully with his adversary to headquarters.

Martín hoped that the young officer on duty would be more reasonable; however, when the officer heard his story, he had Martín detained until the Chief of Police arrived.

VI

While Martín Rivas was sitting behind bars, Don Dámaso Encina's salon was glowing with the usual lighting of his evening tertulias.

On a sofa sat Doña Engracia chitchatting with her sister-in-law, whose daughter was sitting across from them with Leonor and Agustín. Gathered around a card table in the corner of the adjoining chamber were Don Dámaso and a couple of gray-haired gentlemen; and behind them sat Leonor's adoring suitor, the young Mendoza, looking on.

Doña Engracia was bragging to Doña Francisca about Diamela's breakthroughs in the language of Vaugelas and Voltaire, while one of Doña Francisca's younger children, who could only be described as a spoiled brat, amused himself by yanking the tail and ears of his auntie's little gem.

Matilde Encina looked so unlike her cousin Leonor that it was difficult to believe that this fair-skinned, blue-eyed blond was even remotely related to the dark brunette sitting beside her, let alone as first cousins. Sharpening the physical contrast was Matilde's languid, melancholic air, which lacked the self-assurance so becoming of Leonor. And although their dresses were equally stunning, Matilde's beauty paled beside her cousin's.

The girls were holding hands affectionately when Clemente Valencia entered the salon.

"Oh, here comes the vulgar show-off, flashing his diamonds and chains," said Leonor.

The young man dared not sit beside the two cousins in view of the frigid salutation from Don Dámaso's daughter; instead, he decided to join their mothers.

"You know, they say you'll marry him," said Matilde to her cousin.

"Jesus," she replied, "because he is rich!"

"And because they think you're in love with him."

"I don't love him or anyone," replied Leonor.

"No one? Not even Mendoza?" asked Matilde.

"No one, Matilde. Have you ever been in love?" Leonor flatly asked her cousin, who blushed and fell silent. "When you were engaged to Adriano, did you feel that love they all talk about?"

"No," she answered.

"What about Rafael San Luis?"

Matilde blushed again without responding.

"Look, I've never dared to bring this up, but you used to say that you were wild about Rafael, and then you suddenly clammed up. The next thing I knew, you were packing up your trousseau to marry Adriano. Which one of them did you really love? Tell me what happened. It's been a year since your fiancé died, and it seems to me that it's about time you stopped playing the role of an old widow and started opening up to your best friend. Are you telling me you didn't love Adriano?"

"No."

"Then you've never forgotten Rafael?"

"How could I ever forget him?" answered Matilde, fighting back tears.

"Then why did you leave him?"

"You know how strict my father is."

"Oh, no one would have forced me," asserted Leonor proudly, "especially if I loved someone."

"If you've never loved anyone, as you say, then you shouldn't be saying those things," replied Matilde.

"It's true I've never loved anyone, at least, not what I consider true love. I've been fond of a few young men, but not for very long. I abhor how they beseech me to love them back, for it makes me think of the superiority they pretend to have over us, and I just cringe. I have yet to meet a man who has enough pride to despise the prestige of money and enough self-respect not to bow down to beauty."

"I've never thought about it," said Matilde. "I loved Rafael the minute I met him and my feelings haven't changed."

"Haven't you spoken to him since Adriano's death?"

"No, I wouldn't dare. I wasn't strong enough to disobey Papa and so he has every right to despise me. I've seen him a few times in the street as fair and handsome as ever. I swear that I nearly fainted at the sight of him, but he passed me by, pretending not to see me, holding his head with such dignity."

Leonor relished her cousin's excitement and imagined that her ardent and poetic worship must be perfectly sweet for the soul.

"Do you believe he doesn't love you anymore?"

"That's what I believe," Matilde sighed.

"Poor Matilde! I wish I could love like you do, even if I had to suffer as much."

"Oh, if you haven't suffered, don't wish for it!"

"I'd prefer that torment a thousand times over this dull life I lead. Sometimes I think that something is wrong with me. All my girlfriends have been in love and I've never thought about a single man for more than two days straight."

"Keep it up and you'll be happy."

"Who knows?" murmured Leonor ruefully.

The butler announced that it was teatime, and everyone filed into the chamber adjacent to the recreation room where the master of the house was playing cards with Don Simón Arenal, and Matilde's father, Don Fidel Elías. Don Dámaso associated with the sort of men we call parasites in Politics, the sort who live protected by Authority and who profess no more political creed than their immediate convenience and blind adhesion to the great word Order (used in the strictest sense). Our nation's political arena is paved with this kind of man who claims to be in hell for good intentions (not to liken our Politics to hell, although there are innumerable points of comparison). Don Simón Arenal and Don Fidel Elías applauded every blow of Authority and contemptuously called anyone who expressed concern with public affairs without holding a position of Authority either a rabble-rouser or a demagogue. Worst of all, they were vehemently opposed to free press and deemed public opinion Radical rubbish. When they referred to Radicals (or *Pipiolos* as we say in Chile), they meant anyone who dared to raise his voice without owning houses, haciendas, or money.

Their despotic opinions, which they professed by virtue of convenience, had kindled some domestic discord for Don Fidel. His wife, Doña Francisca Encina, had read some books and ventured to think for herself, thereby desecrating the social principles of her husband, who perceived all books as pointless, if not pernicious. Being well-read, Doña Francisca was Liberal in Politics and nourished this tendency in her brother, whom Don Fidel and Don Simón had difficulty converting to the Party of Order, which some graciously referred to as the Energetic Party, back in the old days.

All gathered around the tea table, where the conversation took distinct turns in each group according to age and taste. Doña Engracia recounted the dinner scene to her sister-in-law to prove that Diamela understood French, to which Doña Francisca replied by quoting some French authors on the cleverness of the canine breed. Leonor and her cousin sat between the young men, and Don Dámaso sat at the head of the table with his friend and his brother-in-law.

"You can be damned sure, Dámaso," said Don Fidel, "that this Society of Equality is nothing but a gang of rabble-rousers who want a piece of our pie."

"And that's not the half of it!" said Don Simón, whom the Government had appointed for various commissions. "They're conspiring for our jobs too!"

"But, man," replied Don Dámaso, "what about the schools that our Society founded to educate the people?"

"People, what people?" retorted Don Fidel. "The worst evil that one can do is to teach a bunch of rogues to act like gentlemen."

"If I were Governor, I would ban their meetings," proposed Don Simón. "What are Politics coming to, when the whole toot and scramble gets involved!"

"But they are citizens like you and I!" argued Don Dámaso.

"Yes, but penniless citizens, hungry citizens," said Don Fidel.

"Aren't we supposedly living in a Republic?" asked Doña Francisca, jumping into the conversation.

"Would that we were not!" replied her husband.

"Christ Almighty!" the lady exclaimed, scandalized.

"Listen, sweetheart, women should not talk Politics," said Don Fidel sententiously. This maxim was approved by the demure Don Simón, who nodded in agreement along with her nephew, who added, "Toilette and bouquets are for ladies, Auntie dearest."

"Who would have thought that Europe would have made him a bigger fool?" huffed the lady.

"A while back," said Don Simón to Don Dámaso, "a minister asked me whether you were in Opposition."

"Me!" exclaimed Don Dámaso, "I have never been in Opposition. I am Independent!"

"If my memory serves me correctly, it was to offer you a commission."

Regretting his hasty response, Don Dámaso fell pensive before inquiring, "And what commission was that?"

"I can't recall at the moment," answered Don Simón, "but you know how the Government is always looking for men of merit to hold office and . . . "

"Indeed they should," continued Don Dámaso. "How else would they establish Authority?"

"Look, Leonor, they're already winning your papa over," remarked Doña Francisca.

"No, nobody wins me over, dear," said Don Dámaso. "I have always said that the Government should employ only men of repute."

"I still have hopes of seeing you as Senator one of these days," said Don Fidel.

"I have no such aspirations," said Don Dámaso, "but if the people elect me . . . "

"Here it is the Government that elects," observed Doña Francisca.

"And that's the way it should be," responded her husband. "How else could it govern?"

"If that counts for governing, they might as well leave us all alone," said Doña Francisca.

"I already told you, when it comes to Politics," warned her husband, "you women should stand out of the way."

Don Simón approved a second time, and Doña Francisca turned to her sister-in-law out of frustration.

After tea, the tertulia reconvened in the salon, where the older men obsessed about Politics and the younger men encircled Leonor, who sat next to a table where there was a book inlaid with mother of pearl.

"Look, Leonor," her brother said, "they've already returned your album."

"I thought you had it," Leonor said to Emilio Mendoza indifferently.

"Señorita, I brought it back this evening as I promised I would."

"Did you take it to inscribe some verses?" Clemente Valencia asked of his rival. "I've never been able to brave poetry," quipped the capitalist, rattling the gold chain of an expensive watch.

"Nor *moi,*" said Agustín.

"Let's see your album," said Doña Francisca, opening the cover.

"Auntie dearest, they're literary *morsoes,*" exclaimed Agustín. "Let's hear some musique instead."

"Read to us, Mama, please," said Matilde. "Some of us would love to hear those *literary morsoes*, as my cousin calls them."

"Here are some verses," she said, opening to a page, "and they were composed by Señor Mendoza."

"You write poetry, sport? Don't tell us that you're in love," said Agustín.

Emilio blushed and glanced at Leonor, who pretended not to notice.

"It's a short composition," said Doña Francisca, who was aching to read it aloud.

"We're ready, Auntie dearest," said Agustín.

Doña Francisca read with a ridiculously affected and sentimental voice.

To the Eyes of . . .
Sweeter thou must be,
Casting thy eyes upon me,
For torment it is to see
The fountain of such delight,

Be the source of my blight;
When thy gaze is honey for them,
Yet, for me alone, pure venom,
My mind exasperates
At the cruelty of my fate;
If by loving thee I offend,
Thou may seek thy revenge,
Though thou must comprehend
That either my love or my life
Thou shall bring to an end;
If it is vengeance so vigorous
In requite of my love so rigorous,
I must surrender to this strife,
For life is much too brief
To wallow in such bitter grief.

Emilio Mendoza

At the conclusion of this flowery recitation, Emilio Mendoza looked languidly at Leonor as if to say, "You are the goddess of my inspiration."

"How long did it take you to write these verses?" asked Doña Francisca.

"I finished them this morning," said Mendoza, feigning modesty and guarding the fact that he had merely copied this composition from the Spanish poet Campoamor, who was little known in Chile at the time.

"Here is something in prose," said Doña Francisca.

"Humanity walks toward progress, turning in a circle called love, at the center of which there is an angel called woman."

"Oh, how touching!" said Doña Francisca dreamily.

"Yes, whatever it means!" quipped Clemente Valencia.

Enchanted by each line, Doña Francisca continued flipping leisurely through page after page of shallow phrases and graceless stanzas, each ending with a pitiful plea for compassion from the owner of the album.

"If you leave my aunt with the book, she'll stay up all night," joshed Agustín to his friend Valencia.

By taking his hat Don Fidel signaled that he was ready to leave. Once they were in the street, he said to his wife, "Did you sense that Dámaso was hinting that he would like his son to marry Matilde? Agustín is a magnificent match."

"He is a worthless boy," answered Doña Francisca, remembering how little affection her nephew displayed for poetry.

"Worthless? His father is worth nearly a million! Sweetheart, just think that next year the lease on El Roble expires, and if the owner isn't inclined to renew my lease. . . ."

"I haven't seen that hacienda of yours yield much of a profit yet," said Doña Francisca.

"That is beside the point. I must consider what will happen after the lease expires. Marrying Matilde to Agustín would not only assure our daughter's good fortune, but would guarantee us Dámaso's financial backing on any venture, which he is not always willing to lend us."

"Well, you know what you are doing," his wife replied irritably, for she was incensed by his prosaic calculations.

There was silence the rest of the way home.

Now let us return to Don Dámaso and his family, whom we last saw in the salon.

"What has become of our houseguest?" asked the gentleman, to which a servant replied that he had not returned from his stroll.

"He must have gotten lost," figured Don Dámaso.

"Santiago isn't big enough for anyone to get lost! It's not like Paris, where one can easily *s'égarse!*" exclaimed Agustín.

"I've been thinking," said Don Dámaso to his wife, "that Martín may be able to assist me in keeping my books."

"He seems like a nice young man, and I appreciate the fact that he doesn't smoke," said Doña Engracia.

Martín had said that he did not smoke when he refused an after-dinner cigar that Don Dámaso had offered him during one of his states of Republican rapture. After his friends bade him goodnight, he was somewhat cured of his equalitarian impulses, in view of the news that a Minister had considered him for a commission.

"After all," thought Don Dámaso, as he went to bed, "those Liberals are so extremist."

VII

Martín protested against the arbitrary incarceration, entreating his liberty and promising to return the next day to be judged; however, the officer on guard upheld the initial order with the inflexibility of a Napoleonic foot soldier who would prefer death to surrender.

Tired of protesting and beseeching, Rivas resigned himself to waiting patiently for the Chief of Police to arrive. He was overcome by the heaviness of his heart. The worst of his worries was the explanation that he would have to give to the Encina family the next morning if he were unable to obtain his freedom by then. He imagined Leonor's haughty look, Agustín's insolent chortle, and the belittling compassion of their parents. In his mind, Leonor was to blame for this humiliating fiasco. Recalling her provocative beauty and dreading her disdain, the poor provincial cursed his destiny and asked Heaven to justify the poverty of some and the wealth of others. No sooner had his thoughts turned to the inequities of fate when he felt a sudden, obscure rage against Fortune's favorites.

"I only hope that Leonor looks the other way," thought Martín, "because I'll know how to deal with anyone else who dares to laugh at me."

This singular reflection made it clear that, as much as Rivas wanted to escape the profound feelings that the sight of Leonor stirred in his soul, he could think of nothing but her. He asked himself pitifully, "Will she despise me?"

At moments he considered returning to Copiapó with the paltry sum that he had left. He thought about working up north to support his family, but knew deep down how silly it would be to turn back simply out of dread of being disliked by a woman he had met only once.

The Chief of Police arrived at midnight and allowed Martín to state his case. The provincial's eloquence spoke more in his favor than the poverty of his attire; and for that reason, the Chief set him free. Martín returned to the house at half past midnight, only to find the front door locked. He rapped gently a few times. Nobody seemed to hear, and so he retired with no further ado. Manning himself with patience, he resolved to spend the rest of the night walking the neighborhood.

Santiago used to be a quiet place where people went to bed early. Hence, Rivas saw nothing more exciting than the facade of the homes and the snoring night watchmen on each corner, protecting the residents. He entered the house the next morning when the front door was opened by the valet on his way to the Plaza. His derisive smile was the first of a succession of indignities that Martín was sure to encounter in Don Dámaso's home.

Shortly before breakfast he came downstairs, prepared to face the shame of his situation straight-away, lest he be cast under open fire of suspicion. Don Dámaso observed Martín approaching his study and opened the door for him.

"How have you spent the night, Martín?" he asked, after the youth had greeted him.

"Most unfortunately, sir," he replied.

"How so? You haven't slept well?"

"I have spent the better part of the night in the street."

Don Dámaso widened his eyes and exclaimed, "In the street! And where were you before the door was locked at midnight?"

"I was detained at the police station."

Martín recounted his misadventures blow by blow and watched his guardian struggling to contain his laughter. Don Dámaso, barely convinced of his own sincerity, said, "I feel positively terrible about all of this, but let's put it all behind us. I'd like to speak to you about a project that may interest you."

"I am at your service," answered the youth, without daring to ask Don Dámaso to keep the disagreeable episode a secret.

The gentleman said, "I would like to know if you wouldn't mind looking after my correspondence and bookkeeping, after your studies, of course. I would pay you 30 pesos per month to be my secretary, if the job suits you."

"Señor," Martín replied, "I appreciate this opportunity to return the favor of your kindness and I will gladly handle your correspondence and books. However, I will not permit myself to be compensated for such a simple service."

"But, man, you're poor, Martín. At least, this way you'll have 50 pesos at your disposal."

"I would much prefer your esteem," replied Rivas, earning Don Dámaso's respect for having rejected a salary that many in his place would have craved.

Martín acquainted himself with the tasks that he would undertake in Don Dámaso's study, while the master of the house leafed through some of his papers and thought about how his guest had conducted himself. For some men, an act of generosity revealing indifference toward money is the height of magnanimity. The worship of gold has always had so many disciples that one exception seemed incredible, especially in this day and age. Thus, Don Dámaso admired the heroism of Martín's words, and yet felt somewhat wary of the young man's Quixotic edge. The ambitious host was concerned that his inexperienced houseguest might be an obvious target for those who preached *liberty* and *fraternity*.

"You see, Martín," he said after some rumination, "nowadays Santiago is plagued by men who care only about Politics. If you would allow me to give you some advice, I would caution you against those so-called Liberals. They're always stuck at the bottom of Society. Between you and me, I think all that a man must do to lose himself completely is to become a Liberal. In Chile, at least, I think it is difficult for them to climb the ranks."

By the frankness of this advice, Martín understood the political principles constituting the profession of faith by which Don Dámaso hoped to occupy a seat in the Republican Senate. Absorbed in his studies and removed from social intercourse, Rivas did not know that a great many of his country's politicians cultivated that very profession. His strict judgment and youthful, noble pride led him to the doleful notion that his guardian was politically motivated. This judgment was based solely on instinct because Martín had never stopped to seriously question the issues that burn within humanity like a high fever when the masses lack their vital atmosphere, which is to say: liberty.

Don Dámaso had shared Martín's misadventures with his wife and children shortly before breakfast was served. Petting Diamela, Doña Engracia said, "Which means, the poor boy hasn't slept a wink all night."

"*C'est-à-dire*, Mama," said Agustín, "that he spent the night *à la belle étoile*. What a merry escapade."

"Now listen up," said Don Dámaso. "This boy who went to the Plaza to buy shoes only has an allowance of 20 pesos, and yet he turned down a salary of 30 pesos, which I offered him to be my secretary."

"Oh, Oh! *C'est-à-dire*," exclaimed Agustín, smoothing his mustache, "that he wants to play proud."

"He refused to be your secretary?" asked Doña Engracia.

"No, no, he accepted the position, but refused the salary."

Leonor looked up at her father as if it were only then that she caught wind of the conversation. Meanwhile Agustín, who was lolling upon the sofa and admiring his red slippers and morning pants, remarked, "It's just to be forgiven for the boot escapade."

Just then, in walked Martín, who had been called to breakfast. Agustín greeted him, saying, "I hear you're having a rough time sleeping in Santiago?"

Martín blushed, and Don Dámaso signaled to his son to shut his mouth. Endeavoring to make light of the joke as best he could, Rivas responded, "What can I say?"

"Poor chap," teased the dandy, "shopping for boots at the Plaza. Why didn't you come to me? I would have sent you to a French bootery."

"What do you expect?" answered Martín proudly. "I am a provincial and I am poor. The first explains my misadventure, the latter why a French bootery would be too expensive for me."

"You've never mentioned any faux pas of yours in Paris, and that's why you are so quick to criticize this man."

Without looking at Martín, Leonor spoke these words to her

brother cheerfully to disguise the acrimony that enveloped them. Rivas knew that he should thank the girl for her defense, but felt tongue-tied. Agustín, likewise, was rendered speechless, for he recognized his sister's superior wit and opted to disguise his defeat by petting Diamela who sat in his mother's lap.

"I told my family about the episode," said Don Dámaso, "only to explain your absence last night."

"Rightfully so, Señor," declared Martín, who had regained his composure with Leonor's words. "I hope that these fine ladies," he added, "will excuse my inadvertent absence."

"Of course, young man," said Doña Engracia. "It could happen to anybody."

"Certainly, to anybody," repeated Agustín, seeing that everybody sided with Martín. "No harm intended. It was a *plaisanterie sans conséquences.*"

Leonor nodded in agreement with her mother, and Martín understood this little gesture as absolution for the absurd fiasco.

After breakfast, he enrolled in the legal program at the National Institute. Having run all of his errands, he returned to Don Dámaso's studio and sat down to work at his desk, saying to himself, "She doesn't despise me." This idea lifted the enormous burden weighing on his heart and allowed him to dream of happiness in the distant horizon of hope.

VIII

From the next day forward, Martín began studying with the determination of a young man convinced that education is the only path to happiness, since fortune has denied him wealth. From the first day of school, his poor, rustic outfit made him conspicuous among his fashionable classmates, most of whom came to class dreaming of last night's ball or reminiscing of a rendezvous much fresher in the mind than the precepts of *The Laws of Castile* or *The Handbook of Trials.* This made Martín feel isolated. Among our youth, those whose attributes are not worn on a fancy shirtsleeve for all to see must struggle against much indifference, and even a touch of disdain, before engaging the compassion of others. The other students regarded Martín as a poor devil who deserved no more attention than his tattered clothing and refrained from offering him a friendly handshake. Martín recognized what might properly be called the *impertinence of accouterments,* but remained dignified in his isolation by exhibiting his superior academic faculties whenever an opportunity arose.

Something caught his attention, and it was the absence of a student whose name was often mentioned. Almost everyday someone in class would ask, "Has Rafael San Luis arrived?" After the usual "no," they would talk about the absentee whom the students must have revered, judging by the frequency of their comments.

Two months into the semester, Martín noticed the arrival of that student whom everyone greeted cordially, calling him by that familiar name. He was 23 or 24 years old, and his fair, delicate features (so refined that they were almost womanly) set into relief a fine curve of a shiny black mustache. A full crop of hair, parted in the middle, accentuated the nobility of his head, and behind his small, rosy ears curled shiny black ringlets. His lively eyes (not especially large) seemed to blaze with powerful intelligence and with the fire of a valiant, noble heart. He was of average height and nicely built.

At the beginning of class, Rivas studied this young man, who finally returned the look after speaking to a friend. Just then, the professor asked Martín his opinion about a judicial issue that was being debated, and after his response, he received an irate rebuttal from the student whom he had just corrected. Martín retorted with lofty vigor, causing his opponent to turn red with indignation.

"Who is he?" Rafael asked a friend, who replied, "He's new in town, and by the looks of him, I'd say he's a poor rustic. He doesn't know anybody and he only speaks when the professor calls on him. I'd say he's no slouch."

Rafael observed Rivas and seemed to take interest in the issue that he and his opponent debated.

The student who had shown his humiliation under defeat approached Martín after class with a look of snobbery and cautioned, "You were right to correct me, but don't ever use that tone with me again."

"I will bear no one's arrogance and I will always respond in the tone used with me," asserted Martín, "and having already treated me thus," he added, "I must warn you that I take lessons from no one but the professor and only on the subject of the course."

"This gentleman is right," intervened Rafael San Luis, who ended the argument with these straightforward words: "Miguel, you were rude when it was only his duty to correct you. Besides, this man is a newcomer, and we should at least be polite, if not kind."

Martín approached San Luis somewhat shyly, saying, "Thank you for speaking up for me."

"You're welcome," said Rafael, shaking his hand.

"Well, now that you've come to my aid," continued Rivas, "I'm hoping that you can show me around. I'm new in Santiago and I'm feeling out of place."

"From what I've just witnessed," answered Rafael, "you need little guidance. What rules Santiago is pride, and you seem to have enough nerve to put this town in its place. I must say, though, that I only defended you because they told me you were poor and didn't know anyone in class. Everyone is caught up in frivolous trappings here, and your situation aroused my sympathies."

"I'm pleased to have your sympathies," said Martín, "and would be more pleased if you will allow me to cultivate this friendship."

"You've chosen a sad friend for yourself, Martín," replied Rafael with a melancholic smile. "But maybe I can save you from sadness if you learn from my mistakes. I'll see you tomorrow."

He bade farewell with these words, leaving a strange impression on Martín, who thoughtfully watched him walk away. In truth, there was something mysterious and poetic about this striking young man. Martín observed a sense of dignity amidst the simplicity of his manners and identified with his melancholic air. Rafael's attire also caught Martin's eye because it showed impulsiveness as well as disregard for the style to which the rest of the students conformed. His turned-up collar was not starched like everyone else's and his loosely knotted black tie revealed the smooth lines of his throat, the kind sculptors tend to give to the bust of Byron. Moreover, Martín read in his parting words a slight analogy to his own situation and fancied that Rafael might also be one of Fortune's disinherited sons. This idea encouraged Martín to approach him the next day to continue their conversation.

"When you're free," said San Luis, "we'll go for a bite to eat at a little hotel I know. Where are you staying?"

"At the home of Don Dámaso Encina."

"Don Dámaso Encina!" he gasped. "Are you related?"

"No, I brought him a letter from my father and he took me into his home. Do you know him?"

"We've met," he answered, concealing his agitation. Both fell silent for a few moments until Rafael changed the topic.

After class San Luis invited Martín to lunch at a rundown hotel where a bottle of wine poured more candor into their conversation.

"The menu is not nearly as appetizing as Don Dámaso's," said Rafael, "but you can loosen your tie and breathe easy there."

"You've been to his house?" asked Rivas, who was struck by his friend's nervous curiosity about his host.

"Yes, in better times," he said. "And how is his daughter?"

"Oh, she is precious," said Martín enthusiastically.

"Careful, I'm sensing a potentially fatal admiration in your voice," said San Luis becoming serious.

"How so?" asked Rivas.

"Because the worse thing that a poor fellow can do to himself is fall in love with a rich girl. Studies, future, hopes . . . you can kiss them all goodbye," sighed San Luis, raising his glass of wine. "Yesterday, you asked me for guidance, and now I'll give you some of the soundest advice you'll ever hear. Love, for a poor, young student, is the apple of paradise: forbidden fruit. I'm telling you this because you've got the noble ambition that makes for greatness. If you want to be Somebody someday, Martín, protect your heart with a shield of indifference as impenetrable as rock."

"I don't plan on falling in love," answered Martín, "and I have mighty good reasons, including the one you just mentioned."

San Luis then changed the topic so many times, that it seemed as though he were trying to make Martín forget his advice.

When Martín mentioned his new friend to the Encina family that evening, Don Dámaso said, "That blade is nothing but a schemer, hunting a pretty dowry."

"But Papa," contested Leonor, "you mustn't be unfair. I have a higher opinion of San Luis."

"He's a *parvenu,*" said Agustín. "Papa is right. In *l'époque où nous sommes,* every bloke in the street is digging for gold."

"And why shouldn't they, if there are needy people who deserve it more than many wealthy people?" said Leonor.

Leonor's energetic defense of Rafael from the attacks of her father and brother, compounded by Rafael's caution against love, sparked a flame in Martín's eyes and an eerie discomfort in his heart. He could only infer that his new friend had fallen for Leonor and that Don Dámaso had forbidden him to see her. Thus, disheartened, as if he had just received sad news, Martín set himself to work, distressed by the gloomy prism through which he suddenly beheld the future.

After sending off Don Dámaso's correspondence, his mind ran innumerable laps around the same inference and arrived at this discouraging conclusion: "They must have been in love with each other, and since Leonor defends him, she must still be in love with him."

IX

The notion that Leonor loved his new friend instilled in Martín a certain reservation toward him in spite of the kindness that Rafael had shown him. Over the course of several days he endeavored in vain to allay his suspicions in conversations with Rafael San Luis; however, such confidences never came to pass.

One evening after dinner, Martín was about to retire as usual before Don Dámaso's guests arrived. Just as he was taking his hat, Leonor inquired of him, "Are you fond of music?"

Martín felt a strange twinge. He found it so extraordinary that this haughty girl should address him directly that the sound of her voice made him feel as though he was dreaming. He turned toward Leonor, speechless, as if he were mistaken. Leonor repeated the question with a faint smile.

"Señorita," answered Martín, touched, "I've heard so little that I can't really say."

"It doesn't matter. I'll play something for you. Sit beside me because I must speak with you."

Utterly astonished, Martín followed Leonor. Don Dámaso, his wife, and their son were playing a French game called Patience, which Agustín was teaching them, while Leonor began to play the prelude to a waltz after inviting Martín to sit beside her. The youth gazed ecstatically at her beauty, stunned that this was really happening. Leonor played the prelude and a few bars of the waltz without speaking, and when Martín was beginning to see himself as a plaything to gratify her whim, she gave him a conceited look.

"Do you know Rafael San Luis?" she asked.

"Yes, Señorita," replied Rivas, inferring from this question that his nagging suspicion was about to be confirmed.

"Has he spoken to you of anyone in my family?"

"Very little. I find him rather reserved," he answered.

"Are you his friend?"

"A new friend. I met him a few days ago at school."

"Have you spoken with him lately?"

"Almost every day since we became friends."

"And he hasn't inquired of anyone in particular in my family?"

"No one," he replied. Then, in the hopes of corroborating his growing doubts by reading her expression, he added, "Come to think of it, yes, he asked me about you on one occasion."

"No one else, then?"

"No one else, Señorita."

Leonor played for a while longer with no further comment. Martín felt hot under the collar, trapped, and restless, before the arrogance of this young lady, who only deigned to address him to inquire about another man, presumably someone she fancied. He yearned for an immense fortune, a celebrated name, or striking looks; anything at all that would elevate him to her stature so that he might capture her attention, for it was likely that she thought no more of him than she did of the furniture. Feeling further debased by his obscurity and poverty, he felt himself capable of committing a crime just to occupy her thoughts, even if they were thoughts of horror.

Moments later she looked at him and said, "But, you must know what he does or where he goes."

"I am truly sorry, Señorita, that I cannot satisfy your curiosity," answered Martín somewhat stiffly, "for I have yet to receive confidences from San Luis. We've only seen each other at school, and I can't really say what he does in his spare time."

The music stopped. Leonor leafed through some sheet music, stood up, and walked over to her parents, saying, "You've already mastered that game?"

"As well as I have," said Agustín.

Rivas felt mortified when Leonor walked away without a word or a look, as though it had completely slipped her mind that she was the one who had insisted that he stay. Then, as if it had suddenly registered that she had left him at the piano, Leonor asked him, "Do you know how to play this game?"

"No, Señorita."

After a few agonizing minutes of looking for an inconspicuous way to leave the room, Martín slipped away to his quarters with a knot in his throat. His anguish kept him from rationalizing the rash feelings that overwhelmed him. Sundry imprecations against his destiny and the pride of the rich; mad brews of vengeance; boundless gloom and doom; furious vows to make a name for himself; and a thousand confusing ideas—all flashing through his brain, thundering in his heart, and raining hot tears down his cheeks—made him writhe in his chair and see himself in the mirror with frightened eyes. Then, like a lightning bolt amidst a mighty tempest, cutting through the night sky, was this unspeakable thought that made his heart shudder, "Oh, and to be so beautiful, so absolutely beautiful."

The calm of the storm gradually settled, bringing with it the enchanting reverie of first love. He had forgiven Leonor, for she had suddenly discovered the treasures of his pure, faithful heart and welcomed his tender, submissive adoration. Martín drifted into a world of fantasy, hearing the celestial music of a waltz, to which he and Leonor exchanged vows of everlasting love, vows which defy age and ask for a single tomb so that they may awaken together in life-ever-after. He envisioned an eruption of passion, which could vanquish pride and find the earthbound felicity that only dreams are made of. While Martín watched his love shining like silver in a smelting pot when fire purges it of dross, Leonor and Matilde quietly withdrew to a sofa, away from the main salon where they usually chatted.

"As I was saying the other day," began Leonor, taking her cousin's hand into her own, "Martín dropped the name of Rafael San Luis at dinner, and I had to defend it from my father's slurs."

Matilde squeezed her cousin's hand knowingly, and Leonor continued, "This afternoon I asked Martín to sit beside me at the piano to question him about San Luis. They're friendly, but they hardly know one another. It seems that Rafael hasn't divulged any matters of the heart yet, but I promise that I'll find out. Rivas is smart. I'll gain his trust and find out whether Rafael still loves you."

The two young ladies continued talking until Emilio Mendoza sat himself beside Leonor to pay his addresses, which she neither encouraged nor discouraged in the slightest fashion.

The next day Martín received his friend's salutation with a touch of apathy. San Luis, who felt a genuine warmth for Martín, immediately noticed his reservation and asked him forthright, "What's wrong with you? You look sad."

Martín felt disarmed by the informality, considering that his friend had always maintained a distance from the other classmates. Moreover, he knew deep down that Rafael was not responsible for his torment, and he had sufficient sense to see the absurdity of his jealousy.

"It is true," he said, shaking San Luis's hand, "last night was insufferable."

"Why, may I ask?" asked Rafael.

"What difference would it make? You wouldn't be able to bring me happiness."

"Careful, Martín! Don't forget my advice. Love, for a poor student, is the apple of paradise. If you taste it, you lose it."

"And what can I do when . . . "

San Luis interrupted him. "I don't want to hear another word about it. Love is one of those feelings that grows like wild ivy once you confide in someone. I wouldn't want to let evil take root, so don't tell me anything. Solitude is a deadly advisor, and you spend much too much time alone. You need to be distracted," he added, seeing that Martín remained pensive, "and I'll take care of that."

"It won't be easy," said Martín, who was still dispirited by the lingering impressions of last night.

"It's worth a try. We've got nothing to lose. Come to my place tomorrow night at eight, and I'll take you to see some folks who will show you a good time."

The two friends went their separate ways, Martín heading toward Don Dámaso's mansion.

X

When it was time to dine, Martín entered the salon and found Leonor alone at the piano. Each day the timidity he felt in her presence seemed to increase, and he feared that his feelings would be written all over his face if she caught him alone. Love, which fears no requite, causes even the boldest of men to recoil, and Martín was no exception. He quietly turned around to leave with his cheeks burning red, as he pondered, "Will she take pity on me?"

Leonor had already noticed his entrance and, instead of her customary indifference, she sprung to her feet and hastened to the door to call him. Martín returned, startled, if not daunted, by her impetuosity. Noting his troubled look, she inquired, "Why are you leaving?"

"I thought you were busy and didn't want to disturb you," he answered.

"Disturb me! Why would you ever think that? You heard me call you."

"To my delight."

"Come, sit. We must talk."

To his chagrin Martín interpreted Leonor's affected tone as a means of luring him back to yesterday's subject of interrogation. He followed her into the salon, but maintained a distance when she sat down in an armchair. She warmly waved him to take a seat, and said, gazing into his eyes, "Last night you slipped out before I even noticed."

"Señorita," replied Rivas, recouping his poise, "I thought that you had nothing more to ask me."

"That's not the only reason I wanted you to stay. I admit that I shouldn't have left you sitting there by yourself, but I want you to know that I'm sorry if I've offended you. Forgive me, I wasn't thinking."

All that was missing was the apologetic tone that generally accompanies an expression of remorse. It seemed as though she was struggling against her own pride and as though she wanted Rivas to feel the vast distance between them because her voice sounded more like a command than an apology. Yet this apology was motivated by an inherent righteousness that prevailed in her heart and conscience, in spite of the arrogance her family had cultivated in her. Leonor had perceived in Martín's departure his humility and recognized that he had cause to be offended. Had it been one of her foppish admirers, she might not have noticed the circumstance or questioned the propriety of her behavior; however, since it was a poor, obscure provincial, she regretted the discourtesy and, after thinking it over (though only for a fleeting moment) she opted to excuse herself. But, when it came time to actually do it, Leonor felt that the gesture was not nearly as easy as she had anticipated. It was a rather ungraceful situation to be in, and were it not for the strength of her will, she might not have carried through with her decision. Afraid that Martín might misconstrue her intentions, she spoke in a condescending tone and she looked at him, hoping to read his reaction. She had apparently aroused a bit of resentment, for there were reflections of it in his eyes when, to her surprise, he responded in the same tone that she had used with him.

"As for me, Señorita, I regret that I was unable to provide you further information about the person in whom you seem to take special interest."

"Certainly not for myself!" she exclaimed, losing all semblance of poise and aloofness.

"Oh!" remarked Martín, unable to conceal his satisfaction. "For someone else?"

Leonor, having the profound wisdom of her sex in matters of the heart, recognized the joy illuminating the young man's face.

Feeling faintly shy under his steady gaze, she wondered, "Is he falling for me?" Then, as if she were offended by his relief, she resumed her usual tone as if to punish him for having the audacity to love her. She remarked, "I see, Señor, that you have a lively imagination to make suppositions about what you hear."

He was mystified by her capriciousness, for moments ago she had summoned him to apologize, and now she sounded more caustic than ever. He admitted, "It is true, Señorita, that I jumped to a conclusion and obviously fell very short."

"Why on earth would you presume that I would be interested San Luis simply because I asked about him?"

"I'm sorry, it was a mindless assumption, but I promise that I made nothing of it and I'll give no further thought to it."

"I certainly hope not!" piped Leonor, with her nose in the air, causing Martín to cringe.

At this moment, Doña Engracia entered, followed by her husband, who perceived from the antechamber that Martín and Leonor were unattended. He whispered to his wife, "Why is my daughter alone with this boy?" His wife consequently imparted this remark to their daughter, who exclaimed indignantly, "Papa doesn't think before he opens his mouth, and he overrates that little protégé of his. Martín Rivas may be clever and have a knack for Papa's business, but I'm appalled that my own father would find him worthy enough for my consideration."

Her mother looked down sheepishly and consoled herself over the lack of parental authority by scooping up Diamela, who pounced around her feet, begging for attention.

Don Dámaso, meanwhile, forgot his concern as he listened to the young man's opinion on an important enterprise that he was eager to undertake.

Leonor's assessment revealed that Don Dámaso frequently praised his secretary, who knew enough about the business (through corresponding with the agents in the provinces) to provide sound advice on more than one occasion. For this, Martín had relied on God-given intelligence, rather than business experience, which he lacked almost entirely. Wishing to repay his hospitality, Martín took great pains to make himself useful to Don Dámaso so that he would not wear out his welcome. In the short time that he was of service, Martín enjoyed the high esteem of his host, who invested plenty of stock in his intuitive advice.

Don Dámaso, fully satisfied with Martín's recommendation, looked for a way to express his gratitude. He said, "I've noticed that you don't join us in the salon after dinner."

"Sir, my studies afford me little time," answered Rivas, who was delighted by the prospect of spending more time with Leonor and meeting those who courted her.

"Nevertheless," insisted Don Dámaso, "you should find time to join us. I want you to become acquainted with our Society. Friendships are always an important advantage for a young man dedicated to law."

That evening Martín responded to that invitation to meet those characters whom the reader has already met.

We should note that during his brief stay in Santiago, Rivas had already considerably improved his wardrobe, thanks to some tips from Rafael San Luis. This consisted of ordering articles of clothing from a tailor and paying monthly installments of 12 pesos once the suits were made. Thus, he was able to dress appropriately and still retain 8 pesos for other monthly expenses.

To comprehend the commotion at Don Dámaso tertulia that night, we must set the scene in the Capital at large and explain the ardent political concerns of that era.

The Society of Equality (of which we have already heard mention) was formed in the beginning of 1850 by a few members who saw their ranks rapidly multiplying into rows of men, attracting widespread public attention by the time the following incidents occurred. The name alone would have alarmed the authorities were it not for their ideology and their ardent campaign to call individuals from all social classes to join their ranks. Within a brief span, the Society counted more than eight hundred members and brought controversy to serious social and political issues. This invigorated the inert populace of Santiago, where Politics became the center of every conversation, the preoccupation of every mind, the hope of some, the nightmare of others. One would find passive citizens turning their drawing rooms into a Court of Justice for fiery debates; brothers embracing diverse factions against one other; rebellious sons defying the will of their parents; and rampant political frenzy destroying the peace of many families. In 1850, and later in 1851, there was not a single household in Chile where the irreconcilable voice of political dissension did not resonate, nor was there a single person who was not impassioned by one or another faction. Lycurgus would have had no need to enforce his law against indifference toward public welfare because there was no such offender. The Society of Equality had already held four celebrated sessions by the 19th of August, the date of the notorious session commonly known as *The Clubbing.*

It happened the same night that Martín would first join the evening reception of his host.

XI

There prevailed, as we said, unusual commotion among Don Dámaso's guests on the night of August 19th. It was rumored that the Society of Equality would be dissolved by order of the Government. The evidence was that four armed men had assaulted members of that Society a few nights earlier when Group Number Seven was entering La Chimba.

Martín sat down after Don Dámaso introduced him to his friends, and the conversation, which was momentarily interrupted, resumed.

"The authorities have a right to dissolve any congregation of demagogues," argued Don Fidel Elías in response to an objection someone had just voiced. "After all, what does Authority mean? The right to rule. Therefore, ruling to dissolve, as I have said, is within its right."

Doña Francisca, an opinionated woman, covered her face in horror of her husband's autocratic irrationality.

"Furthermore," added Don Simón Arenal, an old bachelor who presumed to be a man of some importance, "the public should be content with its right to enjoy the holidays and should refrain from that which is beyond its comprehension. If every whippersnapper voiced his opinion on Politics, what would be the point of education?"

Having temporarily abandoned his expectations of being appointed to a Government commission, for which he had been made to hope, Don Dámaso was presently lingering under the influence of the Liberal newspapers, whose articles were fresh in his mind. He quoted, "The right of association is sacred. It is one of civilization's triumphs over barbarism. To prohibit it is to render vain the blood of the martyrs of liberty, and furthermore . . . "

"I'll see if you're still speaking of martyrs and liberty when they come to seize your fortune," interrupted Don Fidel.

"This has nothing to do with the violation of personal property," replied Don Dámaso.

"That is where you are gravely mistaken, my friend," said Don Simón Arenal. "Do you suppose their name was arbitrarily chosen? Society of Equality means that Society will work to establish equality, and what prohibits that more than anything is the contrariety of fortune. In other words, the well-to-do will be roasted ducks."

"*C'est-à-dire,*" said the chic Agustín, "*canards des noces.*"

"There is no doubt about it, sir," agreed Emilio Mendoza, who had hitherto demonstrated his approval by nodding silently.

Don Dámaso fell silent. Arguments against his financial security (which were often used to intimidate the wealthy harboring Liberal tendencies) left him perplexed and taciturn.

Emilio added, "Exemplary gentlemen such as yourselves should lend your support to the Government at a time like this."

"Of course," goaded Don Fidel, delighted to employ another syllogism, "it is what every good patriot should do. The country is represented by the Government. Therefore, to show your support is to show your patriotism."

"But child," said Doña Francisca, "your syllogism is false because . . . "

"Tisk, tisk, tisk," interrupted Don Fidel. "Politics are beyond a woman's comprehension. Isn't that the case, young man?" he asked Martín, who happened to be standing closest to him.

"I am not of that opinion, sir," answered Rivas modestly.

Don Fidel looked at him appalled, exclaiming, "What!" Then, as if struck by a smart idea, he asked, "Are you a bachelor?"

"Yes, sir."

"Oh, well then, my boy, say no more."

At this moment in walked Clemente Valencia, who always arrived later than the rest. He said, "I was coming through Calle de las Monjitas, but I couldn't get through the mobs of people."

"What, a revolution?" Don Fidel and Don Simón asked, withering.

"Not yet, but if there comes a revolution, the Government is to blame," replied Valencia (much to the surprise of those listening, for it was rare that the capitalist did not stumble over his phrases).

"I think that in Politics even boors sound eloquent," Doña Francisca said to Leonor, who was at her side.

"Come on, sport, what's the matter? Spit it out!" said Agustín while Valencia was catching his breath.

"Tell us what's going on," the rest of them entreated of Clemente, who answered, "There was a general session of the Society of Equality."

"We already knew that."

"The session ended at ten o'clock."

"Big news," murmured Doña Francisca under her breath.

"That is what they told me in the streets," he continued.

"And what else," asked Agustín. "Then what happened?"

"The place was raided, and the members who were still there were beaten with clubs."

"Clubs!" echoed the ladies and gentlemen.

"*A coups de bâton!*" exclaimed Agustín.

"What an atrocity!" said Doña Francisca, righteously incensed. "It seems we have lost sight of civilization."

"Woman!" replied Don Fidel, "Woman, keep your nose out of Politics! The Government knows what it's doing!"

"*Oui, oui,* but there are limits," said Agustín. "*C'est un peu beaucoup!*"

"The duty of Authority," exclaimed Don Simón, "is to stand guard for the very tranquillity which that so-called *Society* of rebels threatens."

"But this is positively exasperating!" objected Doña Francisca.

"What does it matter, as long as the Government has the power."

"Well done, I say, well done. They deserve a good beating," said Don Fidel, "and that's what they got for meddling."

"But this could cause a revolution," said Don Dámaso.

"Stop kidding yourself," answered Don Simón. "All they're

doing is trying to teach the rabble some respect. Every Government should flex its muscles from time to time. It's the only way to govern."

"To beat is not to govern," interjected Martín, whose good sense and inherent benevolence opposed these tyrannical arguments.

"I'm with Don Simón," replied Emilio Mendoza. "All force against the enemy."

"Extraordinary theory," said Martín, perturbed. "I was taught that nobility meant generosity toward the enemy."

"Toward another kind of enemy, not Liberals," refuted Mendoza disdainfully. Rivas walked away toward a table to cool his rising temper.

"Don't waste your breath. They won't listen to reason," said Doña Francisca.

The political discourse continued as the ladies and gentlemen gathered around the table upon which the butler placed a tray of hot chocolate. All the while, Martín was mindful of Leonor, but found it impossible to determine her stand on any of the diverse opinions, nor could he ascertain which of her suitors she preferred. Her face revealed nothing but ceremonial civility toward both of them. This revelation, rather than cheering Martín's spirit, cast him further into dejection. He thought that if Leonor looked indifferently upon the stately politician and the pompous capitalist, he would never stand a chance because he possessed no comparable means of seduction. Yet, he felt haunted by the image of this lofty beauty, whom his love had crowned with a halo. All of these thoughts flowing through his mind were nothing but the sentimental syrup of unrequited love, and he reasoned that Leonor was too beautiful to condescend to love any man.

While Rivas restrained himself from looking at Leonor, fearing that those around them would read his mind, Matilde and her cousin found a quiet place to talk by themselves.

"That's the man who is friendly with Rafael," said Leonor.

"I found him interesting," said Matilde.

"You're not unbiased," smiled Leonor.

"Have you asked him again about Rafael?"

"No, because my questions made him think that I was the one in love and, besides, he was offended because I called upon him only to ask those questions."

"Oh, he's proud!"

"Indeed, and I'm surprised he even came here tonight because he never did before. He rarely speaks at the table unless spoken to, and when he does, it's only to refute their vulgar opinions."

"I see that you've been watching him closely," Matilde teased her cousin, "and I think that you're more concerned about him than with any other man here."

"What an absurd notion!" she said.

Yet Matilde's observation made Leonor realize how frequently Martín seemed to drift into her innermost thoughts, which was rarely the case with the other young men who were always accosting her. She blushed when recalling that the same idea had already occurred to her once before: when Martín's face beamed with joyous relief after she had confessed her motives for grilling him about his friend San Luis. The fact that she blushed with humility was not entirely out of character for someone spoiled by nature and her parents. As much as Leonor had professed her desire to fall in love, one could see a great deal of pride under the cloak of indifference that she wore when rejecting Santiago's most eligible bachelors. Mildly flustered that an insignificant young provincial would enter her mind, she resolved to use her willpower to overcome what she determined was an involuntary weakness. A woman's heart delights in these kinds of contests to dissipate the dread of boredom. Henceforth, Leonor regarded Martín as an adversary, without realizing the jeopardy of her own little game, which obliged her to do precisely what she proposed not to; which is to say, think about him.

Martín, meanwhile, had withdrawn in despair. Like everyone who loves for the first time, he did not attempt to resist the passion; rather he resigned himself to the grief it awoke in his soul. He found himself in the realm of woeful poetry, relishing the exotic pleasures of exaggerating the magnitude of his heartache. First love often produces in the soul the kind of vertigo that one experiences when looking over the edge of a chasm, and Rivas envisioned his future as an abyss, devoid of any hope, and felt himself toppling endlessly into its depths.

Distracted by such feelings, Martín had forgotten that he was supposed to meet Rafael the next day, until his friend reminded him after class, "Don't forget that we're going out tonight."

"Where are you taking me?"

"Come and you'll find out. I want to try out a cure."

"On whom?"

"On you. I see very alarming symptoms."

"Why bother?" sighed Martín, as they parted.

Wanting to brighten the spirits of his new friend, San Luis did not breathe his own sigh of grief until he was a few paces away from Rivas.

XII

At eight o'clock that evening, Martín entered an old house on Calle de la Ceniza. Rafael came out to greet him and invited him into his room, which Martín had to admire for the sophistication of its furnishings.

"Welcome to my humble abode," said Rafael, offering him a green leather armchair.

"Passing down this street," said Rivas, "I never would have imagined finding such luxury here."

"Keepsakes of brighter days," said Rafael. "Among the many things that I've lost," he added sadly. "I still have a taste for fine living. But let's talk about something else so that we can both be happy. You know where I'm going to take you?"

"I haven't the slightest notion."

"Well, I'll tell you while I freshen up."

Rafael took a razor, made a rich lather from a bar of soap, and sat in front of a round mirror that tilted back and forth. Then he began to shave, speaking when he could.

"Let me tell you, we're going to be carousing at the home of some pretty girls. If you know what I mean by *carousing,* you'll gather that we won't be rubbing elbows with Santiago's finest. The family hosting the party can best we described as would-be-aristocrats, or simply, *would-be's,* as we say around here."

"And what are the girls like?"

"I'm getting to that—one step at a time. There's a widow with three grown children. Let's start with the fairer sex by order of age.

First, there's Doña Bernarda Cordero de Molina, who is roughly 50 years old and wild about gambling. Her daughters are Adelaida and Edelmira. The elder was named by her godfather, and the younger by her mother who came up with a theatrical name because she was with child when she saw Othello. I'm sure she'll tell you all about it once you get to know her. Adelaida entertains an ambition worthy of a full-staged tragicomedy; she wants to marry a gentleman. The would-be's think that a son of a good family is the ideal man because they tend to judge the priest by the collar. The sisters look alike in some ways. They both have chestnut hair, brown eyes, an ivory complexion, and a pretty smile. Yet the look in their eyes couldn't be more different. Adelaida's expression reveals the stores of ambition in her heart, while her sister's speaks of loving tenderness. Edelmira is as gentle and romantic as a heroine in one of those serialized novels that she loves to borrow from an old shopkeeper. Her sentimental heart, as Balzac said of one of his heroines, is a sponge that swells at the slightest drop of sentiment.

"That leaves us with the 26-six-year-old numskull, Amador, a crass boor, the sort we call *lowbrow.* His mustache and goatee are classic trimmings, and when he plays the guitar, he croons *vida mía.* Loverboy's a sight for sore eyes! Just you wait and see.

"I can only guess how they manage, since no one seems to be toeing the line. Doña Bernarda's late husband, Don Damián Molina, pretended to be of a son of a good family, as you'll hear from the widow herself. He lived hand to mouth most of his life, but they say he left his family 8,000 pesos. The son, having squandered his inheritance, basically lives at his mother's expense and covers the extras by gambling. At election time, he is an active patriot if the Opposition pays a higher price than the Government, and a hard core Conservative, depending on the deal. Sometimes he even serves both parties simultaneously, philosophizing that 'after all, we're all compatriots.'

"With two pretty lasses under one roof, Cupid had to find his way to their house. But you won't believe me when I tell you who has fallen for Adelaida."

"Who?

"The elegant son of your host."

"Agustín?"

"He, himself. Shortly after his return from Europe, a friend of his brought him there. At first, he thought she would be swept away by his smooth talk and fancy suits, but it wasn't as easy as he had expected. The more she resisted, the more he took interest. If she had fallen for him right away, he would've kissed her goodbye already. But, his whim is turning to real passion because she is playing hard-to-get."

"Does her sister have eyes for anyone?"

"Nobody, despite the doleful sighs of a policeman who longs to marry her. I suppose Edelmira dreams of something more poetic like the heroes she reads about because she detests his adoration, which makes him squirm inside his uniform as if he were being held back from a promotion."

With these words, Rafael, who had dressed up, gave the finishing touches to his hair. To fill the silence, Martín commented on a daguerreotype that was hanging over a writing desk. "I've seen this face somewhere before."

"Oh, really? Who knows," answered Rafael, stepping away from the light. "Shall we go?" he added, snuffing out the candle and leading his friend to the door.

"Let's go," said Martín.

They went to a house on Calle del Colegio; the front door was bolted, which was not out of the ordinary given that a party was being held. Rafael knocked loudly until a servant let them in. How shall we endeavor to describe this man without offending the reader's sensibility? There are some images that the pen resists depicting, preferring to leave its production to the brush of a painter like Murillo, whose *Beggar Child* had nothing painterly or pleasant about it. Suffice it to say he was a poor man's servant, wearing a ragged smock that reeked of kitchen grease.

"The carousal's in full swing," said Rafael as they stopped to look inside the patio window.

Martín said, "I wasn't expecting to see so many people."

"They're all friends of the family. Look, there's the aspiring Adelaida. What do you think of her?"

"Very pretty, but there is something hard about her brow, something calculating or off-putting, but maybe you've just prejudiced me."

"No, no, you're absolutely right. It's written all over her face, but most people would find her regal. In fact, Agustín Encina says that she looks like a queen in disguise. Now take a look at her sister, Edelmira, right over there. What a difference between them. Imagine her without the languor of romanticism in her eyes. What an adorable creature she would be!"

"I agree," said Rivas. "I think she is prettier than her sister."

"Look, look!" said San Luis, clutching Martín's arm. "There's Amador, the crass fellow carrying a glass of punch. You must taste it; it's called *chincolito.* Isn't Amador a mighty fine specimen? That white satin vest embroidered with a splash of color by some sweetheart is simply dapper with that red-striped tie, and my, my, my, if he isn't the perfect picture of an angel in procession with those curlicues. Loverboy looks like he's in Heaven, serving that girl some punch."

Just then, someone leaned over and spoke into the ear of the "mighty fine specimen," who then came out to greet them.

"Gentlemen," Amador said, bowing, "would you do me the honor of joining my guests in the ballroom?"

"We were putting on our gloves," answered Rafael, "and we were just about to enter. Señor Amador," he added, pointing to his friend, "it is my honor to introduce you to Don Martín Rivas."

"It is my pleasure," said Martín.

"No, sir, the pleasure is all mine," said Amador, acknowledging Rivas's greeting.

The threesome then entered the adjoining apartment, which Amador had grossly exaggerated when he called it *the ballroom.*

XIII

All eyes turned toward the newcomers, who were led in by Amador. The young men acknowledged them politely, yet cautiously, while the young women whispered among themselves upon introduction. The noisy revelry that Rivas and San Luis had noticed from the patio ceased as soon as they entered, but a sonorous, matronly voice promptly interrupted the hush: "You'd think they all dropped dead! Like they never saw nobody before!"

It was the voice of Doña Bernarda, who was waving her arms in the middle of the room, animating her guests with this eloquent admonition, which made the boys squirm and the girls smile and lower their eyes.

"My lady Bernardita is right," said one guest. "Let's start dancing cuadrillas."

"Cuadrillas, cuadrillas," repeated the others, following his lead.

A family friend sat at the piano, which he had brought there that morning, and began to play a set of cuadrillas, and the couples took their places, regardless of age or social class. A matron of 50 stood opposite her daughter of 14, who was tugging at the cinch of her skirt in an attempt to stretch it longer so that she would look grown-up.

"Stop that! You're gonna tear it," warned her mother, much to the mortification of her dance partner, who was endeavoring to act like a proper lady in the presence of Rivas and his friend.

Nearby, a young swain was declaring his affection at the top of his voice to prove that he was not embarrassed in front of the newcomers.

"Señorita, I say you're a thief," he said, "because you've stolen my heart." To which she softly replied with her cheeks aglow, "Flattery will get you nowhere, Señor."

Doña Bernarda, the blithe hostess, went from couple to couple, complimenting each one of them. When she came upon the mother and daughter partnership, she eyed them with a malicious tone, exclaiming, "Take a look at this ol' broad havin' herself some fun, and with a swankie ol' blade too! I see, my pet, you won't be re-tirin' no time soon."

"Not if I can help it!" she laughed. "Why leave all the fun to the kids?"

Amador was rushing around the room, trying to find a partner. After many refusals, he asked a girl, "And you, Señorita, would you grant me the honor of dancing with me?"

"I've never danced cuadrillas," she answered with a shrill voice. "Ya wanna polka instead?"

"Just keep shakin', Mariquita," Doña Bernarda said to her, "and you'll pick it up in no time. It ain't as hard as you'd think it is."

With a little more nudging, Mariquita finally agreed to dance, and the cuadrillas began to the discordant strains of the piano. The pianist was stomping so hard on the pedals that the stool was skipping about, making as much noise as the instrument itself. The indistinct melody was further stifled by the hooting and hollering of the dancers and spectators, three or four of whom were simultaneously prompting Mariquita and the 14-year-old girl, both of whom were off-step at every turn.

"Through here, Mariquita," advised one.

"Atta girl! Now's a curtsy!" another added.

"Turn *dis* way," a voice screamed, "not *dat* way!"

"Keep your eyes on me, and do what I do," Amador would say to her, waddling forward and backward with his vis-à-vis.

"Hey! Keep your voices down!" bellowed the pianist. "Nobody can hear the music!"

"Take a swig o' mistela to cool ya down," said Doña Bernarda, passing him a glass, while Amador clapped his hands loudly to let him know that he should start playing the next figure.

In the second figure, the young girl began to dance the first figure over again, vexing her mother and causing mass confusion because everyone wanted to set her straight by telling her what to do—all at the same time! This mayhem, which distressed those who wished to lend this affair the respectability of a tertulia, thrilled Doña Bernarda, who with a glass of mistela in hand, applauded the mistakes of the dancers and shouted every now and then, exhilarated by the party's liveliness, "Let the frenzy whisk ya away!"

Rafael San Luis was, to Rivas's sweeping surprise, the life of the party. He was doing all that he could to further entangle the knot of the cuadrilla, occasionally raising his voice over all others and taking advantage of the chaos to snatch someone else's partner and start another figure with her, just when it seemed that order was about to be restored. Martín watched this new side of his friend, which was counter to the melancholic sobriety that he had always noted in him, and believed that there was something forced in San Luis's efforts to seem happier than everyone else.

"He's the pick o' the litter 'round here," said Doña Bernarda, approaching him.

"I didn't know he was so live," responded Rivas.

"Don't let his roar fool you. He's a lil' pussycat. Did he tell you what he did for me?"

"No, he hasn't told me anything."

"You see what I mean? He ain't no braggart when it comes to doin' good. But, lemme tell you, I nearly died last year, and when I came 'round and went to pay the doctor and the 'pothecary, they said I didn't owe them nothin' 'cause he'd already paid for everythin'. If that ain't a good boy!"

Doña Bernarda's expression of profound gratitude struck Rivas and returned his thoughts to the wild joy of San Luis, who had just introduced utter chaos into the cuadrilla. Rafael hastened toward his friend when he noticed that he was being watched. Within the short span of crossing the dance-floor, his usual serene sadness returned to his face, superseding his look of gaiety.

"It all boils down to this," Rafael said. "The more shame we lose, the more fun we have."

"Are you really having fun?" asked Martín.

"Real or imagined, what's the difference? The point is to forget your worries," he said before walking away.

Martín was about to enter the adjoining chamber when he came face to face with Agustín Encina, who was as fastidiously foppish as ever. The two youths eyed each other indecisively for a moment and then blushed.

"What are you doing here, Rivas, my dear chap?" exclaimed the dandy.

"Why are you acting so surprised when you're a regular guest here?" replied Martín.

"I wouldn't say *surprised*, but to find such a reserved chap among . . . Well, I come here because it's the closest thing to a Parisian *grisette*, and there isn't much *amuzement* for a young man in Santiago."

Agustín then stepped away to pay his respects to the hostess, who showed her delight by flashing him the few pearly whites that she had left in her crooked smile. Just then, Rafael, who spotted the young Encina, took Rivas by the arm and walked toward him. Extending his hand, he said to Agustín, "Have you said hello to this fine gent? All the girls go wild over him."

"I'm pleased to see you're in good spirits," answered Encina, a bit embarrassed. He then left for the salon, dangling a thick, gold watch-chain with which he hoped to allure the disdainful Adelaida.

After the dancing had ended, Doña Bernarda called some of her friends, saying, "Let's play some Montecito and have us some fun too."

Several people gathered around a table on which Doña Bernarda placed a deck of cards, and the rest, including Rafael and San Luis, followed the sounds of a guitar coming from the salon. Sitting on a small stool facing his audience, Amador was playing a song, while the servant, who had opened the door for Rafael, carried around a tray of mistela. While the guests eagerly accepted the liquor, Amador set down his guitar to hand Rivas one glass and Rafael another, insisting that they "drink up."

Glass after glass painted glee on every face and endeared every ear to the voice which cheered, "Cueca, cueca, let's hear some cueca!"

Kerchiefs waved in the air, and Rivas was startled to see a girl walking across the room, arm in arm with the policeman who had detained him on the night of his arrest.

"That's the officer who was on duty when they booked me," he said to Rafael.

"And that's the one who is head over heels for Edelmira. He just arrived, that's why you haven't seen him."

Just then the joyous strands of zamacueca sounded under Amador's fingertips, and the couple set off into the dips and turns of this dance, while Doña Bernarda's son, lifting his eyes to the ceiling, crooned the following verses, as old perhaps as the dance itself:

Last night I dreamed an awful sight,
awakenin' in such affright,
two dark an' lovely eyes were slayin' me,
they were yours, lookin' at me furiously.

Many spectators joined in, clapping to the rhythm and goading other couples to dance.

"Ooooh, baby!" shouted a voice, sighing in exaggeration, while someone else gushed, "Oh, oooh. Give it to her, darlin'!"

"Don't let her stop!"

"Sway the kerchief!"

"Show some swing, lil' officer!"

Others joined in with disparate voices as Amador crooned:

Head over heels,
for two pretty lasses,
I'm as happy as my cock
and as tickled as my ass is.

After the final refrain, a frenzied "bravo!" greeted the old-fashioned gallantry of the police officer, who knelt before his lady after the final turn. The drinking continued, raising the spirits of the guests, some of whom shouted bawdy wisecracks at the beaus and threw kisses at the belles. Their initial display of uppity manners (modeled after High Society) was succeeded by this peculiar strain of overconfidence and overpoliteness, which is characteristic of this sort of affair. The people whom we call *would-be-aristocrats* stand somewhere between the general populace (whom they despise) and the gentry (whom they envy and wish to emulate). Their conduct is, therefore, a curious blend of common manners mixed with presumption, to the point of caricaturing the upper echelon of Society, which conceals its absurdities under the latent brass of riches and snobbery.

Rafael relayed these observations to Rivas when dodging someone who was pressuring them to swig another glass of punch.

"That's precisely why," San Luis remarked, "love advances more swiftly in these circles than in the grand salons where it seems to take forever to make the first move. Forget about all those timid tactics like nervous glances. You like a girl? Don't beat around the bush. Speak your mind, but don't expect an easy answer. When it comes to matters of the heart, woman is the same wherever you go. She wants you to oblige her, but she'll only meet you halfway."

"Rafael, I must confess," said Rivas, "this isn't my idea of a good time."

"Hey, I can't force you to loosen up," replied San Luis, "but I'll declare you a lost soul if you're not at least distracted from your thoughts. I'll show you a sight that you've never seen before."

"What would that be?"

"A brassy rich boy at Cupid's mercy. It's a pitiful sight to behold. Just you wait and see."

Rafael called the young Encina, who was sitting beside Adelaida, hyperbolizing his love. His cheeks were tinged by the vapors of mistela and her frigid reception. San Luis asked him, "How's the love-life going?"

"So-so," answered Agustín, fidgeting.

"At the risk of being indiscreet, might I advise you?"

"Go ahead."

"You'll never win her at the rate you're going."

"Why?"

"Because you're courting Adelaida as if she were a lady. If you want to get anywhere with these folks, you have to drop that snobby tone of yours and speak on their level."

"But how?"

"Have you danced?"

"No."

"If you ask Adelaida to dance zamacueca, she'll see that you're not above dancing with her."

"You think that'll work?"

"I'm sure of it."

Agustín found this argument to be logical in his drunken stupor, but voiced this objection, "It's a pity that I don't know how to dance zamacueca."

"That doesn't matter! Didn't you say that you danced the can can in France?"

"Oh, that I can do!"

"Well, it's essentially the same."

Agustín, persuaded by this comment, asked Adelaida to dance zamacueca. A shout of "bravo!" greeted the couple, and Rafael placed the guitar in Amador's hands, who began to improvise in a voice which the mistela made even more sonorous:

I'm suffering, vida mía,
over the cruelty of my fate,
hearing you laugh at my pain,
you wretched ingrate!

Egged on by Rafael, Agustín kicked his leg up so high that he lost his balance and staggered about the room for a few seconds before landing at Adelaida's feet. Then everyone who was clapping along began to mock the forlorn dandy.

"One clown down!"

"Upsy-wupsy lil' guy!"

"You couldn't have fallen in a better spot!"

"He needs a balancing pole to walk a straight line!"

Agustín managed to pull himself up, and started twisting and gyrating to even greater applause, while Amador sang falsetto to the merriment of his listeners:

Jumpin' over a trench,
'Hold my foot for me,'
Said the crippled wench,
'So it won't get drenched!'

Everyone chanted the refrain until Augustín, thinking that they were cheering him on, fell to his knees before his partner to imitate those who had preceded him. Adelaida burst into gales of laughter at this failed attempt at chivalry and dashed back to her seat. There were echoes of laughter from everyone else at the sight of the dandy kneeling by himself in the middle of the floor.

Apparently embarrassed by the behavior of Don Dámaso's son, Rivas left the room, followed by Rafael.

"He's a jackass," San Luis said in reply to something that was voiced in this regard, "and he thinks, as the moneyed often do, that he can afford to be asinine. And since our Society lives in awe of those who gild their inanities, I like to amuse myself at their expense."

Rivas left his friend standing beside the table where Doña Bernarda was leading a card game and found a seat next to Edelmira, who said to him, "You're playing a small role in tonight's diversion."

"I am no friend to noise, Señorita," he said.

"Then you must be miserable."

"No, it's just that this isn't my idea of a good time."

"I know what you mean. Even though I've seen so many of them, I'm never quite at ease."

"Why not?"

"I think we lose our dignity here because the young men who visit us, like you and your friend San Luis, regard us as mere recreation, unworthy of anything more."

"I believe you're mistaken, at least as far as I'm concerned. But, now that you have spoken with such candor, I must say that I knew you were thinking that by just looking at you."

"Oh, it shows?"

"Yes, but it's only because I empathize with your situation."

"As I said, I've never grown accustomed to these affairs, which my sister and mother enjoy. There is too much distance between you and us for there to be any hope of mutual respect."

"Poor lass," thought Rivas upon finding a kindred spirit wounded by the anathema of poverty. This idea led Martín to the supposition that perhaps Edelmira loved as hopelessly as he did.

"I don't understand your despair in light of your youth and beauty. Please don't mistake this as flattery," he added when

Edelmira lowered her eyes sadly. "I was speaking from the likelihood that someone loved you and offered you happiness."

"We aren't loved the way rich girls are loved," replied Edelmira, dispirited, "and the men we're mad enough to fall for are often the ones who offend us the most and make us regret our station in life."

"Are you saying you'll never meet a man who understands your heart?"

"Maybe, but I'll never find one who will love me enough to make me forget my station in life."

"I regret that I don't know you well enough to argue the point," said Rivas.

"And I'm talking as though I've already known you, maybe because your friend has already spoken of you, and you measured up to his description."

"In what way?"

"You haven't tried to seduce me, unlike most young men who want to spend time with us."

Many of the guests began to urge Rivas to dance zamacueca with Edelmira, but both obstinately refused. However, they would have been unable to free themselves of the demands if Rafael had not come to the aid of his friend, assuring the people that the provincial had never danced before.

XIV

While the joviality was swiftly waxing, the mistela was numbing the minds of the drinkers at an alarming rate. As one might expect from such scenarios, they were all raising their voices over each other, and even those who were quiet and controlled at the start of the carousal progressively displayed a loquacity that was only interrupted when the liquor caused them to stammer.

A harpist, who was also a nasal soprano, accompanied Amador as he played the guitar, and the piano was pushed aside to make room for them. She sang a duet with Amador, and a chorus of anomalous voices strained against their slipping faculties to create harmony. From time to time, Doña Bernarda would scream from the next room to restore order, "For Christ's sake! Somebody throw a stone at them caterwaulin' alley cats!"

The moment that Rivas left his seat, the police officer, whose name was Ricardo Castaños, seized the opportunity to free himself from the zamacueca and sit beside Edelmira to whine about the conversation that she had just had with Martín.

Meanwhile, Agustín, forgetting his genteel breeding, guzzled down the entire contents of the glass with which Adelaida had just wet her lips.

"If you weren't interested, then why did you let him talk your ear off?" the officer complained to Edelmira.

"My heart *est tout à vous,*" professed Agustín, "and I surrender it wholly."

The harpist and Amador sang this song:

I won't ever leave you behind,
Thoughts of you never leave my mind,
I'm taking you with me in my soul,
Without your love, I'll never feel whole.

And people wandered around the room, clinking glasses as they sang out of tune:

Without your love, I'll never feel whole.

When Rivas listened to the refrain, it reminded him of the bitter melancholy of his isolation, leading him to believe that he would never know the bliss that Love promises to pure young hearts. He was feeling badgered by the noise and offended by the ease with which the others surrendered themselves to a love improvised by the vapors of liquor.

Rafael, meanwhile, summoned the guests to the patio, where he lit fireworks that exploded in the air, rousing frenetic applause and prolonged cheers to Doña Bernarda, whose saint they were celebrating. Then Amador called the guests back inside the house, announcing, "Now boys, it's the time you've all been waiting for! It's . . . suppertime!"

"Supper!"

"Oh, what a treat!"

"Well, what were you expecting?" replied Doña Bernarda's son. "Take a look around. Can't you see this is a classy joint?"

The rowdy bunch crowded into a small whitewashed room to gather around the supper table. Each sought a place beside the lady of his preference, and behind them stood those who were unable to find a seat.

"Girls and boys," announced Doña Bernarda, "anyone without a chair eats standin' up. Anyone without a fork eats with his fingers."

Her witticism was celebrated with fresh applause, and with this attack signal, everyone charged at the sumptuous display of food. In front of Doña Bernarda, who was sitting at the head of the table, was a golden roasted turkey—the classic Chilean dish in every tier of Society. The fried fish and tossed salad gave the table a traditional touch and complemented the stuffed pork sitting next to a fountain of mouthwatering olives, delivered "fresh this mornin'," Doña Bernarda was pleased to report, by her "dear ol' cousin, who's an Augustinian nun." There were pitchers of the famous Garcia Pica vintage to wash down these hardy vittles and a bowl of punch, that all were invited to dip their cups into as long as they, according to Amador's instructions, kept "their grubby fingers out of it."

The young men indulged the ladies with old-fashioned finesse and courtesies long forgotten in recent times. One suitor offered to trim a feathered slice of turkey, and when pinning his fork into it, declared that his heart was pierced by Cupid's arrow. The police officer refused to drink from any other glass than that which had been graced by Edelmira's lips, and Amador endangered his health by drinking cup after cup of chicha, toasting to the health of the lass beside him. Agustín, having wiled away his loveladen eloquence upon Adelaida, reminisced about the delicacies of Parisian banquets, wolfing down a chunk of stuffed pork.

The heavy drinking began to take its toll on the officer's brain, for he tried to prove his devotion by kissing Edelmira. At the sound of her daughter's shriek, Doña Bernarda's maternal reflex instantly brought her to her feet to reprimand the perpetrator as if she were his grandmother, which was a tad drastic, as one might imagine. Amador also wanted to chastise the audacity of the rash lover, but his knees buckled, landing him on the carpet. This incident momentarily suspended the general gaiety, as did the effect of the mixed drinks on Agustín's stomach, who was carried away as if he were wounded in battle, while the officer began shouting orders as if he were commanding his troops. Others had taken to self-pity and told their woes to the wall with their faces bathed in tears. A group of youngsters, who were swearing eternal friendship, embraced each other in a dark corner, and others urged Doña Bernarda to forgive the "friendly little kiss."

Seeing these characters acting under the influence of liquor (rather than their own will) brings to mind those Flemish paintings which bring to life the grotesque side-effects of Immoderation (or, Drunkenness to be perfectly blunt) and the decadent behavior of carousals. Their figures are often portrayed in a drunken stupor with men drooling and begging for the mercy of some femme fatale.

The few left standing did not want the party to end and hid the gate-key to prevent Rivas and San Luis from going home. The final scene was an argument, which lasted a quarter of an hour between those who wanted to leave and those who insisted on prolonging the festivities. At Doña Bernarda's petitions those who were blocking the gate finally desisted and gave way to the guests who were still able to walk home on their own two feet.

Doña Bernarda and her daughters returned to the encampment, where the officer laid dead to the world among other casualties, whom they covered with blankets. The young heir of Don Dámaso Encina was snoring loudly in Amador's bed, where they had left him unconscious. Doña Bernarda and her daughters retired to a back room, which served as their bedchamber for the night. There they were visited by Amador, who had already recovered some of his senses, being a veteran of this sort of revelry.

"Hey, sis," he said to Adelaida, "I think you finally roped him in."

"But this lil' ninny," said Doña Bernarda, pointing at Edelmira, "playin' the finicky cat with the lil' officer, could learn a lesson or two from her sister."

"But, Mother, I don't want to get married," answered the girl.

"You think I'm gonna support you forever? Girls should get married. Lookie here, the officer makes a nice salary, and his sergeant who's related to the servant, told me he's gonna get promoted."

"Not everyone's lucky enough to catch a marquis like her," said Amador, referring to Adelaida.

"But be careful," warned their mother, "go slowly. Them rich boys only wanna fool 'round. Adelaida, she who blinks, loses everthin'. If he don't start talkin' wedlock, here's Amador to kick him out."

"Leave it all to me," said Amador. "Before the year is up, Mother, those moneybags will be our in-laws."

This said, they bade each other goodnight, trusting the hostess to awaken the invalids from the party early in the morning so that they would all be out of the house before Mass.

All the while, Agustín snored away in a drunken slumber, oblivious to their scheme to rope him into the family.

XV

Martín accompanied Rafael home from Doña Bernarda's house. It was nearly three o'clock in the morning when they arrived at Calle de la Ceniza.

"It's too late for you to leave," Rafael said. "You might as well spend the night here. Agustín is going nowhere tonight, so no one will notice your absence."

Rafael lit two lamps and presented Rivas with an armchair, asking, "You didn't have any fun?"

"A little, I suppose," Martín said, as he fell back in the chair, fatigued.

"I saw you talking to Edelmira. She suffers because she is ashamed of her class and lives in hope of meeting a gentle soul like herself."

"I barely met her and yet I felt sympathy for the poor girl," said Martín.

"You did?"

"Yes, she has a very vulnerable sensibility."

"It's true, but what can you do? She won't be the first person who gets burned for approaching the light of happiness," Rafael sighed. Then he added, running his fingers through his hair, "It's what happens to butterflies, Martín: the ones that don't die in the flame never lose the marks on their singed wings. Enough of that! It seems I'm poeticizing. It must be the liquor talking."

"Go on."

"That damned mistela has set my head afire. Let's talk over

some tea. Spirits always seem to loosen the tongue and expand the heart."

First he lit the stove and then with the same match he lit a cigar. Sitting on a sofa, he said, "You didn't seem to have much fun."

"I can't say that I did."

"You suffer a serious flaw, Martín."

"What is that?"

"You're much too young to be taking life so seriously."

"Why do you say that?"

"Because I can tell that you've fallen in love."

"It shows?"

"Well, it's always good to know the score. Let's take a tally. How high are your hopes?"

"Hopes for what?"

"That Leonor will love you as much as you love her."

"I have no hopes whatsoever."

"Come now, you're not all that unfortunate," said Rafael, standing up. Martín looked at him, baffled, because he thought to love without hope was the worst misfortune imaginable. "I mean," continued San Luis, "not even a timid glance or a hint of a coy smile."

"No, nothing."

"Better yet."

"Do you know Leonor?" asked Martín, whose interest was growing.

"Yes, she is gorgeous."

"Then I don't understand."

"Well, I'll make you understand. Let's suppose she loves you."

"Oh, that would never happen."

"Just suppose, for the sake of argument. You know that a love requited is mightier than one that dwells hopelessly on sighs. So let's just say for the sake of argument that she loves you too. You're on top of the world and you want to marry her. Life couldn't be sweeter, and you thank your lucky stars for your loving angel, and you even forget that you're poor . . . until it's time to ask her parents for their consent, and that's when brutal reality in the shape of her father chases you out of the house like you're a leper or a rabid dog! It happens to the best of us, my friend, in this so-called *civilized*

Society of ours. You wouldn't want to be the next poor chump, would you?"

San Luis ended this rhetorical question with a strained laugh because he had worked himself into a feverish spell. Then he said, while preparing tea, "Believe me, I've been through plenty in my lifetime. I've never told my story to anyone, but the memories are overwhelming me. The moment I met you, I knew you would be a good noble friend, and now I hope you can learn from my mistakes."

"Thank you," answered Martín, "your friendship has been my only joy since I've moved here."

San Luis served two cups of tea, placed a small table beside Rivas, and sat in front of him.

"Well, you're about to hear the story of my heart," he began, "and it's by no means a fantastic novel. If you weren't in love, I wouldn't tell you because you wouldn't understand. I suppose I should begin at the beginning, as they say. My mother died when I was 6 years old. I can hardly recall what she looked like, although sometimes I recognize her in my dreams, but her face escapes me the moment I wake up. Since I can remember, I lived at a boarding school, where my father would often visit me. Childhood passed, and after its happy innocence came adolescence with its solitary introspection. At 18 years of age, I was reading and writing poetry with a burning passion that Descartes would describe as love. Then, I met the girl in this portrait."

Martín looked at the daguerreotype that Rafael showed him. It was the same one that caught his eye several hours earlier. Studying her face closely, he asked, "Is this Leonor's cousin, Matilde?"

"She's the one," said San Luis, without looking at it.

"I saw her last night at Don Dámaso's house."

"It was two years before I told Matilde that I loved her, and yet our hearts had spoken long before either one of us had dared to. By the age of 20, I knew that she was feeling the same toward me, and she had been all along. Like I said, I was on top of the world, and life couldn't be sweeter."

Rafael paused a moment to light his cigar again.

"What more could a man want?" said Rivas, who thought that

the joy of being loved once was worth any disgrace that a man could face.

"I lived in a rose-colored world until I was 23," continued San Luis. "Matilde's parents approved of me because my father was a well-to-do speculator. I thanked my stars for her. She was always tender, and I was happy until a rival came into the picture. He was young, rich, and handsome, and he cast my world into sudden darkness. As much as it pained me, I had to swallow my pride and admit that I was mad with jealousy, for there is no dignity before undying passion. Matilde chased some of my fears away, swearing that I was the only man in her life, but just when I felt that she was mine again, fresh doubts would come and go like clouds across a sunny sky.

"One day my father called me to his room and broke down in my arms. I was so wrapped up in my own little world that I hadn't noticed that his face had grown haggard.

"His first words were these, '*Rafael, I'm ruined!*'

"I couldn't believe my ears.

"'*After I pay my debts,*' he said, '*there'll be nothing left.*'

"'*Don't worry, Papa,*' I said to console him. '*We'll be fine. I'll find some work.*'

"The story of my father's ruin is common these days: cargo ships lost at sea and undersold wheat in California, that gold mine of so few and ruin of so many. In a nutshell, the misfortunes of mercantile speculation. This news saddened me on my father's account, but as for me, it was like talking to the emperor of China about the death of one of his lowly subjects. I was 60,000,000 rich in bliss because Matilde loved me. What did I care about the loss of 5 or 600,000 pesos?"

"She loved you in spite of your poverty?"

"Yet and still. I continued visiting Matilde's home, speaking to her of my love and to her mother of my studies. You know how love is blind. Well, I didn't notice Don Fidel's sudden coldness toward me. One night I arrived to find myself alone with your protector, Don Dámaso, and my blood ran cold.

"'*It is my duty,*' he said '*to relate a disagreeable matter, which I hope that you will receive with the temperance of a gentleman.*'

"'*Sir,*' I answered, '*you may speak freely. I was brought up as a gentleman, and I needn't be reminded to act like one.*'

"'You cannot ignore,' said Don Dámaso, '*that the situation of a young lady is always very delicate, and that her parents must distance her from all that could compromise her. My brother-in-law Elías has learned that Society is concerned about your frequent visits and fears that Matilde's reputation may suffer some consequence.*'

"The tip of the dagger had pierced my heart, and I nearly lost consciousness.

"'*You mean to say,*' I said, '*that Don Fidel is throwing me out of his home.*'

"'*I mean to say that he respectfully requests that you suspend your visits.*'

"My bravado about good breeding turned out to be completely groundless because, blinded by wrath, I jumped on Don Dámaso and grabbed him by the throat. Here I ought to note that I'd heard from a friend that this gentleman was being hounded by Matilde's other suitor, Adriano, to whom he owed a large sum which he was unprepared to pay at the time. He had obtained an extension by promising his creditor that his brother-in-law would grant him Matilde's hand. I had refused to believe it beforehand, but my doubts vanished when I realized he was throwing me out of Don Fidel's house, and I lost my senses.

"Seeing that Don Dámaso was turning blue under my furious grip and starting to choke, I released him, throwing him against the sofa, and fled from the house.

"At home I found my father bedridden. My Aunt Clara, who lives with me here, was at his side, and only left him when he was asleep. I sat at the head of the bed and kept watch throughout the night. I tried to read, but it was impossible. I was choked with grief, and my eyes failed to comprehend the words on the pages because my imagination was seething. My father's shortness of breath, instead of inspiring concern, made me think of Don Dámaso, whom I had punished for being the bearer of gloom. Then my father started coughing so violently that I forgot my sorrows and began to fear for his life. The next day, the doctor diagnosed his illness as pneumonia, which was so acute that it drained him of life within three days. I never left his bedside, holding vigil with my aunt, who came to live in our house. My father's brother visited during the day. Back then, he was poor, but he would eventually make a name for himself. My poor father died in my arms, blessing me. Who on earth could endure so much pain at once?

"A month later, I paid some condolence visits and heard that Matilde and Adriano were engaged. Could it be any worse?"

"I can't imagine," said Martín.

"Do you see why you're better off than you think? Since she doesn't love you, there's still time to forget about her and save yourself from misery."

"It's not easy to forget once you're in love!" exclaimed Rivas. "I prefer to suffer."

"Try loving someone else then."

"I couldn't. Besides, my poverty has shut Society's door on me."

"That's what happened to me," said Rafael. "After a year of mourning, I lost all self-respect in search of forgetfulness, and I learned that to avenge a disgrace upon oneself is to be doubly disgraced. It seemed to me that sacrificing some poor girl was nothing compared to my woes. I neglected my studies, thinking that a law degree was useless if I wasn't going to marry Matilde. I skipped classes and frequented cafés, spending hours at the billiard table and hanging around with a rowdy crowd, the kind of guys who shout at waiters or anyone who will listen to what they have to say. It didn't take long before I was regarded as one of them.

"One day, when I was passing by the Señor de Mayo procession in Plaza de Armas with a new buddy of mine, I noticed three women who stood out in the crowd. One of them older; the other two, young and pretty. There was something about them that set them apart from the rest of their class.

"'*Lovely lasses,*' I said to my companion.

"'*They're the Molina sisters, and the older woman is their mother.*'

"'*You know them?*' I asked.

"'*Of course, they host the best carousals.*'

"Adelaida caught my eye in particular. Her rosy lips seemed to promise me forgetfulness. Her expressive gaze and dark brows; her black tresses over her long shawl; and her petite figure seemed to call my name. I went to her house to introduce myself.

"'*I missed the whole procession in the Plaza and all the other girls because I saw only you,*' I said to Adelaida moments after meeting her.

"Apparently my friskiness didn't offend her because my buddy had introduced me as the son of a good family, which was as good as having a halo over my head.

"At night when I looked at this picture of Matilde's innocent, peaceful face, I would feel ashamed of the kind of life I was leading. But my conscience was weaker than my jealousy. I continued courting Adelaida and pretending I was happy-go-lucky, when I was really tormented by visions of Matilde and the sound of her voice in Adelaida's vows of love. Who would believe that in the middle of the nineteenth century a broken heart can still drive a man to despair? The more things change, the more they stay the same!

"It was depraved of me to avenge the falsehood of one woman through the sacrifice of another, but I couldn't stop myself. Of all the wretched souls on earth, brokenhearted lovers are the first to search for forgetfulness in a degenerate life, for their misery degrades their sense of honor. When two lives are joined as one through vows of love, betrayal deprives the abandoned lover of his reason for living. I should have thought this before hurting Adelaida, but I was blinded by the news of Matilde's happiness, which was described to me in excruciating detail by some people I knew. An old friend of the family even told me about the wedding gifts, like jewelry worth 3,000 pesos. Listen, I know I'm no saint, and since destiny showed no mercy on me, I thought, '*why should I feel morally obliged to anyone?*'

"It didn't take long to convince myself that resignation was the only way to face disgrace because I was so miserable and ashamed of myself. The illicit pleasures, far from healing me, made me conscious of how low I had stooped, making me feel unworthy of Matilde's love, which used to be my highest aspiration.

"Within a few months I was faced with a serious obligation to Adelaida because she had a son. Since then I've broken up with Adelaida, but I've tried to ease her family's financial burdens. I've always known her to be strong, but I was astonished to see how well she took it. In fact, from that day forward she has acted as if nothing had ever happened between us. Does she still love me, or does she despise me? I don't know.

"You're probably asking yourself why I brought you there, and whether it occurred to me that the same thing could happen to you."

"It certainly crossed my mind," said Martín.

"I've learned a great deal at the cost of many regrets," replied San Luis, "and I only meant to steer you away from the mistakes I've made. If I thought you were as frivolous as the rest of our classmates, I would have kept you away from that house."

"Well, you've judged me wisely," replied Martín. "As far as I'm concerned, it's Leonor or no one. I have no reason to complain because she has done nothing to encourage me. But let's talk about you. What would you say if I reunited you with Matilde?"

Rafael sat up, startled, "You? And how would you manage that?"

"I'm not sure, but I know it's possible."

San Luis folded his arms on the table, and put his head down, murmuring, "It's hopeless. Her fiancé is dead, but I'm still poor."

He stood up after saying these words and spent a few moments preparing a makeshift bed on the sofa.

"You can sleep here, Martín. Good night," he said, before climbing into bed without changing his clothes.

XVI

After the attack against the Society of Equality on the 19th, there were fiery debates about Politics in tertulias everywhere. Don Dámaso Encina's salon was no exception on the night of August 21st, for his guests were completely engrossed in the rumors that Santiago would be declared a state of siege.

"The Government must take this measure at once," said Don Fidel Elías.

"That would be ludicrous," replied his wife.

"Francisca," Don Fidel replied adamantly, "how often must I tell you that women should stay out of Politics?"

"It seems to me that Chilean Politics is not so enigmatic that it is beyond comprehension," she said.

"Take heed of what my compadre says," said Matilde's godfather, Don Simón, "for it is true that you cannot fathom a state of siege without having studied the Constitution."

This gentleman, considered to be a man of some capacity (for the dogmatism of his phrases and the eloquence of his silence), generally ruled upon the frequent squabbles between Doña Francisca and her husband, who then clucked, "Precisely, and the Constitution is the foundation of our Government and without it we wouldn't have a Government."

Don Dámaso lacked the nerve to back his sister in this controversy because his friends had convinced him, through the threat of a revolution, to support the Government. Doña Francisca told him, "Thanks for defending me. Oh, George Sand said it aptly: woman is a slave."

"But, dear, given the threat of revolution, I believe that it would be prudent . . . "

"Señor George Sand can say whatever he damn well pleases," interrupted Don Fidel, looking for the approval of his compadre, "but the truth of the matter is that, without a state of siege, the Liberals will take over. Correct me if I am mistaken, compadre."

"It sounds like you fear those poor Liberals," exclaimed Doña Francisca, "as if they were the northern barbarians in Middle Ages."

"Worse than the seven plagues of Egypt," said Don Simón in a pedagogic tone.

"To tell you the truth, I don't know what I would fear more," exclaimed Don Fidel, "the Liberals or the barbaric Araucano Indians because Francisca is mistaken when she says they are from the north."

"I was referring to barbarians from the Middle Ages," said the lady, miffed by the stubborn ignorance of her husband, who insisted, "No, no! Age has nothing to do with it because Araucano Indians have wee folks and old folks, the same as Liberals, but they're all a bunch of thieves, and if I were in power I would declare a state of siege."

"The state of siege is the basis of domestic tranquillity, Don Dámaso, my friend," said Don Simón, seeing that the host was still ambivalent.

"I agree, I believe in Governments which secure tranquillity," said Don Dámaso.

"But, sir," exclaimed Clemente Valencia, biting the tip of his gold-crowned walking stick, "they want to beat us into tranquillity."

"*A coups de bâton*," said Agustín.

"That's the way it should be," replied Emilio Mendoza, who, as we have said, blindly pledged his allegiance to the authorities. "The Government must show itself to be forceful."

"Otherwise, the Constitution would topple tomorrow morning," said Don Fidel.

"I believe the Constitution makes no mention of clubs," observed Doña Francisca, who could not resist the temptation to rebut her mate, who shouted, "Woman, woman! How many times must I tell you . . . "

"But, compadre," interrupted Don Simón, "the Constitution has its amendments, and one of them is military ordinance, which would cover such measures."

"You see what was I saying!" answered Don Fidel. "Have you read the ordinance?"

"But that ordinance refers to the military," objected Doña Francisca.

"Every attempt of opposition against Authority," argued Don Simón dogmatically, "should be considered a military transgression because resisting Authority requires arms, and, therefore, those who resist must be viewed as militants."

"You see," said Don Fidel, impressed by his compadre's logic.

Doña Francisca returned to Doña Engracia, who was petting Diamela, and said, "To argue with those reactionaries can make one's blood boil."

"I know what you mean, my darling, it's stuffy in here and I can hardly breathe," answered Doña Engracia, who, as we said before, suffered from apnea. Doña Francisca, silently cursing the stupidity of her sister-in-law, replied, "I was referring to the heat of these disputes."

"I know what you mean, my darling," she added, "and it's plumb dreadful. All day long my head is burning and my feet are freezing."

Doña Francisca, in order to pacify herself, began to flip through an album belonging to her niece who had retired with Matilde to the other end of the chamber.

Martín was hanging his hat in the cloakroom when Agustín hastened toward him, saying, "My family needn't know how the other half lives, so let's keep the other night our little secret."

Leonor was saying to Matilde, "Tonight I'll see if I can win his trust and make him talk about Rafael."

A circumstance casually arose to further Leonor's project. Doña Engracia's valet entered the salon, carrying some fabrics that he had brought back from town. The instant that Doña Francisca saw the materials, her foul mood vanished (as did her thoughts on

Politics) and she joined her sister-in-law in a dissertation on fashion, while Don Dámaso and his friends continued to debate the destiny of the country, borrowing the tired rhetoric etched in our minds by countless politicians. Agustín was the only one who ventured to join the girls at the other end of the salon, leaving his peers to Politics.

Leonor had announced her motive for speaking to Rivas, as if to excuse herself for thinking about him. She refused to admit that she was intrigued with his whereabouts and eager to test her willpower against him. The poetic expression playing with fire aptly describes Leonor's presumptuous vows to triumph where she had seen many of her friends succumb. She armed herself for the war of love with the pride of her beauty as her main weapon.

Their eyes met as Martín approached the salon, helplessly drawn to her divine beauty, frantically searching for a reason to talk to her, and finding some relief in the excuse that he would be helping his friend by providing Leonor with more information about him. The look in her eyes commanded him to approach, and he acquiesced with the reverence of a subject before his sovereign. To see Martín filled with such emotion made Leonor's heart flutter ever-so-faintly. This subtle reaction made Martín think that he had misinterpreted the look in her eyes and he wanted to curse his awkwardness in a thousand languages, and this humiliation showed in his face.

Fortunately, Leonor regained her composure, looked at Rivas again, and put an end to the seemingly eternal moment in which the young man swore to himself that he would flee from that house forever.

XVII

"My mother interrupted our conversation the other day," Leonor said, "and I was really sorry about that."

Rivas had neither a response to, nor an explanation for, what he had just heard.

Hearing no reply, she continued, "I was really sorry because I was afraid that I hadn't clarified why I was asking about your friend San Luis."

Martín was relieved to know that it was not his imagination that she wanted to speak him. He answered, "You made yourself perfectly clear, Señorita."

"Was it your understanding that I was asking for myself?"

"It was at first, but I stand corrected."

"Oh," remarked Leonor, "have you discovered something new?"

"As you say, I've discovered your intention."

"And my intention is . . . ?"

"To help a friend, from what I can see."

"Well, tell me about it, from what you can see."

"Your friend is interested in Rafael."

"And . . . what else?"

"Certain circumstances have separated them."

"Now I know that you've earned his trust."

"I have."

"And so now you've suddenly decided to be communicative," said Leonor, with a touch of reproach in her voice.

"It was only yesterday that I earned this trust," answered

Martín, who was thrilled to be on friendly terms with the girl who had caused him misery just yesterday.

"Therefore," replied Leonor, "you can answer me."

"I think I can."

"Since you seem to know all about it, you'll understand that I'm interested in finding out one thing. Does he still love Matilde?"

"With all his soul."

"Really?"

"I'm convinced of it. The enthusiasm with which he spoke about his love, the disillusionment it left in his soul, and the discouragement with which he faces the future seem to confirm my opinion."

"You speak as if it were your own heart," observed Leonor, to which Rivas replied with a melancholic air, "I believe in love, Señorita."

The girl sensed danger in this response and felt she ought to say nothing, but her pride made her ask him something that she would have never asked any man under ordinary circumstances.

"Are you in love?"

Martín could not hide his shock at her question, nor his desire to prove to her that the heart of a poor country boy was as worthy of love as those fancy city boys who were always courting her. He said, "A man in my position has no right to be in love, although he has the right to believe in love in order to empower himself for the struggles that destiny may have in store for him."

"Your friend's bitterness must be contagious."

"No, Señorita, but your sudden curiosity about my situation made me think about it. From the little I've seen of Santiago, I'm beginning to believe that love is nothing but a pastime here for the privileged few who have little to do."

"They say the heart obeys no rules."

"I can't speak from experience," answered Martín.

"Then where does that faith of yours come from? You said that you believe in love."

"From the depths of my soul. I've always felt that the heart has a higher purpose than circulating blood; that there is more to life than the gold everyone is digging for; that in the streets and theaters and salons, a young man's heart searches for a higher pursuit than seeing or hearing or partaking in the empty chatter of his peers."

"And that pleasure, that mysterious something, is what you call love. Is that right?"

"I think that if one never finds it," replied Martín somewhat proudly, "he'll either be lonelier or happier than everyone else."

"Happier in what way?"

"He will surely suffer less, Señorita."

"Which is to say that love is a disgrace."

"Everyone views it according to his own position in life, and that's how I see it from my perspective."

"Then you must be in love since you have such firm opinions on the matter."

Her matter-of-factness tinged Martín's cheeks, but instead of recoiling, he found the nerve to say, "I suppose you're not interested enough in this subject to want my sincere opinion, but I'll give it to you anyway. Since I happen to regard love as a disgrace, I am resolved to overcome its influence."

"In other words, you think that you're superior to everyone else."

"I would be nothing more than an egotist if I did. I would simply rather take the path less traveled."

Leonor, who had expected to win her little game hands down, felt thwarted by the way Rivas held his ground. Defending herself with a haughty look and an imperative tone which usually worked with men, she coolly pointed out that he had strayed far from the topic.

"If you have something else to ask me, please do, or if you prefer that I leave . . . "

"Let's talk about your friend," said Leonor dryly.

"Rafael is unhappily in love, Señorita."

"Perhaps you should enlighten him with your philosophy of resignation."

"Actually, he is the one who taught me that it's better to forgo the warmth of the flames than risk the burns of disillusionment."

"You always anticipate disillusionment."

"Which shows that I don't believe that I'm better than everyone else, as you presumed, and that I'm modest enough to acknowledge my influences."

"There are modesties that seem very much like pride, sir," said Leonor, "which in your case would contradict your argument. Perhaps your friend neglected to advise you that one should have a reason to be proud."

She left her seat without looking at him or waiting for an answer. For the first time in her life, Leonor felt defeated in a confrontation that she herself had provoked. In place of the banal, obsequious flattery of the dandies with whom she usually played this sort of game, there was the proud submission of a poor, obscure man who refused to bend his knee before her majesty and who artlessly affirmed that it was not his aspiration to gratify her. She had presumed that Rivas was enamored with her, judging by his reaction when she had denied personal interest in Rafael San Luis; however, this conversation undermined that presumption. Her faith in the supreme power of her beauty was shaken and her vanity rocked (for it was already counting on yet another captive in a long chain of victories). It was no longer enough to simply amuse herself at his expense. Now she longed for outright vengeance and vowed to inspire a passion so fierce that it would bring him to his knees.

Martín was left to wallow in the sadness that always seemed to linger after their encounters. Every time he was more convinced that she was playing games with him and mocking the infatuation his eyes must have revealed when they first met. As she walked away, he regretted his words and cursed his awkwardness for failing to make her see that his heart and mind were worthy of esteem. He was disheartened by her parting words, which clearly confirmed that she considered love and intelligence worthless without riches and reputation. Under this unsettling impression, he prayed to Heaven for supernatural powers, as all unhappy lovers do, not to forget, but to win her proud heart.

Leonor and Martín prayed for the same things in different ways. She was relying upon her divine appearance. He, on a miracle from Heaven.

When Doña Francisca, her husband, and Matilde stood up to leave, Leonor fixed her cousin's kerchief so that she could whisper these words into her ear, "He still loves you. I'll come see you tomorrow to tell you all about it."

Matilde clasped her hands with inexpressible appreciation. She had never returned home so happy and carefree.

Don Dámaso, finding himself alone with his wife, began to recite the Conservative ideas to which his friends had converted him by the end of their debate. He said, "After all, they have a point. What good has ever come from the Liberal party? And their point is well taken, because all over the world the rich have always sided with the Government. Take England, for example, where all of the Lords are rich."

Having thus reflected, he went to bed thinking that this direction would be the quickest way to Congress.

XVIII

We mentioned that Rafael San Luis lived on Calle de la Ceniza with his aunt, Doña Clara San Luis, who was unmarried due to lack of money and beauty. She had taken her nephew into her home when she saw that he was down on his luck and alone in the world. She added her modest savings to his inheritance of 8,000 pesos, which was all that remained after the debts were paid. With no other vocation but to attend Mass and pray the novenas of her devotion, she studied the grief written on Rafael's face with the discernment of a woman who has no other care in the world. Without ever soliciting his confidences, she knew how deeply he was suffering and occasionally offered him some Christian guidance about the virtues of acceptance and prudence.

While we were visiting other characters, Doña Clara busied herself with finding an occupation that would take her nephew away from Santiago, where she watched him abandon his studies and waste away in idleness as he searched for forgetfulness. On the morning of the 21st, while Rafael was sleeping off a hangover, Doña Clara wrapped herself in a shawl and went to visit her other brother, Don Pedro San Luis, who lived on one of the main streets of Santiago.

Don Pedro, as San Luis had mentioned to Rivas, had made himself a nice fortune. He owned two haciendas, not far from Santiago, which he was obliged to lease due to his debilitating health. He had a wife and a son, Demetrio, who was 15 years of age.

En route to her brother's manor, Doña Clara thought of a way to improve her nephew's lot.

Don Pedro, who cherished his family and always answered to their beckoning call, welcomed his sister affectionately and brought her to his study. Once she was comfortably seated, he asked, "How is Rafael?"

"Well, he is the reason I've come to talk to you. You know how I spoil him."

"Yes, and I'd say you overdo it," observed Don Pedro, "and it's a shame because he's a talented boy."

"Isn't he! But, he's seems sadder and sadder, and he's letting his studies slip more and more."

"That's terrible. You ought to advise him."

"I have an idea, but I need your help."

"Mine? Well, let's hear it."

"I've given it plenty of thought," said Doña Clara. "I think that the best thing that could happen to this boy is to take him away from Santiago and set him up on the farm, where hard work and the hope of a better life will shake him out of the misery that is eating him alive."

"You want me to find him a lease?"

"Better than that. Aren't you always saying that you wish your son would start working the land?"

"Precisely. Clara, my boy is no scholar and it's important that he gets to know the land that will be his someday."

"Well then, why don't you put him to work with Rafael on one of your haciendas?"

"Good thinking," exclaimed Don Pedro, who was always a bit worried about leaving his young son on the farm alone. "Do you know if Rafael wants to leave?"

"I've never asked him, but we'll discuss that later. When does the lease expire on El Roble?"

"Next May, and just yesterday Don Simón Arenal was here, on behalf of his compadre Don Fidel, asking if I would promise to extend his lease for another nine years."

"And?"

"I didn't say anything because I've been thinking about sending Demetrio out there."

"Then," the lady rejoiced, "you're going to tell them that you can't."

"That would be the best solution, if Rafael wants to drop out of law school."

"I'll recommend it because I don't see much hope in his studies."

Doña Clara returned home contented and shared her plans with her nephew, who asked for a few days to reflect upon it.

After class the next day, Rafael left the university with Martín, who was wondering whether he should mention his conversation with Leonor, but he decided against it out of his instinctive discretion that cautioned him not to divulge anything without Leonor's consent.

San Luis broke the silence between them with this announcement, "They're proposing a project for me, Martín, and I want to hear your opinion."

"What kind of project?"

"A lease in the country."

"Could you make a living for yourself?"

"Quite nicely."

"Are you fond of your studies?"

"Not like I used to be."

"Then accept it."

"Let me tell you why I'm hesitating. Guess who is currently leasing the hacienda and who wants to continue leasing it? Don Fidel, Matilde's father."

"Oh, now that changes the whole picture. Tell me more about it."

"Don Fidel wasn't always the stodgy, old reactionary that he is today. Believe it or not, he used to be a Radical, like many old-timers who have since abandoned the cause. Don Fidel fought in the war against Conservatism, which unfortunately has no end in sight in this country. He became friends with other Radicals, especially my father and my uncle who struck it rich with real-estate, unlike my father who lost it all on a few unlucky speculations. When my Uncle Pedro moved to Santiago for health reasons, offers poured in on the hacienda, El Roble. Naturally, he preferred to grant the lease to his comrade Don Fidel, who would benefit the most because he already owned some land next to El Roble—

about one hundred acres of alfalfa crop, which would thrive on my uncle's grounds. When it came time to sign the contract, a complication arose, the lack of a guarantor. Don Dámaso hadn't established himself in Santiago yet, and the rest of Don Fidel's friends weren't in the position to back him. My uncle refused to risk El Roble, even for friendship, because most of the money invested in it had come from his wife's dowry. Then, out of the clear blue appeared Don Simón Arenal as Don Fidel's guardian angel.

"Don Simón hardly knew him, but he lent him an exorbitant amount of money so that he could buy Don Fidel's political influence. Back then Don Fidel exercised strong influence over the jurisdiction where he owns land, in fact he still does, and Don Simón wanted to be elected Deputy. Now, why would a rich man like Don Simón want to be a Deputy? Because social upstarts like him are always seeking status so that they can pass their new money off as old money. He's the perfect example of the improvised gentleman, a common sort among us these days. Since then Don Fidel and Don Simón became fast friends; in fact, they became compadres. It wasn't long before Don Simón was sipping tea among Santiago's elite and Don Fidel was talking like a die-hard reactionary to please his new best friend and financial backer, who had learned from years of experience that the only way to prosper in Politics was to uphold the status quo. The friendship between my uncle and his tenant began to break down, but their contract was rock solid. But, now that it's expiring and agriculture is booming again, given the new market in California, Don Fidel will do anything to renew the lease. That's why he sent his compadre Don Simón to obtain new terms. But my uncle has offered El Roble to me and his son, and I'm sure that he'll help us get started. So that's the whole picture."

"I still think you should accept," said Martín.

"I've asked for a few days to think it over," responded San Luis, "and you'll see my weakness. The truth is, I haven't completely abandoned hope that Matilde loves me."

Rivas resisted the temptation to tell his friend what he knew about Matilda; instead he asked, "What difference would that make, since you're still poor?"

"It's true, I'm still poor but if she still loves me," answered San

Luis, "I bet that I could win her father over if I gave him the lease, which means everything to him. That way, we could make up and begin to put the past behind us. Matilde would bring our families together, and my cousin and I would undertake some other business together with the help of my uncle."

Martín thought that his last conversation with Leonor might determine his friend's destiny because he could not imagine that she was asking so many questions out of mere curiosity.

"You're right, but I think you should talk it all over with your uncle, man-to-man. That way you can starting planning, rather than just hoping," advised Martín, knowing that he would report all of this to Don Dámaso's daughter if she asked him about Rafael again.

XIX

Leonor arrived at her cousin's house at twelve o'clock the next day as she had promised. A night of sweet dreams had brightened Matilde's cheeks and eyes, which sparkled in joyous anticipation of the latest word on her beloved.

"Mama has left, so we're alone," she said, instructing Leonor to sit down. "I was beginning to think you weren't coming!"

"As you know, I sent for Martín to ask him for the latest on Rafael."

"And he must have given you an earful because your conversation lasted quite a while," observed Matilde, radiant.

"All of it can be summarized in what I told you last night," said Leonor. "Rafael still loves you."

"How does Martín know?"

"It seems that he confided in him."

"Yes, but saying so isn't enough," exclaimed Matilde, growing dispirited. "Now what am I to do?"

"You still love him too."

"Yes, but we're still separated."

"The ball is in your court."

"Mine? But what am I supposed to do?"

"Who left who?"

"I did, but . . . "

"There are no buts."

"You know very well that I couldn't disobey Papa."

"That's no excuse from his point of view. San Luis, thrown out of your house, without a single word from you, had plenty of reasons to believe that he was forgotten."

"I swore to him a thousand times that I would never forget him."

"How do you explain that you were going to marry someone else? Wasn't that breaking your vows?"

"He ought to know that I was acting against my will."

"Look, Matilde," Leonor said in a serious tone, "I believe that there is nothing more sacred than vows of love, especially when you had your parents' approval. You shouldn't have broken your vows just because he lost his money. You should have kept them."

"You know that I couldn't stand up to my father," said Matilde, on the verge of tears.

"I know, but I want to make you see that if you really loved San Luis, you should make it up to him now that you know he's still thinking of you."

"Yes, but how?"

"Write to him."

"Oh, I wouldn't dare!"

"In that case, renounce your love since you're unwilling to take the first step toward reconciliation."

Matilde covered her face with her hands, bursting into sobs.

"But, sweetheart," Leonor said, using a gentler tone as she caressed her cousin, "you're making yourself sick over nothing. When are you going to stand up for yourself!"

"Oh, that's easy for you to say because you're not in my place!"

"That's not true," said Leonor briskly. "I'll never break my vows once I make them."

"But I wouldn't have the nerve to do it alone. You have to help me."

"How?"

"Let Martín be the one to tell him."

"It's true," reflected Leonor, "I can tell by his answers that he already knows the whole story about Rafael anyway. Let's suppose that Martín agrees to be the messenger. Then what? Don't you have to give San Luis some explanation as to why you treated him that way?"

"I suppose."

"First of all, you have to see if you still feel the same way about him, because you can be sure that once Rivas sends him the message, San Luis will want to see you and hear your reasons for behaving the way you did. You mustn't refuse him that, unless you end it once and for all, because he'll be convinced that he's just a stupid prop in some cruel prank."

"I love him and I'll do whatever I have to, but only if you help me," resolved Matilde, holding Leonor's hand, while drying her tears.

"You've finally made up your mind! I was beginning to doubt your sincerity."

"Oh, believe me, Leonor, I love him more than life itself," she blubbered. "I've cried myself blind, and at times I felt like I would do anything just to see him again and hear him say the things he used to say to me."

"Let's see what we can do about this. I think you should see him, since you don't dare to write to him, and Martín, as we said, can help us with this."

"What is your plan?"

"To tell him that he can meet you at Alameda."

"When?" asked Matilde, unable to hide her rising anxiety.

"Tomorrow. You'll come with me, and Agustín will escort us."

"My God," murmured Matilde, whose body trembled as if she were already in Rafael's presence, "if Papa finds out about this!"

"Leave everything to me," answered Leonor, who seemed to take heart as her cousin gave in to her tears, hugging and thanking Leonor between uncontrollable sobs.

"You owe me nothing, Matilde," she said, hugging her back, "because my love for you is not the only reason I'm helping you."

"There's another reason?" asked Matilde, lifting her head from her cousin's embrace.

"Yes, another reason. I want to make amends for my father's actions. As we both know, he was largely responsible for throwing Rafael out of your house."

Leonor failed to mention her ulterior motive for helping her cousin. Yes, it was true that she wanted to make amends for her father's damage, but she also wanted to regain her self-esteem, which had suffered a disappointing blow in the first round of battle against Martín. This setback, because it was the very first blow to her amour propre, naturally distressed her. Of course she would eventually retaliate, but in the meantime she needed an immediate project to occupy her mind, lest she be tormented by peace and quiet. It was her intensity, in fact, that blinded her to the potential consequences of her plan, which could very well taint her cousin's reputation, not to mention her own.

"What if someone happens to spot us at Alameda and tells Papa?"

Leonor, who was irritated by any sign of weakness, exclaimed, "Matilde, you must make up your mind one way or another. For me, there are two obvious options. Either renounce your love for Rafael, or stand up to your father so he won't pressure you to marry the man of his choice, not yours. My advice to you was based on the assumption that you were completely decided on Rafael. But, if that's not the case, simply put him out of your mind and go on with your life."

"Maybe if I wait, another occasion will arise . . . "

"Tell me, haven't you waited for more than a year?"

"Yes."

"And, in all that time, has San Luis taken the smallest step toward you?"

"No, none at all," sighed Matilde softly, "that's why I thought he despised me."

"And nevertheless, he still loves you. I suppose what keeps him at bay is either resentment or fear. There is one thing for sure, nothing comes of waiting. He will continue thinking that you took him for a fool, and all appearances will support his opinion."

"I know, but I'm so afraid that Papa will find out . . . "

"Well, if I were in your place, I would want him to know. If your love is true and you would never, as you say, love anyone except Rafael, sooner or later what you fear will come true."

"I've resigned myself to suffer in silence."

"But you wanted to know if San Luis had forgotten you."

"True."

"And you told me that you would give your life to have him back."

"That's true too. Oh, I wish I had your courage!"

"You asked me for advice and I gave it to you. If you're not strong enough to overcome your fears for the man you love, then give him up. You shouldn't do anything that might compromise your reputation because Society will despise you."

"You're right, I've already suffered enough and I have the right to seek happiness."

"So let's do it. If I had to choose between suffering in silence at the risk of being scorned, or defending my man and paying the price, I would prefer the latter."

"And so would I," said Matilde firmly.

"Which means that I will speak to Martín."

"What will you tell him?"

"That you still love Rafael. Martín probably suspects as much."

"And what else?"

"And you and I will stroll by Alameda near the fountain between one and two o'clock tomorrow afternoon, so that he can casually greet us."

"Very well," answered Matilde, making an effort to keep her entire body from trembling.

"For that to happen, I ought to be on my way," said Leonor. "I have to catch Martín before he leaves my father's study, otherwise I might not have a chance to speak to him tonight."

They bid each other a tender adieu, and Leonor stepped into her father's carriage, which was waiting to take her swiftly home.

XX

Shortly before his niece departed, Don Fidel Elías returned home, brooding over Don Simón Arenal's news about the lease on El Roble.

Don Fidel entered his wife's sitting room, where she spent an ample portion of her day reading her favorite novelists and poets. She was in the midst of reading *Adam's Dream* in *The Wicked World* by Espronceda, when her husband's droll voice interrupted the climactic moment when the hero begs Salada for a horse (reminiscent of Richard III shouting, "A horse, a horse! My kingdom for a horse!"). Don Fidel's presence awoke her from poetic ecstasy and drew her back to reality.

"My compadre Arenal says that the lease on El Roble is not secured."

Doña Francisca looked at him distractedly, for she had long grown accustomed to withholding her opinions about her husband's affairs when there was no third party to witness her sharper wit.

"Don Simón just told me," he persisted, thinking that Doña Francisca had not heard what he had said, "that Don Pedro San Luis needs to think about it before he can commit himself to renewing the lease on the hacienda."

"Let's wait and hope for the best," she answered, yearning to pick up where she had left off in her book.

"I'm glad to see you're not worried about ending up in the poorhouse," said Don Fidel, sarcastically, "because that is where we will be if I lose the lease."

"We'll find some backers for Don Pedro."

"I've already thought of that, but bloody Politics have ruined our friendship just when I needed it the most."

"I'm sorry to say it, but I told you so."

"You don't have to rub it in. I'll figure something out. But for now, let's forget about the hacienda and talk about another prospect. Do you think that Agustín fancies Matilde?"

"How would I know?"

"How would you not know?" Don Fidel said impatiently. "I'm asking your opinion because I'm too busy a man to notice the sorts of things that a woman is supposed to notice."

"I have seen nothing that would make me think so," responded Doña Francisca, impatiently picking up the book that she had laid on a table.

"Because you're always dreaming of poetry and rubbish while I'm taking full responsibility for the well-being of this family."

"Why should I bother to get involved with anything if you're going to criticize me for it later?"

"It's true, if a man wants something done right, he must do it himself. But I can't do absolutely everything myself. You could at least pick up the woman's share. Agustín is a good match and we can't let him get away. I'll handle this business with Don Dámaso myself because if I don't do it myself, it won't get done."

Don Fidel took his hat and stormed out of the sitting room, convinced that he alone was capable of managing so many items of business at once. His daughter's marriage was, after all, an item of business—as it is for most parents.

Don Fidel's departure made no impact on Doña Francisca because their conversations usually ended as abruptly as this one. She picked up *Adam's Dream*, deploring the lack of poetry in the man with whom she was bound by indivisible ties, and this notion turned her thoughts to George Sand, who also held an aversion for matrimony.

Don Dámaso's carriage, meanwhile, carried Leonor quickly home despite the abominable condition of the pavement of the streets, which have only now caught the local authority's attention.

Leonor glided across the front patio and opened the door to her father's study, after making sure that Martín was alone. During the ride home, she wondered how she would ask for his help and decided that the best approach was direct. Thus, she walked straight up to his desk. He sprang to his feet when he saw who had interrupted him from his work.

"Sit down," Leonor said with a certain tone of superiority.

"I prefer to stand, Señorita," answered the young man, seeing that Leonor remained standing with one hand on the desktop.

To prevent any misinterpretation, Leonor said, "I'm here to discuss the same subject we discussed yesterday."

"I am at your service," he said, with a respectable humility that had caught the girl's attention on more than one occasion.

"When your friend shared his confidences, did he ever name the woman he loves?"

"Señorita Matilde Elías, your cousin."

"Rafael, you say, still loves her?"

"It's true."

"Do you think he would be happy to know that Matilde has always felt the same?"

"I think that this news would make him very happy, Señorita."

"Well then, you may tell him. It seems to me that news like this received from a friend is twice as joyous."

"It will give me endless pleasure to give it to him," said Martín.

The sincerity with which the young man uttered these words showed Leonor that he was capable of true friendship and served to soften her anger over what he had said the previous night.

At some point on the way home, she must have changed her plans because she turned to leave the room at this moment.

"A word, if I may, Señorita," said Martín. "Rafael believes that he has been misled. Will he believe what I'm going to tell him?"

"I don't know, but I think that if he were interested, he would find out the truth for himself."

This said, Leonor departed, and Rivas sank into his chair, put his head into his hands, and said to himself, "I'm little more than a servant to her and much less than a peer."

This bitter reflection (inspired by her imperious tone and serene composure) never left his mind until the end of the workday when he went to tell San Luis, "If only you could give me the news that I'm about to give you."

"News!" said Rafael, with a vague presentiment of the truth. "What is it?"

"Matilde still loves you."

"Martín, please don't tease me about the most sacred part of my life. Though I don't believe a word of it, I want to believe it so badly that it hurts."

"Well, you can believe it. Listen, I wouldn't kid you about something so painful."

Martín then told his friend all about his conversations with Leonor, and Rafael clasped his hands, rejoicing. "You bring me more than joy. You bring me life!"

Rafael began to pace the room, and out of his mouth flowed a river of happy memories and dreams so that within a quarter of an hour Martín knew everything about the romance that rekindled his friend's lust for life.

"I've forgotten about you, my dear Martín," Rafael said, sitting at his side. "Any developments on your side?"

"There is nothing to report," said Martín, who envied his friend's happiness. "The past, present, and future are equally bleak. I should listen to your advice and put the whole mad idea out of my mind. You can already see that I'm nothing more than her messenger-boy."

"Keep your chin up. You never know. Maybe Leonor will fall in love with you someday. The way she looks after her cousin makes me think that she isn't so cold after all, and I'm even beginning to forgive her father for what he did to me."

Martín took his hat as if to leave.

"Don't go," San Luis told him. "Let's have supper with my aunt. She'll be as happy as I am when she hears the good news. Besides, I want to talk to you more about Leonor's last comment. What was it that she said to you?"

"That you should find out the truth for yourself."

"You see! I must find a way to see Matilde. What would you do in my place?"

"I would write to her. It seems very natural to me."

"Can't you think of a better way? Letters are frustrating. If they aren't cold, they're ridiculously affected. Besides, I have to see her."

"You can ask to meet her in a letter."

"But where?"

"Why not leave that up to her?"

"Fine, I'll write to her."

On the way to the dining room, Rafael told his aunt the joyous news that Martín had brought him. He then sent the servant away and told his aunt at the table, "I need you to tell Uncle Pedro what has happened. I'm so glad that I asked for a few days to think about his proposal."

"And what shall I tell him about that?" asked Doña Clara.

"Tell him that it's an excellent way to obtain Don Fidel's consent. I'll grant him the lease on El Roble if my uncle lets me, and that's how we'll reconcile. If Don Fidel allows me to marry Matilde, I'll study for my law degree, or if he prefers, I'll work the land with my uncle's support. I know you'll convince him. My uncle has a big heart, and he won't let me down."

Martín thanked Rafael and his aunt for the wonderful meal and returned to Don Dámaso's house after the Encina family had finished their dinner. As he went upstairs, he heard Leonor playing the piano for her father, which she often did at this hour.

Leonor was disappointed not to see Martín at dinner because she was longing to serve him a piece of humble pie. She assumed that he was visiting San Luis and hoped that he would return in time for the evening tertulia so that she could make him eat his words.

XXI

Agustín Encina pranced into Rivas's chamber at this very moment, humming the melody of a French song.

The egotistical principle guiding most human actions moved him to seek Rivas's friendship after finding him at the home of Doña Bernarda. Although he still looked upon him with the arrogance of the sophisticated Santiagoan toward the unfashionable, he warmed up to the young provincial when it occurred to him that "Martín can accompany me to the Molinas, where he'll be very useful to me."

The expression "he'll be very useful to me" must be clarified within its social context.

Love, the guiding star of youth, leads a young man into a salon where the stillness in the air prevents him from voicing the adoration in his eyes, for fear of being overheard. However, the knot in his throat dissolves when *Simple Admiration* evolves into *Tender Admiration*—to quote Stendhal—because glances no longer satisfy the demands of the heart. It becomes necessary to hear the lady's voice and to confess to her all the sweet afflictions of his lovesick soul. In order to steal an intimate moment to elaborate his choppy, suspenseful phrases, the young man engages an accomplice to entertain her mother or her sisters, who are always quicker to lend an ear to the banalities of a young bachelor.

It is in this context that Agustín thought Rivas could be very useful to him at the home of Doña Bernarda, whose vigilance was all the sharper because the stakes were all the higher, granted that the suitor was the son of a very well-to-do family.

"Have you been back to visit the Molinas?" Agustín asked Martín, offering him a cigar.

"No, I haven't," Martín answered.

"Will you *retourner* any time soon?"

"I haven't given any thought to it."

"They're excellent girls."

"So they seemed."

"I'm planning to pay them a visit tonight. Care to join me?"

"That would be nice."

"What did you think of Adelaida?"

"I thought she was lovely, but not as much as you did," said Martín, grinning.

"Who told you I'm smitten?"

"It's written all over your face."

"Well, my dear chap, it's true. There isn't a single lass in my circle who holds a candle to Adelaida."

"I'm sorry to hear you say that," said Rivas.

"Why?"

"Because you might do something mad."

"What do you call mad? In Paris everybody has this sort of fling."

"I would say it was mad, for example, if you stirred hopes of marriage," he said, recalling San Luis's comments about Adelaida's disposition and her aspiration to marry into money.

"Bah! my dear chap, open your eyes to the world! All those girls know that a gentleman such as myself would never marry them."

Martín argued the moral implications of these Parisian mores, but Agustín simply dismissed him as blind to the ways of the world. To end Martín's reproach, he said, "I'll continue to see her with or without you because *je l'aime de tout mon coeur*. It would be a pity, though, if you didn't join me."

"If you insist . . . "

"I most certainly do! It's important to keep your friends happy and to have some fun, otherwise life is so drab in Santiago. *C'est convenu?* I'm going to get dressed and I'll meet you in half an hour."

"Fine, I'll be ready soon," Martín answered, hoping that a diversion might lift his spirits.

Don Dámaso's son departed and Martín examined his conscience, while preparing for their social call: "My feelings grow stronger as my hopes grow weaker. Maybe I should quench my desire with an easy love like Rafael and Agustín."

As Martín considered applying the remedy "like cures like" to heal his wounded pride, Agustín returned, dressed with an irreproachable elegance, and proceeded to prattle about his ladylove all the way to Doña Bernarda's house.

Meanwhile, Leonor had taken a seat at the piano, which she played zestfully. She was delighted to have shown Rivas no sign of agitation earlier that day and wished that he would return so that she could rile him with her scorn. She could not forget his vow to resist the powers of love because it was the first time that anyone had dared to underestimate the sheer force of her beauty. Bored by the music, she wandered over to the sofa. The sound of every footstep on the patio made her heart rush and she greeted everyone who arrived coldly. The absence of her cousin made the night seem even longer because she wanted to explain why she had changed her plans when she spoke to Martín. She was further irritated by Martín's nonappearance because it denied her the pleasure of serving him a slice of humble pie.

Don Dámaso never noticed that his daughter was aggravated or that his wife was fast asleep with Diamela upon her lap. He was too busy arguing throughout the night against the Ministry, which Don Fidel and Don Simón vehemently supported.

Don Fidel, after arguing against the Opposition in front of his compadre, later asked himself on the way home if switching sides would gain him an extension on his lease on El Roble. At home with Doña Francisca, he continued his reflections aloud.

"It's a slippery tightrope! If I lean to Opposition, I'll lose the support of my compadre. Now that he is hobnobbing with the upper crust, he seems to forget who put him there. Damned Politics!"

Buried in a book by George Sand, Doña Francisca was inspired to voice a theory of her own. She said, "Politics, in the words of what's-his-name, is an inflamed circle . . . "

"What circle, woman! Who gives a damn about what's-his-name! If Don Pedro would renew my lease on El Roble, I would laugh at the whole world."

Doña Francisca rolled her eyes as if to ask Heaven what she had done to deserve such a bore for a mate.

XXII

Rivas and Agustín arrived at the Molina residence as Doña Bernarda was preparing the card table and calling Amador and his friends who were socializing with her daughters. "Com'on, boys," Doña Bernarda was saying, "stop twattlin' and try your luck over here."

Amador's friends beckoned to the call of the hostess, who ushered in the new arrivals with a deck in hand. Doña Bernarda was about to rise and greet them, when Agustín said to her, "Madame, please do not incommode yourself."

"Sorry, sonny, no *commodes* in here," apologized Doña Bernarda.

"What I mean to say is: please don't trouble yourself for our sake," replied the young Encina with a gracious smile. "Simply carry on as you would without us."

"Oh! I didn't catch that fancy lil' French talk," exclaimed Doña Bernarda. "You wanna play a hand?"

"Later, Madame," answered Agustín. "First we must greet these young ladies."

The girls were summoned by their mother "to bring some light so everybody could be together." Adelaida and Edelmira obeyed, and the police officer followed them carrying a candlestick.

"That's why I like men in uniform," said Doña Bernarda in praise of Ricardo Castaños's chivalry as he placed the candlestick on the table and sat down beside Edelmira.

Realizing that it would be difficult to speak a private word to Adelaida without being overheard, Agustín began to encourage Amador to sing.

"Oh, I'm wild about music," he said to the young Molina, who immediately picked up his guitar and asked, "What's your favorite tune?"

"Anything you play," said Agustín.

This response prompted Amador to attune his guitar and sing a few verses to the monotonous melody of this old folk song:

I wouldn't kill myself for nobody
Who wouldn't die for me;
The gal who likes me is the gal I like
And all the rest can take a hike!

Agustín, taking advantage of the noise, pleaded with Adelaida for proof of her love.

"And what proof do you have for me?" she asked.

"Me? Whatever you ask."

"If you love me, as you say, my words would satisfy you and you wouldn't ask for further proof."

"But I can't get enough of your words. We never have a moment alone to speak freely and that is why I've been asking you for that itty, bitty little favor."

"What favor? I don't recall."

"A rendezvous."

"Oh, good gracious! That's more than an itty, bitty little favor!"

"Why?" asked Agustín, as submissively as possible.

"Who stands to lose from a rendezvous? I would, wouldn't I?"

"Don't you believe me to be enough of a gentleman?"

"On the contrary, too much so."

"Why too much?"

"Because you'd never marry a girl like me. Admit it," she said, staring through the young man. It was the first time she had been so frank with Agustín. Reeling from the question, he hesitated briefly, but the elasticity of his morals (whose theories he had expounded to Rivas earlier that day) prompted this flimsy defense: "But, why on earth would you doubt it?"

Adelaida instantly recognized deception, but did not flinch; instead, she pretended to believe him, inquiring, "You swear you wouldn't fool me, would you?"

Roaming in an open field of lies, Agustín replied within a blink of an eye, "On my life!"

And the swiftness of his response confirmed Adelaida's skepticism. With a sentiment that Agustín mistook as innocence, she exclaimed, "Oh, if only you wouldn't lie!"

"On my life, I swear to you that I'm not lying. Promise me a rendezvous so that we can speak in private."

Just then Amador ended his song, and Adelaida answered shortly, "The street door will be open tomorrow at midnight."

Agustín almost fell off his chair. His face beamed with joy, and his eyes sparkled.

"You've made me the happiest man alive," he whispered in time with the final cords of the guitar.

"Step away. My mother is watching us," Adelaida said to him between clenched teeth.

The dandy proceeded to the card table, complimenting Amador on the song he had not heard.

"Com'on, lil' Frenchy," said Doña Bernarda, shuffling the deck, "place your bets."

Martín had been sitting by himself all this time, feeling isolated from those around him, as lovers tend to feel. In his imagination, he was singing incoherent verses of unrequited love to the melody of Amador's song. When the music ended, his eyes met with Edelmira's. The temptation of quenching his desire with an easy love returned when he recognized a sorrow in Edelmira's gaze that spoke of his own affliction. Just then, Amador called upon the officer to ask his opinion on the home-brewed mistela, an honor that Ricardo Castaños could not refuse. Rivas took advantage of his absence to sit beside Edelmira, who remarked, "I didn't expect to see you back so soon."

"Why?" asked Martín.

"Because you looked out of sorts the other night."

"I only came back to have another word with you."

Rivas spoke this line as if to test how an advance would be received.

"Are you like all the rest of them?" Edelmira asked, as though she were offended.

"Why do you ask?"

"Because I thought you were different from all the rest."

Rivas mistook her apparent offense as genuine because he did not realize that her reply was a typical ladylike response to a welcomed advance.

"In what way?" he asked her.

"Sincere with words," Edelmira replied, "but incapable of playing with serious things."

This simple appeal to his integrity had all the bite of an angry reproach, and he saw that he was in danger of taking the same undignified path to remorse as his friend Rafael.

"Please believe me when I say that it was our conversation that made me want to come back. It's the truth," he said. "I was moved by the way you described your position in life because I found it so much like my own."

"I'm glad you changed your tone."

"I meant what I said," said Martín.

"I believe you, but I wish that you'd let down your guard and speak as plainly to me as I did to you the other night."

"I've already begun by saying that we have something in common."

Edelmira, seeing Martín as the kind of storybook hero which romantic girls often dream of, was delighted to find her way into Rivas's heart through friendship—a recourse instinctively taken by sentimental souls who are wary of rehearsed flattery. As they continued chatting, Martín regretted the idea of inspiring an unrequited love and found real sweetness in the romantic friendship that Edelmira offered him. It was not long before his sympathy ripened into an admiration for her exquisite sensibility and her profound disregard for those who believed that they had a right to her love when they were incapable of understanding the delicacy of her feelings. In her disconsolation there was a certain perfume of poetry that rarely fails to move a decent young man. Thus it was that Martín, charmed by Edelmira's sensitivity, came to a point in their conversation where he said, "I must confess that I'm hopelessly in love."

This open confession, which would keep Martín pure by clarifying his position, had a dual effect upon Edelmira. It plucked a sprout of hope and planted in its place what an inkling of confidence plants in any woman—curiosity.

"Let me guess: she must be rich and pretty!" she asked.

"She is very beautiful!" said Martín, unable to contain his enthusiasm. Then he arose from his chair when Amador returned with the officer, who commended the mistela.

"I hope you won't stop coming here to visit me," Edelmira told him.

"With a friend like you," answered Martín, "I need no other companion."

Everyone gathered around the card table, and Amador picked up the deck left scattered by his mother, who was happy to have won 100 pesos.

The player who lost the most was Agustín Encina, who, excited by the good fortune of his *affaire d'amour,* challenged everyone to another round to show Adelaida how little he cared for money. Amador called for another bottle of mistela to cultivate Agustín's high spirits, and the liquor flowed as the stakes rose. Doña Bernarda's son had undoubtedly learned some of the methods whereby a certain class of gamblers manage to procure other people's money—with more courtesy, but no more honor than highwaymen—for within a quarter of an hour, he had swiped Agustín's purse clean.

"I'll play with my word as my credit," he announced, gulping down a glass of mistela when he found himself flat broke.

"As you wish," said Amador, "but I'd quit if I were you."

"Why?"

"'Cause you're having a spell of bad luck."

"It will pass," retorted the dandy, who held his poor opponents in contempt. Amador exchanged a knowing glance with another gambler at the table, then drew two cards, asking, "How much are you wagering?"

"6 ounces on the 7 of diamonds," said Agustín.

After an hour he had lost 1,000 pesos, which then doubled within another half hour. Martín intervened and called the game to an end.

"Bring me a piece of paper and I'll sign an IOU," Agustín said to Amador. The document vouched for 2,000 pesos, but Agustín signed for 4 because he had received an amorous look of admiration from Adelaida just then.

On their way home, the young Encina, transported by his conquest and the vapors of mistela, bragged to Martín in his peculiar dialect of gibberish about the irresistible way he had softened Adelaida's heart.

After their guests had left, Doña Bernarda, Adelaida, and Amador lingered around the card table. Edelmira left the room upon hearing her mother's sermon about the need "to catch a good man while you still can." Amador closed the door behind Edelmira and asked his other sister, "Well, what happened?"

"Tomorrow at midnight," she answered.

"Oh! Oh!" exclaimed Doña Bernarda. "Sweet talkin' Frenchy asked for a date?"

"It's not the first time," said Adelaida.

"Them rich boys think they can use our girls," replied Amador, "but this one's gonna regret it."

"So, you're gonna bring your pal here?" Doña Bernarda reminded him.

"You bet I will," responded Amador.

"And what if he don't wanna?" asked the mother.

"Don't you worry, Mama," answered Amador, taking up a candlestick on his way out. Then he added, leaning toward her, "Don't forget what we talked about."

"You worried I'm gettin' rusty?" she answered.

There was a faint noise behind the door.

"It must be that ninny Edelmira *earsdroppin'*," said Doña Bernarda.

"Who cares if she's listening?" said Amador. "Tomorrow she'll know all about it."

The widow seemed satisfied with this response and went straight to bed.

XXIII

Rafael San Luis was transported so swiftly from the depths of despair to the bliss of Martín's unexpected news that he felt as though it were all a dream.

As soon as Martín left, Doña Clara was sent to convince Don Pedro that their nephew's happiness was entirely dependent upon the terms of lease on El Roble.

Alone except for the furniture that bore witness to his incessant pain, Rafael kissed the portrait of his beloved and reminisced about their happy times, not without a twinge of remorse for the way he had lived after their ill-fated separation. The guilt of having sacrificed Adelaida Molina's honor to console his grief spoke more clearly in his conscience than ever before. Happiness set him back on the path of virtue just as desperation had led him astray. He felt ashamed that he was no longer as faithful and virtuous as the love he would profess, but he strove to nobler thoughts to escape his nagging memory. He could think of nothing but seeing Matilde and hearing her tender vows of chaste love. Leonor's parting words to Rivas suggested that he should request a meeting with Matilde. He sat down and scrawled frantically. An hour later, he had torn up two letters before settling on the following:

I've just received news that you still love me, and I can't describe my joy. If it's true that you've kept our love alive, let me hear it from your lips as it has been my only joy and my only dear thought. I'd beg you on my knees, if only I could see you, but if you turn a deaf ear to me now, I'll know that I've been deceived, and I'll plummet to the depths of depression, never to rise again.

This letter satisfied San Luis because it was the one that came closest to capturing his restlessness. The lengthy terms of endearment that he had professed in the two previous renditions seemed too frigid to convey the feverish state of his impassioned soul.

He thought of no other way of delivering this letter than the one invented, perhaps, back in the days when writing itself had begun. The poorly lit streets allowed him to approach Don Fidel's house at night without fearing that he would be recognized. He trembled at the threshold because his whole life had fallen apart the last time he was there. He asked to see an old maidservant of Doña Francisca whom he trusted. Four reales were enough for the attendant who lived on the porch level to fetch the maidservant, who then brought the letter to Matilde within ten minutes.

When it was time for Don Fidel to visit the home of his brother-in-law with Doña Francisca and his daughter, Matilde pretended to suffer a headache so that she could stay home for fear that someone at Don Dámaso's tertulia might detect the anxiety she felt since reading San Luis's letter.

At eight o'clock the next morning, Leonor emerged from church wrapped in a hooded cloak, escorted by a servant, and went to the home of her cousin, who received her in the same room as the previous day.

"Were you really ill last night?" she asked Matilde, who looked as though she had not slept a wink.

"Take a look at this," said Matilde, handing her cousin the letter.

"And your mama?" asked Leonor, sitting down without reading it.

"Still sleeping."

Leonor tossed back the hood of her cloak and began to read the letter. She raised her eyes to her cousin, who stood before her with the demeanor of the accused before the judge. She said, "You have no clue why San Luis is asking to see you, after our conversation yesterday."

"None whatsoever."

"I changed our plans because I thought it would seem more

natural if we waited for San Luis to request the meeting. This letter proves that I made the right choice. Have you answered him?"

"No, I was waiting to see you first."

"Have you changed your mind since last night?"

"No, I'm still frightened, but I can't falter now that Rafael has written to me."

"You'd better answer him right away."

"What shall I tell him?"

"What we planned yesterday. It's not too late. I'll come back with Agustín at one o'clock, and we'll meet Rafael at two o'clock."

After her cousin took leave, Matilde wrote back to Rafael, following her cousin's recommendations, and sent the letter to him through the same channels that she had received his.

At home Leonor went straight to her brother's chamber, where she rapped thrice upon the door. Agustín's voice asked from within, "Who is it?"

"You're not up yet?" asked Leonor, entering the room.

"My! Aren't you the early bird this morning! Are you coming from Mass?"

Leonor said yes and sat down to ask, "And why are you up so early?"

Although it was joy that had kept him from sleeping soundly (the same way that grief does), Agustín shrugged, "*Je ne sais pas quoi.* The sunlight, I guess."

"Last night you went to bed late."

"I went out with friends," answered Agustín, who was excited to recollect his visit from the night before.

"Where?" asked Leonor, slightly distracted.

"To visit the home of some girls."

"Were there lots of people our age?"

"Some—I went with Martín."

"With Martín!" said Leonor surprised. "At the home of which girls?"

"Oh, little sister, you're very curious. I'll name the miracle, but not the saint."

"I didn't know that our guest was the sort to pay social calls," said Leonor, fidgeting with the Mass book that she held in her hands.

"Like every gent on the block."

"Are the girls pretty?"

"Oh, enchanting!"

His enthusiasm made Leonor feel strangely ill at ease.

"Do I know them?"

"I don't know . . . maybe, then again, maybe not."

Agustín kept his answers evasive. On one hand, he wanted to brag that someone adored him, and yet, he wanted to hide the fact that the girl was a lowborn *would-be.*

"You must fancy one of those girls," asked Leonor.

"The prettiest," answered Agustín proudly.

"And does she fancy you?"

"There is no evidence to the contrary."

Leonor posed these questions so that she would not make her brother wary of the next one. "Martín . . . is he courting one of them?"

"I'm not sure, but I've seen him talking up a storm with the sister of the girl who is *mine.*"

Agustín accentuated the possessive pronoun in sweet anticipation of his rendezvous.

"Is she pretty too?" asked Leonor.

"*Oui, oui,* but not nearly as pretty as *mine,* although she is interesting."

The girl fell silent from the humiliating revelation. It was clear that Rivas had lied when he told her with feigned modesty that he vowed never to fall in love. To think that he was wooing another woman while she was sitting at home waiting to taunt him with her contempt! It occurred to her that the silence might awaken a suspicion in her brother so she decided to turn his attention to another matter—the one that brought her there.

"Oh, I almost forgot that I came here to ask you a favor."

"A favor, little sister," said Agustín, "*je suis tout à toi.*"

"I want you to come with me to Alameda between one and two o'clock this afternoon."

"What for? It's not Sunday."

"I'll tell you later, but first you promise me to come with me."

"I promise."

"Tell me, Agustín, are you really in love with that girl?"

"*De tout mon coeur!*"

"So, if you were unable to see her, you would feel awful."

"Very much so, but I don't think that will ever happen."

"Just imagine that they kept you away from her."

"Caramba, that wouldn't be easy!"

"I know, but just imagine."

"Oh, if we're just supposing. Fine."

"There you are, unable to see her . . . wouldn't you be grateful to someone who would make it possible to see her?"

"Of course! I would thank him with all my soul!"

"Well, for that very reason you're coming with me to Alameda."

"Well, I'll be darned! You've got your little beau too, eh?"

"No, silly, I'm not the one!"

"Well then, who is it?"

"Matilde."

"Our cousin? Not again! When I was in Europe, I knew she was in love with Rafael San Luis, but then you wrote to tell me that she was going to marry another chap, and now she wants us to escort her to Alameda to meet bachelor number three. *Excusez-moi du peu!*"

"There is no bachelor number three. Matilde has never loved any one but Rafael."

"Then why was she going to marry Adriano?"

"Mainly because of Papa."

"Because of Papa? Now, you've lost me completely, little sister."

"Don't you know that Papa was the one who advised Uncle Fidel to throw San Luis out of his house?"

"*Pourquoi?*"

"They say it was because Rafael was poor."

"Well, the reason remains."

"Even so, Papa shouldn't have interfered to cause the disgrace of a decent young man."

"*D'accord.*"

"And I think we owe it to them to do whatever we can to make reparations."

"That seems fair to me."

"Matilde has always loved San Luis and will never love anyone else."

"And that's the way it should be. Constancy is my code of conduct."

Leonor explained the rest of her plan and persuaded her brother to support Matilde in her devotion. Then they said goodbye, and Agustín promised not to be late for their date. It was a day of sweet expectations for the dandy as he blissfully awaited the midnight rendezvous, without giving a second thought to furthering Matilde's secret romance.

XXIV

Shortly before one o'clock in the afternoon, Leonor left her dressing room to wait for her brother in the antechamber. She was dazzling in the pure elegance of her apparel. Beneath a Chantilly lace mantelet, trimmed with black velvet, her delicate figure was clothed in a sheer poplin dress. The numerous pleats of her petticoat flowed downward, enhancing her poise, and the Valenciennes neckpiece, clasped by an opal brooch, blended its pearly trim with her smooth neckline.

Leonor sat down for a moment, toying with a parasol, and then stood up to inspect herself in the mirror hanging over the mantelpiece. She touched up her shiny bandeau with the same meticulous hand that carefully arranged every weave of her fashionable ensemble.

She had not the slightest notion that she was being watched through the window of the door leading to her father's study. The two dark eyes upon her were Martín's. When he had heard the door close (through which Leonor had just entered), he went over to the window, expecting to watch her practice the piano as she often did at this hour.

With his heart racing at the sight of such grace and beauty, Rivas longed to draw nearer to his idol, as any lover would, and invented an immediate excuse to approach her. A strange fascination compelled him to confront her aloofness; it was the same mysterious force that compels every unhappy man to dwell on his woes and every criminal to pursue the dark path that his first transgression leads him to. Aching to suffer her haughty gaze and to compare the privation of his lot with the opulence of hers, he hurled the door open without knowing what he was doing. The girl whirled around and found Martín standing, pallid and troubled, at the door. Instantly recalling her vows from the night before, she received him coldly, which made him realize how brash and rude he had been.

"Excuse me, Señorita," he said gently, "I've come to tell you that I've done what you've asked me to do."

"I was expecting to receive word yesterday," answered Leonor, sitting down.

Martín reached for the doorlatch, as if to withdraw.

"My brother shared certain confidences with me this morning," said Leonor, without allowing Rivas an opportunity to leave, "which explained why my expectations were unfulfilled."

Martín's pallor vanished beneath a rosy flush because he rightly assumed that Agustín must have spoken about their visit to Doña Bernarda's house. He replied, "I didn't realize that you were waiting to hear."

"Did you make your friend happy?" asked Leonor, ignoring his excuse.

"I did, thanks to you, Señorita," responded Martín, bowing his head.

"This is going to be a bad example for you," she said with a faint, derisive smile.

"I don't see why, Señorita."

"Because your friend's happiness may discourage that heroic proposition you told me about the other night."

"Rafael occupies a very different position from mine."

His melancholy was so sincerely expressed that Leonor gazed into his eyes and asked him, "Because he knows that he is loved?"

"Precisely."

"And you?"

"I . . . I would not delude myself," replied Martín. To which Leonor responded with the same derisive smile, "You're very diffident."

"Perhaps my diffidence will shield me from a worse disgrace than never being loved."

"What could be worse than never being loved?"

"Being hopelessly in love."

Martín's voice was so charged with emotion that Leonor, in spite of her self-control, blushed and lowered her eyes from his intense gaze. As soon as she looked away, she heard her inner voice scoffing at this weakness, and quickly lifted her gaze, revealing a flickering gleam of injured pride.

"You shouldn't fret," she said, "because it's rare that a man can't find someone, somewhere, to love him. In fact, you're already on the road to finding yourself in the very situation that you dread you'll never find yourself in. Agustín tells me that one of those girls you visited last night has her eye on you, so you can start placing more faith in your star already."

She arose from her seat like a queen from her throne and dismissed the young man as if he were a court jester who miserably failed to arrest her attention. Then she walked out of the room, calling a servant and leaving Rivas standing baffled by the door. In the distance he heard her say, "Tell Agustín that I've been waiting for him for more than an hour."

With tears of humiliation in his eyes, he returned to Don Dámaso's study, feeling sorry for himself for being an object of leisure and banter.

"Pull yourself together," he reproached himself, placing both hands on his head. "It's time to work." Then he picked up a pen and turned his thoughts to his poor family in order to find comfort, but his heart ached all the more.

Leonor returned to the antechamber and sat on the sofa again. Her eyes hesitated upon the door that the youth had just closed, and she felt as though she could almost see him standing there, pallid, distressed, saying to her with his ardent gaze and emotional tone that suspended phrase, which described the sad state of his soul: *hopelessly in love.* She lowered her eyes reflexively again, but when she lifted them, the glimmer of wounded pride was replaced with a wondrous expression, revealing the dawn of new emotion in her soul.

Without formulating a precise idea, Leonor found Martín's sentimental speech, the eloquent gaze in his dark eyes, and the stirring emotion in his voice, a thousand times more attractive than the tiresome flattery of those dandies who held her hostage every night with their stilted routines. This latest encounter aroused a strange sorrow, which erased from her memory the image of the poor, awkward rustic, and replaced it with a sentimental, modest young man, whose few words allowed her a glimpse at a true and noble heart.

Leonor's drifting reflections, unformed at best, were interrupted by the arrival of Agustín, whose necktie, vest, and trousers were color-coordinated in perfect harmony; whose budding beard was cleanly shaven, leaving a shiny, smooth complexion; and whose hair was perfumed with the finest Portuguese jasmine pomade produced in Paris.

"Have I kept you waiting long, *ma toute belle?*" he asked Leonor, modeling his stylish trousers, tailored by Dussotoy in the capital of fashion.

"Much too long."

They left for Don Fidel's house, where they found Matilde awaiting them as impeccably arrayed as her cousin. Her sudden determination enhanced her beauty (otherwise modest to the point of shyness) with a vivacious splendor.

They set out, putting on joyous airs, which only Agustín truly felt, for neither Leonor nor Matilde could subdue their agitation as they approached Alameda. By the time they arrived at the promenade—the pride and joy of all good Santiagoans—Leonor had recovered her serenity and comforted Matilde, whose spark and sparkle were now smothered by fright.

Alameda was deserted, as expected, for it was a normal weekday. The spring sun was playing with the bare poplar branches, casting golden rays and shadows along the promenade.

The threesome approached the fountain together. The isolation they found there boosted Matilde's confidence, and their conversation gained new momentum when they sat near the maitén tree, which was probably planted in the oval of the fountain by some supporter of National trees as proof of his patriotism.

Soon thereafter, Agustín whispered in Leonor's ear, "Here comes Rafael."

Matilde had seen him coming from afar and made valiant efforts to keep herself from trembling.

San Luis graciously greeted Leonor and her cousin, before offering his hand to Agustín, who received him graciously. Rafael had displayed equal courtesy to both young ladies, without the slightest intimation that one of them had occupied his heart for many years. Rafael then filled the awkward pause that follows every salutation with small talk, giving Matilde the confidence to look at him with all of the luscious emotions of love in her eyes.

Leonor took her brother's arm, Rafael offered his arm to Matilde, and both couples began to stroll at a leisurely pace.

San Luis quickly initiated the conversation that he had dreamed of having every day of his sorrow. He painstakingly described his anguish and made his beloved shiver with delight as he professed his love; and, he joyously welcomed the simple, tender words with which she related the throes of sacrifice that she was forced to suffer at her father's command. In this intimate exchange between two hearts joined by mutual passion and separated by ambition, there was a deluge of emotions, a torrent of utter bliss, with talk of eternity and looks of ecstasy.

"All my sorrows are gone at last! Now I know that my wildest dreams may come true. You still love me!" exclaimed Rafael, after Matilde described how she had struggled to overcome her fears before agreeing to meet with him.

"Nothing can change my mind now," she declared, feeling courageous at this rapturous moment. "With all that I've suffered, I've found the strength to endure anything."

Rafael discussed his plans to win her father over, and mirages appeared before their eyes. The golden wings of hope spread over them and the sky seemed bluer and the air seemed purer than ever as it cradled their words.

It took them nearly half an hour to walk three blocks, during which time Agustín bragged to Leonor about his *affaire d'amour*, recasting Adelaida as the daughter of one of the most prominent families of Santiago. He, of course, omitted any reference to the tryst and fabricated a thousand proofs of violent passion in its place.

At the end of the fourth block, Leonor decided it was time to go. Matilde and Rafael felt as though they had not even begun to speak. The young man bade farewell in the manner in which he had greeted them. He hoped that there would be another meeting, should Leonor agree to escort Matilde again, and in the meantime, he would undertake his plan to secure Don Fidel's consent.

XXV

Let us digress to the day after Doña Bernarda's party to explain that conversation between Amador, Adelaida, and their mother about Agustín Encina's promised rendezvous.

The secret romance between Adelaida and Rafael, which he had disclosed to Martín, had also been disclosed to Edelmira and Amador by Adelaida, who wished to hide the result of her indiscretion from their mother. Edelmira did nothing but weep for her sister's disgrace, but Amador helped to facilitate Adelaida's absence from home during the final month, after which she returned from Renca as though nothing had happened, entrusting Doña Bernarda's younger sister to care for the child.

We shall skip all the irrelevant details about Amador's role in handling this delicate situation. Suffice it to say that Adelaida returned home without the slightest stain upon her reputation. However, Amador was the sort of fellow who liked to capitalize on life's misfortunes; he believed that because fate had short-changed him, it granted him the right to exploit others. Thus, he used his sister's secret as leverage to oblige her to be more availing to the lovesick son of Don Dámaso Encina.

When Agustín walked into Adelaida's home, drawn to her lovely eyes, she could think of nothing but avenging the man who had abandoned her. The dandy, as one can see, was the victim of bad timing, and, naturally, had to suffer a few days of ill-fated scorn before Adelaida softened up to him. Not discouraged by the initial setback, Agustín attributed her first smile to his perseverance, although it was really instigated by Amador, who was conspiring to exploit the son of a good family. Amador's ambitious plot was to unite his poor, common stock with the golden breed of Adelaida's new suitor. She reluctantly agreed to play a part in the comedy her brother had cast her in, with no other hope than possibly bettering her lot, which would thereby improve her chances of avenging herself on Rafael San Luis.

The day after Doña Bernarda's party, Amador entered Adelaida's bedchamber while their mother and sister were shopping. Taking a seat, he asked, "How did it go last night with Agustín? Is he still in love?"

"Head over heels," answered Adelaida, without raising her eyes from her needlework.

"And what are you telling him?"

"Not very much," she said, looking at him with her usual tenacity, "because you haven't told me what to do."

"What to do! Didn't I tell you to sweeten up to him?"

"And why should I?"

"'Cause I'm broke," said Amador, lighting a cigar and flicking the match into the air.

"How you can be broke when you come home a winner every night?"

"When I swipe them clean, they sign me IOUs."

"So why don't you collect on them?"

"The same thing happens over and over. You beat a rich kid, fair and square, and when he won't pay up, you go to his father who throws a fit and threatens to throw you in jail."

"What happened to the money you got from Agustín?"

"Pocket change; it slipped between my fingers."

Since Adelaida said nothing, Amador continued. "Listen, all I want is a better life for us. Tell me, wouldn't you like to marry Agustín?"

"You know that all I want is to make Rafael pay for what he did to me," she said, with intense hatred reflecting in her wounded eyes.

"Hey, listen, don't be hurt. We can help each other. If you do what I tell you, you'll marry Agustín and you'll be rich. What more do you want?"

"You make it sound easy," said Adelaida, who dared not contradict the guardian of her secret.

"Where there's a will, there's a way."

"What's the way?"

"Start cutting Agustín a little slack. Didn't you say he's always asking for a date?"

"True."

"Swell, just promise him one when I say so. Then I'll barge in there with a buddy of mine and we'll force him to marry you."

"Yes, but who will marry us?"

"My dear ol' buddy. Don't worry about it."

"Your dear ol' buddy is just a sacristan."

"So what? Listen to me. Mother won't go along with nothing if she finds out that he ain't legit. So watch your mouth."

"And then what?"

"Afterwards, I'll tell Mother to tell Agustín that you ain't going nowhere with him until he tells his parents that he's married. Surely Mother won't oppose. Agustín will tell his ol' man, who's gotta accept it and tell his friends. Then I'll make sure Agustín tells his family to hold the wedding somewhere in the countryside. Maybe I'll tell him the truth once that's done. He'll hafta tie the knot for real 'cause he'll be the laughingstock of Santiago if word gets out."

"But then he'll always hate me for what I've done to him."

"Why on earth would you admit knowing a damned thing about it? Look, the instant he sneaks in, Mother and I are gonna burst onto the scene. You just play innocent and cry and wail if you feel like it, and I'll force Agustín to marry you. Trust me, he'll think you're innocent."

Adelaida voiced some feeble objections, so feeble in fact that they were ignored by her brother, who in the case of outright resistance would have threatened to ruin her. Besides, there was a certain allure to his scheme; after all, it allowed her to fancy herself the wife of a rich young man, mingling as a peer among High Society. She would be the envy of all her girlfriends. But there was another reason, a deeply seeded reason, why Adelaida yielded to her brother's sordid plan with little resistance. Stricken by her disgrace, she was tempted by the prospect of changing her destiny for a happy life, brimming with the material delights of luxury, a life which so many dream of. Thus, she eventually softened up to Agustín and granted him a rendezvous for which the dandy was preparing himself after his stroll to Alameda with Leonor and his cousin.

Amador was successful in persuading Doña Bernarda to take part in this scheme. Her maternal pride swelled at the thought of having raised a man who was capable of devising the ingenious plan of uniting her family with the rich Encina stock. Rocked in the arms of heavenly hopes, she pledged her cooperation, believing that Amador's friend was a priest licensed to bless the holy union.

"If we don't do this, Mother," Amador said to convince her, "when we least expect it, one of those rich playboys are gonna woo the girl and leave us cold."

"You're so smart, my boy," praised Doña Bernarda, whose eyes moistened at the thought of her rich in-laws showering her daughter with bridal gifts, if not for affection, at least for show.

"It ain't enough that they get married," added Amador, "'cause his family's gotta honor the union."

"But, of course," replied his mother.

"Now, listen to me. You've gotta tell the groom, 'After you tell the blessed news to your family, then I'll let you live with your wife.'"

"What if Frenchy don't wanna?"

"Then I'll threaten him, and I'll tell him it's only gonna get a whole lot worse."

This digression ought to explain the conversation that transpired between Doña Bernarda and her eldest children after Agustín and Rivas departed on the night before the rendezvous.

XXVI

Agustín returned home after his stroll to Alameda, constantly checking the hands of his pocketwatch, which seemed to be inordinately slow—so impatient was he for night to fall. He had arranged with Adelaida that in order to avoid suspicion he would not pay his usual call to Doña Bernarda's house and that she would open the wooden wicket facing the street to indicate when it was safe to enter.

Martín did not appear at dinner that evening; he had received a note from San Luis, summoning him to come and hear all about the stroll and the happiness that was flooding from his heart.

Agustín had sustained the dinner conversation prodigiously, garnishing his phrases with Gallicisms and Frenchisms, some of which the clever Diamela understood, according to Doña Engracia, who interpreted the twitching of her dog's ears.

Don Dámaso, rapt in political indecision, added a few words which were so irrelevant to his son's monologue that one would have thought he was either asleep or deaf, while Leonor day-dreamed of the sentimental image of Martín, standing by the door and gazing at her with that look which simultaneously aroused hot and cold flashes.

After dining, Agustín retired to his suite, where he smoked cigar after cigar to while away the time. He saw in the clouds of smoke swirling toward the ceiling the vagarious whirling of his desires and illusions. When he entered the family salon at nine o'clock, exuding *eau de Cologne* (the fragrance preferred by European princesses and duchesses), the whole room suddenly smelled of the painstaking scrupulousness with which the dandy had perfumed himself for the success of his amorous excursion.

To still his impatience Agustín sat beside Matilde, who had arrived moments earlier with her parents. The joy beating in the heart of Don Fidel's daughter brightened her face and kissed her cheeks with the pure translucence of a woman in love who suddenly breathes new life. Finding his cousin in this state of mind, it was easy for Agustín to start a lively conversation, which quickly turned to the subject of San Luis.

Don Fidel and Doña Francisca, who watched their daughter from different angles, noted Matilde's animation and, presuming to be of great experience, assumed that they were witnessing a prelude to passion. This assumption aroused contrary reflections in Matilde's attentive parents; yet both attributed her beaming joy to the amorous attentions with which her cousin must have been courting her.

"Oh, I don't miss a thing! I've had a hunch that they were sweet on each other," observed Don Fidel, while Doña Francisca mused, "After all, bliss can even grace a vulgar soul, a stranger to the ecstatic raptures of noble souls who journey across untilled existence without finding another capable of comprehending the sublimity to which they aspire. . . ."

In walked Martín, not only depressed by his friend's confidences, but envious of the happiness which seemed unattainable for himself. The aspiration of being loved, forever the dream of youth, consumed his every waking thought.

Leonor, who was worried that he would not show up, denied that she was happy to see him and regarded his arrival as a slap in the face, in light of what had transpired between them in the morning. The spoiled girl refused to accept that in this contest, which challenged her own sentiments and ridiculed the exaggerated power of love, her pride was gradually losing its control to new and bewildering emotions.

After greeting her, Martín sat by himself, not far from the piano, where he could artfully steal glances at Leonor as she spoke with Emilio Mendoza. He was unable to detect the change in Leonor's expression, who, agitated by the sentiments that we have just described, pretended to listen to Mendoza with a newfound fascination. However, she soon grew distracted and bored of feigning interest in the dandy's honeyed words. Seizing the opportunity when Emilio Mendoza answered a question by Doña Francisca, Leonor escaped to the piano, where she ran her fingers aimlessly across the keyboard.

Martín reminisced about the lost joy of his conversation with Leonor a few days ago in that very spot. Hopeless lovers tend to poeticize the most insignificant scenes of the past because they see no hope in the present or the future. And Rivas was no exception; he romanticized their conversation, choosing to forget the pain that it had caused him at the time.

"Martín, the piece I'm looking for is in that book beside you. Be so kind as to pass it to me."

These words, spoken so naturally by Leonor, brought the youth back from his flight of fancy. As he passed her the book, he sought an ulterior motive in her request with the inclination that all lovers have to find a hidden meaning in every word uttered by the person they love. The coolness with which she thanked him as she leafed through the sheet music persuaded him that she had no other intention but to play the piece. Martín, a novice in courtship, was inclined to think the opposite of what some of the beaus swarming our salons would think if they were in his place—that all they needed to do to capture a girl's heart was to cast an ardent gaze upon their victim, like a Sultan waving a kerchief.

Martín was about to leave when Leonor said, "The pages won't stay down."

And she held the book with her left hand and played some notes with the right.

"Allow me to hold it for you," Martín said, drawing near to her.

Leonor, without answering, allowed the young man to place his hand where she had placed hers, and then she began to play a piece that she knew rather well.

"Do you know when to turn the page?" she asked him a few moments later.

"No, Señorita," answered Rivas, nervously. "I'll wait for you to tell me when."

Now that the conversation had begun, it was necessary to

sustain it. At least that is what Leonor thought. Rivas forgot all of his griefs and indulged his eyes with the sight of her, as she concentrated on the sheet music and keyboard.

"You must have seen your friend today," said Leonor, looking at Rivas to indicate that it was time to turn the page.

"Yes, and he is the happiest man in the world."

"So you must pity him," replied Leonor, searching his eyes.

"Why would I, Señorita?"

"According to your theory, one should flee from love like a disgrace."

"My theory referred to hopeless love."

"Oh, I had forgotten. But, is there such a thing?"

For a split second Martín was tempted to offer himself as an example of what Leonor seemed to doubt; to convey to her, with the eloquence of profound melancholy, the torments of hopeless love that were ravaging his spirit; to confess his delirious adoration with words that would describe the treasures of passion, stored within his soul for someone who was oblivious to her absolute dominion over him. Yet his voice was caught in his throat and his courage failed at the sudden thought of the glacial contempt that Leonor had shown him earlier in the day. Expecting that she would mock him with her haughty, sarcastic look, his soul retreated to reticence. These reflections flashed through his mind so swiftly that it was only an instant between Leonor's question and his tempered reply, "I imagine so, Señorita."

"Oh! Which means that you're not certain."

"Not entirely."

"Take your friend, for example."

"Rafael was loved before so there was some hope of being loved again."

"Well, if he had held your views, he would've tried to forget her, but he persevered, and therefore deserves his happiness."

"What good is perseverance to a man who doesn't dare speak his heart?" asked Rivas, encouraged by Leonor's reasoning.

"I don't know," she answered. "As for me, I don't understand shyness in a man."

"It may pertain to his happiness and, perchance, his life."

"Don't men stake their lives upon lesser things?"

"Yes, but sometimes his love means more to him than life itself. I don't believe that Rafael would tremble before an enemy, and yet he wouldn't dare approach your cousin if we hadn't reunited them. True love, Señorita, may make the bravest man cower like a lad, and if it is hopeless, he will tremble all the more."

"They say 'if at first you don't succeed, try, try again,' and I don't see why that wouldn't apply to overcoming shyness. Do you disagree?"

"It seems difficult."

"But there's no harm in trying. Besides, I think you're halfway there."

"What do you mean?"

Leonor skirted the question by saying, "You forgot to turn the page," after she had finished playing the piece by memory.

"I was waiting for you to tell me when," said Martín, embarrassed by the cold look in her eyes.

Starting the waltz again, she inquired, "And what is your friend planning to do next?"

"Well, he can hardly wait to see Señorita Matilde again."

"We're thinking about riding to Campo de Marte. He can see her there."

"I would be truly grateful if you would permit me to give him the news."

Leonor suddenly stopped playing the piano and walked away, giving Martín reason to believe that she had engaged in this conversation only to announce the final sentence (the way that letters often state their purpose in the postscript).

Agustín distracted him from his musings and chatted until eleven o'clock, at which time they both retired.

Soon after, Don Fidel Elías went home with his wife and Matilde.

"Did you see," he asked his wife, "how Agustín and Matilde were talking to each other? What did I tell you? They're in love. I'd stake my life on it. First thing tomorrow, I will speak with Dámaso so that we can start making arrangements."

"Wouldn't it be better to wait and see whether it is true?" cautioned Doña Francisca.

"Wait! Do you think that a catch like Agustín is an easy find? If we wait someone else is bound to snag him. Who knows what company he keeps! No, Madame, we must strike while the iron is hot. Tomorrow I will speak with Dámaso."

At this very moment Agustín touched up his courtly ensemble and sprinkled his clothing with a few drops of the most celebrated fragrances for his rendezvous.

XXVII

Agustín was already waiting outside Doña Bernarda's house half an hour before the rendezvous. All the guests had left, and the servant had closed the street door, which creaked as it swung on its hinges. Officer Ricardo Castaños and two other callers passed by Agustín, who ducked and hid his face in the collar of his overcoat.

Don Dámaso's son was all a tingle when he saw the wicket open; it was the signal that he was waiting for. Fancying himself the dashing hero in some love story, he was flattered to think that a beautiful girl was so enamored of him that she was willing to sacrifice her honor. This reflection raised his self-esteem and filled him with appreciation for the divine creature who had surrendered herself to his irresistible allure.

In the sweet expectation of his godsend, he was startled by the church bells which struck twelve. It was the hour of their tryst, and Agustín, in spite of his gratification, felt apprehensive as he gently pushed the creaking gate open. This noise nearly sent the dandy into retreat, but since nothing stirred inside the house, he advanced with more assurance onto the patio. It was dark, but he could see a ray of muffled light emitting from the bedchamber to the foyer. Adelaida had not mentioned that she would leave a light burning, but this did not discourage him. After a few indecisive moments of peering through the door, the utter stillness in the house prompted him to step inside, which he did ever so cautiously in order to prevent the patio door from making any noise. The instinct of precaution counseled him to leave it ajar so that he could escape should it be necessary.

Agustín was greeted by nothing but candlelight casting shadows behind a green screen. Frightened to find himself alone, the idea of betrayal crossed his mind. Courage was not one of his moral qualities, and therefore, he was obliged to appeal to the power of his passion and to the ounce of resolution that he possessed in order to dismiss the advice of fear, which urged him to turn around and retrace his steps.

Adelaida made her grand entrance at this pivotal point, returning him to serenity and the thought of their happiness.

"I was afraid you wouldn't come," he said, trying to take her hand, which she pulled away from him.

"I was waiting for you in my chamber," Adelaida answered, "until all was quiet."

"How careless to leave a light burning," he sighed, turning toward the table to blow the candle out.

"Don't put it out," Adelaida answered, feigning a squeamishness that filled the youth with pride to see the amorous fright that he inspired.

"Don't you trust me?" he asked, attempting to take Adelaida's hand again.

"Yes, but it's better if we have the light," she answered, pulling away.

"Why won't you offer me your hand?"

"What for?"

"To speak to you of my love and to hold this divine hand which . . . "

A loud clamor interrupted the gallant's declaration and he gasped in shock when the door flung open and Doña Bernarda and Amador appeared carrying lamps. Agustín's first impulse was to flee through the door he had left ajar. Adelaida crouched behind a chair, hiding her face in her hands. Amador raced Agustín to the door, jumped in front of it, and threatened him with a knife. The dandy's face turned as white as a cadaver, and he jumped back in terror at the sight of the blade.

"Now do you see what I was saying, Mother? These are the gentlemen who come to mock poor, decent folk in their own homes. But I won't stand for this!" shouted Amador, as he turned the key in the lock, placed it in his pocket, and advanced to the middle of the room.

"What are you doing here?" he thundered at Agustín.

"I . . . didn't think anyone would be asleep yet . . . and I was walking by the house . . . "

"Filthy lies!" Amador bellowed.

"Oh, Frenchy," cried Doña Bernarda, "how can you break into my home to seduce my lil' girls!"

"My good lady, I have not come here with vile intentions," answered Agustín.

"That strumpet is to blame," shouted Amador, as though he were in the final stage of exasperation, "'cause he couldn't have gotten in without her help. She's gonna pay!"

He pretended to assail Adelaida, frantically swinging a knife at her with such mastery that anyone would have sworn that only the agility with which Adelaida fled from the chair saved her from certain death. Doña Bernarda hurled herself into her son's arms and implored mercy, at the top of her lungs, in the name of a great many saints. Amador turned a deaf ear to her prayers as he struggled in the maternal embrace, which seemed to restrict all movement.

"Well, if she ain't gonna pay, then lemme at him! The scoundrel thinks he can shame us just 'cause he's rich."

He waved the knife at Agustín, who trembled in a corner where he had taken refuge behind some chairs. Hearing these words and watching Amador struggle to extricate himself from his mother's arms, Agustín believed his last moments had arrived and prayed with all his soul that the Almighty would save him from this untimely death.

A hardy shove by Amador sent his mother tumbling across the carpet, and one huge leap later he was towering over Agustín, who begged for mercy on his knees.

"Well, how are you gonna make 'mends?" asked Doña Bernarda.

"However you please. My father is rich and he will pay you . . . "

"Pay us!" roared Amador. "You think my honor is for sale? That's how the rich are! If you've got nothing better to offer, I'll end your pitiful life right now, and I won't give a damn if they shoot me dead."

Terrorized by the sight of Amador's derangement, Agustín pleaded pathetically, "I'll do whatever you ask."

"Marry her or die."

"Very well, I will marry her tomorrow," said Agustín, who perceived this condition as the only means of saving his life.

"Tomorrow? Are you joking? You're just trying to weasel out of it! No, it's now or death."

"I can't right now. What will my papa say?"

"Whatever he damn well pleases. That's what he gets for having a son who tries to ruin poor, decent folk! Speak up. Will you marry her, or won't you?"

"Not right now. It's impossible. . . ."

"Impossible! Don't you see, fool," Amador said to his sister, "he only wanted to use you. Oh, I know your type!" Amador shouted at Agustín. "For the last time: will you marry her, or won't you?"

"On my life, I swear to you that in the morning. . . ."

Amador did not allow him to continue his promise; he began knocking the chairs out of the way and raised his knife in the air. Doña Bernarda managed to grab her son's arm and hold him back, which Agustín did not notice because he was groveling on the floor, promising that he would marry the girl.

"Now it's suddenly possible, eh?" Amador said to him. "Wise choice. If it weren't for my mother I would've thrashed your bloody heart out. I'm gonna get a priest, and you're gonna tell him that you wanna get married."

"Yes, I will tell him."

"But he's only doing it out of fright," bawled Adelaida. "I don't want to get married like this."

"No, fright has nothing to do with it," blubbered the dandy out of shame. "Though I insist that tomorrow would be much, much better, but your brother doesn't seem to trust me."

"Now," Amador insisted, then proceeded to lock each door. He took from his pocket the key to the patio door, which he opened, saying, "Everybody, stay right where you are. I'm gonna get the priest who lives down the road. If you escape," he warned Agustín, "I'm gonna visit your ol' man in the morning and tell him about your dirty tricks, and after that, I'm gonna even the score with you."

"There is no need for concern," answered Agustín, who was mortified in front of Adelaida.

Amador stormed out, locking the street door behind him. They could hear the sound of his footsteps on the stone pavement, as well as the gate creaking open and closed. Agustín snapped out of the daze brought on by Amador's exceptional performance, and he appealed to Doña Bernarda's mercy.

"Madame," he said to her, "I vow to marry your daughter tomorrow if you permit me to leave. If I get married without my papa's knowledge, he'll never forgive me."

"Are you serious, lil' Frenchy!" exclaimed Doña Bernarda, shrugging her shoulders. "Don't you see Amador would kill me if I let you go? And as gentle as he is! You just saw how he nearly stabbed his own sister."

"Madame, in the name of God, I swear to you that I'll marry her tomorrow."

"I'd let you out, if only I could," sobbed Adelaida, glaring at him with disgust. "I don't want to marry you because I see that you were deceiving me."

Agustín pulled at his perfumed hair frantically. Everything was against him.

"You're mistaken. I love you and I want to marry you, but not when they are forcing me. Don't you agree that our love deserves a proper wedding?"

"Go tell it to Amador," Doña Bernarda said to him. "What do you want from us?"

A quarter of an hour passed amidst desperate pleas and unrelenting rebuttals. Agustín resigned himself to hiding his face in his hands, with his elbows on his knees. At times he felt that it was all a terrible nightmare, and he envisioned the daily mortification he would be subjected to by his family and Society.

The sound of footsteps were heard in the patio, and then Amador entered, announcing in a somber, intimidating tone, "The priest is here. Whoever says no or spills the beans gets knifed."

Having warned them all, he opened the door and said, "Come in, Father. Everyone is ready."

In walked a grim-looking priest wearing a black hooded robe. His face was partially covered by a folded kerchief which was tied around his head, as if to veil what appeared to be a massive swelling on his left cheekbone. He also wore a wide pair of green spectacles, which further masked his features.

"Well, get up," said Amador.

Doña Bernarda, Adelaida, and Agustín stood up.

The priest made Adelaida and Agustín join hands, while Doña Bernarda and Amador stood at each side. Then, he brought a lamp closer to a book from which he began to read the formulaic wedding rites in a guttural, monotonous voice. Agustín collapsed into a chair after the benediction. The priest signed the marriage certificate, and Amador escorted him to the street door, before returning to the speechless wedding party.

"Be on your way, Don Agustín," he said. "You're free to go."

"I will never admit to what happened here," answered Agustín gravely.

"Lil' Frenchy's nearly weepin'!" said Doña Bernarda. "What's the matter, don't you love my Adelaida?"

"Because I love her, I would have rather married her with the consent of my family," argued Agustín, who, feeling beaten, wanted at least to destroy the bad impression that his resistance must have made upon his new wife.

"Com'on, it's the same thing coming or going," said Amador. "Instead of telling him about it beforehand, you'll tell him about it afterwards."

"It is not the same thing, and it will be a long time before I'll be able to say anything about it," said the bridegroom, groaning at the thought of a lifetime commitment to someone whom he had viewed as a passing whim just a few hours ago.

"Well, sonny," Doña Bernarda said to him, "don't expect to have your lil' bride 'til you've told your family you're married. There, in your papa's palace, is where you're gonna receive her."

"And if he don't tell them, Mother, I will," said Amador. "Why are you looking so surprised? Did you think we were gonna keep the marriage mum?"

Amador's threat made a greater impression upon the miserable fop than Doña Bernarda's threat, which appeared to have little, if any, impact. Exasperated, he begged, "You must give me time to prepare Papa."

"We'll give you a few days," answered Amador.

"And during this period, you promise to keep quiet."

"No sweat."

"Com'on, it's late," said Doña Bernarda. "You better hurry home to that pretty lil' castle o' yours."

Agustín made his way toward Adelaida, who masterfully feigned heartwrenching grief.

"I see that this act of violence causes you as much pain as it does me. I would have preferred to give you my hand in an honorable fashion."

"And I'm so sorry that . . ."

Here Adelaida's wailing cropped her voice, leaving a stronger impression on the young man than if she had said anything because he perceived that Adelaida was as much a victim of the drama as he was.

"Don't sicken yourself, ninny," Doña Bernarda said to her daughter.

"Her grief," observed Agustín, "proves to me that she is innocent of your wicked deeds."

To seal the belated integrity with which he uttered these words, Agustín departed, clasping his hat firmly upon his head, down to his eyebrows.

"Don't forget the deal," Amador called out to Agustín as he made his way toward the gate, slamming it behind him, as weak people do to exorcise their rage against inanimate objects.

Amador bolted the door and started to laugh, boasting, "I scared the wits out of him! Come to think of it, I even scared the French out of him!"

After commenting upon what they expected would happen next, the children kissed their mother goodnight and went to bed. Adelaida found her sister waiting up for her.

"Why did you play a role in that ugly farce?" asked Edelmira, who must have watched everything without being noticed.

"How can you ask me that question?" said Adelaida. "Don't you see that Agustín would've used me if I let him? Those rich boys think that girls like us were born for their jollies. Oh, if I'd only known, I wouldn't have given my heart away, but now I detest them all the same. This one would've used me just the same if I'd loved him. It serves him right!"

The story of Adelaida's heartbreak is quite common in every Society, especially in the social sphere into which she was born. Like many a victim of seduction who receives a cruel awakening in first love, Adelaida had lost, somewhere between the pain of disenchantment and the violent desire to avenge Rafael's abandonment, the delicate sensibility of her naturally pure and noble heart, which now seemed only capable of hatred and dark passions. Those who did not know her past mistakenly attributed her insensibility to pride.

Because she viewed anyone she met from the aristocracy as a means to indulge her rancor, Adelaida had not had a flicker of compassion for Agustín's afflictions, who after entering his chamber, threw himself upon his bed, giving way to out-and-out despair.

XXVIII

The interim between the scenes narrated in the previous chapter and the Sunday when Leonor planned to ride to Campo de Marte with her cousin (as she had mentioned to Rivas) was unmitigated torture for Agustín. Suffering a severe case of guilt-ridden paranoia, he imagined that every trifle of life was designed to expose his secret to the eyes of the world. A casual question by Leonor about his *affaire d'amour* or an offhand comment by his father about his whereabouts made him extremely touchy. Born into a Society that condones the seduction of the lower classes (a common practice among his peers) but not the honorable act of matrimony to pardon the transgression, Agustín Encina not only feared his father's wrath, his mother's pining and bitter reproach, and his sister's conceited scorn, but among all these swords of Damocles pointed at his throat, he dreaded most of all the merciless, murmuring phantom which rules our civilized Society—that austere, severe judge known as: *What will they say!*

The miserable fop so deeply bemoaned his lustful escapades in the land of the would-be's that he lost his appetite, color, and beauty sleep. He imagined the injurious remarks that his chums would make to the clinking of tea cups by the hearth, with an aria by Verdi or Bellini playing in the background. His genial gaiety and proclivity to Frenchify his speech fell by the wayside, and he expressed astonishing indifference toward the most exquisite garments. The world was now devoid of pleasantries. A black tie around his neck sufficed for a whole day. The flowered crown of

Don Juan and Lovelace, which he was intending to wear upon his head to the envy of all, became the noose of a clandestine matrimony contracted in a vulgar circle! Cowardice alone kept him from suicide. If seduction were glory, the truth would cast him into the gulfs of shame forever, and the more he thought about his predicament, the worse it seemed.

Agustín paid nightly visits to Doña Bernarda's abode, where he played (under Amador's direction) the role of the gallant which the family friends knew him to be, thereby eluding any suspicion with regard to the marriage. On each visit he was accompanied by Martín, whom he was also misleading by talking about Adelaida as though they were still in the earliest stages of romance.

Martín followed him willingly because his conversations with Edelmira refreshed his spirit, and their confidences grew day by day. Edelmira listened intently to his irresistible digressions about the life of the heart. Each conversation brought to light new treasures in his poetic soul, and she crowned his head with the halo that sentimental lasses tend to give their storybook heroes. Let us not forget that Edelmira, in spite of her obscure situation, was an avid reader of serialized novels, which a friend of the family lent her.

Ricardo Castaños resented the interaction between Edelmira and Martín, whom he considered a rival. He endeavored to discredit the provincial by telling everyone about his arrest at the Plaza, but this strategy backfired (as do most attempts by an unwelcome suitor to disparage the favored rival because women have a natural propensity toward contrariness). The harder the officer tried to degrade Martín, the more Edelmira preferred the melancholic young man, who spoke of love in words of poetry that would take any woman's breath away. And yet Edelmira and Martín never breathed an amorous word to each other. Martín felt a sincere friendship for Edelmira, a friendship which grew stronger when he discovered how superior she was to those around her. Edelmira, for her part, began to regard him with that sympathy which often evolves into love in a woman, especially when unsolicited.

Agustín was immensely grateful to Rivas for his companionship. Afraid to exasperate Doña Bernarda's family by his absence, he dared not miss a single night and felt that his absurd plight would be less discernible, for his sake and Adelaida's, if he brought a friend along.

Amador had already begun to reap the fruits of his intrigue, by collecting the gambling debt from his supposed brother-in-law, who, feeling pressured to purchase his silence, asked his father for the money, alleging that it was to pay the tailor. Amador was tickled by the facility with which Agustín had satisfied his demands, and squandered the money with the ease of one who acquires it without having had to work for it. Beyond his immediate expenses, there were other bills that needed to be paid in order to keep creditors from breathing down his neck, for Amador was up to his ears in debt as always. Idleness was the bedrock of his character, and he had no lucrative profession or income to speak of, except gambling. Agustín's gold helped to pave a brighter path to easy living. Donning an expensive watch, which he had acquired by questionable means, and a flashy gold chain, which he had just purchased, Amador now presumed himself to be "a classy swain" and called attention to himself by assuming the airs of a gentleman in the cafés.

Doña Bernarda and Amador had a conversation which would have made Agustín's blood run cold. It was the morning before the Encina family traveled to Pampilla. Amador was trying to sleep off a feverish hangover when his mother shook him, saying, "Let's go, lazybones. You gonna sleep all day?"

"Oh, it's you, Mama," groaned Amador, rolling over in the bed. He stretched his limbs, yawned long and loud, and lit a cigar with the flick of a match.

"I woke up thinkin'," said Doña Bernarda, sitting at the head of her son's bed.

"About what?"

"It's been ages since Adelaida got hitched, and Agustín didn't give her one crummy lil' gift yet."

"It's true—he hasn't given her anything."

"So what's the good o' havin' a rich hubby? Even a poor man would've given her somethin'."

"Say no more, Mother. Leave it to me. If Romeo wants to play dumb, it'll cost him double, and I'm gonna tell him so before the sun goes down."

"It's bad enough he ain't 'fessed up," said his mother, "but now he's gyppin' us o' the weddin' gifts."

"Leave it to me. I'll handle it," vowed Amador.

Doña Bernarda described all the dresses that her daughter would need, without failing to mention those that she would like for herself, designating the boutiques where they could be found. The abundance of scrupulous details indicated that the widow had given much forethought to the matter. Her long list included colorful dresses, a long black skirt, and a chiffon shawl for herself because she could not bear merino wool in the heat. With the little arithmetic that Amador had learned from Maestro Vera (who was clearly remembered as one who did not spare the rod when instructing the child), they tallied enough material for a dozen blouses with embroidered frills and ruffles, two dozen pairs of stockings, a few pairs of French boots, and miscellaneous accessories of the first order so that Adelaida could hold her head with pride when mingling among Santiago's finest.

"But Mother," Amador said to her, "me and Agustín can't buy all of that stuff ourselves. Wouldn't it make more sense if he forks over the money so you can go shopping yourselves?"

"Yes, indeedy!" rejoiced Doña Bernarda.

"I'll tell him that 500 pesos should cover the basics."

"Or 600, 'cause it's always smart to have more than less," said his mother.

When Agustín arrived that night with Martín, Amador called the dandy aside to inquire, "So . . . when are you gonna tell your family?"

"It's all in the timing," he answered, turning pale under the gaze of his browbeater, "because if he isn't in the right mood, Papa will throw a fit and disinherit me."

"That's swell," replied Amador, "but what about your pretty wife? Have you ever heard of a bridegroom who turned up empty-handed?"

"I've been thinking about gifts, but I can't ask Papa for money every day."

"What? A rich kid like you can't scrape together enough money for a wedding gift! I'll be standing on your front doorstep on Monday to collect 1,000 pesos."

"But Monday is too soon!" Agustín exclaimed, terrorized. "I just asked Papa for 1,000 pesos the other day. I can't possibly ask him for it now. What will he say?"

"Papa can say whatever he damn well pleases. Don't be surprised to find me on your doorstep with my palm out on Monday."

"Can't you wait another fifteen days?"

"Fifteen days! Are you kidding? You've already embarrassed me in front of Mama and the girls 'cause I promised them gifts from you."

"That's my intention, but I need more time, or Papa will get suspicious."

"So what if he does? Do you think we're gonna bite our tongues forever? Not telling your papa about the wedding is one thing, but money is another. The ol' man's got money to burn. It ain't gonna hurt him."

"But how can I ask him so soon?"

"I don't know, just do it. I'll be there Monday, without fail."

Amador walked away from the miserable coward, leaving him perplexed and depressed. Agustín's anger at this ultimatum subsided, or perhaps he held it back for fear of seeing his secret marriage exposed. Like all those of weak character who are hard-pressed to find a solution, he deluded himself into believing that time would miraculously save him from his dire straits. Agustín took no comfort in the shower of affection from his purported wife and mother-in-law. At eleven o'clock he walked home speechless beside Martín, who did not mind his friend's unusual silence because, like all lovers without their confidantes, he preferred to walk quietly so that he could devote his thoughts to Leonor.

XXIX

The Sunday had arrived when Leonor and her cousin would ride to Campo de Marte.

Some of the particulars about these excursions are provided forthwith to benefit those readers who have not had the good fortune of seeing the glorious capital of Chile when it prepares to commemorate the historic events of September 1810.

These preparations bring flocks of people to Campo de Marte, where every tier of Society gathers to parade their frills and finery before going to Alameda.

The civic battalions travel to Campo de Marte on Sundays, beginning in June, to drill in the use of firearms and military evolutions for the annual reenactment of their victory over the Spaniards on the 19th of September. On these Sundays, Society, which always needs some pretext to entertain itself, meets at this battleground to send off the troops to Pampilla.

Long before the upper crust of Santiago considered the use of stately carriages to be indispensable, as they do now, the ladies would arrive in calashes and sometimes narrow wagons—vehicles that only the lower classes use today. And before English saddles and horses were high fashion on every side street, the elite would parade around in bulky leather caparisons and old-fashioned country boots with enormous spurs, which have since become the exclusive use of the genuine *huaso.* What has not changed is the reason for attending these parades because the disposition of the Santiagoan has always been the same. It is not the fresh air which brings the ladies out, but the opportunity to flaunt the latest style and the purchasing power of their fathers or husbands to adorn them with magnificent garments.

In the eminently refined city of Santiago, it would be an unpardonable crime to wear the same dress on two consecutive Sundays. This is why only men take strolls every day and women sit home until the Sabbath, when they suddenly feel an urge to breath some fresh air.

Those who have no desire to go to the plains, or lack a carriage in which to do so, walk along the main street of Alameda with the sobriety befitting their national character, and they await the arrival of the battalions, critiquing dresses if they are women or stealing glances if they are men.

Before the drums signal the coming of the troops, the coaches park along the edge of Alameda, and the gentlemen on horseback, craving the attention of those on foot, flaunt their equestrian skills by making their horses caracole throughout the streets.

The critic, a bosom buddy of all good Society, makes note of the exceptional outfits and the extraordinary efforts that the dandies exert to dazzle the crowds. Among the gentlemen, there is invariably a quipster in every group, ridiculing the suits that pass by. The ladies, for their part, set their minds to analyzing the dresses that pass by, noting with commendable precision, the date they were last worn.

"Señora So-and-So is wearing the green hoop skirt that she wore last year on the 18th."

"Look at What's-Her-Name with the same mantel she bought three years ago. She thinks nobody will recognize it if she covers it with the lace from her mother's dress."

"The dress, which You-Know-Who is wearing today, used to belong to her sister before she got married, and before that it was her mother's, who bought it at the same time my aunt bought hers."

These observations, which demonstrate the privileges of a feminine memory, were not without undue compliments for the monstrosities worn by their lady friends.

The troops march past the cheering crowds through the central boulevard of Alameda with officers at the front, so absorbed in the act of saluting to their left and right that at times the soldiers marching behind them would step on their heels.

In 1850, when our story takes place, there was the same enthusiasm for these festivities as there is today, although the north side of Alameda was not completely filled with carriages back then. It is only nowadays that many families attend the parade without ever budging from their soft spring cushions.

When Leonor told her father that she wished to ride to Pampilla with her cousin, Don Dámaso ordered the stable boy to saddle the horses by high noon. There were two handsome steeds with stately trots, one for Leonor, the other for Matilde. There was also one for Don Dámaso, whose daughter had obliged him to join them, and two others for Agustín and Martín.

It was one of the loveliest days of spring.

By three o'clock there were throngs of people at Campo de Marte watching the military drills. Coaches, laden with beautiful women, drove across the green pastures, flanked by regal cavaliers who trotted beside the coach doors hoping to make some friendly eye contact. Happy groups of young men and women galloped every which way, relishing fresh air, sunlight, and life itself. A noticeable party among them was Leonor, her cousin, and their two young chaperons. The trot of their horses was uneven. Sometimes the girls rode alone, and at other times they were surrounded by gents such as Emilio Mendoza and Clemente Valencia, who jockeyed for positions nearest Leonor. Admiring her from afar, Martín lagged behind without noticing the magnificent landscape, for he was captivated by this new perspective of Leonor. The fresh air painted her cheeks with a diaphanous blush; the belligerent clamor of the marching band kindled a flame of excitement in her eyes; and the full-length riding skirt and black wool jacket hugged her bodice and revealed her dainty figure. Unlike her usual contemptuous self, the girl was alive with joy, delighting in the ride and the novelty of the scene, in the beautiful day and landscape, and in the waves of wind lapping her face with the sweet smells of the countryside, moist with the morning dew.

The procession stopped near a battalion, which began to fire its arms. The sound of the first gunshot roused the horses, some of which continued to rear through the sound of the second gunshot. Don Dámaso's horse was among the skittish ones that lost its docile bearing and became uncontrollable.

"But they told me that he was so gentle," Don Dámaso said, turning pale while his horse bucked beneath him.

The continual drumfire made all the animals nervous, some of which became as unwieldy as Don Dámaso's startled horse, which had knocked over a basket of oranges and limes that a vender was offering to the youngsters. This accident caused the riders to shift positions. Whether or not it was unintentional, Leonor suddenly found herself beside Rivas, and Matilde, who was trying to control her horse, heard the voice of San Luis greeting her.

"Let's find a better place," Leonor said to Martín. "Would you like to gallop?"

"Yes, I would," answered Rivas.

"Then follow me," said Leonor, who turned her horse southward and signaled Matilde to gallop away with her.

Don Dámaso, meanwhile, paid for the oranges that had fallen into the hands of the boys who escort the battalions to the plains. When he noticed his party galloping away, he said to Agustín, "Follow them. I'll catch up with you later."

Leonor whipped her horse, which was almost running full speed, so excited was it by Martín's horse racing alongside. Martín felt the first tinge of hope in his heart, for he regarded the girl's invitation to follow her, the informality of her words, and the carefree joy of her ride as happy omens. He contemplated her with unspeakable joy. Exhilarated by the swiftness of her horse and the wind in her face, Leonor's eyes sparkled with childlike excitement, and for the first time she looked like a modest, sensitive girl whose heart was free of its usual pride.

They stopped near the penitentiary, where Leonor waited for the rest of the group to catch up to them.

"We've left them far behind," she said looking at Martín who was happy for the very first moment since he had fallen in love. Inspired by the ideas we have just described, Martín had resolved during the ride to forsake his reserve and stake his happiness on one swift blow of audacity. Upon hearing Leonor's voice, his heart pounded wildly and he found the nerve to say, "I hope you don't mind."

We once again feel obliged to interrupt our narration in order to express an editorial viewpoint about the relationship between Leonor and Martín. When two hearts secretly long for one another (especially when they are alone as they are now), each encounter does one of two things: it either brings them one step closer together, or it sets them one step farther apart. The scarcity of words between them is typical of these encounters, and very few words are needed to bring them face to face. Leonor was far from expecting any such response, which was enough to awaken her pride. She had Martín invited along so that she could be free from the tiresome adulation of her two infatuated dandies who had been particularly dull the last few days. Seeing Rivas as the object of a vanity game, Leonor was expecting his timidity, and perhaps his real or rehearsed impassivity, but certainly not the audacity that his question revealed. She responded with the icy indifference that she had hitherto punished him with. Pretending not to have heard him, she coldly asked, "What did you say?"

The blood to rushed to his cheeks, and although he felt tongue-tied and embarrassed, Rivas strained to answer with confidence, "I asked, Señorita, if you minded being alone with me because I came along for your protection."

"Oh! I didn't realize that I needed protection."

"Assistance, Señorita," he answered proudly, "just in case . . . "

"Just in case what? Isn't it enough that you assist my father with all his business? You mustn't feel obliged to serve the rest of us."

"Señorita," replied Martín, "I'll do whatever I can because I have no delusions about my social standing."

"Are you comparing yourself to someone whom you believe to be superior?"

"With those gentlemen heading our way."

"With Agustín?"

"With Señores Mendoza and Valencia."

"And why with them specifically?"

"Because their position allows them to aspire to that which I would never dare."

"I can't imagine why," answered Leonor with a confidential

tone. "In my eyes a man's worth is not measured by his social position, much less by his money. You see," she smiled, "we rarely ever agree on anything."

She cracked her riding whip and hastened to greet the rest of their party, which was quickly approaching. Martín watched her ride off, asking himself, "Does this strange creature have a heart? Does she really want me to think better of myself? Or is she just teasing me?"

The other riders came upon Martín while he lingered with these afterthoughts, so unlike the usual doubts he experienced after speaking with Leonor. Hope had begun to spread its golden rays over the horizon of his mind, shedding light on new sensations surging through his spirit, and these rays of hope brought joy to Martín.

While Leonor and Rivas were engaged in the preceding conversation, the rest of the party approached them, as we said, at a short gallop that slowly tapered into a trot. Rafael was riding beside Matilde, saying the kind of things that he had already said in their first conversation—the kind of things that lovers tend to repeat over and over again. But, he momentarily abandoned the topic of eternal love to discuss some obstacles in the real world.

"My uncle," he said, "is ready to help me. If your father wants to lease the hacienda again, then I'm confident that we'll be together. Will you have the courage to tell your father how you feel?"

"Yes, I will," answered Matilde. "I'll never belong to anyone, if not to you."

"What wouldn't I give to hear you say that!" replied Rafael. "My love for you is stronger than ever. Some people say that suffering makes the heart grow fonder."

Thus, the lovebirds returned to their idyllic songs, voicing endless variations on the same theme. When they came upon Martín, San Luis shared a few words with him and Leonor, and then galloped off when he spotted Don Dámaso approaching.

Don Dámaso had paid for the spilled oranges and set out to join his party. At his age, when one rides infrequently, the body quickly tires from the abrupt movements of a horse, especially if it is skittish like the one he was riding. When he caught up with his children, Don Dámaso wanted to rest a moment, but Leonor darted off again and everyone followed her, to the disappointment of her father, who was beginning to look sluggish under the heat of the sun.

Among the many horses and buggies near the battalion, they found Doña Engracia's carriage, where she was sitting with Diamela on her lap and Doña Francisca at her side. After assuring his wife that he was not tired, Don Dámaso and his party enjoyed limes, oranges, and sweets, which were handed to the riders from the carriage.

To his dismay, Leonor seemed inexhaustible, and obliged her father to follow her on other excursions until it was time to return to Alameda.

They rested near Doña Engracia's carriage for ten minutes, until Don Dámaso felt that he was ready to ride. However, as soon as he mounted, his aching body was overcome by fatigue; and, the stride of his horse in spite of its ease made him groan, so much so, that the good gentleman vowed never to ride again. He swore this to his daughter repeatedly as they took lap after lap around Alameda, stopping only for brief intervals, which Don Dámaso spent straightening his cravat (because it would inch its way to the back of his collar) and placing his hat back in its proper position (because it would also slip around his neck).

As he dismounted his horse at home, Don Dámaso made a few indicative gestures of his lamentable state and implored Leonor not to invite him on any such excursion for the rest of the year.

XXX

Agustín Encina relied on tremendous patience and repeated pleas to obtain a few more days of repose in order to meet Amador's demands. With no other prospect than procrastination, he solicited a postponement, fearing that a request for more money would arouse suspicions, leading to the discovery of his clandestine marriage. Agustín's primary objective was to keep it secret for as long as possible. Encouraged by the vague hope of those who find themselves in trouble, he trusted time, rather than his own capacities, to solve the problem.

His feelings for Adelaida, based upon the elastic morality of most young men, drastically changed the moment he believed the relationship to be permanent. His burning desire ended when he found himself with a wife in place of a lover. Agustín thought very little about Adelaida and much-too-much about what Society would think of him. He was haunted by the dread of mockery.

Thus passed the days until the 10th of September, when Doña Bernarda reminded her son that they had nothing new to wear on the 18th. Across the social spectrum of Chile there is a law that nobody wishes to break, that of buying new clothes for national holidays. Doña Bernarda observed this law religiously and thought that she and her daughters would be better dressed than ever this year, if only Amador would collect the money that Agustín owed them. Both mother and son agreed to demand payment without further delay.

Later that evening, Agustín visited Doña Bernarda's home with Rivas.

Amador notified his supposed brother-in-law that his time had expired and warned that he would appear the next day without fail to collect the funds. Amador turned a deaf ear to Agustín's pleas and threatened to divulge the matrimony.

In the meantime, Edelmira conversed with Martín whenever she could break free from Ricardo. Unbeknownst to Martín, the hopeless romantic grew more enamored of him every day, but sought nothing but the melancholic voluptuousness of unrequited love that she had read so much about.

Agustín nearly crumbled on the way home. If it were not for his amour propre he would have cried out for Martín's help, but he managed to hold himself together until he made his way safely into his bedroom suite.

Martín also retired for the night without attending the tertulia. After the ride in the country, he clung to the glimpse of hope that Leonor's words had planted in his soul. Her deliberate play of indifference deterred him from declaring his love, yet the things she said to him at Pampilla when he had asked her that pointed question granted him a glimmer of possibility.

Don Fidel, in the meantime, had mulled over his plans to marry Matilda off to Agustín. Although he usually ignored any opinion that was not his own, he found Doña Francisca's observation about the premature nature of his project persuasive enough to wait, but was unable to stretch his patience much beyond the 10th of September. This union, he figured, was an advantageous match because his nephew would inherit at least 100,000 pesos. He rendered his calculations with the precision of a man for whom the illusions of the world become evermore enticingly metallic the longer he lives. Don Fidel was, therefore, unlikely to neglect his interest in El Roble. Ambition had him digging for gold at both ends of the rainbow. It was an ingenious enterprise, he thought, to marry his daughter into money, and, at the same time, extend his lease for nine more years on the hacienda. And so he implored Don Simón Arenal to make another attempt to obtain the lease from Rafael's uncle.

Without waiting for his compadre's reply, Don Fidel rushed to his brother-in-law's estate on the 11th of the month in order to catch Don Dámaso before he left for his afternoon stroll around town to shoot the breeze with other businessmen, a favorite pastime of many capitalists in Santiago.

While Don Fidel makes his way there, let us turn to Amador Molina, who has just arrived at the Encina mansion. He was as punctual as any bill collector and he never looked more like the prototypical lowbrow than he did now.

Picture this: An old, well-brushed hat, tilting over his right ear like a hustler. A colorful cravat with big, bold blotches like the wings of a monarch butterfly. A homemade shirt, stuffed with a red satin cushion that some pretentious boors used to wear in those days to enhance the build of their upper bodies. A clashing vest, buttoned only halfway in order to display a pair of suspenders, woven by some lover for his birthday. A white handkerchief peeping out of his coat pocket. A ragged pair of pearl trousers, which were a bargain, even though they were floods. A pair of lambskin boots, mended at the tip of the right pinkie toe and polished with prodigious care. And, to top it all off, a fat walking stick twirling between his fingers like a windmill, and a hand-rolled cigarette, resting between his thumb, index, and middle fingers—with a thin band on his ring finger, which said in black enamel: *Viva mi amor.*

Now you have the perfect picture of Amador standing on the doorstep, where he could hear the sound of Leonor practicing the piano. He tweaked his mustache and stroked his goatee like a bully preparing to intimidate a weakling.

Shortly after brunch, Don Dámaso and Martín generated some business correspondence, while Agustín kept a restless watch to see who might come knocking. His sunken eyes and pale face not only marked his present terror, but an agonizing night of insomnia. When he saw Amador through the window, he flung the door open and ushered him in at once. Without waiting to be offered a seat, Amador plopped himself down on a chair and tossed his hat on the carpet.

"Caramba!" he said, as he surveyed the furnishings and adornments. "Getta load of this joint!"

Agustín shut the door while Amador struck a match to light his cigarette, which had gone out.

"Well, is the money ready?"

"Not quite yet. You see, Papa will hit the ceiling if I ask him for more money."

"Well, then, he has two fatherly duties: first he can hit the ceiling; then he can fork over the dough."

"But we might lose everything if he's unwilling. Why not wait a few more days?"

"If I were living the sweet life in a place like this, with all your fancy furniture and servants, of course I'd wait. But, dear brother, my family is poor and your wife can't be seen dressing like she's a nobody. Besides, he'd only be mad 'cause he didn't know you were married. But, I'll make him swallow that pill if you're so uptight about it. So quit stalling."

Agustín turned in despair to the door facing the patio and noticed that Don Fidel Elías was entering his father's study. He regarded this visitation as a gift from Heaven.

"Look," he said to Amador, "there goes Uncle Fidel into my father's study. How do you suppose I can ask him for money now?"

"We'll wait until Uncle Fidel leaves. Got any tobacco or liquor? So we can talk like good brothers."

Agustín handed him a Cuban cigar and prepared a tray of liquor. Amador lit the cigar, poured himself a glass of cognac, guzzled it down, served himself another, and looked at his prey with satisfaction.

"Not bad," he said to him. "So this is how the highlife tastes. To think a guy's gotta fill his belly with plain ol' anise!"

Let us leave them for a moment while we visit with Don Fidel, who has just led his brother-in-law to the far end corner of the study, away from Rivas who was working at the other end of the room.

"I've been thinking about something for a few days, and I've come to tell you about it," he said quietly. "It concerns both of us."

"What is it?" asked Don Dámaso with the same mysterious air that Don Fidel had used with him.

"If you had kept your eyes wide open, you would have noticed."

"Noticed what?"

"Your boy and my little chickadee are," Don Fidel whispered into his brother-in-law's ear, "lovebirds."

"Really?" asked Don Dámaso surprised. "I haven't noticed."

"But I have, because I don't miss a thing. I'm sure that they're in love."

"Then they must be."

"Well, that's why I'm here, so we can make the necessary arrangements. I think Agustín is a good boy, and he won't make a bad husband."

"But he is much too young for marriage!"

"What about me? How old do you think I was when I married your sister? Not a day over 22. It's the perfect age. Only rakes want to marry late. If you want an idle life for your son, leave him a bachelor and you'll see that it will cost you an arm and a leg. Oh, I know what I'm saying! I wasn't born yesterday."

"Perhaps, perhaps," replied Don Dámaso, who tended to agree with whomever was speaking. "But first we must hear what Engracia says. You know that it's not solely up to me to give my son away."

"Oh! So you're looking for excuses," said Don Fidel impatiently, forgetting to speak quietly.

"For God's sake," said Don Dámaso, "I'm not looking for excuses. But isn't it only natural that I consult my wife? After all, she is Agustín's mother."

"All I want to know is what you think. Do you or don't you approve of the match?"

"As for me, I would be delighted."

"And will you see to it that your wife consents?"

"I'll do my best."

"Remember what I told you: if he stays a bachelor for much longer, he'll lead a reckless life and it will cost you an arm and a leg. I know how these boys are nowadays, and I never miss a thing."

After obtaining renewed promises from Don Dámaso, Don Fidel went home, congratulating himself on the way that he had conducted this business.

Don Dámaso was left to ponder the frequent handouts that he had given to Agustín lately and muttered to himself, "He is already costing me an arm and a leg." Then he put his hands in his pockets and started to pace the room.

Amador, meanwhile, grew impatient and stood up to see when

Don Fidel would leave. "Time's up," he said. "Your uncle is leaving."

Agustín watched Don Fidel, crossing the patio with a self-congratulatory air. With him went Agustín's hope for another day of reprieve. He pleaded for a postponement, but Amador proved inflexible.

"What are you waiting for? You want me to talk to Papa myself? You're beginning to bore me."

"Why don't I stop by your house tonight? I'll bring the cash or Papa's consent."

"No thanks, I'm cozy right here," answered Amador, sitting down and lighting another cigar. "Stop playing me for a fool. Talk to Papa and bring me the money."

Raising his eyes to Heaven, Agustín implored its divine intervention as he proceeded to Don Dámaso's study like a martyr approaching the cross.

XXXI

Don Dámaso continued to pace and reflect. The prediction of his brother-in-law seemed to be a timely warning to focus on the conduct of his son. Martín finished his tasks and withdrew from the study, leaving his host to his thoughts. When Agustín entered, Don Dámaso looked at him, preoccupied.

"Agustín, where have you been?" he asked.

Agustín, who had already rehearsed his opening line, was startled by his father's question, which he feared was an indication that Don Dámaso had already caught wind of the marriage.

"Who, me?" he stammered. "Oh, I come and go, here and there, as you know, and . . . "

"It's about time you started to think about some line of work," Don Dámaso interrupted him.

"Oh, I'm very willing to work. If I could, I'd start right this very minute!"

"Good, I'm pleased to hear you say that. Youngsters shouldn't be idle. They'll just squander time and money."

This observation was not encouraging to Agustín. However, the fear of Amador walking through the door to expose his dark secret gave Agustín the strength to persevere. He said, "You're right indeed, Papa, and that is why I want to work."

"Very well, my lad, I'll look for an occupation that will suit you."

"Thank you. When I'm working, I won't think of spending like I do now, for I can't even tell you how it is that I owe 1,000 pesos."

Agustín spoke these words as gently as possible and watched

the effect they produced on his father, who stopped in his tracks and stared at his son as though Don Fidel's prediction had already come true.

"1,000 pesos! But I gave you that just a few days ago!"

"That is true, Papa, but I don't know how . . . I can't remember . . . between my friends and the tailor . . . "

"Fidel is right. Boys today spend like there's no tomorrow. Good Lord, 1,000 pesos! That's 2,000 pesos in less than two months. Caramba, young man, you're worse than your mother."

"You'll see that once I'm working, everything will be different," pleaded the dandy in a honeyed tone.

"Really? What kind of work are you planning to do? Children today are spoiled rotten. Not one of you gives a second thought to spending your father's hard-earned money. Yes sir, Fidel is right, you'll end up costing me an arm and a leg."

"I promise you that I'll work, and once I've paid the debt, I won't spend another cent."

"Your promises are worth nothing, my little friend. Do you know what time it is? It's time you settled down in life."

"*Oui, oui,* Papa, I'm perfectly willing to . . . "

"I've heard enough of your '*oui, oui*'s. No more promises, my little friend, settling down means getting married. Do you understand me?"

The panicked youth dropped his eyes, unnerved by this sudden swerve in conversation. There was no turning back; all he could do was stall. Don Dámaso presumed that his son had lowered his eyes out of obedience and submission, and, therefore, sweetened his tone when he added, "You should really start thinking about marriage."

Don Dámaso, who was rarely incensed for long, was pleased to see that his parental authority was respected. His son's change in attitude won his fatherly affection. As Agustín continued staring at the carpet, Don Dámaso spoke more softly when he said, "Agustín, let's talk as friends. I appreciate your respect, but I also want my children to trust me. What do you think about your cousin?"

"My cousin?"

"Yes, Matilde. She is a pretty girl."

"Oh, pretty as a picture!"

"And a nice personality. Don't you think so?"

"*Oui, oui,* Papa, a most exquisite personality!"

"Wouldn't it be nice to take her as your wife?"

"*Oui, oui,* Papa, a dream come true!" said Agustín, who thought that he might be dismissed if he were complacent enough.

"Well, my lad," Don Dámaso exclaimed merrily, "your uncle was just here, telling me that nothing would delight him more than to see you married to his daughter."

"If it seems fine to you, I . . ."

"It seems fine, my lad, fine indeed. It's important to make up your mind early in life if you want to be a happy old man some day."

"Of course, Papa, but I was going to tell you that Matilde doesn't care for me."

"Bah!" replied Don Dámaso, punching Agustín on the shoulder. "I thought the same thing before I got married. Your cousin is one of those girls who is too shy to let you know how she feels, but if you talk to her a little, she'll come out of her shell. I'm sure that she adores you. Well, to be honest, I'm not one hundred percent sure, but, your uncle is."

"No, Papa, it can't be. Matilde loves someone else."

"Don't you believe it, son. All girls have little infatuations until a fellow starts talking marriage."

"Well then, Papa," replied Agustín, unwilling to contradict his father under the present circumstance, "I think it's not a pressing matter, however . . . "

"Pressing, and pressing indeed," insisted his father in a tone less doting than before.

"First I must find out whether she loves me, and if . . . "

"Fine, but I must keep you from squandering all my money in the meantime. You must give serious thought to this matter."

"Without doubt, Papa, and as soon as you cover my debts . . . "

"How much?"

"1,000 pesos."

"Nothing else?"

"Nothing else."

"Don't come back later and tell me about something you've forgotten to mention."

"It's all that I need."

"Very well, my lad. Tomorrow you will bring me the bills and your decision about your cousin, and I will settle everything. Go then, you are dismissed."

Agustín stared at his father who left the room before his son had time to respond.

"The bills and my decision about Matilde! Now I'm worse off than before. How am I going to get out of this hole?" Agustín said to himself.

In desperation he returned to the sitting room and answered Amador's interrogating gaze by saying, "Don't you see, now you've ruined everything with your haste."

"How? Why? What happened?"

"You've ruined everything," repeated Agustín, falling into an armchair, defeated.

"Spit it out! What happened in there?"

"Papa was upset."

"Upset? What a pity! And then what?"

"He said he wants to see the bills."

"What bills?"

"The bills I told him I owed."

"So why the panic? Bring him the bills."

"But how can I bring him what doesn't exist?"

"Calm down, pal, you nearly died on me. I'll make whatever bills you want."

Agustín was horrified by the ghastly serenity with which Amador suggested forgery, and he envisioned himself lost on the shameful path of lies and treachery that Amador so casually invited him to follow. This thought was enough to make him shudder and restored his inherent decency, which until then had been strangled by fear. Before he would become an accomplice to someone who was inciting him to beguile his own father, he much preferred risking a complete confession.

"Forget about the documents," Agustín said. "I'll make sure Papa pays tomorrow."

"Tomorrow is the end of the line. If you turn up empty-handed, I'll start chirping like a lil' birdie. See you tomorrow."

With a sinister wave, he quit the room.

Agustín held his head in his hands and stood motionless. Then, as if struck by a brilliant idea, he dashed upstairs to see Martín, who was having difficulty concentrating on his studies. Agustín startled him when he burst into the room and began pacing the carpet. After his first lap around the room, he stopped and looked at Martín speechlessly, before lamenting, "Friend, I'm utterly disgraced."

"You!"

"Yes, if only I'd followed your advice I wouldn't be where I am today: lost forever."

Martín offered him a chair and said, "I see how upset you are, Agustín. Have a seat. If you've come to confide in me, you can be sure that I will keep your trust and do whatever I can to help you."

"Oh, *merci beaucoup,* my dear chap. I've suffered so awfully these last few days that I nearly crumbled from the pressure of keeping everything inside. But then I remembered your advice, which I regretfully ignored, and I've come to unburden myself because I trust you're a good friend."

Martín was moved by the profound pathos in these words. The dandy, having borne his burden alone, bared his troubled soul with such candor that Rivas felt a genuine concern for him.

"Tell me what happened. Perhaps your troubles aren't as bad as they seem."

"No, no! They couldn't be worse! Would you believe I'm a married man?"

"Married!"

"Yes, till death do us part. And guess who I'm married to."

"I can't even begin to imagine."

"To Adelaida Molina."

"To Adelaida? When did this happen? I am truly stunned."

"Listen to what I get for not heeding your advice."

Agustín recounted to Martín the whole story with excruciating up-to-the-minute details, including Amador's latest demand for money.

"Amador may be flexing his muscles, but I doubt there is any power in his punch," observed Martín. "Are you sure that the man who performed the ceremony was a priest?"

"I don't know. I had never seen him before."

"Did he present a license before he married you?"

"I don't know. I was so distressed that it was all a blur."

"There is something we must do right away."

"What is it?"

"We must search every parish and examine every registry since the day you were married."

"And for what reason?"

"To see if the marriage certificate exists because I have a gnawing feeling that this is a hoax."

"Oh, if only you're right!"

"If the marriage is not registered in any parish then your marriage is null because it was obviously performed without the proper sanctions."

"If you save me from this, I'll owe you my life."

"Amador said that he would return tomorrow?"

"Yes, at the same time."

Martín then designated the parishes he would visit and assigned others to Agustín, saying, "You mustn't leave any stone unturned. We must have certainty before Amador returns, and we must forewarn your father."

"My father. What for?"

"To prevent Amador or anyone else from beating you to the truth."

"And what if the marriage is legitimate?"

"You must be honest and strong. Wouldn't Don Dámaso have the right to be angry at you if he heard about it from someone else?"

"It is true."

"Furthermore, if the marriage is valid, warning your father might allow him the time to repair the damage in a way that might not have occurred to us."

"True," repeated Agustín, admiring the way that Rivas's mind worked.

"Well, let's go. We must get moving."

"I'll go to my room and get some money, 200 pesos, which we'll split."

"The sooner the better," said Rivas.

Shortly thereafter they set out in different directions to pursue their investigations.

XXXII

Don Fidel Elías returned home congratulating himself, as we mentioned, on his ingenuity and mastery in business.

This sort of man, whose every step in life is motivated by money, is common among us. The businessman regards as superfluous anything which does not translate into immediate profit. Art, History, and Literature are, in his eyes, nothing but a waste of time. Science is valuable only when it turns a profit, and Politics, likewise, merits attention from a commercial point of view, and so he seeks and develops friendships around his financial ventures. He holds serious contempt for anyone who looks beyond material interests and finds the price lists to be the most interesting column in the newspaper.

Among the worshipers of the Church of Business, one can find, as the reader has seen, Don Fidel Elías in the 1850s, which is to say, ten years ago. Over the course of this decade, the number of converts to this religion have multiplied due to propaganda and widespread examples.

Don Fidel, as we have already mentioned, regarded the marriage of Matilde to Agustín Encina as a wise business venture. Which is not to say that he loosened his grip on the lease on El Roble. At home he learned that Don Simón Arenal had stopped in to see him, and without removing his hat, or telling Doña Francisca about his interview with Don Dámaso, he headed to Don Simón's manor full of curious excitement.

Doña Francisca was relieved to see him go, like most wives who find themselves free of their husbands for a few hours. In fact, most husbands are crosses that their wives bear patiently, but lay down readily. Doña Francisca was reading George Sand's *Valentine*, and Don Fidel was as cold-blooded as a toad compared to the passionate Benedict. Thus, Doña Francisca was quite content to lay down her marital cross and pick up her book.

Don Fidel cared no more for George Sand than for the needy in the hospices, and so he departed without noticing the reflections of romantic rapture in the eyes of his consort. He arrived at the home of Don Simón with bated breath and his doubts a flurry. Don Simón offered him a seat and a fine cigar, assuring him that it was one of the best from Reyes Tobacco Shop, located at Plaza de San Agustín. (It may be said that the cigar is one of the most popular and acclaimed agents of sociability, for most conversations among men begin with one in hand.) Don Fidel Elías lit his cigar and anxiously waited for his compadre to tell him why he had paid him a visit.

"Did they tell you I stopped by to see you?" asked Don Simón.

"Yes, and as soon as I heard, I came straight here."

"I wanted to tell you that I did what you asked of me."

"Oh, you spoke with Don Pedro San Luis?"

"Last night."

"And what does he say about the hacienda?"

"The man has new conditions in order to renew the lease."

"What kind of conditions?"

"Complicated, as you can imagine."

"Tough terms?"

"Depends on your position."

"Give it to me straight, compadre. It's the only way to do business."

"Don Pedro told me that he wants his son to start working."

"What is the catch?"

"He wants his son to work with his nephew."

"With San Luis?"

"Yes."

"I still don't see what this has to do with me."

"He is considering granting the lease on El Roble to his son and nephew in case you don't consent to what Rafael asks of you."

"What is he asking?"

"For Matilde's hand in marriage."

Completely dumfounded by what he heard, Don Fidel wrinkled his forehead like a man lost in profound reflection and said after a moment, "Really! I'm flabbergasted!"

"These are his terms."

"And if I agree to giving her away?"

"In that case he would lease you El Roble and set his son and nephew to work on another hacienda."

"And what do you think about this, compadre?"

"Oh, it is not for me to say. This is family business."

"So it is," mused Don Fidel, "so it is."

Having already invested most of his money in El Robe, Don Fidel preferred to grant his daughter's hand to Rafael than to Agustín. Don Fidel figured that it would be many long years before the latter would inherit his father's fortune, given Don Dámaso's clean bill of health. Furthermore, the support of his brother-in-law was always problematic and not nearly as advantageous as a nine-year lease extension on El Roble.

"Did you know that Rafael was once engaged to Matilde?" he said after these considerations.

"So I heard," responded Don Simón.

"But my brother-in-law put a stop to it," continued Don Fidel. "Rafael had no money, but he is a good young man."

Don Simón nodded in agreement.

"And if his uncle backs him, he wouldn't be a bad match," continued Don Fidel.

"So it seems."

"It would be best not to make a rash decision. We have time to think about it."

They changed the topic of conversation, and Don Fidel went home half an hour later. His arrival interrupted Doña Francisca, whose heart was swept away by the suspenseful passage where Benedict finds himself in the alcove with Valentine. Don Fidel relayed his two visits of the day: his quasi-commitment to Don Dámaso and the unexpected terms of the lease on El Roble. Doña Francisca discarded the mundane references to business and pondered the poetic side of Rafael San Luis's perseverance. Under the influences of *Valentine,* she readily agreed to Don Pedro's proposition, exclaiming, "Oh! Now this is what I call true love!"

"And working the land," added Don Fidel, "this little fellow will make a handsome catch."

"It's proof of a faithful heart!" she remarked enthusiastically.

"Because Don Pedro's other hacienda is a nice piece of property," observed Don Fidel, willing to suffer his wife's sentimentalism for the first time because he perceived that they happened to be of the same opinion.

"Oh! I am sure that he will make Matilde happy."

"He'll reap a bundle with three thousand cattle."

"I think we needn't hesitate, my child, for we will all be happy."

"I agree with you. This hacienda yields at least 5,000 to 6,000 bushels of wheat."

"Rafael, besides, is a clever young man."

"Not to mention the wool and coal, which are nothing to sneeze at."

"Must you reduce everything to money?" exclaimed Doña Francisca, horrified that her husband was busy calculating his future profits when Matilde's happiness was the matter at hand.

"Sweetheart, the rest is sheer trifles," answered Don Fidel, who was growing impatient with the maudlin reasoning of his companion. "When a family man is light on capital, he should concentrate on the positive. I know what I'm talking about. I wasn't born yesterday. If he were unable to support his family, what good would it do us if Rafael were as much in love as Abelard?"

"Money is not the root of happiness," said Doña Francisca, raising her dreamy eyes to the heavens.

"Just give me the gold, and I'll laugh at all the rest. You can all live happily ever after with your noble hearts and your insufferable novels."

"Well then, let's change the topic because my convictions are set in stone."

"Why do I even bother discussing anything with you!" fumed Don Fidel, frustrated that his wife avoided discussion instead of converting to his doctrine.

Doña Francisca returned to her book, seeking consolation in some idyllic thought.

"So, we agree that we ought to accept Don Pedro's terms," said Don Fidel after he paused to calm down.

"Do whatever you please," sighed Doña Francisca.

"And that's precisely what I intend to do. Nobody is going to tell me what to do because I know exactly what I'm going to do. A nine-year lease on El Roble will do more for us than anything your brother can do for us."

"But you should speak to Dámaso first, so he knows what is happening."

"I'll simply tell him that Matilde's devotion has persuaded me, and . . . anyway, I'll think of something."

He left the room and Doña Francisca went to share the happy news with her daughter.

Don Dámaso, meanwhile, sought Leonor's opinion on Agustín's marriage to Matilde.

"And you, my girl, what do you have to say about this?"

"Papa, I think that you shouldn't rush into anything."

"Isn't that what I just said?" fussed Doña Engracia, who, like any mother, was opposed to the thought of her son getting married.

"But this boy will cost me an arm and a leg if he doesn't settle down. All he learned in Europe was how to squander good money," complained Don Dámaso who, as a capitalist and former banker, looked at things from the materialistic point of view.

"We will try to correct him," answered Doña Engracia, petting Diamela's head.

"We're swimming in money. What are you worried about?" said Leonor, chastising her father with a haughty look.

"I've given him until tomorrow to answer. So we shall see," said Don Dámaso, who then left to take his daily stroll through the business district.

"You must speak to Agustín, my darling," entreated Doña Engracia, who counted more on Leonor's influence than her own.

"Trust me, Mama," answered the girl, "this marriage will never see the light of day."

Doña Engracia embraced Diamela to express her mirth, and the little pooch responded to her caresses by wagging her tail every-which-way.

The family gathered in the antechamber when it was time to

eat. Martín, who arrived at this moment, was called to supper just as he was ascending to his quarters.

Agustín arrived soon thereafter to join his family at the table, where his eyes searched for some sign of hope from Rivas, who was, unfortunately for the dandy, distracted by the presence of Leonor.

Doña Engracia attempted to disrupt the monotonous silence with her favorite pet tricks. While Diamela played dead, her adoring mistress trampled over her belly with her knuckles, which were supposed to be horses and carriages running wild. This trick, which was taught to lap dogs in every home in Chile, drew little attention from Agustín, who wavered between fear and hope, and much less from Martín, who watched his idol with the hyperbolic reverence only first love can inspire.

As he left the dining room, Agustín approached Rivas, who always stepped aside to allow the family to pass.

"Meet me in my chambers," he said in a mysterious voice, like an actor calling a tryst to reveal the birth secret of the protagonist.

Agustín's anxieties of late had caused him to abandon his usual affectations and silly expressions. His spirit was shrouded with somber shades of melodrama, and thus this cryptic tone. Martín followed him to his suite and sat in the chair which Agustín offered him.

"How did it go?" was Agustín's first question, after turning the key in the lock.

"Very well," answered Rivas, "in every parish and court that I visited, there is no marriage certificate to be found. Have you come up with anything?"

"Not a thing," rejoiced Agustín.

"I'll have the certificates by morning."

"And so will I."

"Don't you see? It was all a hoax. Now we must ensure that the secret stays in the family."

Agustín, unable to contain his joy, embraced Rivas, telling him, "You're my savior, Martín."

Just as he had uttered these words, they heard a knock at the door. Agustín asked who it was, and Leonor answered from the other side of the door.

"Shall we open up?" the dandy asked.

Martín nodded, and Agustín opened the door for Leonor who remarked, "It must be a juicy secret if the door is locked." Then she asked Martín, who had stood up as if to leave, "Why are you leaving?"

"Perhaps you would like to have a word with Agustín," replied the young man.

"Yes, I would, but you're not in the way."

Leonor sat down on a sofa beside Agustín, and Martín took a chair farther away.

"Papa," announced Leonor, "told us everything before dinner."

"Everything about what?" exclaimed Agustín.

"Uncle's visit and his intentions."

"About what?" asked Agustín.

"Hasn't Papa spoken to you about settling down?"

"Yes."

"With Matilde?"

"Yes."

"That is why Uncle Fidel visited."

"Oh, yes, I knew that," said Agustín.

"What are you planning to say?"

"That I can't do it."

"Papa expects the contrary."

"That's partly my fault because I wasn't clear when I spoke to him earlier today," said Agustín, glancing at Rivas.

"And now?"

"Tomorrow will be another story."

"Why is that?"

"I'm sorry, *ma belle,* but there is a secret I can't share with you."

"A secret?"

"All that I can tell you is that I was in serious danger and if it weren't for Martín, I'd be completely lost."

Leonor looked at the young provincial, whom her father was always praising and who now seemed to be her brother's savior.

"I'll get to the bottom of all this," she vowed to herself upon seeing the submissive way Martín returned her glance.

She continued the conversation for a while longer, encouraging her brother to stand up to her father. Then she switched the topic to music, her piano studies, and the latest pieces that were in fashion, asking Agustín and Martín for their opinion before concluding with these words, "Tonight, I'll play you a new waltz that you may not have heard."

Martín considered this an invitation because Leonor had looked directly at him when she made this announcement. Under this impression, he presented himself at Don Dámaso's tertulia, from which the Elías family had abstained, having judged it prudent not to attend that evening. Moments after Martín's arrival, Leonor made her way to the piano and called the young man with a glance. He approached trembling. The subtle invitation that he had received from her and the way she invited him to the piano filled him with emotion.

"This is the waltz," Leonor said to him, propping a sheet of music upon the stand.

She began to play, and Martín remained standing to turn the pages.

"From what I see," Leonor said to him, playing the first measures, "you've become the savior of our family."

"I, Señorita?" asked Martín perplexed. "How so?"

"My father says that you're his right hand in business."

"He overstates the modest services that I'm able to extend to him."

"Furthermore, Matilde would probably be eternally miserable without you."

"I played a very minor role there too."

"You were certainly very reserved at the beginning."

"It was my friend's secret, not my own."

"And you assumed I was interested in him simply for asking . . ."

"An involuntary assumption, which was instantly corrected."

"On top of everything, now Agustín says that you're his savior."

"Another exaggeration, Señorita. I've done very little for him in light of what I owe your family."

"The way Agustín describes it, it mustn't be as little as you say."

"It is little in comparison to your father's generosity, which I will never be able to repay."

"All that talk of danger gives me goosebumps."

"I am not as worried as Agustín is."

"Is it so awful that you're unable to speak it?" asked Leonor, beginning to grow impatient with Martín's evasive answers.

"Again, Señorita, it is not my secret."

"I thought," replied Leonor, her haughtiness returning, "I had given you enough examples of my trustworthiness for you to confide in me."

"I would if only I could."

"Which means that no one can persuade you?" Leonor said sarcastically.

"No one, except you, Señorita," replied Rivas, accompanying this bold retort with a fiery gaze that Leonor felt without actually looking at him.

She continued to play the waltz without speaking another word and left the piano when it was finished. For the rest of the evening, she avoided eye contact with Rivas; instead, she engaged in a lengthy conversation with Emilio Mendoza, who, on leaving, fancied himself her favorite.

Leonor went to bed, realizing that she had been defeated by the obstinacy with which Rivas had guarded his secret; yet, this sudden insight, void of any self-deception, inspired an admiration for this loyal, chivalrous man, who preferred to face mockery rather than betray a friend. She was high-minded enough to appreciate the delicacy of Martín's reserve and to respect it more than her own desire to enslave the young man, a desire which was, until now, motivated by her pride and ruled by her will.

XXXIII

At eight o'clock the following morning, Agustín and Martín began to gather the certificates that they had solicited from the parishes in Doña Bernarda's district, and they met each other an hour later. With proof in hand, Agustín became his cheerful self again and pledged to Rivas a thousand oaths of friendship and eternal gratitude.

"I'm eternally grateful," he said, reading the certificates. "These papers are going to knock Amador out. Now let's see who is going to play the tough guy!"

"I insist," said Martín, "that we tell your father everything."

"I can't disagree with you more."

"Based on what you've told me," argued Martín, "Amador will probably go straight to your father when you refuse him the money."

"That is true."

"And, in that case, it will be very difficult to explain yourself to Don Dámaso after Amador's version of the story has taken its effect on him."

"I know you're right, but I haven't the nerve to face my father with the truth."

"I'll go and tell him everything."

Agustín expressed his gratitude to Rivas for this new service, speaking in his peculiar dialect of Spanishized Frenchisms.

Martín proceeded to Don Dámaso's study because he knew that he would find him there working before breakfast. He wasted few words in recounting Agustín's misadventures, excusing his conduct whenever possible. Don Dámaso listened with the apprehension of a father who sees his son's honor, as well as his own, compromised. He did not give a damn about the honor of the Molina family and shuddered at the gall of these ragtags who, in order to preserve their own honor, wished to marry into a respectable family. Martín then explained all the steps that they had taken to prove the nullity of the marriage, which allowed Don Dámaso to breathe a bit more freely.

"With this substantiation," he said shuffling through the ecclesiastic records that Rivas had presented him, "I believe we can put this matter to rest."

"The girl's brother," said Martín, "will stop by again today, demanding money."

"How do you think we should receive him?"

"I think you should turn the tables on him," answered Rivas.

"How?"

"By going to their home and telling his mother that the marriage is invalid."

Don Dámaso, who was accustomed to following Martín's business advice, heeded this personal guidance, asking, "When should I go?"

"Before Amador comes here after breakfast. He should be here at noon."

"Will you come with me?" asked Don Dámaso of Martín.

"I would rather not, sir, because I owe this poor family some courtesy," replied the young man. "They're decent people except for Amador. Adelaida is an unfortunate girl."

"If this works out like I hope it will," said Don Dámaso, "I will be further indebted to you."

"I pray that you won't be harsh with Agustín. He has suffered enough these last few days to last a lifetime, and he is truly repentant."

"On your account, I will not."

The butler announced that breakfast was served, and Don Dámaso walked to the breakfast room talking about other business with Martín.

Rivas sought in vain to lock eyes with Leonor at the table, but she was cooler and coyer the more she took interest in him. Last night, amidst the quiet of her inner reflections, just when sleep was about to close her long lashes, a dauntless question flashed through her mind like a bolt of lightning, "Am I in love?" Her eyes darted open and a thousand incoherent ideas chased her drowsiness away. Like the rising sun that sheds bright light on some things while leaving others in shadows, this radiant idea of love, with all its astonishing reflections, enlightened part of her soul while casting the rest of it in confusion and darkness. It had always seemed to her that love was an enchanted, adventurous dream, but she would have never considered loving a poor, obscure provincial who had never drawn any woman's attention. Her ears began to ring at the thought of what Society would say behind closed doors when they heard the name of Martín Rivas together with hers. Who would believe that this conceited girl, who had scorned so many young gentlemen, would fall in love with a humble lodger whose sole income was a paltry allowance of 20 pesos? She knew that her girlfriends, who had always revered her as the belle of the ball, would undoubtedly marry sons of good families to whom they would proudly offer their arms on a Sunday stroll along the promenade.

"I'll give no more thought to this madness!" was all that Leonor could tell herself, as she tossed and turned in bed, endeavoring to muffle the wild beating of her heart.

The following morning, Leonor confused the fatigue of insomnia with the triumph of her will. The daylight, which dissipates the fantastic proportions that ideas generally take during the night, dulled her mind. She mistook this dullness as her usual indifference until Martín walked into the breakfast room with her father. Instantly flustered by his presence, she felt her head and heart newly and vigorously at odds against each other.

All of this soul-searching was unbeknownst to Martín, who noted nothing about Leonor's indifference but the tyranny of the stars above and their pattern of interminable misfortune.

Silence reigned over the breakfast table, except for occasional interactions between Doña Engracia and her darling Diamela. Agustín studied his father's face, trying to determine his reaction to the deep, dark secret, but Don Dámaso was so preoccupied by the interview recommended by Rivas that his son could sense nothing. Agustín was still uncertain after breakfast as to whether he had been forgiven.

Don Dámaso and Martín went to the Molina residence together.

"This is where they live," Rivas said, pointing to the house.

Don Dámaso left Martín outside and entered the home of Doña Bernarda, who was busy sewing with her daughters in the foyer.

"Señora Doña Bernarda Cordero?" inquired Don Dámaso.

"That's my name, Señor," replied Doña Bernarda, who jumped up to offer Don Dámaso a chair because she judged by his appearance that he was a gentleman.

"Señora," said Don Dámaso, "which of these young ladies is Adelaida?"

"This one, Señor," she said, pointing to her eldest daughter.

Adelaida had sensed that the gentleman had come for some matter concerning her marriage to Agustín, and his inquiry confirmed her presentiment.

After looking the girls up and down, Don Dámaso said to their mother, "I wish to speak to you in private, if I may."

Doña Bernarda sent her daughters out of the room.

"I have come here, Señora," said Don Dámaso, "because I wish to settle a disagreeable matter with you."

"What would that be, Señor?"

"An indignity was committed here which may have serious consequences for you and your family."

"And who are you?" she asked, startled by what she heard.

"I am Agustín Encina's father, Señora."

"Oh! You don't say!"

"I wish to suppose that you acted in good faith when you allowed your daughter to marry Agustín."

"Who let the cat out o' the bag? Well, what am I s'posed to say, Señor? Your son was wrong to come here, and it was only right that he marry her."

"But perhaps you don't know that the marriage was unsanctioned."

"Huh?"

"That is to say that Agustín and your daughter are not married."

"Who are you kiddin'? Married, married till death do them part."

"Well, I have proof otherwise."

"There ain't no such proof. Stay right where you are. Amador, get in here!" she hollered into her son's bedchamber.

Amador, who was sprucing up for his visit to Agustín, answered his mother's call and withered upon seeing Don Dámaso, whom he recognized at once.

"Son, listen to what this gentleman's got to say."

"What is it?" asked Amador, sheepishly.

"He says it ain't true that his son's married to Adelaida."

Unprepared to argue, Amador attempted a contemptuous smile that congealed upon his lips. He tried to smile again, thinking there was no better defense than obstinate denial.

"Too bad he missed all the action."

"You have committed an act of violence," declared Don Dámaso, "and I have documents to prove that you roped my son into a phony marriage."

"Lay the proof on the table then," prompted Amador.

"Here they are," said Don Dámaso, showing the papers that Martín had given him, "and I will make use of them if need be."

Amador recognized that he was skating on thin ice, but lacked the nerve to strike a deal in the presence of his mother.

"Well, if you've got proof, so do we," he bluffed, "and let's just see who can prove what."

Don Dámaso, preferring to end this affair as amicably as possible, stated, "The proof in my possession is incontestable. The marriage is invalid any way you look at it, but since my reputation is at stake, as well as my family's, I have come to settle the matter with this lady quietly to avoid any scandal."

"What scandal? They're married, ain't they?" said Doña Bernarda, consulting her son's expression.

Amador evaded eye contact with his mother, lest he betray himself.

"I acknowledge," said Don Dámaso "that my son was wrong to seek a rendezvous, but he was lured here and trapped."

"Like we're s'posed to look the other way!" shouted Doña Bernarda. "Like poor folk ain't got no honor! Like we're s'posed to let him take the girl as his mistress! Ave María!"

"Calm down, Señora," Don Dámaso said to her. "It is important to see the matter for what it is."

"I see what it is. Why can't you? They're married and that's all there is to see."

"I can bring this matter to the courts and prove the nullity of the marriage. And, if I do, I will not rest until I see the guilty parties punished for entrapping an inexperienced young man."

"Inexperienced? He snuck into my house in the middle o' the night!" shrieked Doña Bernarda. "What's the matter with you?" she added, looking at her son. "Cat got your tongue?"

"You'll see, Señor, that my mother is right. You can't prove it's phony 'cause we've got proof it ain't."

"What proof?"

"That's for me to know and for you to find out in court."

"Is there a marriage certificate registered in any parish?"

Amador fell silent, and Doña Bernarda asked him, "Didn't you tell me it was turned over to the priest?"

"Let it be, Mother," he answered, feeling cornered. "He'll find out in court how much proof we've got."

"Don't you see, Señor? We've got proof they're married, so you better start gettin' used to the idea," exclaimed Doña Bernarda.

"What my mother says is the God-honest truth, but we won't breathe a word of it until you're ready and willing."

"Ready and willing? I'm ready and willing to file charges against all of you today."

"File away! We ain't scared," answered Doña Bernarda, checking her son's demeanor once again.

"Go ahead," Amador said to appease his mother.

Impatient, Don Dámaso stood up and declared, "Your obstinacy will cost you everything. I am prepared to offer a fair amount of remuneration for my son's reckless escapade if you agree to keep this matter quiet. However, if you oblige me to seek judicial intervention, I will not rest until the guilty parties are punished."

"Listen," Doña Bernarda insisted, "nobody's gonna convince me that I didn't see them get married with my own two eyes. Ain't that so, Amador?"

"That's right, Mother."

"Think it over carefully," advised Don Dámaso, "because I'll take this matter to court if I don't receive a favorable reply tomorrow."

He left without bidding them adieu and crossed the patio, prey to mortal anxiety. He was utterly baffled by Doña Bernarda's earnest convictions and Amador's wavering testimony. Despite the certificates that he held in his possession, it appeared that Doña Bernarda and Amador also possessed evidence that might prove him wrong. Under the weight of such fears, he arrived home with his face reddened and his mind vacillating amid terrible doubt.

XXXIV

Don Dámaso Encina, incapable of making his own decision in any matter of transcendence, immediately called upon his wife and daughter to ask them what to do next. Shrieking in horror, as waves of heat sent blood rushing to her cheeks, Doña Engracia nearly fainted when she heard the story.

"Married to a filthy brute!" she gasped, nearly strangling her little pooch, whose yelps formed a painstricken duet with her mistress's and accentuated the impact of her words.

Don Dámaso dropped his head into his hands exclaiming, "But, honey, the marriage is invalid. Don't you see we have proof?"

"What will they say, by God, what will they say?" repeated Doña Engracia, squeezing Diamela even harder, who growled impatiently this time, only to vex Don Dámaso even further. He turned to Leonor, who was as collected as her parents were flustered. "Tell her, child," he said, "that the matrimony is invalid and that we have proof of it."

"That's a far cry from enough, a far cry!" shrieked Doña Engracia. "Once the tongues start wagging, we'll be the laughingstock of Santiago!"

"Papa," said Leonor, "didn't you say that Martín was the one who thought of searching for the proof that you have there?"

"Yes, my child, it was Martín."

"Then I think we should call him. Perhaps he'll know what to do next."

"Good thinking."

Don Dámaso sent for Martín, who came at once. Don Dámaso relayed his visit to Doña Bernarda's house and the obstinacy that he encountered there.

"And now what are we supposed to do?" were the words that ended his narration.

"I am convinced that they're bluffing," said Rivas. "If they really had the proof, they would have laid it on the table, especially Amador, who doesn't have a modest bone in his body."

"We must be absolutely confident that the proof is irrefutable, and then we must buy their silence," Leonor said to Martín with preemptory resolution, as though she and he were solely responsible for straightening out the family chaos.

"You're quite right," Martín said to her. "It's simply a matter of money. I have a hunch that Amador is at the bottom of this, and I agree that money will keep them quiet."

"My father is prepared to spend whatever is necessary, I believe."

"Of course, whatever it costs!" exclaimed Don Dámaso.

"1,000 pesos will suffice," said Martín.

"Will you straighten it out? " asked Don Dámaso.

"I promise to do whatever is humanly possible to settle this matter," answered Rivas emphatically.

"Excellent," remarked Don Dámaso. "Should I give you a bank draft to bring with you?"

"It would be worth more than any promise that I could give," Martín said to Don Dámaso, who went to his study to sign a check against his account.

Doña Engracia was struggling to overcome a fit of apnea, while Diamela was squirming to free herself from her mistress's grip and jump on the dais.

Leonor walked over to Martín and said, "Well, I found out the secret that you tried to keep from me."

"I hope that you'll understand that the secret was not mine to divulge."

"I understand," replied the girl presumptuously, "that it was in your best interest to hide the secret, rather than divulge it, as you say."

"My best interest? How so?"

"You keep the same company as Agustín."

"It is true that I have accompanied him there on many occasions."

"My father tells me that there are two pretty daughters, and I understand that Agustín was only wooing one of them."

Martín was unable to justify himself before this immodest insinuation because he was, as we have often noted, beside himself in Leonor's presence. Disturbed by the subtle accusation, his response was more emotionally charged than he might have preferred it to be.

"I will never set foot in that house again," he promised. "What else can I say to justify myself?"

"What an enormous sacrifice!" Leonor said, smiling coyly.

Just then, Don Dámaso returned with the bank draft, and Leonor retreated to her mother's side. Martín listened only half-heartedly to the recommendations of his host because he was more absorbed in Leonor's sarcasm than the task at hand.

"She is too proud to allow a man of my position to love her," he lamented to himself, with the renewed belief that he was nothing but a plaything to entertain her fickle heart.

The wings of this sad reflection carried Martín to the open field where unhappy lovers breathe the perfumed air of the pale flowers of melancholy. All suffering has a poetic side for young lovers, and Martín was swept away by the poetry of disconsolation, vowing to serve Leonor's family in spite of her disdain. Rather than wish for the magical waters of Lethe to grant him the calm of forgetfulness, which broken hearts often thirst, Martín clung to the idea of sacrifice, as if it would make the most of his heartwrenching misfortunes.

"I'd rather suffer for her," he would say to himself, "than feel nothing."

He set out to fulfill his promise to Agustín's family, thinking, "If I straighten this out, she'll have to be grateful to me. After all, she must be concerned about her family's peace of mind."

At the Molina residence, there was a meeting in session after the departure of Don Dámaso.

"Somebody had to teach them rich folks a lesson," Doña Bernarda said, without noticing the trepidation painted upon the face of her children. "Don't worry your lil' head, Adelaida, we'll make the ol' man swallow the pill even if he writhes like a hanged man. He's gotta accept you as his daughter no matter how much it pains him, and he'll hafta bring you home 'ventually."

Doña Bernarda withdrew after offering this consolation to her daughter, who hung her head in order to conceal the fear which seized her.

Amador and Adelaida exchanged knowing looks once they found themselves alone.

"Someone's been stirring the pot," said Amador. "Agustín ain't bright enough to figure this one out by himself. It wouldn't surprise me if it weren't that lamebrain Edelmira!"

"Meanwhile," said Adelaida, "if they do figure it out, we're sunk. What are we going to do if they bring us to court?"

"That's all we need," said Amador, scratching his head. "Somebody's flipped the tortilla on us."

"You've gotten me into this mess," replied Adelaida, already squirming under the pressure, "so you better get me out of it."

"Hey, if I got you into this, it was for your own good," exclaimed Amador, "and it's not as bad as you think, 'cause the ol' man wants to keep it under the rug. I bet if I 'fessed up, he'd thank me for it."

"Then what are you waiting for?"

"For the ol' man to pay us to keep our traps shut."

"I don't want money. I just want to get out of this mess."

"Don't worry, I'll get you out of it."

Adelaida withdrew after making her brother promise that he would do as she asked. Amador figured that there was more to be gained by accepting Don Dámaso's proposition than simply getting himself off the hook. He said to himself, "I'll appease Mama with a nice gift so she won't blow her stack when I tell her the truth, and I'll pocket the rest."

Animated by this prospect, he resolved to write to Agustín to request an interview. No sooner had Amador picked up a pen when Martín knocked on his chamber door. Unable to guess the purpose of this visit, Amador put on serious airs when greeting Martín, who declined an invitation to sit down.

"I've come on behalf of Don Dámaso Encina," Martín announced.

"He was here this morning," noted Amador, waiting for Rivas to deliver a message from his host.

"He has charged me to speak with you in private."

"I'm all ears."

"He told me that he was unable to come to an agreement with Doña Bernarda this morning."

"You know my mother. Stubborn as a bull."

"Don Dámaso found you more approachable than the lady."

"You know my mother. When she's angry, she sees red."

"I've come to try to settle this disagreeable matter about Agustín with you directly."

"It can't get more settled than it is already!"

"Don Dámaso has asked me to remind you of the consequences should this be brought to court. None of you can prove the validity of the marriage, but Don Dámaso can prove that an act of violence was committed, and he'll demand punishment. If, on the other hand, you confess that it was all a hoax and offer some assurance to Agustín's family that we can bury this matter, Don Dámaso will offer restitution for his son's offense, though Adelaida was partly responsible."

"If you had a sister," said Amador after a few silent moments, "and some Romeo was waltzing around and well . . . wooing her, ain't it true that you'd try to teach him a lesson?"

"Without a doubt."

"Well then, that's all I was doing to Agustín."

"You took it too far."

"So that he won't ever try that number again."

"You can put a stop to this matter right now," said Martín, taking out Don Dámaso's bank draft. "Read this."

"What is this?"

"Yesterday you asked Agustín for 1,000 pesos. His father offers you this sum in exchange for a letter."

"A letter? What does he want me to say?"

"What you've just told me: that you arranged a phony marriage to chastise Agustín."

Amador did not argue the word phony because he believed that he had already displayed sufficient resistance. The check, worth 1,000 pesos, was certainly more enticing than a lawsuit. "Besides," he figured, "I already squeezed a fair amount of juice from this lemon."

"Go ahead, then," he said, grinning, "tell me what to write."

Martín dictated the letter, explaining Amador's reasons for wanting to teach Agustín a lesson. Then he asked, "Who was the priest?"

"A buddy of mine."

Martín continued to dictate the letter, adding to Agustín's version of the story Amador's explanations, including the name of the sacristan who had pretended that he was a priest.

"Promise you won't bring him to court?" asked Amador when he named the sacristan.

"You have my word of honor. This letter is only for Don Dámaso's eyes. It won't be used to implicate you or anyone else. Whoever reads this letter will see that someone was trying to teach a good lesson to a young man who was about to go astray."

Amador signed the letter in exchange for the banknote, which he devoured with his eyes.

"After all," he thought, folding it, "it's a nice chunk of change, and it was a snap to earn."

Rivas returned to Don Dámaso's manor in joyful anticipation that Leonor would appreciate his successful mission.

XXXV

Amador held the banknote as though it were a holy relic and headed directly to Adelaida's chamber.

"It's all settled," he said to her, recounting all the details about Martín's visit, except the reference to the check that he had slipped into his pocket. 1,000 pesos was an enormous sum for Doña Bernarda's son. However, the facility with which he earned it far from satisfied his greed. "If someone hadn't squealed on us," he complained, "we'd be sitting pretty. I bet Edelmira put a flea in Martín's ear."

Adelaida ignored Amador because she was sorry to have ever participated in this intrigue and was relieved to find a quiet way out of it.

"Who else could it be?" Amador continued ruminating. "I'm gonna fix her wagon."

"You should tell Mama what happened," Adelaida advised, "before they do."

"It's all too fresh right now. She'll blow her top. We ought to wait a few days and tell her after the 18th."

Amador and Adelaida agreed not to ruin the holidays. Well-acquainted with their mother's violent constitution, they presumed (rightfully so) that the news would make her so angry that she would ground them during the holidays.

"If I tell her now, she'll throw me out on the street. But, it'll be worse for the both of you," Amador said, "'cause she'll lock you girls in the basement on the 18th."

This argument can only be appreciated by those who know how exhilarating our Independence Day is across the social spectrum. Not to celebrate the 18th is torture for any young person in Chile, especially in Santiago, where people flock from all around to witness the pomp and circumstance of this festive occasion.

Among all of the characters in this story, he who cared the least for the coming of this great day was Don Fidel Elías, whose only concern was the lease on El Roble. Resolved to accept the proposition that he had received by way of Don Simón Arenal, Don Fidel visited Don Pedro San Luis to have a man-to-man talk about the business. Within minutes, he promised that Rafael could marry his daughter on the same day that the lease would be renewed.

"Will you object," Don Fidel asked him, "to my nephew visiting your home again?"

"Of course not! You must know that it was only by undue advice that I denied myself the pleasure of receiving your nephew. He will be welcomed with open arms," assured Don Fidel.

"As soon as I'm free," responded Don Fidel, "Rafael and I will visit your place together."

Meanwhile at Don Dámaso's house, Agustín impatiently awaited for Rivas to return.

Leonor entered her brother's room and brought up the topic that was ailing the entire family. Agustín, who had recovered some of his talkativeness, recounted the details of the affair to Leonor, who inquired, "And the other sister, what is she like?"

"A pretty lass," answered Agustín.

"Didn't you say that one of them liked Martín?"

Notwithstanding his gratitude for Martín's favors, Agustín took it upon himself to assertively affirm that which he only vaguely assumed. He said, "Edelmira is her name."

Leonor remained thoughtful.

"Here comes Martín," exclaimed the dandy, seeing Rivas crossing the patio toward Don Dámaso's study.

Agustín called Rivas up to his suite, where he and his sister asked him concurrently, "How did it go?"

"Perfectly. I brought you a letter that will set your minds at rest," announced Rivas, presenting Leonor with the letter from Amador Molina.

"May I read it?" asked the girl. "Or is this a secret too? I'm only asking," she added, winking at her brother, "because this gentleman is so reserved with me."

"Hurry up and read it, *ma cherie,*" said Agustín. "*Curiosité* is killing me."

"It seems your French is coming back to you," she laughed.

"Martín's news tickles me *oeillet!*" exclaimed the dandy, embracing her.

Leonor read the letter aloud while Agustín gushed after each paragraph, "Oh, perfect, perfect!"

"You said that he was uncouth," said the girl, after reading the closing signature, "but this letter is very well written."

"Well, dearest, I don't know why the letter flows," replied Agustín, "because Amador is as low as lowbrows go!"

"Then someone dictated it to him," observed Leonor, laughing at Agustín's rhyme. Then she riveted her eyes upon Rivas and said, "Perhaps it was Señorita Edelmira?

"Ooooh, aaaah," cooed Agustín, who was giddy from the good tidings. "Or is it Mademoiselle Edelmira, or someone close to her, eh, Monsieur Martín?"

"Amador wrote it in my presence," answered Martín, blushing.

"*Ça m'est égal.*" said Agustín. "What's important is that *moi, je redeviens garçon.*"

"Aren't you the master linguist!" Leonor teased her brother.

Leonor and Agustín brought the letter to Don Dámaso, who was speaking with Doña Engracia, while Diamela tumbled upon carpet. As Don Dámaso listened to the letter, his face grew brighter with every phrase, the way the rays of the morning sun spread over the sleeping prairie, little by little. Doña Engracia scooped up her fluffy dog to express her delight and squeezed her little darling with every nod of approval from her husband.

"Papa," said Leonor, "I think this letter was dictated by Martín. Don't you think it's well written?"

"You're right. You see that my sister Francisca, a lady of letters, is right when she says: 'Style makes the man,' according to what's-his-name, the bloke who wrote. . . . Anyway, it doesn't matter. Thanks to Martín, everything is settled. What would we do without him? Leonor, you should make him accept a gift because he won't accept anything from me."

"I'll try," answered the girl, "but it won't be easy."

Agustín was then called aside by Don Dámaso to receive a severe reprimand for his ridiculous caper.

"What can I say, Papa? *Il faut que jeunesse se pass.*"

"Yes, but there are more seemly ways to live and learn," replied Don Dámaso, sounding like an old grouch. "What we ought to do," he added, quietly addressing Doña Engracia, "is find him a nice wife. Fidel's proposition couldn't have come at a better time."

The lady gave Diamela a tight squeeze to express what every mother feels at the thought of her son leaving her for another woman.

Martín had hoped to find himself engaged in one of those conversations by the piano that were as much a pleasure as they were a torment, but Leonor asked Emilio Mendoza to turn the pages that evening.

There came a moment when Agustín, who found a seat beside Rivas, called his sister to join them. "Come and help me cheer Martín up. He's got the blues."

"I bet you're regretting that big promise you made. You really should've thought about it first."

"What promise, Señorita?"

"The one about never setting foot in the house of *Señorita* Molina," Leonor said derisively, accentuating the word which we have italicized.

"Since I made that promise to myself, I could easily break it without affecting anyone," replied Martín, piqued.

"What lofty intentions," the girl said. "How remarkable."

"What intentions?" asked Agustín. "Fill me in, please. I don't want to miss anything."

"You already missed his promise never to fall in love," said Leonor.

"Is that right, sport?" laughed the dandy.

"And, yet, it seems that Señorita Molina was starting to chip away at his resolution," Leonor added wryly, before Rivas could answer the question posed to him by Agustín.

And with these words, the girl turned her back on them and went to sit beside her mother.

"Leonor is naughty, isn't she?" remarked Agustín, as he watched his sister withdraw.

"She is cruel!" Martín said to himself, before he left the salon humiliated.

On this same night, Don Pedro and his nephew paid a visit to the Elías family. Don Fidel rolled out the red carpet for his future son-in-law, and Doña Francisca welcomed the guest of honor with a spree of romantic theories, influenced by her favorite author.

"A woman in modern civilization is no less a slave than she was in pagan times," his future mother-in-law said. "She is a flower that comes to life under the sunlight of love," she added enthusiastically, "and man has abused his power by restricting the liberty of her heart. You will understand what I am saying because, judging by the proof of your persistence, your soul is superior to that of the average man whom we must live with day after tedious day."

And San Luis, sailing freely on the open sea of love and fantasy, took these theories seriously and replied to the lady in the same syrupy tone.

On the other side of the salon, his uncle remarked to Don Fidel, "It wouldn't be a bad idea to wait a month for the wedding. By that time, I'll have made the arrangements for Rafael to work with my son."

Thus, while the sweethearts were professing their undying love to each other, it was agreed by their elders that they would be married sometime in the middle of October.

After the guests had taken their leave, Doña Francisca was drawn back into reality when she heard the new projects that her husband was planning for El Roble, assuming that the lease was a fait accompli. To switch from theories about the emancipation of women to calculations of bushels of wheat which this or that pasture would yield was a transition far too drastic for her poetic imagination. She suggested between two long yawns that Don Fidel ought to visit her brother, and then she and Matilde went to bed.

The next day Don Fidel arrived at the home of Don Dámaso, just when the family was about to eat breakfast.

"Uncle, *je suis enchanté* to see you here," said Agustín.

"Likewise," said Don Fidel, who then called Don Dámaso aside.

After hemming and hawing, he finally explained the reason for his visit, thereby ruining the plans of his brother-in-law, who was longing to see Agustín "settled down with a nice wife."

XXXVI

The holidays arrived with flags, fanfare, and ceremonial salvos at the Fortress of Hidalgo. The civic soldiers proudly modeled their uniforms for the belles, whose hearts fluttered at the sight of all the fantastic outfits, parades, and diversions. Everyone dreamed of the evening banquets as they listened to the patriotic toasts and the national anthem. Santiago shook off its usual lethargy to celebrate the anniversary of its Independence with paramount exuberance. The patriotic festivities on the 17th and 18th—including the cannonade at the crack of dawn, the national anthem sung by little schoolgirls and country bumpkins alike, the formation in the Plaza, the blessing in the Cathedral, the parade to Alameda, the fireworks display, and the theater performances—all build toward the climactic event on the 19th: the procession to Pampilla.

Santiago, on the 19th of September, is not the proper daughter of her solemn founding fathers. She drops the affected Spanish sobriety that characterizes her throughout the year and laughs her heart out as she frolics in popular festivities. She rides horses and models gala dresses and sings the story of Independence and parades around in stylish carriages and plays the guitar and quaffs drink after drink. The old-time customs and the modern practices walk arm in arm like sisters, tolerating their respective weaknesses and joining voices to sing hymns to the Liberty of their beloved country.

A point-by-point description of these holidays would be tedious for the citizens of Santiago, as well as the readers from other provinces who have either heard stories about the festivities from travelers or have celebrated these traditions in their own towns. Therefore, we will omit some of the particulars and return to the incidents of our story.

After the speeches ended on the 18th, the fireworks began. Each skyrocket that exploded high in the air was greeted by a thousand cheers of *Oooh!* and *Aaah!* from the sovereign masses assembled in the Plaza. A rowdy crowd of Doña Bernarda's family and friends was appraising every skyrocket and greeting every person who passed by. Amador offered his arm to Doña Bernarda, Adelaida welcomed the arm of a friend, and Edelmira reluctantly accepted the arm of Ricardo Castaños, who took advantage of this occasion to profess his unfaltering love for the girl.

Just then, the Encina family and the Elías family entered the plaza. It was Leonor's idea that they should attend the fireworks together. Doña Engracia and her husband were the tail-end of the group, and to their left was a maidservant who carried Diamela in her arms. At the head walked Matilde and Rafael in affectionate conversation, and behind them followed Leonor and Agustín, chatting away. Rivas walked along arm in arm with Doña Francisca, who was bent on establishing a poetic conversation with him.

Agustín described Parisian fireworks in a very loud voice so that everyone around him could hear his opinions. When four little rockets burst through the air, he exclaimed, "Oh, in Paris the fireworks are truly breathtaking!"

"Oooooh! Aaaaah!" shouted the masses in unison, as a signal of approving admiration.

"Oh, a dud! Hide Diamela!" screamed Doña Engracia.

The crowds applauded the commotion which the dud created, whizzing by the spectators from one of the trees.

"How they would applaud if they were to see the Parisian bouquets!" remarked Agustín, "That is what I call truly magnificent!"

"Oh, let's get away from here," cried Doña Engracia, taking the pooch into her arms. "Mama's little gem is trembling like a little birdie!"

"I never feel more alone," Doña Francisca was saying to Rivas, "than in the middle of a maddening crowd. When one lives for the mind, all diversions seem insipid."

A sparkling dud skimmed overhead and saved Martín from having to respond.

"An accident is waiting to happen," said Doña Engracia, hiding Diamela under her cape.

In order to pacify the lady, the party moved toward a safer place, passing by Doña Bernarda and her party.

"Who's that on Rafael's arm?" asked Doña Bernarda.

"The daughter of Don Fidel Elías," answered Amador.

"Thinkin' he's so smug and won't say hello to nobody," replied Doña Bernarda.

Adelaida nearly fainted when she spotted Matilde and Rafael walking together. Just then, Agustín pointed her out to Leonor, saying, "Look, that's the girl they wanted me to marry."

"And the other one is her sister?" asked Leonor.

"Yes."

"Is she the one who is Martín's girl?"

"She's the one."

"She is pretty," said Leonor.

Martín passed by with his partner and waved to the Molina party. Edelmira swallowed a sigh and waved back at him.

"If I knew that you liked that boy Rivas," the officer said to her, "I'd go after him."

"Look at lil' Frenchy, pretendin' he don't see us," said Doña Bernarda.

Then the major fireworks suddenly erupted and captivated everyone's attention until the show ended with the battleships firing back at the castle. Nothing else happened to the characters of our story, some of whom returned home peacefully, while others brooded over the encounter that had just taken place.

Doña Bernarda, for one, could not bear to see Agustín disrespect her family. She said, "If he keeps his nose in the air, I'll tell the whole world that he's my son-in-law, and Troy can burn to the ground for all I care."

Amador endeavored to placate her, assuring his mother that he would settle the score immediately following the 18th.

At the theater that evening, Martín witnessed from his seat in the orchestra the commotion that Leonor caused among the patrons. Nearly every pair of opera glasses was turned to the balcony where she was sitting, exquisitely dressed. The praises of her beauty from those surrounding him inspired a soft melancholy in him. He imagined hearing, in the strains of music and in the murmur of the audience, a friendly voice telling him that someday she would be his. Like a mirage of an oasis in the eyes of a weary traveler, this presage of love disappeared as soon as Rivas tried to assure himself that it was real. When he considered the distance between them, the mirage drifted and faded into the hazy fog of a distant future.

Recognizing her tremendous success, Leonor began to toy with the idea that she could turn a poor obscure provincial into the envy of the most debonair gentlemen of this perfumed assembly by choosing him over all the rest of them. This idea arose from her conceited and capricious spirit, which was always fond of a challenge. Enjoying this reverie, Leonor looked for Martín in the audience and blushed when their eyes locked in a fiery gaze. She felt that she could make him the happiest man in the theater if she wanted. She proudly lifted her chin and frowned on the audience, as if to defy the power of its criticism.

The first and second act passed, while Leonor struggled, without knowing it, between love and pride. When the curtain dropped at intermission, she signaled Martín to join her in the box, a signal which she did not need to repeat. Leonor moved over a seat so that Martín could sit beside her.

"It seems," she said to him, "that you're not enjoying yourself tonight."

"What makes you think so?"

"You were looking distracted, and I started wondering whether . . . "

"Whether what?"

"Whether you were regretting the promise you made the other day."

"I don't recall what promise that was."

"The one about not returning to the Molina residence."

"I am sorry to disappoint you," replied Martín, using the same sarcastic tone that Leonor had used with him, "but I assure you that I had forgotten all about it, which shows how little it costs me to keep it."

"I saw the girl in the Plaza, and I commend your taste. She is very pretty."

"Only someone of your stature can praise another woman's beauty so sincerely."

"Why?" asked Leonor.

"Because only those who are secure about their own superiority can admit beauty in others," responded the youth.

"I see that you've been working on your flattery."

Leonor disapproved of Martín stepping outside the role of a timid and respectful admirer. She glared at him and asked, "Do you think of me as her rival?"

Rivas's heart ached at her reproach, and he wondered how someone so beautiful could be so heartless.

"I had no such thought," he answered with melancholy dignity, "and I am truly sorry if there was any room for misunderstanding in my words."

From the balcony, Edelmira watched Martín talking to Leonor in the box.

"I am sure that Martín is in love with that lady," the police officer said to Edelmira, whom he never let out of his sight. She swallowed a sigh, thinking that his jealous remark was probably true.

Meanwhile, Doña Bernarda was saying to her eldest daughter, "Lookie here, Adelaida, next year on the 18th, you'll be sittin' in the balcony with your lil' Frenchy too."

After Martín's deeply felt response, Leonor fell silent, and the young man left the box.

"I've been too severe," Leonor reproached herself as she watched him leave, promising herself that she would make amends over tea later that evening. But Martín did not return to his orchestra seat, nor did Leonor find him in the salon when she arrived home.

"Has Martín returned?" she asked the butler who was carrying a tray of tea and biscuits.

"He arrived a while ago, Señorita."

As she went to bed, Leonor had forgotten all about her popularity at the theater and the flattery she received from various bachelors throughout the night, including the excessive gallantry of

Emilio Mendoza and the timid adoration of the wealthy Clemente Valencia. She could not stop thinking about Martíns dignified response to her conceited glare.

"I've been too severe," she repeated to herself. "He has suffered, and yet he holds his head up proudly."

Her own proud disposition could not deny the admiration that she felt upon encountering more dignity in a poor provincial than in all the moneyed gents of the capital who were willing to bow to her every whim.

XXXVII

At ten o'clock in the morning on the 19th of September, the Molina family traveled together with their friends in an ox-drawn wagon that had quilts for curtains and a canopy of cattails; it was the kind of vehicle that one would expect to find on the road to Pampilla.

Doña Bernarda, rested her right rump against a basket full of cold cuts and her left side against a basket full of bottles. Across from her sat her two daughters. Reclining beside Edelmira was Ricardo Castaños, who had been granted special holiday leave by the Chief of Police, and sitting beside Adelaida was another suitor. To make this the perfect picture of the 19th of September, we have Amador Molina, sitting up front, holding his guitar in his arms and dangling his lanky legs off the tongue of the wagon. He played a song apropos to the occasion, ending with the verse:

Take us away, driver, away.

The others formed a jovial chorus, using their hands and mouths to mimic the sound of trotting hooves, and they quaffed glass after glass of Amador's wicked punch.

We will not follow Doña Bernarda's family along their entire journey. Suffice it to say that they made their way to Campo de Marte and parked their wagon on one of the streets facing the penitentiary, among numerous families who also arrived in covered wagons.

In the courtyard of the Encina estate, two beautiful horses hoofed the pavement until Rivas and Agustín mounted them at two o'clock in the afternoon. The two young men went to Alameda by way of Calle de la Bandera and followed a procession of horses and buggies that were traveling to Campo de Marte.

"You need to lighten up," Agustín said to Martín, while rearing his horse to flaunt his equestrian skills in front of the residents of Alameda who were watching from their front doorsteps. Under the pretext of cheering him up, Agustín had coaxed Rivas into joining him on this excursion.

"Will your family join us later?" Martín asked.

"I don't think so," Agustín replied. "Mama is afraid to go out on the 19th."

Meanwhile, the Molinas amused themselves thoroughly. The zamacuecas came one after another, and so did the libations that lifted the patriotic spirit of the dancers to remarkable heights. Amador was acting like the ring leader; Doña Bernarda was swilling glass after glass, toasting to the health of the dancers; the police officer was improvising an ingratiating tribute to Edelmira; and curious onlookers, surrounding the wagon, were applauding the dancers and guzzling the punch with blithe remarks and gales of laughter. Exhilaration was painted on every face. The exception was Edelmira, who reluctantly attended this outing, which was so contrary to her delicate, sentimental nature.

Undaunted by her listlessness, Ricardo Castaños reached dreamily for Edelmira's hand. However, Doña Bernarda caught him just as she was about to take another swig of mistela, and she threatened him half-seriously.

"Lookie here, lil' *fossficer.* Try that trick again and I'll have you thrown in that *plentytentiary* over yonder."

Great applause celebrated Doña Bernarda's admonition, and when she pointed to the penitentiary across the street, the crowds shouted the misnomer that the widow had used to designate the institution. Their applause captured the attention of Agustín and Rivas, who happened to be riding by the wagon.

"This sounds like a merry crew," said Agustín, spurring his horse. Martín followed close behind.

Doña Bernarda instantly noticed the two young men and came

forward exclaiming, "Hey, lil' Frenchy! Señor Rivas, how are you? Last night the both o' yous tramped 'bout town with your noses in the air, like you forgot your ol' friends."

"How can it be, Madame." said the dandy. "Last night, did you say? I regret that I did not have the pleasure of seeing you."

"Sure, sure, stop your clownin'," replied Doña Bernarda.

"I give you my word of honor . . . "

"You ain't got no honor, sonny." She offered him a glass and muttered, "Let's toast to wifey. So, when's Papa gonna bless the marriage, eh?"

Amador, who had just noticed the young men, heard his mother's question, but had insufficient time to impede Agustín from responding.

"I believe that everything has already been settled, and Papa believes the same."

"Settled? What the heck's he sayin'?" Doña Bernarda asked her son.

"We'll discuss it later, Mother," said Amador. "There's much too much fun to be had right now."

"That's just swell with me," said Doña Bernarda, feeling light-headed from too much liquor. "Just swell. Frenchy, you're part o' the family now, so hop off your high horse and have a lil' toast with us."

"I genuinely regret that I am unable to . . ." began Agustín, whom Amador was signaling not to contradict his mother.

"Genuinely, schmenuinely!" said Doña Bernarda, grabbing the reins of Agustín's horse. "You're a part o' the family, ain't you? Well, speak up."

Amador recognized by Doña Bernarda's tone that his secret compromise was on the verge of exposure and that it was absolutely imperative to assuage his mother, lest he be obliged to explain his arrangement under these inauspicious circumstances.

"My mother's still in the dark," he whispered to Agustín, "and if you don't play along, she'll make a big stink and embarrass all of us."

"But I can't," answered Agustín, who was ashamed to be seen with them in public.

The crowds surrounding the Molina party had dispersed when

the dancing had come to an end. Doña Bernarda, all the while, kept a tight grip on the reins of Agustín's horse and obliged him to dismount.

"Tell him to come down," Amador pleaded with Martín, "please."

Martín knew that Doña Bernarda would only calm down if they dismounted, and he was further moved to do so when Edelmira asked, "Are you ashamed to be seen with us?"

"Com'on, Frenchy, get off your high horse, or I'll drag you down myself."

Martín dismounted, followed by Agustín, who accepted a glass from Doña Bernarda. Just then Ricardo Castaños smashed his glass against the tongue of the wagon in protest of Edelmira's conversation with Martín.

"You've forgotten us," she was telling Rivas, with a look more lovelorn than before.

"I haven't forgotten you," he responded, "but out of respect for Agustín's family I promised not to return to your house."

"Why must I suffer for another's offense?"

"You! Why in the world should you suffer?"

"More than you can imagine and more than ever lately."

Before Martín could respond, his eyes fell frightfully upon a carriage that seemed to appear out of nowhere. In it were Leonor and Don Dámaso. Agustín, turning beet red, did not know which way to look. Don Dámaso ordered him to approach.

"You! With these people!"

"Papa, let me explain," sniveled the dandy, hanging his head in shame.

"Mount your horse and follow us," demanded Don Dámaso in an austere voice.

Leonor leaned back in the carriage, after staring down at them with disgust.

Edelmira was saying to Martín, "You told me that you would trust me."

"And I meant it," Rivas replied, making heroic efforts to conceal his utter abashment.

Edelmira stared him straight in the eye and trembled with emotion when she asked,

"Do you love that lady?"

"What a question!" exclaimed Martín, forcing himself to smile. "I would be looking way over my head."

"Let's go, let's go," Agustín urged him. "Papa says we must go."

After uttering tangled excuses, they mounted their horses and followed Don Dámaso's carriage.

"I'll get to the bottom of this," Doña Bernarda said to herself.

Holding back tears, Edelmira took the guitar that Amador handed her so that she might play a zamacueca. Then to distract his mother from her thoughts, Amador shouted, "Long live Chile!"

And the crowds of people on foot and horseback cheered, "Hurrah! Hurrah!"

Rising over the noise of drumfire and rowdy picnickers, this patriotic ovation sounded like sarcasm to Martín, who galloped away, cursing his star for leading him to this catastrophic confrontation.

Brokenhearted, Edelmira reluctantly sang the verses of the zamacueca. The dancing and laughing and drinking promptly resumed at the sound of the music and continued throughout the afternoon until the troops withdrew, thereby dropping the curtain, so to speak, on this holiday scene.

XXXVIII

The two young men were surprised to see Leonor at Campo de Marte because she had mentioned during breakfast that she was only going to Alameda, which was her intention at that time.

She regretted her behavior at the theater the night before and wished to be alone to meditate upon the recent state of her heart. For the first time, her mind was free from the frivolous occupations of the humdrum existence in which the greater part of Chilean women watch their best years slip away. We did not arbitrarily select the word *humdrum* to describe the daily lives of our beautiful compatriots. Like most of her peers, Leonor, having no more experience than her schooling, believed that the principal occupation of her sex was to be versed in the latest fashion and the narrow views of her immediate circle of family and friends. Her only objective was to be as elegant as she was beautiful. Her popularity had kept her mildly entertained until Martín walked into her life. Since then, we have witnessed the transformation of her conceited heart to the point where she would wake up thinking about the poor provincial after spending most of the night dreaming about him. After announcing that she would not go to Pampilla, she regretted having toyed with his feelings, and, like a spider moving up and down the same dangling thread repeatedly, she spent an hour wondering how she should atone for her sarcasm.

As impulsive as she was impatient, Leonor wanted to console him with a gentle word or look, but felt as though an entire century would pass before nightfall would provide the occasion. In the glory of love, ordinary measures of time are insufferable and every delay feels like a century. Leonor obliged her doting father to take her to Campo de Marte, where they happened to catch Martín and Agustín at a very awkward moment.

When Leonor saw Rivas chatting with Edelmira, a chill ran up her spine and she vowed to herself that she would forget him completely. However, she could think of nothing but him during the whole trip back to Alameda. Why was Martín more attractive now that another pretty, young belle was in love with him? It remained a mystery to Leonor as she looked out the window at the hordes of people, celebrating in the streets of Alameda. Passing before her eyes were ladies modeling their new dresses, military troops marching through the middle of the street to the fife and drum, and civic troops from Renca and Nuñoa marching along the side streets in their queer, threadbare uniforms. Her thoughts were as jumbled as the view. Feeling sad for the first time in her life, she returned home in a foul mood.

Martín did not attend the theater that night.

Leonor listened with repugnance as her brother explained to Don Dámaso what he was doing by the wagon that afternoon.

During a lengthy conversation at the theater with Matilde and Rafael about love in general, she wondered in the back of her mind whether Rivas had broken his promise and slipped away to Doña Bernarda's house. Her mind was so bent on this suspicion that when she went to bed her pride dismissed the fact that her rival was a lowly would-be. In fact, the next morning, her heart sank when she heard Agustín say that Rivas was going to skip breakfast so that he could join Rafael San Luis for brunch. The very air in the breakfast room turned to ice.

Martín had searched for a pretext to be absent because he dared not face Leonor after what had happened at Pampilla. When Rivas returned from Rafael's house, Agustín said to him, "Leonor doesn't believe a word I said. You must convince her because whatever she believes, Papa believes, and he's still giving me the cold shoulder."

At dinner that evening Martín was truly surprised when Leonor addressed him with warmth and kindness, and he did not know what to think at first. But, upon careful consideration, he came to this forlorn conclusion that typifies a hopeless lover: "She despises me, but she isn't in the mood to mock me."

"Now is a good time to clear my name," Agustín said, as they left the dining room.

"I barely have the nerve," answered Rivas, who wished to speak to the girl, yet needed someone to nudge him to do so.

"Do me this favor," pleaded the dandy, leading his friend to the salon. "She respects you. Look, this morning she asked me why you weren't at the theater last night."

Saying this, Agustín led his friend to the piano where Leonor was seated and then walked away to leaf through a book on a table. Martín quickly regained his composure the moment he was alone with Leonor. As we have observed, he often felt a surge of energy in the face of difficulties, despite his lovesick reticence.

"I didn't see you last night at the theater," Leonor said so softly that the young man dropped his guard.

"The trip had worn me out," he answered.

"Nevertheless," she leered at him, "you chose a convenient place to dismount and rest your weary self at Pampilla."

"Agustín told me that you didn't seem to believe his explanation as to how we found ourselves there."

"You can't really blame me, can you?"

"You must have a very poor opinion of us."

"Actually, I have a very high opinion . . . of your ingenuity."

"What do you mean by that, Señorita?"

"Agustín couldn't have thought of that excuse by himself because it was much too clever. Therefore, I can only conclude that it must have been your idea."

"Your compliment, as much as I appreciate it, is unmerited because Agustín was telling you the truth."

"Yet he was unable to explain something that I saw with my very eyes."

"What is that?"

"An intimate conversation between you and Señorita Edelmira."

"Now that you have mentioned something that directly concerns me, permit me to answer with complete frankness."

"A secret?" asked Leonor, striving for indifference while struggling against anxiety.

"No, Señorita, an explanation about what you saw."

"I already know that your explanation will be perfectly satisfactory because I recognize your powers of invention."

"You may qualify it after you have heard me."

"Try me."

"It's true that I was engrossed in conversation when you saw me with Edelmira yesterday."

"My! I see you're finally beginning to trust me with your secrets!" said Leonor with an enigmatic tone. She avoided eye contact with Rivas and seemed unnerved by the topic. Her breathing became so visibly strained that a precious cameo pendant embedded with pearls swung back and forth on the chain around her neck like a skiff rocking on the waves of the sea.

"There is no secret, Señorita. All that I want to tell you, as I have said, is the simple truth."

"Try me. I'm listening."

"I respect her integrity, and that is why I showed interest in her, and always will."

"Be careful, you're speaking very fervently of your appreciation."

"I am impassioned in my regard, Señorita."

"That is why I said to be careful. They say that appreciation is a blink away from love."

"I wouldn't worry about it."

"Why wouldn't you?"

"Because I know that I could never love her."

"You're very presumptuous, Martín," Leonor said.

"Why?"

"Because you have too much faith in your strength of will."

"If only I could count on it," remarked Rivas with a sincere touch of sorrow in his voice, "I would be a happy man."

Leonor swerved from this course of conversion like a hummingbird that avoids the beauty of the rose for fear of its thorns, contenting itself with harmless daisies instead.

"Let's see," she said, "if you are as honest as you say."

"Try me, as you would say."

"Does she love you?"

Only very discerning eyes would have detected the trace of anguish in her smiling face.

"I believe not, Señorita," answered Martín firmly.

"Be sincere. Agustín has already told me so."

"I know nothing about it. If it were true, I will say at the risk of appearing immodest that I would truly regret it."

"Why?"

"For the same reason you have already accused me of being presumptuous: because I could never love her."

"Because you aspire to higher realms and you think she is too obscure for you."

"Not at all. I believe the heart is free and social hierarchies shouldn't matter when it comes to love."

"Then it's a mystery why you wouldn't love her."

"No, Señorita, it is no mystery at all."

Again Leonor suddenly strayed from this line of inquiry because it occurred to her that he might be in love with someone else. Instead of raising the question, she changed the topic again, saying, "Last night, I was a bit terse with you."

"I try very hard, Señorita, not to displease you when I have the honor of speaking with you, but I confess that I'm never quite successful."

"Is that what you think?"

"These moments mean a great deal to me," answered Martín in a voice charged with emotion.

The cameo pendant began rocking again like a skiff over the waves of the sea, and Leonor missed a note of the waltz that she knew by memory. She glued her eyes to the sheet of music and said to him, as she corrected the mistake, "Perhaps you take things too seriously."

"I seriously try to avoid displeasing you."

"Good gracious! Is my temper really that bad?" she exclaimed, endeavoring to conceal her agitation.

"Perhaps it's my own insecurity."

"Let me say what I believe I said to you before. I don't see any reason for your lack of confidence. Would we be having this conversation if I found you displeasing?"

With these words, Leonor skipped to the end of waltz and played the final notes. Her hands were trembling as she closed the piano, and without further ado, she went to the table where

Agustín was still leafing through a book. More shaken was Martín, who remained precisely where he had stood during their entire conversation. It felt as though a ray of light had illuminated his mind, only to leave him in complete darkness a moment later. Interpreting her kind words as a sign of hope, his heart shuddered as though he were standing in front of an abyss. There she was: the ideal beauty, as majestic and proud as ever, wealthy and admired by all.

"What madness!" he said to himself in a cold sweat.

Agustín turned to Leonor and wrapped his arms around her waist, saying, "I hope that Martín was able to convince you, little sister."

"Of what?" asked Leonor, blushing as though his question had touched upon a nerve.

"That we had no choice but to dismount our horses."

"Oh, yes, entirely," answered the girl, leaving the salon.

"I'm glad," Agustín said to Rivas. "Now she'll convince Papa so we can put this all behind us."

XXXIX

When the haze of liquor lifted from Doña Bernarda Cordero's brain the morning after the long journey to Campo de Marte on the 19th, she began to reflect on what Agustín had said. She clearly gathered from him that there was some sort of an arrangement with regard to the marriage. The slippery excuses that Amador offered at the time raised her suspicions further. What arrangement could that be? And why had they kept it a secret from her? After all, wasn't she the mother of the bride? After serious deliberation, she swore to solve the mystery herself so that no one would, to borrow her colorful expression, "make a thumb-suckin' booby out o' this ol' broad."

She interrogated her son, who, desirous of postponing the explanation as long as possible in the hopes that his mother's fury would dwindle as time went on, offered sketchy answers, which far from easing her mind, only raised her mistrust.

Doña Bernarda reiterated pointed questions, but Amador answered with new subterfuge. Every now and then, he would feed his mother a morsel of truth. He was convinced that a system of gradual explanations, over the course of a few days, was the best way to admit what had occurred. In this manner, the magnitude of the deception would not incite her wicked temper, which he rightfully feared would explode if he openly admitted that his dirty scheme had backfired, leaving her among the wounded.

Unsatisfied by her son's half-baked excuses, Doña Bernarda Cordero decided to take the matter into her own able hands. One day in early October she went to visit the father of the man whom she presumed to be her son-in-law. She had spent enough time thinking about what she would do and what she would say and how she would reject any proposition that was not based upon the recognition of the marriage by the entire Encina family, who, being "loaded with dough," should have enough good manners to "invite them over," as she would say, "to pull up a chair and break some bread."

Don Dámaso offered her a seat, and Doña Bernarda began the conversation, saying, "Señor, I hafta talk to you 'bout . . . you-know-what."

"Surely, Señora," answered Don Dámaso, "I don't know what you're talking about."

"I bet you do, Señor. Only you-know-what would bring me here."

"Would you please be so kind as to explain yourself."

"Tell me, Señor, did the weddin' slip your mind already?"

"Señora, I find it most peculiar that you have come to speak to me of this matter."

"Well, what am I s'posed to say? Ain't I her mother. What are you thinkin'!"

As one can see, Doña Bernarda displayed from the start of the conversion the energy and clarity that she was determined to display in order to conclude this affair quickly.

"Whether you are her mother is not a issue. No one denies that, but I'm puzzled as to why you're acting as though we hadn't settled all of this, as though there were something more to discuss."

"Ain't that what I just said? I'm gettin' dizzy, runnin' 'round in circles here. Since it's all settled, they should start livin' together."

"Who should live together?"

"Lord above, grant me patience! Our children, o' course, Agustín and my daughter. Who else would they be?"

"But, Señora, it appears that you don't wish to understand. Let me repeat that everything has been settled."

"Sure, sure, that's what Amador keeps tellin' me, but I wanna know how."

"What! Don't you know?"

"If I knew, would I be here askin' you?"

"Your son, your very own son, has confessed that the marriage was a farce."

"What? Are you tellin' me I didn't see it with my own two eyes? With God as my witness! You think I'm a thumb-suckin' fool? And what 'bout the priest who married them?"

"The priest wasn't a priest; he was a friend of your son."

"Says who?"

"Amador himself."

"Are you mad? I would've heard 'bout it!"

"The fact is that he has already confessed it."

"To who?"

"To me."

Don Dámaso then proceeded to his writing desk to show her Amador's letter.

"You see this?" he said to her. "Your son wrote this confession that explains the whole ordeal."

"Lemme see what it says," grunted Doña Bernarda, who was unwilling to admit that she was unable to read.

"It is all right here in black and white."

Don Dámaso read Amador's letter aloud from the date to the signature, leaving Doña Bernarda stunned by this revelation. The worst scenario that she had imagined from Amador's befuddled excuses was that he had agreed to allow the Encina family to postpone their acknowledgment of the matrimony. But this letter shattered all of her expectations and veiled her tortured face with shame.

"If that's the case," she said, shaking with indignation, "they're gonna pay for it."

Bidding adieu to Don Dámaso, she rushed home to unleash her rage upon her children.

During the period that Doña Bernarda had spent forming her resolution to visit Don Dámaso (sometime in early October as we mentioned), there was no incident worthy of mention with regard to the other characters in this story.

Matilde and Rafael spent happy and peaceful days together, enthralled by their mutual devotion, yearning for the day that they would be married. Having been promised the second lease on El Roble, Don Fidel now welcomed the repeated visits by his daughter's fiancé with the most affectionate benevolence. Doña Francisca indulged herself in long romantic conversations with her future son-in-law, who accompanied her, with the complacency of a happy man, to the land of dreams where Doña Francisca loved to escape from the prosaic life of the capital.

The Molinas, conversely, did not breathe the free and easy air that the Elías family enjoyed. Adelaida wept in silent desperation when she caught wind that her ex-lover was engaged to be married. It is no wonder how Adelaida Molina learned of this news. In our Capital, rumors spread at an alarming rate through every circle and hierarchy of Society. Furthermore, Adelaida belonged to a social class that lived in envy of the upper class, and therefore, studied its every move and criticized it with gusto. It is not out of the ordinary, therefore, that the wind, so sonorous in frivolous societies like Santiago, should whisper in Adelaida's ear that Rafael would no longer be in the position to offer her reparation for his impropriety.

Beside Adelaida sighed her sister in the melancholy of an unrequited love. Edelmira was one of those people in whom absence makes the heart grow fonder. During the days that Martín had refrained from visiting her home, her feelings for him grew like wild flowers that receive no more water than the rain from the skies. What kept her love alive was an overly sentimental imagination that was further incited by the comments that the officer had made to her in the theater. She thought it must be impossible for a young man to keep from falling in love with such a gorgeous woman. And to think that Martín lived under her roof! The thought that someone else loved him made him all the more attractive, for—as the saying goes—the fruit growing on someone else's tree always looks sweeter than one's own.

The misery eating away at her lonely heart was compounded by the nuisance of an unwelcome suitor who hounded her daily.

Ricardo Castaños stood strong in the face of her scorn and was supported in his pursuit by Doña Bernarda and Amador, both of whom considered him an excellent match. Men are not always able to appreciate the antipathy that a woman feels when pursued by an inopportune lover because our hearts lack the strands of subtlety that would allow us to feel as they do. The perseverance of the young Castaños was abominable to Edelmira, now that she had heard the celestial music of first love playing in her soul. Edelmira did what many a lonely, imaginative lass might have done in her position. She wrote Martín many love letters, which she never sent, but which fanned the flames of her illusion. In them, beams of passion shined through the cloudy paraphrases of her favorite romances, stored in the recesses of her imagination. These Calypsos, in the absence of a lover, offer sundry enchanting recourses to memories and fantasies.

Edelmira wrote a stack of letters by the beginning of October (the point in the narration where we now find ourselves), but soon grew tired of this exercise.

Martín Rivas had not the faintest idea that he was an object of such passion. He grew more fond of the girl during their brief conversation at Campo de Marte, where she showed concern for his absence, but he did not suspect, except vaguely, that under that surface of her friendly questions lurked a deeper feeling for him. Martín brought his reflections upon this matter no further than the supposition, "If I were to court her, she might love me."

He was too absorbed in his own love to notice someone else's whom he had not seen much of lately. Leonor's behavior kept him from drifting into despair; in fact, their last conversation allowed him a glimpse of hope, which Martín at times dismissed as delirium and other times embraced as reality.

Leonor abandoned her usual fickle coquetry, as well as her plot to exasperate Martín. In her silence, and with a few choice words, she was as sincere as if she had frankly declared her love. This was an unprecedented, exceptional situation for Leonor. Accustomed to that which may be called *social consideration,* surrounded by dashing rich suitors from whom she could take her pick, Leonor would have to overcome ideas rooted in her spirit since childhood in order to declare her love for Martín. She found it necessary to measure his worthiness before braving the prejudices and violating the codes of behavior in her Society. Hence, her frequent conversations with Rivas and the vacillations with which she sometimes uttered words of hope that were sincere to her, but dubious to the young provincial whom she had toyed with for quite some time.

XL

We last observed Doña Bernarda Cordero on her way home after Don Dámaso had revealed the secret her son was concealing from her.

With every step she took, her exasperation rose (as may well be imagined). The more she thought about this devastating news, the angrier she grew at Amador for fostering and shattering her ambitious dreams, which seemed even more precious now that they were lost forever. And so she stormed into the house, tossed her cloak over a chair, and called her elder daughter in a harsh voice.

Adelaida came at once.

"Where's your brother?" Doña Bernarda asked her.

"He must be in his room."

"Go get him. I hafta talk to both o' yous."

A few moments later Adelaida and Amador stood before Doña Bernarda, who scowled at her son in unbridled rage.

"You think you can pull the wool over my eyes?" she said, cocking her head and placing both hands on her hips.

"Who? Me? Why would I think that?" answered Amador, withering as he feigned ignorance the way the guilty usually do.

"If you don't know, then I don't know. I must be a thumb suckin' fool if my own children can trick me. That's all I needed. Adelaida's got herself a nice hubby, ain't she?"

"But, Mother, I've been trying to tell you that everything's settled."

"Nice settlement! Don't bargain for another, and we'll be just swell. We might as well be poor blacks. How are we s'posed to show our faces in public? Even the lil' tots are gonna point and laugh at us in the streets."

"Your moods!"

Doña Bernarda, who was already aggravated beyond reason, exploded at her son's impertinence. She yelled deranged curses, vile insults, and abominable threats that decency prevents us from transcribing. Adelaida, more timid than Amador, excused herself pathetically, "It ain't my fault, Mama."

To which Amador retorted sarcastically, "Sure it ain't. It must be mine then. Was it me who was getting hitched? I ain't got nothing to hide, little bride."

"Well, then, who does?" exclaimed Doña Bernarda. "It was all your idea. Why did you lie to your own mama? You must've reaped some benefit."

"What benefit would I get out of it? A fine slur, indeed!"

"But she swears it ain't her fault," retorted Doña Bernarda, pointing at her daughter.

"Well, if she says so, it must be so."

"In the letter you say you brought a friend dressed up as a priest."

"In what letter?"

"The one you wrote to Don Dámaso."

"That's true, but I didn't do it for myself. I did it for Adelaida."

Doña Bernarda turned toward her daughter with the eyes of a charging bull.

"It ain't my fault," insisted Adelaida.

"The thanks I get! Swell, go ahead and blame me now," huffed Amador. "If it ain't her fault, then ask her why I did it."

"Well, let's hear it then," Doña Bernarda said to Adelaida.

"How should I know? You said it was best for me."

"Like I said the first time," exclaimed Doña Bernarda, "it's all your fault."

The widow then fired another round of brutal insults at her son who sought shelter behind these words: "If you only knew what went on under your own roof, you wouldn't be cussing at me for nothing."

Adelaida looked at her brother beseechingly, but he was too concerned with saving his own hide to think of his sister's.

"What goes on under my roof?"

"Ask Adelaida why I did it for her own good. She's quick to say it ain't her fault, but I ain't the one who's got something to hide. She does."

Afraid of what her brother might say next, Adelaida instantly claimed full responsibility; but it was too late now that Amador had led his mother to the trail. Adelaida swore in vain that she had begged her brother to marry her to a gentleman, but Doña Bernarda only repeated, "Yeah, but what were you doin' under my roof?"

Had Amador corroborated his sister's claim at this critical juncture, Doña Bernarda's skepticism would have been put to rest, but he held his tongue so that the blame would not return to him.

"You better 'fess up," Doña Bernarda threatened her son, shaking her fists at him in a fit of hysteria, "or I'll have you enlisted for bein' *dissabedient.* Remember, you ain't 25 years ol' yet."

Amador was not daunted by this threat because he could always leave his mother's home. However, the idler par excellence would have to work for a living. It was easier to confess the truth and forsake his sister than to wrangle with his mother, who always kept a roof over his head and sometimes saved his neck by paying his debts. The slackening of his habits had long since deprived him of noble sentiments, and, therefore, he never thought to brave the indignation of his mother to protect his sister. Thinking only of himself, he blurted out the secret love affair between Adelaida and Rafael, and its consequences. After the damage was done, he attempted to soften the blow with a few sympathetic words on behalf of his sister.

Doña Bernarda turned white, and then she hurled herself at Adelaida. Shrieking at the top of her voice, she flung her daughter around the room by her hair. Edelmira and the servant tried to rescue Adelaida from Doña Bernarda's clutches with Amador's belated assistance. Then the servant ran into the patio to lock the street door so that the neighbors would not hear all the ruckus.

Doña Bernarda displayed extraordinary brute strength for her age and sex. She was dragging Adelaida around the room with her left fist, while furiously punching Edelmira and Amador with her right. A casual bystander to this grotesque, domestic drama might have lost sight of compassion to laugh at the inanity of this brawl, which ended as abruptly as it began. Doña Bernarda swung at Edelmira, who heroically seized both of her mother's arms, forcing her to release Adelaida's tresses. The driving force of Doña Bernarda's right hook was so mighty that it sent Edelmira crashing into a chair. And then Doña Bernarda tumbled into the middle of the floor. With nothing to break her fall, the old widow laid senseless and motionless from complete exasperation and the impact of her fall.

All three children carried Doña Bernarda to bed, where her servant rubbed her feet, her son doused water on her face, and her daughters wept in each other's arms.

The widow eventually regained consciousness and shed bitter tears over the loss of Adelaida's honor. The excessive commotion depleted her physical and moral strength, as do all extraordinary displays of force, and she felt so weak the next day that she remained in bed to recuperate. Now that she knew the wretched truth, hatred and vengeance replaced the gratitude that she had always felt for Rafael San Luis. She spent the whole day trying to think of a punishment that would fit the crime. But, as her meditations proved fruitless, she opted for reconciliation which would, perhaps, return joy and honor to the family.

Thus, several days later, she paid Rafael San Luis a "friendly lil' visit."

It was 10 o'clock in the morning. Rafael was alone in his chamber. The widow's unexpected visit was surely not a blessing, yet he tried to appear nonchalant as he welcomed her affectionately. He sensed that his guest was also trying to hide her agitation. After she sat down in an armchair that Rafael graciously offered her, she reproached him with a friendly smile, saying, "We've missed you at home lately, you know."

"Oh, believe me, my dear Bernarda, I've missed you too."

"There's gotta be some reason. How does that lil' song go? 'If somethin's rattlin' funny, it must be missin' a screw, honey.'"

"Nay, what reasons would there be! Absolutely none. You know how much you mean to me."

"Of course, and you've always been the apple o' my eye. You see, I was just askin' Adelaida 'bout you the other day. 'What's wrong with Don Rafael?' I said, 'What've you done to chase him away?'"

By singling out her eldest daughter, Doña Bernarda confirmed his premonition that there was an ulterior motive to this unexpected, 'friendly lil' visit.'

"I'm indebted to your kindness," he answered.

"So what's keepin' you away?"

"I'm busy almost every night, and although I would love to go, I really don't know how I'll find the time," said Rafael, who wished that she would plainly state the reason for her visit.

"Yes, well, that's what we were askin' ourselves. 'Will we ever see his face again? Is he ashamed to visit our house now that he's swingin' with them rich folks?'"

"Ashamed! You're mistaken, my good lady."

"Well, the proof is that you don't wanna come no more," replied the lady, whose friendly tone was quickly fading.

Rafael noticed the change in her demeanor and allowed his impatience to escape.

"I didn't say that I don't want to," he insisted. "I said that I can't."

"What's the difference? The fact is that you ain't comin' 'round no more and I know why," she declared with heightened discontent. "The buzz 'round town says you're gonna get married."

"Is that what you've heard?"

"Just yesterday. Is it true?"

"Perhaps it is."

"You don't say!"

"It's a very old commitment, arranged before I had the honor of meeting you."

"It may be old, but, what can I say? You broke your 'mitments at my home," retorted Doña Bernarda, glaring at Rafael with adamant resolution stamped upon her face.

The young man turned pale as he listened. Despite his misgiving about the nature of her visit, he never imagined that she would dare to attack him so openly.

He stammered, "I . . . I don't know what you're referring to."

"What do you mean? You should know better than anybody. Why don't we cut to the chase, eh?"

"Señora, please be plain. What do you expect of me?"

"To marry my daughter," declared Don Bernarda, "'cause you dishonored her."

"Impossible," said the young man, "I'm engaged to a young lady who . . . "

Doña Bernarda interrupted furiously, "And what 'bout my family? My daughter's a lady too and you lied to her. If you was a gentleman, you'd marry her like you promised."

Rafael searched in vain for arguments and reasons to excuse his offense, but Doña Bernarda reiterated her argument over and over again.

"For the last time!" exclaimed Rafael rankled, "it's impossible that I marry your daughter, and the best you can do for her is accept the proposition that I'm going to make."

"What *propersition?*" asked Doña Bernarda.

"I have 12,000 pesos that I inherited from my father. I promise to recognize the child as my own and give half of the money to Adelaida."

"I ain't after your money," cried Doña Bernarda, before shouting a thousand recriminations that Rafael was obliged to receive with humility. Then she concluded with this threat, "You don't wanna marry her, eh? Well then, I'm gonna take you to court and we're gonna see who loses what. My daughter's already lost face. I ain't afraid o' standin' up for her. If you want war, we'll give it to you. Don't worry your pretty lil' head 'bout that."

And she quit the room, leaving Rafael in a state of panic. He wrote to Martín, asking to meet him at the gateway (which we now call the Old Gate of Bellavista to differentiate it from the gateways of Tagle and Bulnes). The two friends met an hour later and walked toward Alameda.

"I need your advice," said Rafael, taking hold of Martín's arm.

"What is it?"

"Just when I thought the coast was clear . . . you won't believe who just paid me a visit."

"Adelaida Molina?"

"Doña Bernarda! She knows everything and wants me to marry her daughter."

"She is right," answered Martín coldly.

"I know she is," Rafael replied uncomfortably, "but I didn't ask your opinion on that matter."

"Well, go on."

"I couldn't find any way out of it, so I offered her half of everything I own, but the old hag turned down 6,000 pesos."

"In that case, you should offer her everything. Give her 12,000."

"She won't accept it. She won't hear of anything, except my consent to marry her daughter. What's the point of saying it's impossible? I would never marry her, even if I weren't on the brink of happiness."

Martín remained silent, thinking, "If girls could only hear what men really thought, they could save themselves from unhappiness!"

"What would you do in my situation?" asked Rafael.

"If she won't hear of anything but marriage, I wouldn't give her the opportunity to stop yours."

"How so?"

"I would get married at once."

"You're right, but there is still a risk."

"Of what?"

"Doña Bernarda threatened to take me to court."

"Do you think that she would dare?"

"I fear she would. She is violent and unforgiving. I think that she would rather avenge me than protect her daughter's reputation."

"There may be a way out."

"Please show it to me."

"Amador will do anything for money."

"Yes, if he had a soul, he would sell it."

"Pay him 500 pesos to convince his mother to drop the threat."

"Could you talk to him?"

"Gladly."

"You would do me a great service. You know how much I've suffered. If my conscience were clean I wouldn't tremble at her threat, but as you say, the poor woman is right and my remorse means nothing to her."

"Well, we'll do what we can."

"I already owe you for reuniting Matilde and me. If you manage to keep Doña Bernarda quiet, how will I ever repay you?"

"Aren't there other things we can talk about. What are friends for?"

"Fine, let's talk about your love-life."

"There isn't one to talk about," said Rivas with a smile that failed to rid his expression of sadness.

"I doubt it's as bad as you think," replied Rafael.

"Why? Do you know something?"

"Matilde says that her cousin is constantly talking about you. That is a good sign."

"She probably drops my name among many others."

"What's remarkable is that she only speaks of you. Tell me what you and Leonor talk about. Maybe I'll have better insight."

Martín welcomed the opportunity to recite every conversation that he had ever shared with Leonor, recounting the slightest occurrences with the precision of a man in love. He spoke passionately of his most recent hopes and woefully of his overall discouragement.

"Without a basis for certainty," Rafael said, "there is nothing to rest your hopes on. If I were you, I would try to find out."

"How?"

"I would write to her."

"I would never risk insulting anyone in her family."

"Martín, my friend, you belong to another century."

Martín's sole reply was a muffled sigh.

"Do you mean that you're resolved to live in doubt?" replied San Luis.

"Yes, I admit that I'm intimidated by her splendor. Sometime I find the courage to speak up, but it leaves me whenever she does. I feel so obscure and unworthy when I think of the vast distance between us."

"Well, I trust your judgment," said Rafael. "When do you think you can help me out of my predicament?"

"Today, if I can. I'm going to write to Amador. How much can I offer him?"

"Whatever you think will work. I'm prepared to give up everything I have."

At Calle del Estado, each went in opposite directions.

Amador Molina, meanwhile, was sitting in his room when Edelmira's lovelorn suitor paid him a visit.

"Amador, I've come to speak with you," Ricardo Castaños announced.

"Well, buddy, here I am," answered Amador, shaking his hand. "What can I do for you?"

"You know that I'm in love with your sister."

"I had a hunch. Everybody's in love with somebody."

"But I sense she doesn't care very much for me."

"Good Lord! What more could she want?"

"What do you think?"

"What do I think? I think she's head over heels for you."

"Then why doesn't she say so?"

"Don't you know nothing about women? Straighten up. You're acting like a schoolboy! There ain't a woman alive who don't play games!"

"Then you think that she would marry me?"

"I swear to you, buddy, there ain't a woman alive who don't want a husband. All you gotta do is start flashing your shiny lil' badge and they'll start giggling."

"What about your mother, Amador. What would she think?"

"She'd be tickled pink, of course. There ain't a mother alive, rich or poor, who don't want a son-in-law for her girls."

"Can you speak to her for me?"

"Sure thing, brother," answered Amador, shaking Ricardo's hand.

"I'm not too swift at this sort of thing," replied the officer, "and I thought of you. 'Amador will know what to do,' I said to myself, and so, I dashed right over."

"You did the right thing. Leave it to me. I'll talk to my mother tonight."

A few moments later, each fellow went his way, both contented. The officer with the hope that he would marry the girl of his dreams. Amador with the hope that he would make up with his mother. Since the bombshell of his failed intrigue, Doña Bernarda had only acknowledged Amador's presence in order to berate him. His thoughts were adrift when he heard a knock at his chamber door. A servant delivered a message that Martín Rivas wished to meet him at Alameda to discuss a matter concerning the entire Molina family.

Amador wrote back to confirm the meeting. He wondered why Rivas wished to see him and sensed that he should wait until he met Martín before fulfilling his promise to Ricardo.

Slightly before the appointment, Amador wandered into the Oval at Alameda where Martín joined him moments later. Martín went straight to the point and offered Amador 200 pesos to convince Doña Bernarda to drop her threat.

"You say that Rafael offered my sister 6,000 pesos and my mother turned it down?" asked Amador in disbelief.

"Yes," answered Rivas.

"Well, I'll tell you, my mother is still furious at me about the letter. The thousand pesos they paid me wasn't worth the brunt I had to bear."

"Will another few hundred pesos satisfy you?"

"And what about Adelaida and her child?"

"8,000 pesos. Rafael can't give more than he has."

"Well, I'll see what I can do."

"When will you have an answer for me?"

"I don't know. Who knows what my mother will do?"

"As soon as you know, please write to me."

"Swell."

Amador returned home after this conversation and found his mother sewing with his sisters.

"Mama," he whispered in her ear, "Let's go to your room. I've got something to tell you."

"What now?" asked Doña Bernarda when they were alone in her bedchamber.

Amador began justifying the past and swearing that he acted in the best interest of the family.

"I didn't want to bring it up, until I had some news for you," he added.

"What kind o' news?"

"Good news, of course. I'm always thinking of the family. Are you still mad at me?"

"Depends on the news."

"Wouldn't you like to marry off one of your daughters?"

"What a question!"

"Do you like Ricardo?"

"Sure."

"He wants to marry Edelmira."

Doña Bernarda's face lit up with joy.

"Ricardo takes home a nice paycheck, and he's gonna climb the ranks."

"That's music to my ears!"

"Then you'll speak to Edelmira?"

"I'll speak to her tonight."

"You hafta be tough with her 'cause Ricardo says that she doesn't like him."

"She better not act dogged with me."

"That's right, 'cause a good man like Ricardo is hard to find."

"Just let her try to act snippety."

"There's one other thing."

"What?"

Amador relayed his recent conversation with Martín and said that he offered 7,000 pesos for Adelaida's child if Doña Bernarda would drop her accusation.

"I already know it won't pay to take him to court," said Doña Bernarda. "I asked a lawyer I know, a friend o' your father, and he told me that we'd be lucky if we gotta *a'lowance for pr'visions*."

"Besides, why gamble in court when we can get 7,000 pesos up front?"

Amador twice mentioned 7,000 pesos, instead of 8 because he planned to pocket an extra 1,000 pesos for himself.

"You'll be 7,000 pesos richer," he added, "and nobody will need to know why."

"Who gives a damn if they know why! The servant already knows."

"How do you know that?"

"She told me, and she probably blabbed to who knows how many others. The one who keeps the child knows and so must everybody else. Cursed fop! I hope he pays dearly for it."

"But it's better, Mama, if we take the money up front."

"Well, then go and take care o' it," piped the widow, returning to her sewing and cursing Rafael to damnation.

The next day Amador reported that his mother agreed not to file charges (based on advice from the lawyer who was a friend of her late husband) provided that Adelaida would receive 8,000 pesos. Amador, who was planning to skim 1,000 pesos for himself, was thoroughly dismayed to find that Martín had deposited the money under the name of San Luis in an investment house that would forward the monthly annuity to Adelaida.

Having fulfilled these obligations, Martín went to tell Rafael how he had settled the affair.

"But, don't think you're out of the woods," he cautioned, "until you're married."

"That's precisely what I was thinking," answered Rafael, "and that is why I asked my uncle to shorten the engagement. I hope to be married within the next two weeks."

XLI

Doña Bernarda was in no hurry to speak to her younger daughter about matrimony until she found adequate revenge for the outrage done to her elder daughter. Therefore, she left the topic of Ricardo Castaños for the following day and devoted her thoughts to devising a punishment for Rafael San Luis. Her reflections must have been fruitful because Doña Bernarda awoke with new serenity the next morning. When she called Edelmira, her voice lost the harshness with which she had addressed every member of her household since her visit to the home of Don Dámaso Encina.

Edelmira shivered at the sound of her name because she could not imagine anything pleasant coming from her mother, considering her dark mood of late.

"Sit here," Doña Bernarda said to her, pointing to a chair beside her. "Good luck is rappin' at your chamber door," she added after a brief silence.

Edelmira looked up at her mother with fainthearted curiosity.

"You saw what happened to your sister for actin' like a fool. It's partly my fault for lettin' those cursed fops in my house. But you've got better judgment, and that's why God's rewardin' you now."

Doña Bernarda took a break from her moral exhortation to light a cigarette, while her daughter held her breath, dreading what would come next.

"Ricardo," continued Doña Bernarda, "wants you to be his bride."

Edelmira turned pale, trembling in the chair.

"He's a good boy," declared her mother. "He earns a nice salary and he's gonna climb the ropes. We're poor, and when a catch like this swims by, we've gotta reel him in fast."

Doña Bernarda waited a few moments to allow her daughter to respond, but Edelmira hung her head in silence, staring at the carpet to fight back tears.

"What do you think, sweetie?"

"But Mama . . . " she stammered, lifting her eyes as though she were praying for divine intervention, "I don't love Ricardo."

"What? Nobody's askin' you to love him!" piped Doña Bernarda. "Where did you get the idea that love matters? You sure didn't hear it from me! Lookie here, my lil' princess, you ain't exactly the model o' grandeur. But, we'll keep our eyes open for a duke if you like. Now, don't tell me you're hidin' some popinjay too!"

"Not me, Mama!" cried the girl, frightened that Doña Bernarda might detect in her eyes the love that she felt for Martín.

"Well then, what more do you want? If every gal had your luck!"

"I don't want to get married, Mama."

"Sure, that's just swell. You can't live off your poor mama forever. Lovely daughters. One . . . well it's already out of the bag. . . . Blessed be the Lord! The late Molina was saved from seein' it. The Lord was good to take him away. And now this one don't wanna get married! She'd rather break her poor mama's back. You don't wanna be an ol' maid, do you, sweetie?"

Doña Bernarda concluded this tirade with a gloomy laugh that struck more terror in her daughter than any threat would have. Edelmira bowed her head in order to avoid the unbearable look in her mother's eye. Doña Bernarda lit another cigarette to calm her nerves and asked, "Well, what do you say?"

"I wasn't prepared for this," responded Edelmira, unable to hold back the tears.

"Who said you hafta get married tomorrow? Nobody's rushin' you. I'm just tellin' you what's good for you, and who knows better than your own mama?"

With these words Edelmira recognized that obstinate resistance would only heighten her mother's irritation to the point of exasperation, and she thought it was best to wait until her mother's rage subsided before arguing her case.

"All I'm asking, Mama," she said, "is for a month or so to think it over."

"You mean . . . string him along till he gets bored and changes his mind. You think that in a month's time I'll go soft on you. It ain't gonna happen. Like I said, you ain't gettin' married tomorrow, but you hafta answer him soon."

"But, Mama . . . "

"Don't '*But Mama*' me. You think I'm gonna let him go? Seems you don't know your own mama. Go tell it to the saints."

"I'll do whatever you say, Mama."

"That's what I wanna hear. Now you're talkin' like a good daughter."

"But I need a few months to prepare myself."

"One month is more than enough. End of discussion. So stop your fussin'. Be polite to him, but not snooty. Wear a happy face, and you'll live happily ever after."

Edelmira returned to her bedchamber after hearing this insufferable speech from her mother. She sat by the headboard and hugged her pillow, the confidante of her solitary love. With tears streaming down her face, Edelmira bade a tender adieu to the shapeless hopes, the melancholy joys, and the chaste aspirations of her secret devotion, which had been the only joyful reprieve from her dreary existence. With her dreams suddenly shattered, all she could do was cry her heart out into her pillow like a child.

Now that Doña Bernarda had secured the future of one daughter, she was prepared to avenge the ruin of the other, whom she began to regard as more sinned against than sinning. The sight of her beautiful grandson, whom she brought home to raise, did not quench her thirst for revenge. Quite the contrary. Doña Bernarda became obsessed with her covert plot to ruin the man who had ruined her daughter. She made friends with the servants of Don Fidel Elías so that she could stay on top of all the wedding preparations and spy on the happy bridegroom, who was so wrapped up in his own glory that he was oblivious to the widow's threat.

What is there to report on Leonor and Martín? Nothing much has happened between them. Wounded pride on one side and excessive delicacy on the other kept both parties at bay. They exchanged bashful looks and tripped over their words when expressing their feelings. They cautiously approached the flourishing path of hope, where they felt themselves apart from everyone else, hearing glorious music in the silence, sensing marvelous premonitions in the balmy air, and finding the whole of nature in perfect harmony with their feelings. And, yet, they were not at all happy.

Leonor watched the spectacular panorama of love develop before her very eyes and began to grow impatient with Martín's shyness. She was too proud to take the first step, and he was too reverent to lower his idol from her pedestal; and yet both were madly in love. Out of pure frustration, Leonor, falling back on her pride, swore to forget Martín; and Martín, failing to rise to the occasion, asked the heavens to efface her image from his mind and his love from his soul. However, a single glance made her forget her vow, and him, his prayer. Like butterflies drawn to a new light, they returned to the sweet warmth of their vital atmosphere at the risk of singeing their wings.

XLII

There was plenty of commotion in Don Fidel Elías's home now that both families had agreed to shorten the engagement.

Matilde's relatives were already sending their bridal gifts.

Descending to the ordinary details of life, Doña Francisca and her daughter were examining the patterns of the dresses in vogue. They paid frequent visits to the couturier to try on the wedding gown and other luxurious accessories, entrusting themselves to the ingeniousness of this artiste.

They argued intensely about the jewelry, opening and closing the velvet-lined jewel cases that came from a German jeweler on Calle Ahumada.

Visitors would arrive, and their conversations, which always began softly, would inevitably turn to the adornments, at which point their voices would crescendo as in the aria of Don Basilio. The wedding gifts would be displayed, one pattern would be praised over another, and the diamond cross (which every bride-to-be wears until the bridegroom becomes the heavier cross to bear) would be assessed by all.

Their guests would then leave, and before the family would finish putting everything away, others would arrive, and the whole ritual would begin anew.

And so passed the days.

For those who marry for love (unlike those who marry out of obedience or resignation), illusions can be likened to the sun shining gloriously on a clear spring day. The delicate petals of Matilde's illusions flourished under the tenderness of love and perfumed the breeze that seems to whisper divine promises to lovebirds everywhere. Thus, for Matilde, the past was a bad dream; the present, pure bliss; and, the future so bright that at times she had to look away from it to keep the light from blinding her eyes.

"Because you're not in love," she would say, holding Leonor's hands in sweet surrender, "you can't understand my happiness."

Leonor stared blankly as though she were lost in her own thoughts.

"When I'm away from Rafael, I'm at a loss for words. I can't even describe what I'm feeling. Oh, but what do you care about all of this!" she added, noting that Leonor was scarcely paying attention.

"Of course, I care," answered Leonor, smiling gently.

"You don't know what I'm going through."

"I know exactly what you're going through."

"Why, are you in love?"

The vivacity of Matilde's inquiry indicated that she was more woman than lover because her curiosity about her cousin's love-interest took precedence over her own.

Leonor denied it with equal vivacity, blushing, "Who, me? No, darling, don't be silly!"

"You're fibbing."

"Why?"

"Leonor, you've changed. You were never as dreamy as you've been lately. Tell me, don't be so secretive. Hmmm, let me guess. Which is it, Clemente or Emilio?"

Leonor turned her nose up and pouted. Matilde named dandy after dandy but received the same response until she blurted out, "Then it must be Martín."

"You must be joking!"

Leonor's cheeks turned crimson.

"And why not," replied Matilde. "Martín is interesting."

"You think so?" asked Leonor, putting on a nonchalant air.

"I think he is, and so what if he is poor?"

"Oh, that doesn't matter to me," exclaimed Leonor, lifting her head proudly.

"He has a noble heart."

"Who told you so?"

"You did."

Leonor dropped her eyes, pretending to have poked herself with a sewing needle.

"You've also told me that he is talented," continued Matilde. "Are you going to deny that too?"

"No, I won't."

"You'd better not because I remember it clearly."

"You're just singing his praises out of gratitude."

"Actually, I was just repeating what I've heard from you."

"The whole family is thankful to him."

"Including you."

"That's true."

"Besides, who else can it be since you've spoken about him more than any one else?"

Leonor had nothing to say in response.

"You know I have good reasons to be mad at you," said Matilde.

"Why?"

"Because you don't trust me, and I've always shared my secrets with you."

"What do you want me to say?"

"That you're in love with Martín. Can you deny that?"

"I've denied it to myself for a long time."

"At last—you admit it!"

"It's true. I can't stop thinking about him."

"I'm sure that he has been in love with you for a long time."

"Who told you so?"

"It's written all over his face."

Vanquishing her natural reserve, Leonor recounted in vivid detail every conversation that she shared with Martín, without omitting a single circumstance, not even her impression that he might have eyes for another woman.

"Oh, you're even jealous!"

"I'm not jealous, but if I were sure that he liked someone else, I would put him out of my mind completely."

"You mean that he has never dared to tell you how he feels?"

"Never."

"And neither have you?"

"I don't know what to do. At times I feel like telling him, but then I change my mind."

"Poor Martín! You should be more compassionate with him."

"You think so?"

"Let him know you're fond of him. What have you got to lose?"

"I'm telling you, he is very proud. Maybe pride is holding him back."

"Or modesty. You would know better than I would."

This observation set Leonor's thoughts in motion. After a few moments, Leonor looked at her watch. It was 2 o'clock in the afternoon.

Her curiosity satisfied, Matilde quickly resumed her favorite topic (Rafael) until Doña Francisca entered the room with the wedding gown in her arms. We shall leave the Elías women to admire the couturier's exquisite needlework in order to escort Leonor home.

Leanor bade the good ladies farewell, climbed into her father's lavish carriage, and ordered the driver to take her swiftly home.

When she stepped out of the carriage, she noticed a shabby-looking maidservant in the entrance hall bearing a letter for Martín. Assuming that the letter came from Rafael San Luis or another schoolmate, Leonor walked past the girl with little regard.

The entrance hall attendant delivered the letter to Martín in Don Dámaso's study. It stated the following:

Martín,

You're my only friend and trusted companion. My own family has forsaken me. I can't believe what is happening. My mother is pressuring me to marry Ricardo Castaños. I don't know how this all happened because I've never given him a thought. Please advise me, knowing that I will be eternally grateful if you would dry my tears with some words of wisdom.

Edelmira Molina

Martín read the letter twice and failed to notice each time that the simple sincerity of her phrases harbored timid expectations. He called the attendant to inquire, "Who delivered this letter?"

"Some maid who said she'd be back for an answer," he replied, with an almost inconspicuous smile that those of his class use to show their masters that they are fully aware of what is going on around them.

"Good, I'll give you the answer right away."

The attendant left the room, and Rivas wrote the following:

Edelmira,

I was truly surprised by your letter and deeply grateful for your trust in me. However, I'm hardly prepared to offer my opinion on a matter of this nature because I have no experience from which to draw advice.

You asked me to advise you without considering, perhaps, how extremely delicate the subject is. Before all, I must confess that my sincere friendship precludes me from being impartial. If you asked me to offer a prayer for your future, I would pray with all my heart and soul for your happiness, but you're asking me to guide you in a decision that could determine your fate, and I can't make that determination. Listen to your own heart, Edelmira, for no one is a better judge than oneself. Your heart will tell you what to do.

If, aside from this, my words have any power to comfort you, or if you think that I can be of some service, please don't hesitate to honor me with your trust and confidence.

Sincerely,
Martín Rivas

Martín sealed this letter and gave it to the attendant, charging him to deliver it to the maid who would come for it.

Thanks to Agustín's nonstop talking, Leonor was able to speak to Martín several times during the dinner conversation, which revolved around Matilde's wedding.

As he left the table, Agustín took his friend's arm and both accompanied Leonor to the salon, where she played the piano, while the two young men stood beside her.

"I was with Matilde today," said Leonor, resuming the dinner topic, "and she was walking on clouds."

"I can imagine, Señorita," remarked Martín.

"The French always say," added Agustín, "*l'amour fait rage et l'argent fait mariage;* but here loves makes for both *madness* and *marriage.*"

"I think she is the happiest girl in Santiago," said Leonor.

"Why don't you follow her lead, little sister," said Agustín. "You can be as happy as she is whenever you please. You've bewitched two fine gents, haven't you?"

Martín gazed at her and turned pale.

"Only two?" she laughed.

With these words, Martín's face turned from white to red.

"When I say two," said Agustín, "I'm referring to the gents who visit you most often, *ma belle.* We all know that you can take your pick among the wealthiest."

"What do I care about the money?"

"Would you choose a poor man, little sister?"

"Who knows . . . "

"You're not of this century then. I pity you."

"There are many things worth more than money," said Leonor.

"Serious error, *ma charmante.* Money is a mighty thing."

"Do you agree with Agustín?"

"I think that there are times when it is a necessity," said Martín.

"For instance?"

"For instance, when the lack of money prohibits a man from approaching the woman he loves."

"You have a poor opinion of women, Martín. Not all of us are dazzled by the glitter of gold."

"Not by gold itself, perhaps, but by the luxury it buys," said Agustín, who then wandered away.

"I speak of an obscure man with high aspirations," resolved Martín.

"If the man himself is worthy, he should find someone who understands him and appreciates him. You have little faith," she said, rising from the piano.

"Because I am as obscure as the man I offered as an example."

"Please note that as far as I'm concerned," said the girl, filled with emotion, "money is no virtue, and many other women would agree with me."

Leonor immediately withdrew upon speaking these words, perhaps out of fear of what Martín might say next. With his heart pounding in his ears, he watched her disappear, scarcely able to believe what he had just heard.

At this very moment a messenger from the home of Don Fidel Elías entered, asking for Leonor. He came to deliver this frantic note:

Come at once. I need you. The pain is driving me mad. Please hurry. Matilde

To understand the events that prompted this letter, we should return to the home of Don Fidel Elías, where we last left Matilde with her mother.

XLIII

Rafael, Don Fidel Elías, and Don Pedro San Luis arrived shortly after Leonor had left Doña Francisca and Matilde to admire the wedding gown.

While their elders conversed among themselves, Rafael walked Matilde to the piano, where she ran her fingers dreamily across the keyboard. The happy couple talked about themselves, and only about themselves, as though they were the center of God's great universe. They repeated what they had already sworn to each other a thousand times until they drifted into silent adoration of one another, with their joyous hearts beating as one.

When they least expected it, stormy clouds rolled across the clear blue sky of their happy future. A maidservant entered the salon and approached the piano.

"My lady," she whispered into Matilde's ear, "a woman wishes to speak with you."

"With me?" said the girl, awakening from her golden trance.

"Yes, my lady."

"Who is it? Ask her what she wants."

The servant departed.

"Who would want to speak with me?" asked Matilde, gazing into Rafael's enamored eyes.

Moments later, the maidservant returned to announce, "She says her name is Doña Bernarda Cordero de Molina."

It was if a thunderbolt had struck Rafael lifeless.

Matilde repeated the unfamiliar name to herself and said, "I'm sorry, but I don't know anyone by that name."

Then she looked at Rafael, who seemed to be petrified in his chair. The consequences of this visit flashed before his eyes and the shock strangled his voice. He recognized that he had to act fast in order to prevent the havoc that he envisioned. Pretending to be annoyed by the inopportune interruption, he said to Matilde, "Tell her to come back another day."

Disturbed by her fiancé's apparent distress, Matilde asked him lovingly, "What is the matter with you?"

"Who? Me? Nothing, nothing at all."

"Ask her what she wants," Matilde said, turning to the servant.

"She says that she must speak with my lady."

The girl looked indecisively into Rafael's eyes, who urged her to "tell the woman to come back another day."

"Tell her that I'm busy and to come back later," Matilde repeated to the maidservant, who then took leave.

"Maybe it's some poor widow," said the bride-to-be, smiling.

"Maybe," her fiancé muttered between clenched teeth.

Rafael strained to hear what was happening outside the door and fidgeted as though he were sitting on pins and needles. He counted every second that it would take the servant to deliver Matilde's message, Doña Bernarda to voice her objections, and the servant or the feisty widow herself to enter the room. It was five minutes of mortal anguish for Rafael and mysterious silence for Matilde, who searched his expression for the romantic bliss that she had perceived just moments ago.

Finally, the door swung open and the frightened eyes of Rafael watched Doña Bernarda make a grand entrance with curtseys and bows that were so low as to be grotesque.

Matilde and the rest of the onlookers watched with morbid curiosity. The widow's queer costume was nothing short of appalling. It must be noted that Doña Bernarda had made an earnest attempt to pass herself off as a lady of high standing. Over the garish housedress that she had recently worn on the 18th of September hung a colorful, frumpish shawl, purchased secondhand from a servant of an elderly woman who had worn it in better days. From a mile away, she reeked of the would-be-aristocrat; however, Doña

Bernarda thought it was the perfect outfit to show the present company that she was "a classy broad." She exaggerated her ladylike gestures so that they would note her good upbringing and would not think this was the first time that she found herself in such elite circles.

"Who in the world is she?" Matilde quietly asked Rafael, who stood up, scowling at Doña Bernarda.

"Which o' *yous* is Doña Francisca Encina de Elías?" she asked.

"I am, Señora."

"A pleasure to meet you, Señora. This gentleman must be your hubby, no? And she must be your lil' girl. Ain't she the spittin' image! Oh, how are you, Don Rafael? I know this young man o' course 'cause we used to be as thick as thieves. Oh, I hope you don't mind if I rest my weary feet. The years, you know, Franny, take their toll like everythin' else on this good earth. How's the rest o' the family?"

"Fine, thank you," said Doña Francisca, looking around at the others, all of whom were equally baffled by this bizarre apparition.

"Is she mad?" Matilde asked Rafael. Then she turned to him and saw such anguish in his expression that an inexplicable panic seized her heart.

Doña Bernarda, seeing that no one was speaking, feared that if she remained silent they would think her ill-bred.

"Well, now, Señora," she quickly resumed, "lemme tell you why I'm here askin' to have a word with your lil' girl. You see, I ain't the type to wash my dirty clothes in public, 'cause in polite circles we keep our privates private. But they sent me away, which wasn't very nice 'sidering I ain't no spring chicken and I barely made it here as it is, sweatin' like a mule. I wasn't 'bout to go back home without seein' nobody. Like a dog with its tail between its legs! Like I came beggin' for somethin'! Thanks be to the Lord, we've got enough to eat. So I was tellin' myself: it's now or never 'cause they're gonna get married any day now, and that's why I'm here."

As soon as Doña Bernarda paused to catch a breath, Doña Francisca jumped in to ask, "And to what honor do I owe this visit?"

"The honor's all mine! Really, I was just 'bout to say so, but I was tryin' to catch my breath. They tell me your lil' girl's gonna get married. Just look at her. She's your spittin' image!"

"Yes, Señora," answered Doña Francisca.

"And to this gentleman, ain't that so?' replied Doña Bernarda, pointing at Rafael, who would have liked the earth to swallow him whole in order to end his mortification. He said to Doña Bernarda indignantly, "Señora, what is it that you presume to do?"

"I was just gonna tell Franny, if you hadn't *innerrupted.*"

"You should not permit this woman to continue ranting madness," Rafael said to Doña Francisca.

"Madness, did you say?" bellowed Doña Bernarda. "Well, now, let's just see if it's madness. Lookie here, Señora," she turned to Doña Francisca, "tell the servant to fetch the girl who's waitin' outside with a baby. Just you wait and see if I'm rantin' madness."

"But, Señora," exclaimed Don Fidel, assuming an authoritative position, "what is the meaning of all this?"

"Well, it's as clear as day," replied Doña Bernarda. "You're gonna marry your lil' girl off to a man who ain't got no honor. Just you wait and see."

Then the widow jumped to her feet and went to the door, hollering, "Peta, Peta, come and bring the baby!"

Everyone looked at one another in disbelief, except Rafael, who leaned against the piano with clenched fists, enraged.

Doña Bernarda's maidservant entered carrying a baby boy in her arms.

"So, here you go. This is the child," said Doña Bernarda. "Now, let's hear Don Rafael say it ain't his son. And let's hear him say that he never fooled a poor, decent girl."

"But, Señora," said Don Fidel.

"So, here's the proof," declared Doña Bernarda. "Madness, eh? So, here's the proof. Go ahead, deny he's your boy. Go ahead, say you ain't never promised to marry his poor mama."

A dead silence followed these words. Everyone riveted their eyes upon San Luis, who trembled with anger as he crossed the room, shouting, "I've given your daughter everything I had to secure the child's future! What more do you want from me?"

Matilde collapsed into a sofa, covering her face with her hands, while everyone else stood dumbfounded.

"Lookie here, Señora," appealed Doña Bernarda. "I ask you if you think it's right to disgrace a gal just 'cause she's poor. What would you say if, God forbid, they did somethin' like that to your lil' girl? It could happen to anybody. Even if she's poor, she's got her honor, and he promised her, but never kept his word."

"There is nothing that we can do about this, Señora," said Don Fidel, while Don Pedro San Luis approached his nephew and said, "I think you should leave. I'll take it from here."

Rafael snatched his hat and left the room, looking back at Matilde who tried to stifle her sobs. Then Don Pedro San Luis approached Doña Bernarda and said to her quietly, "Señora, I will look after this child's future, as well your daughter's. Please be so kind as to leave and come to my house tonight. You will set the conditions."

It is difficult to say whether Doña Bernarda found Don Pedro's promises less rewarding than the revenge she had so scrupulously planned over the course of many days, or whether her proletariat pride was bent on humiliating the aristocrat for the way that he and those of his class offered money in order to censure her voice. She glanced at him, lowered her eyes, and then bawled, "I ain't askin' you for nothin', sir! I came here to see if these kind ladies are gonna let a poor girl, who ain't done them no harm, to go on livin' in shame with this lil' angel o' God growin' up a bastard. Don Rafael's got an *ogligation* to marry my girl once he cools down and sees that he ain't been actin' like a gentleman."

"But, Madame," interjected Don Fidel, "it seems to me that Rafael is free to do as he feels and you ought to settle with him."

"I wasn't askin' your 'pinion, thank you kindly," replied Doña Bernarda with her voice growing more threatening. "All I what I wanna know is," she added, looking at Matilde and her mother, "if these ladies are gonna let my girl live in shame. They've got the luxury o' money and honor, unlike us poor gals who ain't got nothin' if we ain't got honor. Who can live with somethin' like that on her *concents*," she continued after a prolonged sob. "If he gets away with it, he'll just do it again. God is just and the good are good. What more can I say? I ask *yous* to listen to your *concents*. Would you marry a man who ruined a poor, innocent girl and left his own flesh-n-blood like a Godforsaken orphan?"

Doña Bernarda's sermon ended in sobs, as she raised her eyes and hands to the heavens, and blew her noise like a bugle, repeating her favorite lines.

"Señora," said Doña Francisca whose romantic imagination was moved to empathy, "you see, how it is not possible for us to decide upon a matter of such importance right now. We will see Rafael when he has calmed down tomorrow, or the day after, and then we will decide."

"Well, you ladies need some time to think it over," said Doña Bernarda, "'specially the lil' bride-to-be who thought she caught herself a free man. I won't ask what's gonna happen to my poor lil' girl who's been deceived. That's the luck o' the poor, but thanks be to God that we're honest folks, and we ain't chasin' after Rafael's money. My ol' man, Señor Molina, was a business man and didn't owe nobody nothin'."

"All will be taken care of soon," said Doña Francisca.

"Very well, then, Señorita, I trust you. I figured, it's better to come to you directly than to take it to the judge. Why drag your names through the mud? It ain't your fault, after all. 'If they're ladies,' I said to myself, 'they'll wanna keep this under wraps and act like Christians toward the poor.' It's better to have friends than enemies. That's for sure, and when a pretty, rich gal loses her man, a hundred others will come runnin'. But it ain't so easy for a poor gal once she's been dumped."

"Very well, Señora, we'll try to settle this matter."

Doña Bernarda, undone by wailing, began to restate her argument, taking better care to formulate the threat that she was prepared "to take it to the judge"; after which, she made her grand exit, leaving her captive audience in the greatest consternation.

XLIV

Matilde broke down sobbing in her mother's arms.

"Come now," said Don Fidel, "I hope no one is taking that old crow seriously. How are we supposed to restore her daughter's honor? What say you, Don Pedro, my friend?"

Don Pedro replied, "I'll go and speak to the woman and try to appease her."

"That's a good idea. Thank you. What a crazy old bird! Not even Don Quixote would have tried to repair her daughters' impropriety, so how could we! She should have watched over them instead of coming here to complain about the seduction when it's too late! As if they were pure as the driven snow anyway . . . "

"Honey, for Christ's sake!" exclaimed Doña Francisca, scandalized by her husband's tasteless comments in front of Matilde.

"What's the matter? I know what I'm saying," retorted Don Fidel, who was irritated by any objection posed by his wife. "That old crow is stark raving mad, and who knows what else! As if I didn't know the wicked ways of this world!"

"But, honey," repeated Doña Francisca, who used a persuasive look and gesture to implore her husband to respect their daughter's anguish.

Poor was Don Fidel's judgment, for he was so preoccupied with the lease on El Roble that he did not realize that he was making his daughter feel worse. Presuming that she was merely worried about losing her bridegroom, he gently stroked her shoulder, saying,

"Don't fret, my little chickadee. No one is going to take your husband away from you."

Don Pedro San Luis seized this interruption in the marital dispute to reassure the family that he would cooperate to the best of his ability, and then he bade them all farewell.

As soon as his compadre quit the room, Don Fidel expressed what he was really thinking.

"Pull yourselves together in front of Don Pedro. I've got everything under control."

"And what are we supposed to do?" asked Doña Francisca, indignantly.

"What are you supposed to do? Nothing at all. Be nice to him and simply insist, as I will, that we're paying no mind to that crazy old bird. And shower him with the kindest respects because I'll be in a pickle if I lose that lease!"

"I am in no position to be thinking of leases," argued Doña Francisca, pulling her daughter away and leaving Don Fidel to his ambitious deliberations.

Matilde threw herself in her mother's arms the moment they found themselves alone. They had withdrawn to the girl's bedchamber where they could speak in private.

"Oh, Mama, who would have believed it!"

A long silence followed this painstricken cry of disillusionment. Doña Francisca dried her daughter's tears and covered her with tender caresses, saying, "Calm down, my sweet angel, for Heaven's sake, calm down. Everything will be just fine."

"Just fine! How can you say that? Do you and Papa really think I'm grieving the loss of a husband? As if I didn't love him! As if I could go on loving the man who made me believe that I was the only woman in his life, when he only came back to me to free himself of an obligation to someone else, who he was tired of! Oh, I don't care about a husband; it's my love I'm grieving! Did you see me in such despair when I first lost Rafael? I suffered courageously because I thought him worthy of a sacrifice. They kept me away from him, but they couldn't make me stop loving him. But now, everything has changed.... "

Her voice was interrupted by sobs, and she clasped her hands to her aching heart.

"Don't cry, my sweet angel, please don't cry," were the only words that Doña Francisca could muster, knowing that there was nothing she could say to soothe her daughter's pain.

"Even if my love could survive this," said Matilde, gradually regaining her composure in her mother's warm embrace, "and even if I could forget what I've seen and heard today, could I ever live peacefully beside him? Wouldn't it be selfish of me? How could I ever be happy, knowing that a poor girl was living in shame and misery because someone deceived her? Wasn't I deceived by him as well believing that he had never loved anyone but me? Oh, Mama, this is torture. The more I think about it, the worse it is. I don't love him. I abhor him! Would I ever know for sure that he chose me over the mother of his son for money, and not for love? Would I ever really know whether he wanted me or my father's riches?"

The last of these cruel conjectures seemed to twist the blade of disillusionment into her very heart, for she stopped speaking, looked around with frightened eyes, and began to moan. Doña Francisca searched in vain for the gentlest of words to soothe her daughter, whom she rocked in her arms and begged not to surrender to such thoughts. But Matilde did not hear or feel her mother's support. Swept away by the doubts that she had just voiced, she recalled all the blissful days, eternal vows, and sweet glances, and as she walked through the field of happy memories, she cut the stem of each flower one by one with the blade of disillusionment.

Over the next several hours Matilde would begin to settle down, but her imagination would soon stoke the coals of her conscience, causing her grief to rise again. Misery, like happiness, must always find itself a confidante; and so, Matilde, seeing that her mother could never understand what she was feeling, scribbled the frantic note that Leonor received after planting a seed of hope in Martín's soul.

XLV

Half an hour after receiving Matilde's note, Leonor arrived at her cousin's home accompanied by Don Dámaso.

Leonor dashed to Matilde's room, while Don Dámaso waited in the foyer, where he was joined by his sister and brother-in-law as soon as they learned of his arrival.

The two girls embraced each other tightly without uttering a word until Leonor ended the silence by asking, "What is the matter with you? Your letter frightened me out of my wits."

Matilde tried to steady her trembling voice as she narrated the ghastly scene that Doña Bernarda had caused. Leonor commiserated with her cousin, but secretly wondered whether Martín was in love with Doña Bernarda's other daughter. "After all," she thought, "birds of a feather . . . "

"What would you do in my place?"

"Me? Truly, Matilde, I'm completely stunned."

"But put yourself in my place. What would you do?"

Dodging the question, Leonor asked, "Would you ever be able to forgive him?"

"I could forgive him," she replied, "but I couldn't love him anymore."

"It's very difficult to give advice on such matters," replied Leonor.

"I'm not asking for advice. I want to know what you would do in my place."

"I would scorn him."

"You should know that Papa will stop at nothing to keep us together."

"Then I would break it off myself," said Leonor, with her characteristic resolution.

"That's just what I will do then. What's the worst thing that could happen? There is nothing that Papa can do to make me to suffer more than I've already suffered."

They remained in a prolonged silence until Matilde added, "But how shall I do it? Papa will forbid me to say anything about it to him or his uncle."

"Write to him, then," said Leonor.

"You're right. I have to end it before Papa gets involved."

Matilde sat down and wrote her lover's name. A teardrop landed in the crease of her stationery and she asked Leonor meekly, "What shall I tell him?"

"Take your time to think it over."

"No, no. I've already made up my mind, and there is no turning back."

"I think a few words will suffice."

Matilde began to write furiously and after a few minutes, she straightened herself up and read aloud:

It's over between us. It's pointless to have to justify a resolution that is so powerfully motivated by my conscience. I'm writing to avoid any explanation that I'm not disposed to hear or read.

Matilde Elías

"That will do it," said Leonor.

Matilde called a maidservant and charged her to bring the letter to its destination without allowing anyone at home to notice her departure. Then she sat beside her cousin, saying, "I needed you at my side because you give me strength. Aren't you proud of my courage?"

Then she burst into sobs, hiding her face in her hands.

"We can still call the servant back, if you want. It's not too late," said Leonor.

"Yes, it's too late because everything is over!"

Don Dámaso heard all the outrageous details from his sister, who was constantly interrupted by Don Fidel, who seemed to think he could better explain the ordeal.

"I've been saying it all along," exclaimed Don Dámaso, who had never forgotten the fierce grip of Rafael's hands around his throat, "that boy is bad news."

"Come now, who hasn't tried something like it? We were all boys once."

"Jesus Christ, Fidel, what principles!" exclaimed his better-half.

"Look, sweetheart, women don't know the ways of the world like we do."

"But we know morality."

"Are you insinuating that being philosophical makes me immoral? I'm wiser to the world than you are. Even your own brother can tell you that."

Don Dámaso, who was a master-weaver, as we say in Chile, not only in matters of Politics, but in all matters great and small, agreed, "It's true that many boys make similar mistakes. I cannot deny it."

"Ha! What did I tell you?" Don Fidel taunted his wife. "When I tell you that I'm wise to the world, you ought to show your husband some respect. Rafael committed a wee, little peccadillo, and everyone will forget all about it."

"I doubt that Matilde will soon forget it," answered Doña Francisca.

"Of course she'll forget. If I know women like I know women, it will all blow over in a couple of days."

"We will see about that," said Doña Francisca.

"Indeed, we will. I am never wrong."

While Don Fidel looked for a box of matches to light his cigar, Don Dámaso approached his sister, saying, "I'm telling you that the boy is bad news."

"And I'm telling you that Matilde will not forgive him," maintained Doña Francisca.

"It's a blessing in disguise. Your girl deserves better. If I were in your position, I would oppose the marriage right now."

"But you should support me on this issue," replied Doña Francisca, to which her brother promised, "Oh, you can count on me."

Don Fidel returned, and shortly thereafter Don Dámaso went home with his daughter.

That evening Leonor told Martín what she had learned at Don Fidel's house.

"Poor Matilde is miserable," she said to him, "and I'm beginning to believe that you're wise to practice your theory of indifference."

"Unfortunately, one cannot always master his own heart," said Rivas. "Therefore, the theory is still a theory which has yet to be proven possible."

"Oh, so you've already changed your mind. Señorita Edelmira must have influenced you."

"She is not the one who changed my mind," replied Martín.

Satisfied by his sincerity, Leonor walked away, leaving him to wonder, "Will she ever feel love?"

Martín went to visit Rafael, only to learn from Doña Clara that had he left an hour ago.

"Please tell him that I'll return in the morning," Martín said, before bidding the lady goodnight.

Meanwhile, Don Fidel went to visit Don Pedro San Luis to advise him to expedite the wedding so that they "could get it over with and put the past behind them."

"Well, I believe that we should wait and see what they want to do. But, first I must settle the matter with the old widow, lest she cause a scandal."

"I'll see to it that the children get together tomorrow morning," insisted Don Fidel, who perceived a postponement of the wedding as a delay on the lease.

Just then Rafael walked into the room, disheveled and forlorn. The way he dragged his feet and slumped his listless body into an armchair rendered Don Pedro and Don Fidel speechless.

Don Fidel ended the awkward silence with these words, "Don Pedro and I were just saying that the best thing to do is speed up the wedding. I speak for my daughter's happiness. What say you?"

"It is useless, Señor," answered the young man in a hollow voice.

"Useless, how?"

Rafael took a letter from his pocket and passed it to Don Fidel, saying, "Read it yourself, and you will see."

Don Fidel read Matilde's letter, then folded it, exclaiming,

"Bah, childishness! You know she doesn't mean it. Come with me and you'll see how different she is."

"No sir, I will never go back," Rafael said solemnly.

"What a notion! You see, Don Pedro, my friend, what lovers are made of? Glass. They crack under the slightest pressure."

Don Pedro took the letter from Don Fidel to judge for himself. He concluded, "This letter is very serious."

"If you knew girls like I know girls, Don Pedro, my friend," replied Don Fidel, "you would know that they're never serious. They just want to hear us begging! Rafael should come home with me and see for himself."

"I will never go back, sir," repeated San Luis. "This letter, which seems to have been written without your consent, clearly states that it is over."

"It can't be. Trust me. How can you pay heed to a rash girl! I'm sure that she is already sorry for having written it."

"I appreciate your concern," said Rafael, "but I urge you to respect Matilde's wishes. If she ever regretted having written it, she would say so because she knows that I would throw myself at her feet."

"All I want," said Don Fidel, concerned with the lease, "is for you to remember where I stand and how much I long to have you as my son-in-law. If by some disgrace this should not come to pass, I hope that you both will bear witness to my efforts and my good will."

"Oh, we have no complaints," said Don Pedro.

"Formality is the only way to conduct business," declared Don Fidel, "and that is why when I make a deal, there is nothing on earth to keep me from upholding my end."

"I never neglect mine either," said Don Pedro.

Don Fidel understood Don Pedro's reply as a formal promise to renew the lease and dismissed everything else as secondary. He returned home, intending to coerce Matilde into retracting her letter so that he could formalize the lease more readily. However, despite her tears, Matilde had prepared herself to defy the imperious voice of her father, who realized that it would be impossible, but for an act of violence, to see the marriage through since it was broken in such an abrupt and freakish fashion.

Don Fidel took some comfort in knowing that the lease was secured in any case, and went to visit Don Dámaso. On his way there, he congratulated himself on an idea which suddenly struck him.

"To obtain the lease and marry Matilde off to Agustín would be a stroke of genius."

He walked into the salon and called Don Dámaso aside to set his plan into motion.

"Forget what I said in front of my wife today," he said. "I simply said those things in order to get my way on a larger issue. For the sake of my daughter's happiness, I made a compromise with Don Pedro San Luis against my own better judgment. But now everything has changed."

"How?" asked Don Dámaso.

Don Fidel relayed the contents of his daughter's letter and the majestic display of her resolution.

"Magnificent!" rejoiced Don Dámaso.

"All along I wanted her to be Agustín's wife," said Don Fidel, "but it's too early to broach this touchy subject right now."

"Since she broke it off herself, it's a different story."

"I couldn't agree with you more, though we ought to let a few days pass."

"Oh, of course."

When Don Fidel went to bed that night, he gave thanks to Doña Bernarda for what he had considered in the morning to be a catastrophic visitation.

XLVI

Martín, unable to fall asleep that night, anxiously awaited the break of day. Distressed by Rafael's predicament and Leonor's comments, he tossed and turned throughout the night until, completely exhausted, he nodded off shortly before sunrise. In spite of his weariness, he awoke at seven o'clock in the morning and studied, as he generally did, for two hours.

He went to visit Rafael at nine o'clock, but found the house locked. He knocked on the door leading to Doña Clara's quarters. When the lady, who had just returned from church, opened the door for Martín, he asked, "Has Rafael gone out so early?"

"Haven't you heard?" asked the lady, wringing her hands with worry. "Rafael has left us!"

"Where did he go?"

"To the Franciscan Recoleta," said the lady, who in spite of her apprehension, showed an uncanny air of satisfaction.

"To Recoleta?" repeated Martín. "When?"

"At the crack of dawn."

"What made him do such a thing?"

"Then you haven't heard?"

"I heard what happened at Don Fidel Elías's house yesterday."

"After that Rafael received a letter from the girl, telling him to forget about her, and that's all it took. Poor boy! You should've seen him last night, crying like a baby. What tears. Dear Lord, it nearly broke my heart."

"Poor Rafael," said Rivas.

"The boy told me everything last night. Dear Jesus! The life of youngsters today! Part of me is relieved that he went to the monastery, for he must reconcile himself with God. How can anyone expect happiness, living like that?"

The lady's simple piety appealed to Martín's noble sentiments; however, he was moved to defend his friend.

"You know how deeply he regrets his behavior. He knows that he was wrong."

"Yes, my poor boy," said the lady, whose eyes filled with tears.

"I'll go and visit him today," said Martín.

"Please don't bother because he told me that he won't receive any visitors. Oh, I almost forgot something. He asked me to give you this letter. I have it right here."

The lady handed Rivas a sealed letter, which he took home to read after bidding her farewell. At the home of Don Dámaso, the servant handed him another letter, saying with a knowing smirk, "The same maid delivered it and she'll be back later for your answer."

Rivas went upstairs to his room to read Rafael's letter, which stated:

Dear Martín:

When you come to see me tomorrow, my aunt will tell you what I've decided to do. In the quiet of the night, I've reflected on this terrible day. I have lost her! There are no words to describe my pain. Do you remember when we studied the life of Martín Luther and I called him a coward because he joined a religious order for fear of God when his friend was struck dead at his side by a bolt of lightning? It was my vain insolence speaking. You, who defended him at the time, will understand the upheaval in my soul. A thunderbolt parted the heavens and struck me senseless. Through the core of my heart! Burning to the roots every last godsend in my life. Only once before, when my father died in my arms, did I feel my soul turn to ice. It's the realization of being completely alone in this world, of knowing that the love that kept my heart alive has perished, of feeling that there is nothing and no one on earth to console me!

Martín, her letter was three lines long, and yet, those three lines poured through me like lava, devastating everything in its path. In those few words, she spared me none of her terrifying scorn. There was no trace of yesterday. No trace of any hope of forgiveness that every God-loving soul allows for human frailty. My blessed angel despises me, Martín. She abhors me. I used to believe that I could bear any fate, but it was only because I thought that there was no fate worse than death, and I never imagined that this could happen to me.

I've spent hours wondering what I should do, and one thought keeps haunting me: it's God's punishment! After all, I had no right to aspire to happiness when I've brought misery to an innocent, frail person. I'll never be disrespectful or morally lax again, and I'll fall on my knees before God's mercy, if the sins of the world are forgiven. Although I've heard sermons on this from many a pulpit, my miserable soul only listened to the truth half-heartedly during my carefree days, and now I'm suffering the consequences, which are more than I can bear.

I don't plan to spend the rest of my life in penitence, atoning in a cloister. I'm going to search for peace and to strengthen myself with models of virtue so that I can forget her and mourn her as though she had ceased to exist. Who knows what I'll do after time has healed my aching wounds with scars of melancholy. Without her, I don't know what else there is to live for.

Please don't think that I've forgotten about Adelaida. I can't blame her or her mother for my disgrace. I forgive them and pray that they do the same for me. I'm very aware that I could make amends and restore her honor in the eyes of the world; but, Martín, you know, that I don't love her. It would be a monstrous union that would inevitably end in suicide, which would only bring more disgrace. I could give her my life, but I could never make her happy. Though, I will give much more thought to all of this.

In my retreat from society, I will see no one. I'll write to you when I can, and my aunt will forward my correspondence. A priest, an old friend of the family, has taken me in as his spiritual disciple.

Goodbye for now,
Rafael San Luis

Martín put his head in his hands and surrendered himself to the sad meditations inspired by this letter until he was called downstairs to dinner. When he crossed the patio, he opened the second letter, but only had time to read the signature; it was from Edelmira Molina.

Before revealing its contents, we must step back to when Edelmira sent her first letter to Martín, which we have already read.

After Edelmira had reluctantly agreed to marry Ricardo Castaños, she destroyed the letters that she had secretly dreamed of sending to Martín. Her mother's violent demands awoke the girl from her fantasy of living happily ever after with her romantic hero. Although Edelmira initially recognized the folly of her secret passion, her incessant wishful thinking began to crystallize into actual hope. In this state of *Crystallization*—to make use of Stendhal's picturesque theory of love—Edelmira thought that to oblige her to marry anyone else was to brutally sever her hope before she had the chance to make it a reality. In protest against this act of violence, she found the courage to write to the man of her dreams. Although this act may be considered risqué for a respectably young lady, it was not altogether inappropriate considering Edelmira's social upbringing. Although a woman's instinct is the same regardless of her class, the would-be-aristocrat leads a coarser lifestyle that chips away at the modesty that makes a woman in love tremble like a frightened dove. The language of seduction is more vulgar among the would-be's and more apt to make a favorable impression on a young girl through sheer force of habit. Through the revelry of their carousals, the would-be's learns about the baser side of human nature long before their highborn sisters who live sheltered lives in what we call *good families.* Thus, Edelmira, even though she was more cultivated than most of her peers, found nothing improper about probing Martín's feelings. It may be true, on the other hand, that every woman finds a way—some more subtle than others, depending on her class—to overcome her shyness in order to find out whether the man she loves happens to feel the same way.

Edelmira's first letter could be read as an innocent plea for sympathy. When she read Martín's reply, she dearly wanted to believe that his friendly words of advice veiled a deeper attachment, but found no other tone than that of a dear friend who might be inclined to lend a hand if she decided to defy her mother.

Encouraged by his offer, she wrote the second letter that we saw Martín opening on his way to dinner.

There was little conversation at the table that evening because Don Dámaso wished to respect Martín's friendship to San Luis.

After dinner, Agustín lit a fine cigar and offered one to Martín, asking, "And what's become of Rafael?"

"He ran away to Recoleta early this morning."

"What a romantic! He has my deepest sympathies," exclaimed Agustín.

"He wrote me a letter. He is desperate," added Martín.

"I can't see how he could possibly be desperate," interrupted Leonor, who was working on an embroidery, "when he has a lover on every corner."

"There are loves and there are lovers. We mustn't confuse them, *ma cherie.*"

"Oh, excuse me," replied Leonor.

"It's the difference between *amour* and *passion,*" observed the dandy.

"I find that there isn't a man alive who is capable of true love," said Leonor, peering at Rivas, who silently protested with his eyes, while Agustín begged to differ.

"*Au contraire, ma toute belle. Pas mal de gens* have lived their whole lives *follement amoureux.* And we mustn't forget Abelard, whose tomb I visited at Père Lachaise in Paris."

"Why are you so quiet?" Leonor asked Martín. "You must be thinking in Spanish what he's thinking in French."

"I think you judge men too harshly," answered Martín.

"But doesn't the example of your friend San Luis justify my opinion?" asked the girl.

"But there are exceptions," replied Martín.

"Of course there are exceptions," said Agustín, "I just gave you Abelard at Père Lachaise, and the list goes on."

"The list goes on?" Leonor said to her brother, while casting her eyes upon Martín. "Go ahead and start naming them."

"*Fie-toi à moi,* little sister," said the dandy, "I know plenty of them. Take Martín *par exemple.*"

"Really? Did you know you were on the list?" she asked him, smiling, while Rivas blushed.

"Señorita," he replied, "at the risk of sounding immodest, yes, I think I am one of the exceptions."

"You think or you know?"

"I know that I am," answered Martín, gazing so ardently at the girl that she was obliged to look away at the embroidery.

"Are you in love, Martín?" asked Agustín. "Let's hear all about it, my dear chap."

"You're going to force him to lie!" cautioned Leonor, controlling a stiff smile as she embroidered a few stitches.

"Why, Señorita?" asked Rivas in the same lighthearted manner.

"You wouldn't want to commit yourself to the one you love," replied Leonor.

"Unfortunately, I will never be able to make such a commitment. She is so above me that she can't hear my voice," he stated, just when Agustín walked toward the patio to toss out his cigar.

"If you speak clearly she will hear you, even from a distance," Leonor answered with a gentle smile she could barely hide.

"In that case," replied the young man, "if you ask me what Agustín has just asked me, I will tell you the truth."

Leonor looked down at the embroidery again, and Agustín returned to his seat.

A few moments later, Martín left for Don Dámaso's study, having long forgotten Edelmira's letter that he had tucked into his pocket.

XLVII

Leonor's reply inspired Martín's imagination to wander with the inexhaustible voracity of someone who believes that his wildest dreams may come true after all. The story of the little milkmaid who builds a castle in the clouds to amuse herself while walking to the marketplace can best describe the luster of such high hopes, which are always in danger of crashing to the ground like the pitcher of milk. Fortunately for Martín there was nothing in his path on which to stumble. The expression in Leonor's eyes and the nervous energy in her words encouraged his joyous reverie.

Only after half an hour did Martín remember to read Edelmira's second letter, which stated the following:

My Dear Friend:

Thank you for your kind words. Your letter was a great comfort. I'm so thankful that I have someone to turn to because my family has turned against me. I tried to recall what I wrote to you because I couldn't understand why you refused to advise me in my despair, and then I realized that I was holding something back from you. There are two reasons why I find that marriage repulsive. First, I have no feelings for Ricardo. Second, it's difficult for me to say this, especially to you, but my heart is not at liberty, and I could never be happy without the man I love with all my soul. Now that you know this, Martín, please advise me because time is passing quickly and with every moment my sorrow grows along with my aversion to marrying the wrong man.

Forgive me for troubling you, but you're my only friend and confidante, and I'll never forget your kindness.
Edelmira Molina

"Poor girl," Rivas said to himself, as he took a piece of paper to answer her letter. From his reply, one can sense his elation following his recent conversation with Leonor.

My Dear Friend:
How can you be unhappy when you're in love? If you seek strength in your love, you'll find the courage to resist. At first, I thought I should limit myself to offering my friendship, rather than my advice, so as not to interfere with a decision that would affect your whole life, but I didn't know that you loved someone else 'with all your soul,' and that you were asking whether to obey your mother and betray your love by giving your hand to someone you'd never give your heart to. As for me, I believe true love is so precious that we must defend it at all costs, and to betray it in the name of obedience is mere weakness. Anyone who takes this lightly will have nothing but painful regrets later in life. Why not throw yourself at your mother's mercy and speak your heart? She was once young and she will understand. If you're afraid, then send for me. I'm sure that I will be able to soften her heart when I plead your case out of sincere friendship. After all, what more could a mother want than the happiness of her children?
On the other hand, Edelmira, a love, which I think you're capable of feeling, should find its strength in its innocence and abandon its secrecy. A mother's heart is a sanctuary where one can keep a relic until it's ready for the eyes of the world. So you must trust in her and not spend your tears on a secret passion that should be the pride of a noble soul like yours. Or trust in me, if you feel that I can help you find your way to happiness, as ardently as I desire.
You apologized for troubling me, but I insist that I'm the one who seeks your confidence in the name of our friendship.
Forever yours,
Martín Rivas

Later that evening Martín's letter found its way to Edelmira's hands by way of the maidservant who was entrusted to be the messenger. Martín's brief but eloquent theories of love set Edelmira's passion ablaze. His heart was a treasure and she longed to possess it. The sentimental shapes of her romantic desire grew so distorted that she managed to persuade herself that Rivas was veiling a secret love for her behind his friendly words of advice.

Edelmira did not respond for a few days, for she was lulled by the sweet delusion that her dreams would come true if she wanted them badly enough.

During this period, there was no other intimate episode between Leonor and Martín that would allow either party to make a long-awaited, decisive move. To distract himself, Martín put his mind to Don Dámaso's business, which progressively became his responsibility entirely. He also studied religiously for his final examinations because, like most Chilean students, he had neglected his coursework to enjoy the festivities around the 18th. And yet, Martín still found time, as lovers always do, to spill his feelings in long, gushing letters to Rafael San Luis. In them, he would relentlessly repeat the perpetual theme of love in a variety of ways, painting the same feeling in a wide spectrum of colors.

But days passed without any response from Rafael.

Ten days later, the servant brought him a letter with a knowing smirk that suggested that the author was Edelmira. The letter (which we have purged of a few distracting grammatical errors) read as follows:

Your letter has consoled me, but as much as I appreciate your advice, I could never tell my mother what I've told you. Yes, I'm afraid she'll take it badly because she expects us to obey her, plain and simple—especially given what has happened to Adelaida.

You tell me to seek strength in my love, and it's true that it gives me courage to suffer anything before marrying against my will, but that's the extent of my strength. I wouldn't dare tell my mother that I love someone else. The reason for this may be—something I didn't mention in my last letter—that my love is, and may always be, unrequited. I haven't written to you in a while because I didn't want to trouble you and didn't dare admit what I'm now confessing. But now that you know my heart as well as I, please continue to guide me with your advice. It's my sole source of comfort and support in my affliction as I dread the day that I must answer my mother.

Rivas commiserated with Edelmira's circumstances because they were not unlike his own.

Edelmira, I never knew that the fate of unrequited love could befall someone as beautiful and noblehearted as you, whose love would fill any man with pride. After your confession, what can I say? I wouldn't ask you to name the man who is blind to his happiness because he is blind to your love. I'm sure that he is a worthy man, capable of understanding you and honoring the treasure you've blessed him with. I don't think that I'm mistaken. And so, the best advice that I can give you is: keep your love pure and it will keep you pure. Heaven blesses those who harbor beautiful sentiments without straying from the path of virtue.

I still urge you to confide in your mother because the day that you must decide is nearing. It's better to prepare them now than to invite disaster by surprising them later. I can't emphasize enough how willing I am to help you find your way to happiness. You may count on me. I am at your service.

Edelmira sighed deeply upon reading this letter. She had exhausted her resources and had arrived at the point where she would have to name the man she loved. As we said before, deep down she was hoping that one of Martín's phrases or some unforeseen incident (which lovers, who have blind faith in chance, always anticipate) would invite her to reveal to Martín the whole secret, which she had only half confessed. However, neither his reply nor chance allowed for such an opportunity. Now what? A deep sigh was the only answer to this sad question. These letters, which she read repeatedly, shed heavenly light on Martín's soul. What a mirage for a young woman in love! It was as if she had caught a glimpse of Paradise, without being able to pluck one of its flowers. Edelmira watched their vivid blossoms swaying in the fragrant breezes, inebriating her senses, until the question "Now what?" suddenly appeared like an archangel with a flaming sword to expel her from the gates of Heaven. She could not decide what to do and trusted time to make the decision for her.

A circumstance favored this indecision. Ricardo Castaños had asked Doña Bernarda to postpone the wedding until he was promoted to Captain at the end of November. They planned the wedding for mid-December, which seemed like a distant future to Edelmira.

Edelmira shared this good news with Martín, who congratulated her, but insisted, to no avail, that she advise her mother if and why she would object to the marriage.

To Edelmira's surprise, the distant future arrived in no time. One fine day, Ricardo announced that his promotion would be finalized within four to six days. He made this announcement on the 29th of November. Therefore, there were only a few days left to prepare for the wedding, which was set for the 15th of December. This opened the wounds of Edelmira's agonizing struggle between her love for her mother and her aversion to the young Castaños, who thought that with three braids on his sleeve he offered his reluctant sweetheart an irresistible empire. Edelmira recognized that her trust in time had been misspent and that it was necessary to make a drastic move, lest she give her hand to the wrong man and live unhappily ever after.

XLVIII

Although he was not exactly happy, Rivas managed to keep his spirits up and distract himself with hard work and study. At the beginning of December, he was pleased to announce to his family the happy results of his examinations. Martín was free until the new year, but told his mother that he could not afford to visit her during his vacation as he had planned.

What really kept Martín in Santiago was the fear that his absence would lessen his chances of being loved by Leonor, who occasionally insinuated that there was, indeed, room for such a possibility.

We have watched Leonor slowly learn to accept the notion of loving a man who occupied a social position far beneath her usual suitors, who were growing more persistent each day. Yet, she felt somewhat disconcerted by his timidity toward her when he seemed to display such serenity and determination in all other facets of life. Hence came a reserve, unnatural to her character, and with it came the decision not to take another step forward until she had irrefutable proof of his love. Perplexed as to why he had declined numerous invitations to speak his heart, Leonor shared her concerns with Matilde. Leonor had been her cousin's confidante in times of bliss and sorrow, and now it was Matilde's turn to reciprocate. Although she was still hurting inside, Matilde wished to repay Martín for his kindness.

The whole family admired the courage with which Matilde recovered from the vicious blow that had ended her happiness so abruptly. Something she had said to Leonor demonstrated the integrity that no one had expected from the meek and timid girl who was, until now, vexed by the slightest tension. Matilde said, "If I had one ounce of respect left for Rafael, nothing would console me. But I'm not in torment over his deception, which I can forgive. I'm grieving because my love for him has died."

In essence, she was mourning her lost love, while pardoning the one who had destroyed it.

"Martín condemns Rafael's conduct," she would say to Leonor at other times. "He is an honest man. If he ever tells you that he loves you, you can believe him over anyone else."

Preparations were being made in the Encina household to vacation in the country during the summer. It had been agreed that Matilde would accompany her cousin when the family stayed at Don Dámaso's hacienda near the coast, which is frequented by many Santiagoans during the swimming season.

In joyous anticipation of the trip, Martín wrote the following to San Luis in a long letter:

I'm going to help Don Dámaso, but there will also be time for me to spend with her. Perhaps we can go places together, and it wouldn't matter where as long as she is there. And if she grows bored and acts on some childish whim like she did on our ride to Campo de Marte—maybe there will be a chance to tell her that I'm in love with her. All of this makes my head spin and my heart race. I've tried not to be so excited, but my will is lost amidst the craze of my passion.

Destiny, nevertheless, had something quite different in store for Martín.

On the eve of her wedding, Edelmira gathered all of her courage to implore her mother's mercy, in the name of God, not to oblige her to marry someone she did not love.

"Where's your head!" roared Doña Bernarda, raising her hands to the heavens. "If every gal had your luck! What a disgrace! We're ready to marry her off to a Captain, but no, he ain't good enough for the lil' princess! No sireee! She won't settle for nothin' but the Chief! Like we're s'posed to make him a widower!"

"But, Mama, I'll never be happy with that man," agonized the girl.

"Oh, how would you know that? Are you a fortune teller? You think you know better than your own mama? If you don't love him now, you'll learn to love him later when he's your hubby. Like I'm gonna roam the streets lookin' for your soulmate! Like I'm gonna carry you on my back your whole life! Give an ol' lady a rest! I didn't love the late Molina when we first got married. Love comes later, but I ain't gonna argue with you. What I say goes!"

Edelmira sought Amador's support, but he refused to intercede on her behalf, saying, "Mother knows what's best, and there ain't a saint in heaven who can change her mind. So stop your whining. What more do you want than a Captain?"

Her family's inflexibility made her turn to the only person she could count on.

"If all others abandon me," Edelmira thought, as she lifted a pen, "Martín will rescue me."

Edelmira, seized by panic, envisioned herself walking to the altar with Ricardo, under the imperious gaze of Doña Bernarda, bidding farewell to her inner peace and her chaste love for Martín. This vision had been her nightmare for two months; now it was becoming a terrifying reality. Under these impressions, she wrote to Martín, telling him about her futile supplications to her mother and brother. She voiced her desperation with the persuasive power of truth, reminding him of his promise to assist her. She asked him to help her execute a plan that she conceived as the only viable solution. The plan was to run away from home and take refuge with her aunt in Renca, who had sheltered Adelaida when she was forced to hide her condition from Doña Bernarda.

My aunt has a good deal of influence over my mother. Mama denies her nothing because she has a nice estate in Renca and helps us, especially when it comes to money. I would've asked my aunt to come to Santiago, but she never likes to visit because she was widowed here and misses her husband terribly. Besides, my mother would have talked her out of it. But, when she sees the drastic measures I'm taking, she'll defend me. Since she is much younger than my mother and was raised with us as if we were sisters, she loves us very much, and I'm sure that she'll welcome us.

Edelmira declared her resolution irrevocable and asked Martín to send a carriage to meet her at seven o'clock the following morning at the Church of Santa Ana, where she would await him under the pretext that she was attending confession.

Martín received this letter the day after he had written to San Luis, sharing his plans to travel with Don Dámaso's family to the seaside. After imploring Edelmira to think carefully about her decision, he replied:

If you insist, tomorrow the carriage will be there at the time and place you have indicated. Permit me, though, to accompany you to your aunt's home, so as not to leave you at the mercy of the driver. You can leave the church whenever you feel ready, and you will find me there. Be careful. And please allow me the honor and pleasure of escorting you.

Edelmira kissed the letter when she found herself alone that evening. She carefully guarded her intentions and waited until Adelaida and everyone in the house was fast asleep before packing her personal belongings. She carefully packed all of her letters from Rivas, wrapping these treasures with a ribbon. Then, she laid down to think about her destiny and waited until it was time to go to church the next morning.

XLIX

Edelmira and her maidservant left the house at half-past six in the morning and arrived shortly thereafter at Santa Ana.

In the church square there was a horse-drawn postchaise; its reins were held by a postilion who was mounted on one of two Cuyo horses, a very popular breed.

The postilion, while cracking his whip from time to time, crooned a popular tune in a monotonous, nasal voice—sotto voce.

Edelmira felt her body tremble when she spotted the carriage she would make her escape in, and, without thinking, she hesitated to inspect it. Edelmira and her maid seemed to rouse the postilion's sense of chivalry because he interrupted his tune to say, "What brings these morning stars out today? Perhaps I can be of assistance."

"*'Sistance wit what?*" reacted the servant.

Edelmira snapped out of her momentary daze and hastened toward the church door.

"Goodbye," said the postilion, watching them scurry. "Off they go, leaving me in darkness. So hot-headed and pretty-eyed!"

"Ain't he a fresh one," replied the servant, while Edelmira, frightened by their exchange, hurried away.

They were a few paces away from the stone steps of the church when Rivas appeared; he must have been watching Edelmira's arrival from some nearby place. She became nervous and pale to see him so close. He pretended to be surprised to see her in order to prevent any suspicion on the part of the servant.

"What are you doing here, Señorita, at this hour?"

Edelmira stammered and slowly backed away from the maid, who seemed not to be displeased by the flirtatious of the postilion, for she kept turning around to look at him.

"You see, I'm here on time," Martín told Edelmira softly. "Are you sure about this?"

"Very much so," she answered with a look that seemed to ignore the fear and grief that had caused her face to wither.

"And will you permit me to accompany you?"

"Why would you trouble yourself for me?"

"It's no trouble at all. As I've told you in my letter, I refuse to leave you at the mercy of the driver who is a stranger to us both. Furthermore," added Rivas, "you've extended me the privilege of your friendship, which I'm honored to reciprocate. Accompanying you is far from a bother. Indeed, it is a great pleasure."

Edelmira was enraptured by the fine manners of this young man upon whom she had placed all of her attentions of late and was relieved not to be left alone with the coachman whose inordinate informality startled her.

"Don't you trust me?" asked Rivas.

"Oh, more than anyone else."

"Then I'll wait for you inside the coach. As you see, I'll stay perfectly out of sight there."

"I'll be ready as soon as I can."

The servant did not notice her mistress's passage into the church because she was thoroughly engaged in a splendid exchange of glances with the saucy coachman. When she saw Martín depart, she reluctantly came looking for Edelmira, who pointed to a pew and said to her, "Wait for me here. I'm going to look for the confessor, and I'll be back soon."

Martín, meanwhile, waited inside the postchaise.

Edelmira kneeled on a mat in front of the altar and fervently prayed to Heaven for protection and shelter. Then, after praying for courage to take the next move, she stood up, folded the mat, and proceeded to the confession booth, where she could keep an eye on her maidservant, who was passing the time inspecting the saints on the altars and thinking about absolutely nothing, which is typical of our lowest tier of Society. Edelmira took advantage of this distraction to sneak out of the confessional and leave the church.

The devout, who were beginning to arrive, wearing cloaks and skirts similar to Edelmira's, facilitated her escape, as they came and went throughout the sanctuary, which many of them regarded as their home.

Edelmira made her way to the church square with her heart racing and her body trembling. To avoid the suspicion of any bystander, she decided it was best to act confident and walk directly to the postchaise. The door opened, Edelmira climbed in, and Rivas told the coachman, "Onward."

At the snap of the whip, the horses began to trot away.

Edelmira's servant, tired of looking at the altars, turned her eyes to the layman who was lighting some candles and compared him to the postilion, whom she deemed a finer looking fellow.

The postilion, who was quick to win the servant's favor, possessed the impudence natural to our commoners and, therefore, made lewd insinuations about the couple he was driving. He improvised a variation on a popular love song, cracking his whip:

I won't ever leave you behind,
Thoughts of you never leave my mind,
I'll take you with me in my soul,
If you nuzzle with me in my cubbyhole!

Edelmira was hiding her face in her hands and struggling to control the sobs rising in her throat. Martín waited until the sobbing subsided and only spoke when he saw that his travel companion seemed calmer.

"It's not too late to turn back. Just say so, Edelmira, and I'll do whatever you please."

"Don't think that I have any regrets," answered the girl, drying her tears. "I'm only sorry that I'm being forced to run away from home."

"If you trust your aunt," replied Martín, "I think everything will turn out the way you want it."

"It's far from what I want, but it's better than getting married."

"The rest may follow."

"Who knows!"

This exclamation was followed by a sigh of grief.

"You must be passionately in love," said Rivas, who was interested in Edelmira's situation given that, as we have said, he found it similar to his own.

Edelmira blushed and lowered her eyes when answering, "Didn't I say so in my letter?"

"And hopelessly?" asked Martín.

"Hopelessly," repeated the girl, with another heavy sigh.

At this moment the coachman's voice could clearly be heard singing the refrain:

I'll take you with me in my soul,
If you nuzzle with me in my cubbyhole.
In my cubbyhole, yippee yah yeah . . .

And his voice mingled with those of the fruit vendors who were coming to the city to sell their scrumptious wild strawberries from Renca.

"Do you remember hearing this song?"

"Your brother sang it the night we met," answered Martín, "but Amador didn't spoil it with the last verse."

"You have a good memory."

"Why, have you forgotten that night?"

"Oh, no, I remember it vividly. Most of all, I remember speaking with you."

"Perhaps because he was there," Martín said, smiling.

"Who?"

"You know, the one we've spoken about."

"Oh, no. I didn't care for anyone then."

In spite of the innocence of her response, there was so much sorrow in Edelmira's voice that Rivas asked, "Do you regret telling me about him?"

"Of course not!"

"I pose the question only because I want to help you."

"What more could you do for me? You've gone far out of your way already."

"Perhaps I could do more if you told me his name."

"No, nay, never!"

"Do you think I'm asking out of mere curiosity?"

"No, no, but . . . "

"Well, I certainly won't insist. But, please, believe me that I wasn't asking out of curiosity. I only wanted to help you."

"I believe you, Martín. Forgive me for not answering, but I can't right now," said Edelmira. Then she added in a softer apologetic tone, "I'll tell you later, if that's fine with you."

"Tell me only if you think that it will be useful for me to know."

"Fine."

"But we can speak of him without naming him," said Martín, assuming that there could be no other conversation more amenable to Edelmira than this.

"Oh, yes," she said with a smile.

Then they chatted cheerfully, and Edelmira seemed to forget her predicament as she told her story simply and eloquently without explaining how her love began because she herself was unsure. Her recollections were music to Martín's ears because they played upon his own experience. Thus, they arrived at the home of her aunt, who, after hearing Edelmira's account, lavished Martín with attention.

"If you don't mind," she said, "we'd love for you to stay and eat with us."

Rivas gladly accepted and joined Edelmira and her aunt for brunch. In the dishes that they served him; in the large basket of wild strawberries that filled the whole room with a delectable aroma; in the furniture that decorated the house; in all that surrounded him; the young man found a rustic charm that made him feel at home. In this frame of mind, he accepted the widow's offer to take the horse for a ride, which Martín did for a couple of hours. Sometimes he would gallop, other times he would stop to admire a pasture or a field that reminded him of Leonor, and he would forget the rest of the world, imagining himself holding her hands and confessing his love.

Edelmira accompanied him to the postchaise when it came time for him to return to Santiago.

"While you were riding, I did what I promised I would," she

said to him, handing him a letter. "Here's the name that you asked me for on the way here."

Rivas took the letter and said goodbye, without noticing her nervousness.

"Don't open it until you're far from here," she said as the coach began to pull away.

Rivas waved to her again and departed.

The horseback ride through the countryside and the satisfaction of having assisted Edelmira put Martín in a very good mood. Reclining in the coach, he dreamed about the trip he would take to the coast with Don Dámaso's family and only thought to read Edelmira's note when he was far away.

It stated the following:

Martín,

You know the whole story of my love, except his name, but you'll understand why I couldn't tell you it during our journey once you know that his name begins this letter.

Edelmira Molina

"I'm the one!" exclaimed Rivas, astonished. Then, after reading the letter for the second time, he remarked with deeply felt compassion, "Poor Edelmira!"

For the rest of the journey he could think of nothing but this shocking revelation, and he arrived in Santiago sorry for having been, though involuntarily, the cause of Edelmira's grave adversity. He stepped out of the coach at Plaza de Armas and walked to Don Dámaso Encina's stately mansion. On his way upstairs, he heard Agustín's voice calling him.

"Man," he said excitedly, "where have you been?"

"I've been away from Santiago. Why are you asking?" answered Rivas uneasily.

Agustín closed the doors to his suite and turned to Martín with a mysterious tone, whispering, "You won't believe your ears when I tell you what happened."

L

To understand what Agustín proceeded to tell Rivas, we must relate what transpired during his absence.

The maidservant who accompanied Edelmira to Santa Ana early that morning was busy comparing the layman who was lighting the church candles to the flirtatious postilion who had flattered either Edelmira or herself. The servant was inclined to believe that it was she who had captured the postilion's eye, and as we have said, she preferred him over the layman who was lighting the candles. However, he soon departed and she had no one else to make comparisons with, and so, she occupied herself by counting the altars and the candles on top of them, and at the end of three-quarters of an hour, realizing that she had not said her prayers, she recited a couple of *Hail Mary's* and a few dozen *Our Father's.*

After an hour, she began to think that Edelmira's sins were not so small since they took so long to confess, and when she grew bored of wondering what they might be, she stopped thinking altogether and fell fast asleep. A church elder awoke her half an hour later to ask if she had missed the Gospel of the Mass.

The maidservant promptly replied, "Ain't seen nothin' come by here."

The elder departed, saying, "God bless you," and the maidservant yawned a few times.

Tired of waiting, she went from confessional to confessional, and then from pew to pew, peeking at the devout faces under each veil. Unable to find Edelmira, she went out to the church square, where her mistress was nowhere to be found, and sadly noted the absence of the friendly postilion. Then she hurried back into the church, looking around at the worshipers who thought she was nosy, and ran back to the plaza feeling distraught. The first thing one encounters in any square in Santiago is a uniform, and so she found a policeman who was blowing a harrowing whistle at a passersby.

"What time is it?" she asked the policeman.

"'Round ten, I reckon."

"Oh Lord, ten o'clock!" cried the servant, who then started to run home.

It was fifteen minutes after ten o'clock when she arrived at home, where Doña Bernarda impatiently awaited breakfast.

"Where's Edelmira?" the widow asked.

"She ain't back yet?"

They searched the house for Edelmira and then gathered to discuss her possible whereabouts. Countless suppositions and an hour later, they sat down to eat. Then they waited another two hours without the slightest suspicion that she might have run away from home. Doña Bernarda summoned the maidservant, who, when obliged to account for their trip to church, appeared fidgety when omitting the encounter between Edelmira and Martín. Her nervousness awoke Amador's vague suspicions, which he relayed to his mother, who in turn threatened violence if she did not unearth the secret of her daughter's absence.

"These filthy brutes are rotten to the core," Doña Bernarda declared, "and that's how you gotta treat them."

The maid was summoned before the family tribunal once again and soon found herself tangled in Amador's webs. The threats proved successful: half an hour later, the maid had accounted for every step of the morning's excursion.

"Mother," said Amador, when he was alone with Doña Bernarda, "I wouldn't be surprised if she ran off with Martín."

"God save her!" the widow bellowed, clenching her fists, "for I'll send her straight to *'Crection.*"

By that she meant the House of Correction for Women.

At this moment Ricardo Castaños arrived, and when he heard what had transpired, he made a suggestion that was unanimously agreed upon: that they go directly to Don Dámaso's home. When Amador and Ricardo arrived there at half-past three in the afternoon, they discovered that Martín had left the house before seven o'clock in the morning. The timing was suspicious. The two fellows looked at each other.

"Shall we come back later?" asked the Captain.

"We should tell the ol' man what's going on. If Martín ain't mixed up in all this," Amador said, "then what's he doing strolling the churchyard so early in the morning?" Then to play on Ricardo's jealousy, he added, "And what a coincidence that he happens to bump into Edelmira at the same time, eh?"

"Let's go," Ricardo resolved, as if they were united against a common enemy.

"Step aside," answered Amador, who embraced the opportunity to harass Martín in retaliation for having meddled in Adelaida's affairs.

Don Dámaso Encina was in his study reading a newspaper article by the Opposition. Amador and the Captain greeted him cordially, and Doña Bernarda's son began to explain the reason for their visit.

"I don't believe that Martín is capable of such an act," said Don Dámaso, when Amador concluded his tale.

"Señor, you don't know him like I know him," replied Amador. "He acts like he couldn't hurt a fly, but when you least expect it—wham!"

Don Dámaso called his son to see whether he knew of anything, but Agustín said, "*C'est une indignité,* and I don't believe a word of it."

"Then why did Martín leave so early?" asked Amador.

"Can't a man take a walk *de bonne heure* without trying to snatch up some girl?" answered Agustín who seized this occasion to ridicule the fellow who, not so long ago, had bullied him into a mock wedding.

"We're not joking around here," Ricardo Castaños retorted.

"I say what I think," replied Agustín, "and if you're sure that Martín has run off with the girl, you better start looking for her somewhere else."

Don Dámaso interposed his authority and declared that if

Martín had any hand in her disappearance that justice would be served for the honor of the household. This said, Amador and the official departed.

"Papa, they're just after money," said Agustín.

"Whatever they're after," answered Don Dámaso, "the fact is that there is some reason to suspect Martín, and if there is any truth to the matter, I will not permit a young man who sets such a bad example to live in my house."

Leaving his father feeling self-satisfied for taking a stand, Agustín went to tell his sister. "You won't believe your ears!"

"What is it?"

"They've come to accuse Martín of eloping with Edelmira Molina, my would-be ex-sister-in-law."

Leonor dropped the book that she was reading, and jumped to her feet as white as lace. Agustín repeated all that he had just learned.

"And what do you think about all of this?" Leonor asked him anxiously.

"It doesn't take a long stretch of the imagination," responded Agustín, who, as we have seen already, believed that there was some affection between Edelmira and Martín.

Leonor felt like bursting into tears, but managed to restrain herself.

"But Martín has always denied that he was involved with that . . . that *girl,*" she said contemptuously emphasizing the word we italicized.

"What do you expect, *ma belle?* In this cold world everyone's got a little secret to keep himself warm."

"That is unpardonable hypocrisy," exclaimed Leonor, scarcely able to control her anger.

"Hypocrisy, little sister, call it what you will. But, a man is a man after all."

"Why deny the way he feels?"

"Why? *La belle affaire!* Because some truths are better left unsaid, *ma cherie.*"

Leonor fell back onto the sofa.

"I see," he added, "that you could be gentler with poor Martín, who has been so good to all of us. Go easy on him, little sister. Isn't a woman's heart all-embracing, like they always say?"

"And what should I say?"

"I don't know, but I'm surprised to see that you're taking this so *sérieusement.*"

"You're mistaken, Agustín," replied the girl, with convincing serenity. "I couldn't care less about any of this. I was just worried about what will happen to him. In spite of all he has done for us, as you said, Papa and Mama won't be lenient with him."

"Oh, now you're talking like a good girl! I was going to punish you by smoking, but I've pardoned you."

And Agustín left the room, lighting a fat cigar as he returned to his quarters. Rivas arrived shortly thereafter, and Agustín called him aside (as we observed in the previous chapter).

"You won't believe your ears," he had said, after mysteriously closing both chamber doors.

"Let's hear it," said Rivas, sitting down.

"Amador and Edelmira's fiancé came looking for you."

"Really?" asked Martín, quickly changing color.

"They told Papa that you ran away with the girl."

"Scoundrels," cursed Rivas between his teeth.

"That's exactly what I said. I must confess that I found it quite amusing. Be assured that I defended you with sword and shield. All you have to do now is rid my father of any doubt."

"What for?" asked Martín coldly.

Agustín looked at him aghast. "Well," he said, "you must admit *c'est un peu fort.*"

"I don't see why."

"You don't see why? Good grief! The truth is never enough, you must convince Papa of your innocence."

"I fear that would be difficult."

"Difficult?"

"What Amador says is partially true."

"True? You ran off with Edelmira!"

"I chaperoned her."

"Where?

"To Renca."

Agustín stood up, put on his hat, and saluted Rivas, saying, "I applaud your talent. Look, if I had done that with Adelaida, no one would have laughed at me! You're a brave man, dear chap. I tip my hat to you; you're a master."

"Why?" asked Martín, laughing at the comic airs of his friend.

"Why! It seems you plucked yourself a pretty posy. How modest you are!"

"All I did was escort her."

"Clara or Dara . . . what's in a name?"

"You don't understand," replied Martín.

"I understand all too well, Casanova."

Rivas reconstructed the course of events without mentioning that Edelmira was enamored of him. Agustín lit his cigar, which had gone out, and remarked, "Well, now that changes everything. In other words, you sacrificed yourself in the name of friendship."

"I don't see what the sacrifice is."

"Anyone can get the wrong idea, even girls who think themselves *insouciant.* Just think, even Leonor was fuming."

"Oh?" said Rivas, disturbed, "She knows about it too?"

"Everything, and she thinks what I thought, although I tried to excuse you."

They were presently called to dinner.

"Are you going to deny everything to Papa?"

"I have committed no crime to have to deny my actions."

"You're a free man," Agustín said, opening the door. "I'm merely offering you my humble opinion."

They proceeded to the dining room. Agustín worried for his friend, who walked confidently although his heart beat wildly; Martín feared nothing but Leonor's scorn. When they entered, the family was already seated around the table.

LI

Complete silence reigned over the table when the two young men sat down to eat. Don Dámaso tasted the stew with an affected air of solemnity, and Doña Engracia cut a bite-sized morsel of beef for Diamela. Leonor stared out one of the windows, adorned with tapestry drapes, under which hung another curtain of white lace. Martín sought in vain to make eye contact and sensed her disapproval by the way she held her head up with singular haughtiness. Nevertheless, this silence was too awkward to endure for very long, and, naturally, the one with the weakest character ended it.

Don Dámaso gradually lightened up and decided to address Martín more warmly, given that no one else broke the silence that was bothering him.

"Have you been out today?"

"Yes, sir," answered Martín.

No other question occurred to Don Dámaso, and the awkward stillness returned. However, Agustín, who had trouble keeping quiet for any length of time, took his father's lead and said, "There's no place to picnic around here like there is in Paris."

Then the fop began to rave about Lake Enghien, Saint-Cloud Park, and various other parks around Paris. Since the others at the table were not inclined to interrupt him, he continued rambling through most of the meal, tossing in Gallicisms and Frenchisms to add touches of local color.

"Over there, they know how to live it up," he exclaimed zestfully, before concluding, "but over here, *les environs* are so drab in Santiago. No parks, no castles, no nothing."

The meal ended without Leonor seeming to notice Martín's presence at the table. Afterward, Doña Engracia said to her husband, "I hope, dearest, that you will speak to Martín because this cannot continue."

"There's plenty of time. I will speak to him tonight," answered Don Dámaso, who, being very mindful of his digestion, used it as the excuse to avoid broaching the unpleasant subject of Edelmira.

"Fine, but, don't forget to do it. I will not stand for any scandal under my roof," insisted Doña Engracia, petting Diamela as if to make her a witness to her decency. The little dog growled in agreement, and they withdrew from the antechamber through which they had passed. Behind their parents came Agustín and Leonor. Rivas was the last to leave the dining room and the first to retire to his bedchamber.

"You know there is some truth about Martín's affair," Agustín said to Leonor when they found themselves alone.

"Said who?" asked the girl, who was aching for Martín to clear his name.

"Martín said so himself."

"Oh my! He didn't dare to deny it!" exclaimed Leonor with a furious look, which seemed to speak of vengeance.

"But he was acting out of friendship."

"Sure he was," she said sarcastically.

"Just think, the old woman was forcing the poor girl to marry against her will."

"And Martín, merely out of friendship, as you say, appointed himself her knight-errant, is that so? That's a pitiful excuse from the long lost age of Don Quixote."

"Damn!" exclaimed Agustín, who had inherited his father's facility to change his mind at any given moment. "You know, you've got me thinking. Maybe you're right."

"You mean you believed him!" added Leonor, unable to conceal her indignation. "You have an uncanny ability to fall for anything. Let's see, what would *you* have done in his place. You would've admitted it because it was a very serious offense. A girl has honor whether she is rich or poor."

"Everything that you're telling me seems as true as the Gospels, *ma belle.* I'm so gullible. Martín baited the hook and I swallowed it."

"Hook, line, and sinker!"

Agustín departed, muttering to himself, and Leonor retired to her suite. Unwilling to admit that she was furious, she entertained herself by trying on a hat that she bought for the country. As she looked in the mirror, two hot tears trickled down her flushed cheeks.

Don Dámaso observed that Martín did not attend the salon that evening, and so, on the insistence of his wife, he sent for his lodger and spoke to him privately in the antechamber. Judging from the looks on their faces and the way that Don Dámaso struggled to start the conversation, one would have thought that the host was the accused. After waiting patiently while Don Dámaso sought a thousand ways to disguise his agitation, Martín decided to break the ice.

"Sir, I have spoken with Agustín," he said, "and I know from him what accusation they have brought against me."

"Oh, so you already know. Well, man, then I'm relieved. Imagine, two blokes show up on my doorstep, claiming you-know-what about you-know-who, and I, of course, didn't believe a damn word they said, but here the lady of the house . . . "

"Before you continue, sir," Martín saved his host from having to defend himself, "I should advise you that their accusation was not completely unfounded."

"What did you say?"

"I said, that their accusation was not completely unfounded. There is some truth to it, although my accusers have misconstrued the larger picture."

"I am perplexed."

Martín told him the same story that he had told Agustín before dinner.

"If it were up to me," replied Don Dámaso, "you know that I would look the other way, but you can see that I have a family here, and the lady of the house is very strict and easily scandalized, unlike me, especially when it comes to . . . "

"Sir, I appreciate your indulgence," answered Martín. "However, my conscience is clear so there is no need for pardon. From what little you've said, I understand that the lady is upset and given that I'm greatly indebted to you for your hospitality, I will certainly not be the one to upset the tranquillity of your family. I understand what I must do. Tomorrow I will take leave so that the good lady may regain her serenity."

"Man, don't say that!" exclaimed Don Dámaso. "You must understand my embarrassment. The lady will say that it's not true, and then . . ."

"I have never given you any reason to doubt my veracity," said the young man with a presence that commanded respect.

"Of course not, and nobody doubts you . . . furthermore . . . well, you know how my wife is . . . "

Martín remained firm while Don Dámaso entangled himself in his own excuses, without saying anything conclusive.

"If he leaves, I'll miss him awfully," he thought, as Martín walked into the salon where the usual tertulia was in session.

Leonor was speaking with Matilde, who frequented her uncle's house since calling off her engagement. Rivas walked straight toward them with an adamant look of resolution, which was remarkable for an encounter with Leonor. His gaze was as confident as his gait. Leonor grew faint at the sight of his determination, but looked at him with glacial indifference, which did not succeed in intimidating him. As he walked away from Don Dámaso, Martín had sworn to himself, "I don't know what I'll do if she doesn't believe me, but I must speak to her no matter what she thinks."

With this conviction in mind, he sat next to Leonor casually so that no one would conceive his behavior as premeditated. Leonor turned her cheek toward her cousin with an insulting pretense that Martín ignored.

"Señorita," he said unwaveringly, "I wish to speak with you."

"With me!" Leonor exclaimed in a voice that betrayed her restlessness. "Didn't you already speak with my father?" she added, expressing a majestic arrogance that would have intimated him under any other circumstance.

"For the very reason I have spoken to him, I hope that you will kindly permit me to speak with you."

"Really! Your tone of voice is frightening me," she said, pretending to be filled with as much indifference as disdain.

"Perhaps I'm nervous, forgive me. What has happened to me is so consequential for my future that I'm beside myself."

"What has happened to you?" asked Leonor with a smile that challenged the young man's solemnity.

"You know what has happened, Señorita."

"Oh, your affair with Señorita Edelmira? I could hardly believe it."

"Agustín must have told you my explanation."

"Yes, Agustín mentioned something about a service you wished to provide the young lady. A pitiful excuse that my brother obviously invented."

"Señorita, that which you call an excuse is the simple truth."

"Really? Forgive me. I assumed he was trying to make me laugh."

"Do you believe that there is no man capable of such a service?"

"Well, whatever I used to think must be wrong because now I see that there is such a man, and that man must be you because if you say it's true then it must be true."

"Are you patronizing me, Señorita?"

"Do you think that I would waste my time putting on airs?" Leonor asked, as she lifted her radiant face proudly.

"I think that you needn't waste your time on my account, but I had hoped to see more earnestness in your words because I value your opinion of me."

"If you really held my opinion in high esteem, you should've consulted me on this little escapade or elopement, or whatever you wish to call it, because I would've come up with a better story."

The degree of sarcasm in Leonor's voice made his blood boil.

"Señorita, you are cruel to mock me. If you believe, like your mother, that by helping a friend, which I would do all over again if need be, I've been inconsiderate to your family, you could at least be kinder to me now that I've come to explain myself."

These words piqued Leonor's conscience because she had assumed that his defense was nothing but a frivolous alibi.

The young man continued. "Your mother had led me to understand through Don Dámaso that I should leave this house. Indeed, the insinuation was completely unnecessary because your displeasure was cause enough. Furthermore, I was already decided on the matter, but didn't want to leave without explaining what really happened. But you receive me with sarcasm. Why didn't you allow me to cherish my impression of you? It would have been more comforting to remember you with appreciation rather than grief, because no matter what, I will always remember you."

The young man's melancholy moved her in spite of herself.

"My papa must have explained it wrong," she said in a voice that seemed more timid than proud.

"I don't know. I didn't inquire. All I want is to justify myself in your eyes."

"You have succeeded. The girl was your beloved, and it was only right to serve her as you did."

Martín was unable to discern whether Leonor meant what she said, but recognized that she wished to end the conversation.

"Perhaps one day," he said to her, "time will clear my name."

"Can't you do it yourself instead of expecting time to do if for you?" Leonor asked him eye to eye.

"I can't, Señorita, for there is a secret that I must respect."

Leonor's mistrust came to a peak—sarcasm returned to her voice and haughtiness to her eyes. She glared at him, inquiring, "A secret of your ladyfriend, I suppose. What can we do but wait for time to clear your name?"

"I flattered myself with the notion that you would believe me."

"So it seems," she answered dryly.

"How can I continue? She despises me!" was all that Martín could think.

Then, to finish the discussion, Leonor turned to address Matilde, who was deep in conversation with Agustín.

Martín would have liked to throw himself at Leonor's feet and pray to Heaven to justify him without having to resort to Edelmira's letters as proof. He sought refuge in his chamber, where he threw himself into a chair, giving way to tears. After a quarter of an hour, he remembered Edelmira's letter, which he took out of his pocket. "Poor girl!" he said, bearing in mind the comparison that he had always found between his lot and hers. Then, remembering his temptation to use her letters as proof to end Leonor's doubts, he removed them from a box and burned them all.

"Now I'll be free from temptation," he said to himself, staring at the flames as though he were hypnotized and numbed beyond weeping and suffering itself.

That night was a night of martyrdom for Martín. To distract himself he took his time preparing his luggage, which did not take very long given his few possessions. Then he pined, leaning his forehead against the window overlooking the patio. From there he relived every incident of his life since he had first crossed that patio, poor but carefree and hopeful. In this all-too-familiar elegy to lost hopes, Rivas bade farewell to the golden dreams of first love. And yet, he did not yield to the prospect of an unhappy future. He found in his own suffering the strength that many others would lack. He thought of his mother and sister and felt that he owed it to them to pull himself together. Invigorated by their memory, he sat down to write a letter to Don Dámaso, thanking him for his generosity and hospitality, and another to Rafael San Luis, recounting the history of events leading to his decision to return home until the new year when he would continue his studies at the National Institute.

Then he deliberated long and hard as to how he should respond to Edelmira's letter. Although he feared that the truth would hurt, his better judgment kept him from fomenting an unrequited love. Out of a strong sense of decency, he decided it was best to write to Edelmira and relate the story of his heart since coming to Santiago. He did not identify his beloved, but he might as well have spelled her name in capital letters because it was clear on every page that it was Leonor. Rivas concluded his letter to Edelmira without alluding to what had transpired that day, sharing only his plans to return to the capital after an absence of two months.

At six o'clock the following morning, Martín brought his luggage to the inn where he had spent his first night in Santiago. He immediately entrusted the servant of Don Dámaso to distribute the letters that he had written at night, remunerating him generously to assure their prompt delivery.

Then Martín found a seat on a freight coach and left for Valparaíso at ten o'clock in the morning.

LII

Don Dámaso's family spent the beginning of the new year at his hacienda on the coast.

Matilde was invited along to share Leonor's room overlooking the orchard.

Agustín and his father went horseback riding every morning and joined the family for brunch, after which Leonor would play the piano, while Agustín, having nothing better to do, would lavish his cousin with attention.

Doña Engracia was pleased to see her son spending time with Matilde, whom everyone in the family truly adored, and was equally pleased to see how extremely well the country air suited Diamela.

Don Dámaso avidly read the newspapers that were delivered from Santiago. He would lean toward the Ministry or the Opposition, depending on whichever article he read last. When sending off his correspondence, he would often think of Martín, who had so efficiently saved him from this drudgery.

The solitude and monotony of the country life, where weeks passed by without incident worthy of mention, had diverse effects upon both girls, who, despite their intimate living arrangements, kept their feelings to themselves.

As we have already seen, Matilde had wept from the disillusionment that had brought her respect for Rafael San Luis to a bitter end, and with it, her love. Time away from the old scenery slowly healed her wounded spirit, leaving only the scars of melancholy that precede the complete cessation of pain. In this state of mind, Matilde found solace and forgetfulness in Agustín's elegance and youthful exhilaration, and she eventually began to enjoy his company.

Leonor's mind-set was quite the contrary. The more she thought about the relationship between Martín and Edelmira, the less likely it seemed to be amorous. She recalled the conversations and the glances with which Martín might have confessed his love had he the nerve, and these recollections seemed to support the veracity of his alibi. Ingenious is the mind when it wants to find reasons to support what the heart desires. Leonor decided to believe Martin, reasoning that if he were guilty he would have better defended himself by denying everything. Naturally, these reflections gave rise to feelings of regret for having received him with sarcasm. In the distance, all of these ideas came back to her in vivid colors so becoming of Martín that, by the time the family returned to Santiago at the end of February, he had regained his place in her heart without having to defend himself. She had realized that her false accusation arose from the same foolish pride that always seemed to keep Martín from speaking his heart.

Feeling the brunt of this gradual return in favor of Rivas were the many suitors of Leonor, including Emilio Mendoza and Clemente Valencia, who came to visit Don Dámaso's hacienda. One would have thought that Leonor had made vows of fidelity because she was startled by their romantic advances, which she used to receive with contemptuous laughter. She eluded any occasion where she would find herself alone with any one of these callers. Furthermore, when joy and confidence filled the salon, she would steal away to the orchard and dream of the days of yore in Santiago, wishing for their return.

Around this time, Rafael San Luis wrote to Martín:

Dear Friend:

After two months of silence and solitude, meditation and tears, I am the same as I was before: I love as I loved before. Nothing has had the power of the mythic waters of Lethe—not prayers to Heaven, not mystical contemplation, not beautiful models of virtue—nothing can make me forget her. I won't be fatalistic and say "it was written in the stars," but I will always ask myself with my hand over my heart, "Is this God's punishment?"

I am haunted by the memories of happy days lost forever and by the image of her face. Sometimes she looks at me with love, to my sorrow, and other times she repeats the cold words of her last letter. The solitude of the cloister, far from extinguishing the fire in my bosom, has only fanned its flames. In this icy air, I'm burning with fever, unable to breathe because there isn't enough air, or light, or space, or life itself to ease my tormented spirit.

I didn't want to abandon my retreat without giving it time, the same way that I didn't want to make a rash decision when I came here. I didn't feel any different after the first month, so I waited through the second month of seclusion before deciding to return to my dear aunt, who with all the faith in the world, believed that religion was setting me straight.

I'll leave tomorrow and manage the best I can. I have a prospect better suited to my character. It may turn my life around, and maybe yours as well if you come and join me. Let's not plant our hopes in the future, as we did before. Let's break the stems of those dried flowers. For me the sun of happiness began to shine too brightly and withered its blossoms, but we must go on. I'll show you the way that we can consecrate the vigor of our souls.

Rafael San Luis

Around the same time, Rivas received the following letter from Edelmira Molina:

Dear Friend:

I won't deny my sorrow at hearing that you love someone else. Whoever she is, I pray that she returns the love you deserve. Although I've wept for my unhappiness, I'm much too indebted to you to want anything but your happiness. I also pray that I will someday be able to prove my sincerity by returning the kindness you've shown me.

I'm writing to you from my aunt's house, and I'm going to tell you why I haven't returned to my mother's. Two days after you brought me here, Amador came to get me, but my aunt objected and wrote to tell my mother that I would only return if she would leave me at liberty to marry whomever I pleased, or not at all. Although my mother promised that she would, my aunt asked me to stay and spend some more time with her, just in case.

I bid you farewell, wishing you complete happiness, and reminding you that you will always have a friend in . . .

Edelmira Molina

Now that you have read these letters and the explanations that preceded them, we may move forward in our story to the beginning of March 1851, when Martín Rivas returned to the Capital.

LIII

In following the personal lives of this story, we have strayed from the public commotion that was stirring at the end of 1850 and the beginning of 1851, which those who were living in Santiago at the time will clearly recall. In the early chapters we broached the divisive political spirit of Chile, especially in Santiago, which was the focus of the liberal propaganda planted by the Society of Equality. Without entrenching ourselves in history, we shall sketch the political situation that was building toward a great public event of enormous consequence to many of our characters.

The rising tension in the air came to a peak when it was reported that the people of Aconcagua had revolted on the 5th of November 1850. Those with foresight feared that other, bloodier uprisings would ensue, while ultra-Radicals prepared for battle and the Government kept a close watch over them. This raised the bloodthirsty fury of the Press and deeply rooted, fervent animosity on both sides—an animosity that thrives as vigorously today as it did when the battle began 10 years ago. The Liberal Press (defending the right of insurrection) and Public Opinion (which is the consolidation of many isolated opinions into one prophetic voice) spread the belief that the movement in San Felipe would have frightful repercussions in Santiago. By February there was already talk of a coming revolution. They said that the masses would rise to the first call of duty and that the civic troops would "join their brothers," to quote the popular expression, "in the people's crusade against tyranny." Nearly all the armed forces garrisoning the capital were expected to revolt.

In short, this was the situation in Santiago at the beginning of March 1851, when Martín Rivas returned to the inn where he had stayed two months before on his way home to Coquimbo.

He changed his clothes and left the inn to visit Rafael San Luis. A quarter of an hour later, the two friends embraced each other warmly. As they sat down, they searched each other's faces for traces of the sorrow they had experienced during their separation. Rafael found in Martín's face the same youthful, thoughtful expression, the same pure, dark complexion, the same engaging gaze, and the same noble face. There was no trace of grief in Martín's serenity. Martín, on the other hand, noted that something in Rafael's stark gaze, furrowed brows, and sunken cheeks marked the heartbreaking struggles that his friend had endured. Their mutual, involuntary inspection lasted but a fleeting moment.

"Well, how have you been?" asked Rafael, affectionately.

"You can imagine," answered Rivas, "aside from the joy of embracing my mother and sister, everything else was sad."

"You haven't forgotten about *her*, have you?"

"Not for an instant!"

"Poor Martín," said San Luis, taking his hand. "Do you remember my prognosis when we first met?"

"Very clearly, but it's much too late now."

"Did you receive my letter?"

"Yes, and I gathered from it that your life as a recluse is over."

"I mentioned a prospect that I've been mulling over."

"Yes, what is it?"

"A new love," said San Luis, with a mirthless smile.

"Who has replaced Matilde?" asked Rivas.

San Luis approached his friend, pointing to his black hair.

"Look," he said, "do you see any gray hair?"

"Yes."

Rafael took a deep sigh without any hint of sentimentalism.

"Politics, my new love is Politics."

"Oh! I remember you were involved in it when I first met you."

"We struck up again. A few days after I wrote to you up north, two of my buddies from the Society of Equality sent me a letter.

Here it is," Rafael added, reading aloud:

We hope you've recovered from your amorous fever. Your country needs you and the time has come to prove your love. Are you as worthy of the faith you used to profess? You know where to find us.

"In spite of my loneliness, I dreaded coming back," continued Rafael, "until they set me straight and showed me a new direction, one that would point me to forgetfulness, or at least remove the thorn of memory. In Politics there are always two sides at war: the old regime of resistance, exclusivity, and force, on one side; and those who crave reformation and assurances, on the other. There is no room for hesitation if one genuinely feels the patriotism that many claim to feel. I embrace the latter and I'm willing to sacrifice my life for it."

Rafael then described the political state of Santiago, which we have just touched upon, and expounded his Liberal theories with the ardor of a passionate heart, full of faith in the future. The fire of his conviction soon kindled Martín's noble spirit.

"You are right," he said to San Luis. "Instead of crying over our troubles like women, we should consecrate our lives to a cause worthy of men."

"Tonight," said Rafael, "I'll introduce you at our meeting and acquaint you with our plans. As for me, I'm convinced that the time for peaceful protests is over. It's time to fight, and I can't understand what our leaders are waiting for. As a soldier, I'm resigned to wait, but impatiently."

During this conversation Rafael had lost all vestige of discouragement; his pale cheeks were flushed and his large eyes were sparkling with excitement. After a long conversation, the two friends went their separate ways, agreeing to meet later that night.

Martín arrived on time, trying to suppress the memories that the streets of Santiago brought to mind, but he could not resist passing by Don Dámaso's mansion, which he stopped to admire for a few moments from the street corner.

At the meeting, Martín heard avid speeches denouncing Government policies and met young enthusiasts, dandies turned activists, desirous of devoting their energy to the country and awaiting the call of duty to offer their lives. Rivas was inspired by the idea of helping to realize the glorious political and social theories that those young men demanded for their country. As they left the meeting at eleven o'clock at night, Rafael took his arm, saying, "Let me ask you something."

"What is it?"

"Since we hit it off from the start," San Luis began, "I've been meaning to ask you to come live at my place, but I knew it couldn't compare to living in that mansion where you could see Leonor every day. But now that you're alone, why don't you come and live with us. You know my aunt is a saint. You'll feel right at home, and we'll spoil you rotten."

The sincerity of this offer convinced Martín instantly and he thanked his friend profusely.

"Fine," Rafael said gladly. "You'll have my bed starting tonight, and tomorrow we'll send for your luggage."

"I was planning to take a little trip in the morning," answered Martín, "so I would rather come tomorrow afternoon. That way I won't have trouble finding a coach early in the morning."

"It's up to you. Where are you going?"

"To Renca, to see Edelmira."

They said goodnight and went their separate ways.

At ten o'clock the next morning, Martín set off on the road to Renca. The familiar scenery conjured the hopes that he had felt during his last trip, when the landscapes offered his eyes the promise of happy days spent with Leonor in the country. Now, without the image of his beloved, all else faded away, condemning him to grief before knowing happiness. As soon as he saw the ranch where he had left Edelmira, his own preoccupation dissipated and he turned his thoughts to the fate of this poor lass whose friendship he cherished.

He stepped out of the carriage and walked to the front door. Edelmira had seen him from a window and came running to greet him. Martín's tender salutation caused a blush to fade from her cheeks when she saw herself so close to him. Then they filled each other in on what they had done over the past two months.

"I really want to go home to Mama," said Edelmira, "but I must wait to be sure that Ricardo has left our house for good."

No mention was made of Edelmira's last letter during this conversation, which her aunt joined in, showering Martín with kindness. Two hours later, when Rivas was saying goodbye, Edelmira stood up with a sudden look of resolution, as though she had spent some time agonizing over a decision that she was about to announce.

"I have something to ask you," she said to Martín, as soon as her aunt had stepped away.

"Just name it."

Edelmira replied, blushing, "I would like you to be as frank with me as I have been with you."

"I appreciate your honesty and promise that . . ."

"Don't promise me anything. Simply answer my question. Is Leonor the one you love?"

"Yes."

"That's what I've always thought. When my brother recently told me about the visit he paid to the young lady's father, I realized that you might have jeopardized your own situation to improve mine."

"There is some truth in that," said Martín, endeavoring to smile.

Edelmira's aunt returned, and the young man bade them adieu.

Edelmira escorted him to the carriage as she did the last time and stood watching until it drove around a bend in the road and Martín was out of sight. Then she went inside to tell her aunt, "Didn't I tell you? Martín sacrificed his happiness for me, but I'm going to do everything I can to give it back to him so that I can repay his generosity to me."

LIV

On the 15th of April, Matilde and her mother visited Leonor's home, dressed in their Sunday best. They were coming from church at nine o'clock in the morning. Doña Francisca entered her brother's room, and Matilde, Leonor's.

"What are you doing?" Matilde asked her cousin, who was gazing out the window instead of reading the book in her hands.

"Nothing. I was reading."

"Guess why I've come to see you at this hour?"

"Tell me."

"Guess who I ran into this morning as we were leaving San Francisca."

"Who?"

"Guess."

Leonor wished to hear the name Martín Rivas, but dared not speak it. "I can't imagine," she said.

"Martín Rivas," said Matilde, "and he recognized me immediately and said hello."

"He is back in town!" Leonor exclaimed. "Papa has been looking all over for him. How is he?"

"More handsome than ever."

"Was he alone?" Leonor asked, anxiously.

"Yes. But even if he were with Rafael, I assure you that I wouldn't have cared. You know it's all over between us."

A few moments later, Doña Francisca came looking for her daughter and they said goodbye to Leonor, who kept thinking about the news her cousin had just brought her. She knew that if she announced Rivas's arrival to her father, he would make every effort to bring him back to the house; but her joy at the thought of seeing Martín again in the intimacy of her private life reminded her of the reason that he had left the house. The proud belle, to whom the most distinguished suitors of the capital continued to pay homage, humbly asked herself, "How will I know if he loves me?"

Love made its impression on her proud resistance like drops of water falling on a rock over time. Her righteousness yielded to the reign of passion because she was more of a woman than a child spoiled by her parents and Society. This lofty beauty who toyed with so many submissive admirers now accepted the role of the slighted lover. There was seductive pleasure in devoting herself to someone she used to regard as a lowly country bumpkin. During this gradual transformation, the pale flowers of sentimentalism had blossomed in her soul, which not long ago scoffed at those who surrendered to Love.

After breakfast, Leonor fondly recalled her conversations with Martín and all those trivial incidents which mean everything to lovers, as she played the music that she used to play more frequently in those days. Thus occupied, she was interrupted by a maidservant who announced, "There's caller who asks to speak with my lady."

Leonor opened the curtains and looked out the patio. She saw a girl standing there, whose lovely, youthful face made Leonor ask herself, "Where have I seen her before?"

"Ask her what her name is," she said to the servant, who went away with the message and returned with the following reply, "Tell her that I am Edelmira Molina and that I must speak with her in private."

"Edelmira!" exclaimed Leonor. Then, after a thoughtful pause, she looked up and said, "Show her to my room."

When the servant went back to the patio, Leonor glanced reflexively at one of the hanging mirrors and touched up her French braids before meeting with Edelmira. Leonor responded with regal haughtiness to the meek greeting of her presumed rival, who said somewhat nervously, "Señorita, I've come to pay a debt."

"Please sit down," said Leonor, who saw the effort that Edelmira was making to overcome her nervousness.

Edelmira sat down and began to say, "I'm greatly indebted to a young man who lived in your house last year. Only a few days ago I learned why he had to leave, so I came here as soon as I could. My brother," she added, "brought me here and he is waiting for me outside."

"What do I have to do with any of this?" asked Leonor dryly.

"I'm appealing to you because I wouldn't dare approach your mother. But I knew that I had to come here to clear Martín's name."

The name of the young man whom both girls were in love with seemed to echo in the room.

"I heard," continued Edelmira, "that your family was led to believe that Martín eloped with me. My brother and another young man convinced your father of this the day I left for Renca, where I've been living until now."

"Oh, did you go alone?"

"No, Martín was kind enough to escort me, and that is why they believed he was involved with me and that he had run off with me. But none of that is true. I ran away to Renca because my family wanted me to marry the officer who accompanied my brother here that day. Martín was kind enough to escort me, and if it weren't for him, I would be miserable today."

"Señor Rivas has been remarkably unselfish," said Leonor, "to act this way even though you don't love him."

"I never said that I don't love him!"

"Oh!" exclaimed Leonor, whose eyes gleamed with jealousy, causing Edelmira to sigh from the realization that Leonor might be in love with Martín too.

"Yes, Señorita, I love him, but he doesn't love me and never has."

"I don't know if it's your candor or modesty speaking, and I'm sorry that Martín isn't here for me to intercede in your favor."

"I haven't come here to ask any favor," replied Edelmira proudly. "I've come here to clear Martín's name because I, perhaps, am the reason for his misery."

"Oh, is he miserable?"

"Yes, he told me so just a couple of days ago."

"Where have you seen him?" asked Leonor, forgetting to project indifference.

"He came to see me at Renca."

"How sweet!" Leonor snapped. "How can you say that your love is unrequited!"

"He came because he is noble and promised me his friendship."

"Don't lose faith—there's a fine line between love and friendship."

"No, Señorita, he is only a friend, and I have proof of that."

"Proof?"

"Yes, and I brought the proof with me because, as I just said, I want to defend him because he has been so good to me."

Edelmira brought out Martín's letters and handed them to Leonor, saying, "If you would take the trouble to read these letters, you would see that I'm telling you the truth."

"But this seems to be a reply," Leonor said with a contemptuous smile, after reading the opening lines of the first letter.

Edelmira explained what she had written to Martín, and Leonor continued reading, dropping her usual contempt out of curiosity. Such was the manner that she learned of the integrity of the relationship between Martín and Edelmira, and the piety with which he had handled that affair. Leonor had difficulty hiding her joy upon reading the letter that Rivas had sent to Edelmira before he had left for Coquimbo.

When Leonor looked up from the letters, the terse irony in her expression was replaced by lovingkindness. She said, "These letters leave no trace of doubt about his generosity, and yours."

"Señorita," Edelmira answered, "no sacrifice for Martín would be too much. I'm not speaking out of my love for him, for you see that these letters leave me with no hope. Rather, I speak out of sincere gratitude and an obligation to return his favor to me."

"I must thank you for trusting me with this. My whole family owes Martín for considerable services. My father will be very happy to see him. Do you know where he is living?"

"With San Luis, a friend of his."

Saying goodbye, Leonor accompanied Edelmira to the patio and offered her hand affectionately. These heartfelt gestures convinced Edelmira that Rivas's love was not unrequited after all.

Then Leonor went to visit Agustín in his suite.

"I'm presently indisposed," said the dandy, who was engaged in the serious concerns of his wardrobe. "But *je suis à toi à l'instant.*"

A moment later the door opened, through which Leonor entered, saying, "I have good news."

"Have you seen Matilde?" asked the young gentleman, who was growing more fond of his cousin every day.

"No, it's real news. Martín is back in Santiago."

"I haven't thought about him in ages. Such a good sport. I've missed him. Where is he living?"

"In San Luis's house."

"That's a shame."

"Why?"

"Because, as you know, I may be his successor to our cousin's heart."

"That doesn't matter. You must bring Martín back home."

"Gracious, *ma cherie*, I dare say that you seem eager."

"Have you forgotten how Martín left this house?"

"No, no, it was Papa's fault for paying heed to slander."

"Well, now it's up to us to make reparations and let him know that we're not ungrateful."

"Little sister, how you've changed your opinion!"

"Yes, I have."

"The King of France said it best: *Souvent femme varie*. There isn't a French book that doesn't quote it, little sister, because *c'est la vérité pur.*"

It was agreed that Leonor and Agustín would remedy the situation with Don Dámaso, and since their father was delighted by the news and claimed that he missed Martín more every day, his son went straight to Rafael's house, only to find that they were both out for the evening.

Agustín decided that he would return the following day. It is very significant to bear in mind that the following day would be the 19th of April, 1851.

LV

Martín and Rafael returned home at midnight on the 18th of April. It was clear that political passions had raised their spirits because there was zest in their glances and gestures and zeal in their speech when they supported the Liberal Opposition to the Government (which was ending its second term) and to those who were endeavoring to reinstate it.

Passionately embracing the cause of the people, Martín found that the dark cloud of melancholy, hovering over him during the past few months, was beginning to lift. Endeavoring to stifle the voice of love amidst the hue and cry of Politics, he had managed to turn Leonor's image into a sweet remembrance instead of a constant thorn in his side. To keep himself in this frame of mind, Rivas lived among his books by day and his political co-religionists by night.

Rafael, who had abandoned his studies, lived immersed in clandestine activities for which he gave no account, not even to Martín. Sometimes ostensibly cheerful, other times quietly somber, he spoke in secret with people who visited the house, and often went out alone after just returning home with Martín from their secret society. Rivas noticed something mysterious in his friend's behavior, but refrained from asking.

The names *Leonor* and *Matilde* were rarely mentioned by the two young men, both of whom seemed to want to deny their secret grief.

They arrived home, as we said, at midnight.

Lighting a lamp on the table, San Luis found a note, which he brought closer to the candle before passing to Rivas. "Agustín Encina," was the heading, under which it was written in pencil, "I'll stop by tomorrow morning at eleven."

Martín sat down, distracted, while San Luis lit a cigar and began to pace the room. The vivacity of their conversation as they entered suddenly seemed to vanish upon reading the card. After a few moments, Rafael asked, "Why do you think he stopped by?"

"I haven't the foggiest idea."

"But you're thrilled."

"Not really."

"He'll ask you to go and live with them again."

"I don't think so."

"Supposing he did, would you go?"

"I couldn't."

"And what if it weren't just his parents, but his sister who also wanted you back?"

"It would make no difference."

"You'd be doing the right thing," said San Luis, who started pacing again.

"I can't deny that I'm deeply indebted to the family," replied Martín after a brief silence. "I came to Santiago poor and alone. Not only did they give me—a complete stranger—a room of my own in their home; they treated me with respect and kindness as though I were a member of the family."

"Have you forgotten the services you provided Don Dámaso, including rescuing his son from the snare he was caught in?"

"Even if I had done more, it wouldn't be enough."

"Then go back and live with them," Rafael said bitterly.

"I already told you that I won't go back," Martín said dryly.

Silence returned but was interrupted for the second time by San Luis, who revived the subject of Politics; however, Martín did not partake with the same vigor that he had displayed before reading the card. San Luis, noting his distraction, said goodnight and withdrew.

Agustín was punctual the next morning. He entered Rivas's chamber at eleven o'clock, announcing, "I've come to get you and bring you fond regards from everyone at home, starting with Papa, who sends a warm embrace, all the way down to Diamela, who longs to nip at your heels."

"Agustín, my friend," said Rivas, "how can I thank your family? I'll always be grateful, but as you can see, it's impossible for me to accept your gracious invitation."

"Give me one good reason."

"Because Rafael wouldn't forgive me if I left him alone."

"Your first home was our home," insisted Agustín.

"I know that, and I'll never forget all that your family has done for me."

"Likewise, my dear chap. But, if you don't come along, we'll call you *ingrate* in every language known to man."

"I would never be, and that's why I'm sorry to have to decline your offer," said Rivas, patting the dandy's shoulder.

"Let's go, man, *pas de façons* . . . Look, I've promised someone that I wouldn't return without you."

"Who?" asked Rivas with interest.

"Leonor—she is the one who told us where to find you. I don't know how she found out, but you know what the French always say: What a woman wants, God wants."

"Please tell your sister how much I appreciate her concern and how sorry I am that I can't accept your family's generosity."

"Yes, she'll take that very well! You know that when Leonor decides what she wants, Leonor gets what she wants. And she has decided that we must make reparations for having misconstrued your good deeds."

"Oh, so I've been cleared!" cheered Rivas.

"You've won us over. The opinion is unanimous, except for Politics because I can never tell where Papa stands. Today he stands for the Opposition and tomorrow against it. But don't let that stop you from coming. Papa says he needs you very much."

Martín excused himself, restating his promise to San Luis.

"You'll have to come to the house and excuse yourself in person. When can we expect to see you?"

"I'll try to stop by tonight," said Rivas.

Satisfied by this concession, Agustín spent the next hour babbling about his fondness for Matilde and his hopes of it being reciprocated. Then he left Martín surrendered to thoughts of

Leonor. Recalling past scenes at the Encina mansion and the way that Leonor had slighted him, he was wrestling whether or not to yield to his desire to see her. By four o'clock that afternoon, Rivas was still undecided as to how he would respond to Augustin's invitation when Rafael returned home in seemingly high spirits.

"Did Agustín stop by?"

"Yes, and he stayed a while."

"Did he try to convince you to stay with them?"

"Very hard."

"And what did you say?"

"That I would try to pay them a visit tonight."

"Wrong move," said Rafael in a bossy tone that he had often used with classmates, but never with Martín.

"That is for me alone to judge," retorted Rivas, who rebelled against any sign of tyranny.

"I hope that we're close enough to be completely honest with each other," said Rafael, softening his voice.

"Fine, tell me what you have to say," said Martín.

"I think you shouldn't go there, at least not yet."

"And why not?"

"Because you'll run the risk of more heartache. You're much too nice to throw yourself at the feet of some spoiled, fickle girl, who'll walk all over you again as though you were just another sacrifice to her beauty. Besides, there is nothing to be gained by visiting her tonight because as timid as you are with women, when you finally dare to look at her, you'll find some pretext to enslave yourself again."

San Luis paused, anticipating a response from Martín, but continued. "I have some news that may steer you away from your romanticism."

"What news?"

"Let me ask you something first."

"Go ahead."

"Did you mean what you said at our meeting, or were you just venting?"

"I meant every word of it, otherwise I wouldn't have said it."

"Which means you're committed to our cause, come what may?"

"Come what may."

"And how do you regard the pact you made to carry out any order that I assure you is from our leader?"

"I regard it as sacred."

"Not even Leonor can keep you from it?"

"No one could keep me from it, not even Leonor."

"You're the man I've always known you to be," said San Luis, sitting down in front of his friend.

"After such ceremony, I can hardly wait to hear the news."

"My news is this," he said, lowering his voice. "Everything is ready. The revolution begins tomorrow. Only four of our brothers at the club know this secret, and between us we've distributed the posts to the rest of the men. I've chosen you as my second in command if you accept."

"I am honored," said Martín, exhilarated.

"Now you'll understand why I was opposed to your visit to Leonor. I'm wary of her influence and don't want our brothers to think you're a coward."

"You're right. I won't go to see her."

"Many believe that there will be no bloodshed and all the forces will flock to our side. I disagree, but I think we'll triumph in the end."

"How many men can we count on?"

"The surest bet is the Valdivian battalion, and we'll bring in reinforcements from Chacabuco and maybe the artillery barracks. For me, the only one to count on is Valdivia. If they're well commanded and backed by the people, then we can take over all the barracks, starting with the arsenal where we can seize the weapons to arm the people. Bilbao, and many others you know, are brothers of the revolution, and I've promised them that you would be one of us."

"Thank you for your faith in me," said Martín, taking his friend's hand. "I'll make sure that you won't regret it."

"Before we go, since we have all night to talk this over," said San Luis, "I'm going to tell you what I've been thinking you should do about Leonor."

"What is it?"

"Even if you went back to live with them, you'd never find the nerve to tell her how you feel."

"Maybe I would if she weren't so rich and I weren't so indebted to her father."

"Well, considering that she still is and you still are, you'll be too shy to say anything and she'll be too proud to take your hand and say, 'Martín, I've read in your heart what I'm feeling in mine.' It's not going to happen."

"I know," sighed Martín.

"So, you only have one option."

"Well, let's hear it."

"You ought to write her a love letter and have it delivered in the morning."

Martín remained silent.

"Would you rather keep it a secret forever?" asked Rafael.

"Of course not!"

"Well, then, you'll never have a better occasion than now to tell her. The looming peril will excuse your audacity. If she loves you, she'll forgive you. If she doesn't, then you'll lose nothing. Since you didn't go to her house, they won't be able to accuse you of disloyalty."

San Luis did not need to argue any further to convince Rivas, who ignored the peril of tomorrow to surrender to the long-awaited pleasure of unburdening his heart.

"I have to leave," Rafael said, "I'm going to get the latest orders and I'll be back at midnight."

He closed the door, and Martín sat down to transcribe the letter that was already written in his mind with blazing letters.

LVI

It was the most solemn occasion of Martín's life. He was going to confess his love to the woman of his dreams on the eve of staking his life on a noble cause. It was not fear he felt, but the anxiety that the idea of imminent death strikes in the most courageous spirits when healthy vigor seems to anchor the soul with an instinct for self-preservation. In this state, he took up a pen and wrote:

Señorita:

By the time you receive this letter, I may be in grave danger of losing my life, if I haven't already. Only under this dire circumstance would I dare ask you whether you know that I love you. Out of shyness and deference to your family, I've tried to keep my heart a secret, but it has been extremely difficult. I must confess plainly and sincerely that you're the only woman I've ever loved. My better judgment knew to resist this feeling, but I couldn't help but surrender to its power over me, even though I saw it was hopeless. I've struggled against my love and made every effort to hide it from you and everyone else, but I can't bear this secret burden, knowing that my life may end tomorrow. Forgive my audacity. Please receive my confession as the final words of a dying man who speaks his heart in devotion to you, with the hopes that you will not scorn or mock him, for he has worshiped no other star than your love.

There is one other thing that I must say to you. I haven't had the opportunity to clear my name since I left your home. Although I trusted time to clarify my position, I longed for the opportunity to justify myself as I suffered undue incriminations. This may be my last chance to convince you that I was telling you the truth. I hope that you will believe me, knowing how serious I am at this moment.

Martín added a few words of his appreciation for her family and avoided, as he had throughout the letter, the sentimental drivel typical of a love letter in a novel. Although he revered her as a goddess, he spoke straight from his heart without resorting to the fanciful phrases that spill from the pens of lovers. He read this letter several times and felt relieved that he would not die without Leonor knowing his heart and giving him at least some respect for his faithful love.

At eleven o'clock that night San Luis entered the room, announcing, "Everything is moving as planned. I brought our weapons."

Saying this, he held out two belts with two revolvers and two swords that he had carried under his cloak. He handed one of each to Rivas, saying, "Here you go. Now you are armed to defend our country."

Masking their worries under nervous smiles and jokes about their improvised roles of revolutionaries, they inspected their weapons, divided the ammunition, and tried on their swords. Then Rafael explained everything that he knew about the battle plans. They talked until two o'clock in the morning. Every noise in the street startled them, and they would fall silent for long intervals, as if straining to hear any movement of the sleeping masses.

"It's time to take our positions," said Rafael, when he saw that it was three o'clock. "Do you have your letter?"

"Yes," answered Martín.

"I paid Don Dámaso's servant one peso to wait for me," added San Luis, "and promised him another 8 to deliver your letter."

Rafael stepped out for a few moments and returned looking pale and troubled.

"Poor aunt," he said, "sleep peacefully."

Rafael looked around the room at the furniture, witness to his joys and griefs, and like someone who wants to distract himself from oppressive memories, he said, "Let's go. God willing, we'll return victorious."

They walked toward the street, hiding their weapons under their cloaks, and silently approached Plaza de Armas, which they crossed heading toward Don Dámaso's estate. When they arrived, San Luis said to Martín, "Wait for me here."

He walked to the front door and knocked softly. The servant answered at once.

"Please deliver this letter to Señorita Leonor," Rafael said, handing over Martín's letter. "You must give it to her the minute she wakes up. Here is your tip," he added, repeating his instructions and making the servant promise to fulfill his orders faithfully.

Rafael and Martín walked to the breakwater, and from there to an old house. Rafael pushed the door open and directed Rivas to enter a dark patio. Groups of two or three men began to arrive armed with revolvers under their cloaks. As time went on, more groups came through the same door and filled the patio.

San Luis organized the men into two groups as close to military formation as he could. He conferred the command of one group to Martín and the other group to another young man, reserving the position of Commander for himself. San Luis appointed other members of the secret society subordinate positions, and once his men were in battle formation, he gave them a fiery speech on Chilean valor. He ordered one of the officers to go to the Plaza and send word when the armed forces arrived. The emissary returned after ten minutes announcing that the Valdivian battalion was on its way.

San Luis ordered his men to take their positions, which they secured shortly after the arrival of the Valdivian battalion, which would play a momentous role in the historic events of April 20th.

San Luis met with Colonel Don Pedro Urriola, the mastermind of this insurrection, and conferred with all the other leaders, most of whom expected that the armed forces and the civics would join their ranks. Rafael was among those who argued most fervently for immediate action to raid the fire barracks and arm the people at once. Precious time was lost in debate. At half past five in the morning, the revolutionary troops, whose numbers remained relatively steady, were still waiting for orders at Plaza de Armas, where they had been since four o'clock that morning. They finally decided to attack and dispatched San Luis's troops with another squad of soldiers to seize the fire barracks.

These soldiers and their compatriots began firing the first shots of battle, which, given the precious time lost in discussion, must have been one of the bloodiest in the history of Chile's capital.

LVII

We shall take a few paragraphs from a newspaper published the day after the battle to explain how the warfare began on April 20th.

> *Colonel Urriola led his men to the Plaza and succeeded in ambushing the citadel, for it was only guarded by three soldiers; the rest were on duty inside the building.*
>
> *They also raided the fire barracks and armed the people. Many guards banded with the rebels, as did the soldiers from Chacabuco who were in the citadel.*

The fire barracks posed little resistance to the rebels, who seized the weapons and returned to the Plaza in greater numbers.

Formidable news awaited them there: two Valdivian sergeants who marched with their squads to raid the barrack of Battalion Number Three of the National Guard suddenly revolted and shot their commanders, leaving one dead and another gravely wounded; after which they led their units to strengthen the ranks of the Government.

This news spread grim premonitions among the revolutionaries, for this example of defection could be contagious throughout the Valdivian battalion, the only veteran force that until now supported the uprising.

The cries of revolution resounded in the farthest corners of the city, and people flocked to Plaza de Armas, where the leaders of the insurrection were preaching mutiny, unable to arm many of those who came forward to join the cause. The same news reached the Government through various sources and allowed the administration to plan their defense while the revolutionaries were spending precious moments quarreling and proselytizing. The call to arms was played in every barrack and the artillery was prepared for counterattack. The Civic corps that could get hold of weapons converged in Plaza de la Moneda, and the Government forces, surrounding the neighboring streets, seized Cerro Santa Lucía.

Those in the Plaza, seeing that there were no enforcements coming to their aid and that there were insufficient arms for the people, resolved to attack the arms and ammunition depot, a critical point in determining their victory. According to the aforementioned publication,

> *The artillery barrack sits at the foot of Cerro Santa Lucía near Cañada, in a rental house, a very vulnerable military position, on the corner of Calle Angosta de las Recogidas and Cañada. Widely exposed on three sides, there was a cross-street eight yards from the main door, which would readily lay bare the artillery behind it. Almost opposite its main entrance is Calle San Isidro, making it easy for enemy gunfire to rip through the door.*

The revolutionaries took Calle del Estado toward Cañada, where a bloody combat erupted. We will describe some of the gory details after relating the situation at the Encina mansion, which was located on one of the central streets in Santiago.

The cries of revolution jolted the family out of their deep sleep at the crack of dawn.

Don Dámaso leaped out of his bed when he heard the servants in the adjacent rooms screaming, "Revolution!" His wife leaped out right behind him with admirable agility, when she heard her husband shouting (while searching for his trousers), "Honey! Revolution! Revolution!"

The darkness heightened the terror of Don Dámaso's cry. He not only frightened Doña Engracia out of her wits, but startled himself with the sonority of his own voice. The couple scrambled around their bedchamber, looking for articles of clothing that they were already holding in their hands.

"My boots, my boots, what have I done with my boots?" Don Dámaso was mumbling, as he fumbled around the room in search of them.

"Look, man, you're wearing my petticoat!" screamed Don Engracia, who having lit a candle, stood at the foot of the bed, trying to cover her half-naked body.

The candlelight allowed Don Dámaso to see that he was wearing his wife's petticoat over his shoulders, and, wanting to get rid of it as quickly as possible, tossed it at Doña Engracia's head. Trying to catch it with one hand, while holding a chemise over her bosom with the other, she knocked the candlestick onto the carpet, casting them in darkness again. This mishap started Diamela, who began howling in unison with the terrorized couple, heightening the bedlam and the clamor, as each voice seemed desirous of drowning out the other two. At last, when the candle was lit again, Don Dámaso found his boots, Doña Engracia put on her petticoat, and Diamela curled up quietly in the warm bed that her masters had vacated.

"We must dress quickly," said Don Dámaso, telling his wife to do what he himself was unable to do, for each article of clothing seemed to elude him in this harried trance.

Then they heard knocking on the door.

"Who goes there?" asked Don Dámaso, turning pale.

"Papa! Papa," Agustín cried. "Get up! There's a revolution!"

"I'm coming," answered Don Dámaso, opening the door for his son.

While they finished getting dressed, Don Dámaso and Doña Engracia fired a line of questions at their son, who having no information about the revolution, asked his parents the same questions that they were asking him.

Frustrated by his son's inability to calm his anxiety, Don Dámaso finally asked, "What about Leonor?"

The threesome proceeded to Leonor's suite, where she was dressed and sitting quietly beside a table.

"Child, there is a revolution," Don Dámaso said to her.

"So I've heard," Leonor responded calmly.

"What shall we do?" her father asked, astonished by Leonor's courage.

"What do you want to do? It seems to me that the best thing to do is wait right here."

Don Dámaso could neither sit still nor comprehend how anyone could be so calm at a time like this. He rushed out, ordering the servants to bolt all the doors and returned to Leonor's chamber, shouting, "This is what happens when you pander to a bunch of bareback rogues. Cursed Liberals! They start a revolution because they have nothing to lose. Oh, if I were Governor, I would shoot them dead on the spot."

The distant sound of gunshots ended his speech and cast him into a sofa, nearly fainting. Doña Engracia, terrified as well, threw herself into her husband's arms, forgetting that she was holding Diamela, who howled at the excruciating, sudden torture.

"Papa! Mama! Let's be rational. Oh, shut up, Diamela!" said Agustín, trying to appear confident, although his knees were knocking.

The only person who seemed truly calm was Leonor, who implored them (without emotion or consternation) to calm down.

Time passed in this fashion until the light of day hushed the commotion troubling every member of the household except Leonor.

A maidservant entered the room, whose voice was choked by panic. "Señor! They're knocking at the front door!"

One would have thought that she had announced that showers of bombs were about to come crashing through the roof, for Don Dámaso covered his head with both hands, yelling, "They've come to get us! It's all over!"

Leonor, ignoring her father, advised her brother to go and see who was knocking.

"Who? Me? That's easy for you to say. What if the bad guys are out there? I'd defend you if I had to, but why should I have to? Let's just keep the doors locked."

"You make me feel so safe," replied the girl, leaving the room and heading to the front door, where the knocking was redoubling in an alarming manner.

Those who were knocking were Don Fidel Elías and his wife, Matilde, and her younger siblings. They rushed inside, all talking at the same time about what they had witnessed in the streets. On their way to the inner quarters, Leonor was approached by the attendant who had let them in. He said to her, "Señorita, I have a letter for my lady."

The girl opened the letter mechanically. When she read Martín's signature her jaw dropped open and her voice cracked as she said, "Very well, attend the door and advise me if someone calls."

Her face recovered some of its serenity as she thanked him, and only its slight pallor indicated that she was under intense duress. Leonor stole away to an empty chamber, closed the door, and swiftly opened the letter that she had tucked into her pocket. Upon reading the contents, the girl lost all semblance of the courage that had distinguished her from her family. Her face was drained of color; her eyes were full of tears; and, her breathing was quickened by the violent beating of her heart.

"My God! What will I do?" she cried at the horrifying thought that Rivas might be in danger at this very moment. Then she jumped up, as if struck by a worse blow, and asked herself, "And what if he is already wounded? Or dead?"

To the heavens she raised her eyes, which wept the first tears of love. Then she prayed for Martín's life; it was a sublime supplication of an enamored soul—awkwardly worded, yet eloquently expressed. And then, as if she suddenly realized the impotence of her pride and the barren vanity of her beauty, she wept like a child, completely oblivious to everything except her love. After struggling to regain her composure, she straightened her dress (which an instant of complete desperation had disheveled) and emerged from the room holding Martín's letter over her heart.

Don Fidel recounted the news that he had just heard in the streets alleging that the revolutionaries had seized the arsenal and were heading to Casa de Moneda, the Government's last stronghold.

"It may already be over," Don Fidel concluded.

Everyone then proceeded to the upper floors of the mansion to observe the movement in the streets from the balcony.

"What's going on down there?" Don Fidel asked two men who were running by.

"The people are victorious! Colonel Urriola has seized the artillery!" shouted one of them.

"Long live the people!" cheered the other.

"Long live the people!" repeated Don Dámaso, who was always rooting for the victor. Then, as if to vindicate his seditious outcry, he added, "It's about time justice was brought to our poor brothers, dwelling under oppression."

"What makes you think that they won't oppress *us* now?" retorted Don Fidel, who was horrified by the thought that the rabble would rule Chile.

"It is only proper that our brothers should reclaim their rights," said Don Dámaso assuming a sudden patriotic tone, forgetting that half an hour earlier these newly adopted brothers were "a bunch of bareback rogues."

While they continued quarreling and wondering what would happen next, Leonor slipped away to Martín's old room, where she felt closer to him surrounded by the furniture he had lived with. She prayed that God would keep him safe, clasping the letter against her bosom.

Gunshots resounded from the artillery barrack, warning the curious onlookers to desert the balcony and run for cover, lest they fall victim to stray bullets.

Rather than follow them as they make their frantic way down the spiral stairwell, we shall return to the battlefield, where some of our characters are counted among the belligerent.

LVIII

We last saw the revolutionaries on Calle Estado marching toward Alameda en route to the arms and ammunition depot, which they counted as an easy victory. San Luis marched at the head of his troops, whose numbers multiplied on the way, although many of those who joined the ranks were unarmed. Martín, as serene as though he were walking in a parade, kept his men in line, exhorting them to observe military formation.

Cheering masses were already filling Alameda and the sidewalks. As the revolutionaries approached, they spotted numerous Chacabucoan units strategically positioned at Cerro Santa Lucía and hastened to scale the hill in order to drive the soldiers out of their posts. When the Chacabucoan army saw the rebels advancing, they fled down the hill toward Cañada beside the southern fortress, swiftly seeking refuge in the arms and ammunition depot, which opened its doors to them, thereby fortifying the few remaining soldiers defending the structure from within.

In spite of their speed, the revolutionaries arrived at the arsenal seconds after the door was already bolted shut behind the Chacabucoan soldiers.

The revolutionary troops were ordered to attack the barrack, which they did amidst the hue and cry of the people, most of whom were standing by as onlookers (perhaps for lack of arms, or perhaps for lack of leaders without which our masses rarely take initiative unless guided by the ruling class, whom they invariably regard as naturally superior in spite of the propaganda of Equality).

Rafael San Luis's troops attacked the flank, and the Valdivian army assailed the front of the barrack. Then the besieged, having saved their ammunition until they were in closer range, opened fire. While the veteran troops sent a storm of bullets at the doors and windows, the improvised army of rebels hurled rocks at the roof and labored to demolish the main door, opening a hole near the lintel. Amidst the rapid fire, some men led by Martín Rivas managed to break down a door facing Calle de las Recogidas.

"Let's go, men!" he shouted, brandishing a sword in one hand and a revolver in the other.

And saying this, Martín Rivas attempted to lead his men into the building, but they were met with such a murderous fusillade that most of them retreated at once. Martín endeavored in vain to urge them onward by speech and example until explosions were heard from across the street, where the Captain of the besieged had positioned a cannon. There was a hail of bullets over the fields and a thunderous barrage of cannon fire that decimated the revolutionary ranks.

The sound of these explosions warned the families of Don Dámaso and Don Fidel to leave the balcony and run for cover. At the very moment that Leonor was calling out Martín's name in fervent prayer, he was charging into the thick of the battle, like the knights of old, with his beloved's image in his mind and her name upon his lips.

In spite of their courage, the besieged saw themselves in grave danger under this constant bombardment, when a brigade under the command of Colonel García appeared at the end of Calle Agustínas, as reported by the aforementioned newspaper. This brigade, composed of as many National Guardsmen as the Government could gather, advanced down the street and found itself caught between two lines of fire. Valdivia's army was ordered to attack its rearguard, while the rest of the rebels turned their fire toward its advance. The courageous zeal of the revolutionaries equaled that of the National Guard.

Rivas and San Luis fought with the same courageous zeal. They put their swords back in their belts and picked up their guns to fire at the enemy as their soldiers did. The commanders' orders could not be heard among the earsplitting detonations, the excruciating screams of the wounded, and the angry curses of those who were forced to retreat.

In the height of warfare, a fatal bullet struck Colonel Urriola, the leader of the revolution, whose dying words were, "I have been deceived!" Words that History quotes as evidence that the revolutionaries were not expecting the powerful opposition that they encountered. The news of Colonel Urriola's death wounded the morale of his troops, who eased their fire, shifted from offense to defense, and retreated to Cañada opposite the main door of the barrack. Reunited in dense formation, there they renewed their gunfire almost more ferociously than before.

Then, two cannons came rolling out of the main door of the barrack, firing back at the rebels.

From the end of Calle San Isidro, Martín, Rafael, and their men fired at the soldiers who emerged from the barrack and ordered those who lacked arms to use the weapons of the fallen soldiers.

It was, without doubt, the bloodiest moment of battle. The enemies, standing only paces away from each other, were close enough to fire with certainty and witness the deadly effects of their gunshots. The noise was deafening and men were dropping left and right. The curious bystanders, who had been watching from the sidelines since dawn, fled from the gruesome spectacle, leaving the enemies at war among themselves. Both factions seemed to forget that every bullet spilled upon Chile's soil the generous blood of one of her own sons. Brazen courage in the face of danger, obstinate tenacity in offense and defense alike, and unrivaled ardor and heroic assurance were the attributes of national character displayed on both sides. The cannon fire stopped when the hailstorm of bullets ripping through Calle San Isidro downed both officers operating the cannons and most of their support. The commander of the arsenal replaced both officers, who were laying seriously wounded at the foot of the artillery, one of which was his own son. However, when the commander arrived, a furious crossfire wiped out nearly all of the artillery corps left standing, and the revolutionaries advanced through the smoke to seize the cannons, which death had left unguarded. Martín and Rafael were the first to place their hands on these guns that had caused so much devastation to their troops.

"Victory! Victory!" shouted San Luis.

And his men cheered along, dragging the cannons to their side. No sooner had the cheers of victory ceased when the main door of the barrack opened again, whence a barrage of bullets massacred the rebel forces.

Rafael clutched Martín's arm and shouted at his men, "Fire! The enemy is at its end!"

These words were drowned out by another fusillade, and the young man who spoke them threw his arms around Martín's neck, saying, "I'm wounded. I can't get up."

Martín held his friend around the waist, pulled him out of the line of fire, and carried him to the nearest house. Martín kicked the door open and dragged Rafael, whose clothes were soaked in blood, into a room where he found an old man and two women.

"Señora," Martín said to the woman who appeared to be the elder, "please see what you can do for this man."

They all helped to remove Rafael's coat and found two bullet holes in his chest that were gushing with blood with every breath he took. Rafael took his friend's hand, saying, "Leave me here. I won't make it. There isn't much time left for me."

Martín's eyes, which blazed with the fire of battle a few moments ago, now glistened with tears.

"You're wounded too," said Rafael said to Martín, whose right arm had been hit by the same fusillade that had felled San Luis.

"It's nothing. I can hardly feel it."

"Victory will be ours," Rafael strained to say. "Listen to the guns. Enemy fire is dying down."

Rafael struggled harder with every word and his voice weakened the more he bled. Martín tried in vain to stop the bleeding with kerchiefs and makeshift bandages. After straining to hear what was happening on the battlefield, Rafael clutched Martín's hand and made an effort to sit up.

"Say goodbye to my poor aunt for me," Rafael said tenderly, "and if you see Adelaida, tell her to forgive me, and remember me, Martín, because . . . "

The effort that Rafael had exerted to finish this phrase seemed to spend his last breath of life, for the words died upon his lips and his head fell back on the pillow that the women had placed beneath him.

"Dead! Dead!" cried Martín, holding him in his arms. "Poor Rafael!"

Martín broke down, sobbing over his friend's corpse, but collected himself after a few moments and kissed San Luis on his pale cheeks and forehead. Martín promised the women that they would be well rewarded if they brought the body to the home of Pedro San Luis, and he left the room, vowing, "I will avenge your death!"

There was an eerie light in Martín's eyes when he clutched his sword, drawing it as he departed. When he returned to the battlefield, there was pandemonium among the revolutionary forces. One of the Chacabucoan soldiers who was taken captive at the citadel escaped to the artillery barrack and other soldiers followed his lead, which spread mass confusion among the ranks. The revolutionaries gradually ceased fire, and when they saw Rivas return to the barrack, they entered the building, believing themselves to be victorious—walking right into enemy hands. Martín also entered the barrack under the same misconception and found Amador Molina (who had been hiding during most of the fray) standing in the entrance, denouncing the rebels whom he had supported at the start of the battle.

One of Martín's comrades approached him, saying, "We're defeated. Our men are deserting us. We have to run."

Just then Amador yelled, "Ricardo, I've got a couple of rebels over here!"

"Coward!" Martín shouted, taking him by the throat. "If I didn't pity you, I'd kill you!"

Then he hurled Amador across the room.

"Run, it's our only hope," said the young man who had just spoken to Martín, and he pulled him away as people began to crowd into the room.

At first Martín resisted but Amador ran inside, calling the police who had helped to defend the arsenal. When Amador came running back with Ricardo Castaños and some soldiers, the youth insisted, "Quick, let's go. We can't let them capture us."

Martín shook his comrade's hand goodbye, and then ran toward

Don Dámaso Encina's home, while Amador and Ricardo searched for him among the people who had just filed into the entrance. This allowed Martin to gain a lead on his pursuers, who ran into the street after he was already a block away.

"Let's go look for him at Don Dámaso's," Amador told the police, "and if we don't find him there, we'll search the entire city."

LIX

Having brought to light the principal events of the bloody battle that erupted in Santiago on the 20th of April 1851 (endeavoring to be concise by excerpting official passages from the newspapers), we shall now turn our attention to the main characters of this novel.

The entire Encina household suffered hours of mortal anxiety, with the thunder of the battlefield rumbling through their quaking hearts and arousing panic in everyone, especially Leonor.

Doña Engracia gathered everyone into one room to pray the Rosary. Don Dámaso and Agustín recited *Ora pro nobis* with exemplary devotion, while Leonor withdrew to the upper floor. There, on the balcony, listening to the commotion throughout the city, Leonor prayed for Martín's life and strove to divert her thoughts from the morbid premonitions that the sound of every bullet brought to mind. She dared not question the people passing by in the street for fear of receiving fatal tidings. Keeping her eyes fixed upon the battlefield, she saw a group of men running toward her home. As they passed under the balcony, one of them stopped to catch his breath.

"Señorita," he said to Leonor, "we've been defeated. The Valdivians were turncoats!"

Then he ran off, trailing the others who had already gained considerable distance on him.

A sudden chill rushed through her veins at the thought that Martín must have been captured, if not killed. Lifting her voice to

Heaven, she began to pray aloud, calling out Martín's name among torrid words of extemporaneous prayer. Just then she noticed a man running toward the house. For a moment she thought that she might be delirious, but then squealed with joy and ran downstairs. It was Martín!

The patio was empty and the street door was bolted with a weighty crossbar. Leonor turned the key in the lock, pulled back the unwieldy crossbar as if it were weightless, and opened the door within seconds. Rivas arrived just then and found himself face to face with Leonor, more beautiful than ever, with her clothing in disarray and her face drained of color. The young man, who had just faced a thousand perils in three hours of deadly combat, suddenly felt dismayed in the presence of this pale girl who looked at him with tears of happiness.

"Señorita," he stammered, "I have come . . . "

Leonor took both of his hands into hers and said, "Come inside quickly before they see you."

And Martín obeyed the soft pressure of her hands and the sweet sound of her command. Leonor locked and bolted the door with the same strength and swiftness with which she had opened it.

"Follow me," she said.

They crossed the patio and, bypassing the room where everyone else was praying the Rosary, Leonor opened Agustín's door, rushed around the second patio into her own suite, and locked the door behind Martín.

"No one saw us," she said, breathlessly.

Martín stood in the middle of the room gazing at Leonor as though it were all a dream. This beautiful girl, whose name he had invoked so many times during the thick of the battle, was now at his side in her bedchamber, which he had always considered a sanctuary. And this haughty girl, who had hitherto turned a proud face and contemptuous gaze upon him, now looked at him lovingly, with a gentle, nervous smile.

"Sit down," she said, offering him a chair. "I received your letter this morning and . . . "

She gasped in horror and took his bloodstained arm, saying, "Oh, you're wounded!"

"It's nothing. I can hardly feel it."

"Let me see. Remove your coat."

The shirt sleeve was clinging to the wound and soaked in blood.

"It's nothing but a scratch," said Martín.

"Let me dress it," she said. Then she took a fine linen scarf, which she was wearing as a cravat around her neck, and tied it around the wound after rolling up his sleeve.

"You made me suffer this morning more than I've ever suffered in my entire life. Why didn't you come last night like you promised my brother?"

"Señorita, I lacked the courage. Despite the time I've spent away from you and my devotion to the cause I've risked my life for today, my love for you overpowers me, and I would have faltered today if I saw you last night."

"To risk your life like that! " rebuked Leonor, lowering her eyes. "Why didn't you ever tell me what you wrote in your letter?"

"Because I would never have had the courage. Besides, haven't you misconstrued my intentions?"

"It's true, but Edelmira enlightened me by showing me the letters you wrote back to her."

"My position also obliged me to remain silent."

"Who cares about your position if I love you!" exclaimed Leonor, looking deeply into his eyes.

"Oh, say it again, Leonor," entreated Martín, taking her hands into his with delirious joy.

"Yes, I love you and I won't hide it from anyone. This morning I relived every day since you first walked into my life, and I saw how cruel and proud I was. If you had died today, I never would have forgiven myself. Even if I hadn't received your letter, no one would have been able to convince me that your rash decision wasn't my fault in some way. That was wrong of you, Martín, to risk my life to endless tears."

"Could I ever dream of happiness after you dismissed me from your house?"

"It was only because I loved you. Why else would I care if you loved some poor girl!"

"I had hoped it was true, Leonor, but how could I be certain?"

"By asking me!"

"You seem to forget," he said, smiling, "how you can make the bravest man cower with one cold look, a look which I have seen too often."

"Chastise me, it's only fair," she answered, adoringly.

"But this moment is worth everything I've suffered," said Martín, and without thinking about what he was doing, he knelt before Leonor, taking her hands into his.

"We've been so foolish, Martín," she said, losing herself in the reflection of his rapturous gaze. "How often did we tell each other with our eyes that we were in love? Oh, you're right. It's my fault. Of all the men in my life, you were the humblest in position, but the noblest in spirit. I was afraid to admit it to myself, but now that I'm proud of our love, I promise to make it up to you."

"I don't know whether I'm the most deserving," said Martín, "but I certainly love you the most. How could I defend myself against your beauty? I yielded to it without asking myself what I could ever hope for, and yet I wanted to resist the passion that overwhelmed me, but nothing could stop it—not the feeling of dignity, not the lack of hope, not even your scornful look—only death. And that's why I risked my life this morning. I thought you despised me."

The girl listened avidly and allowed Martín to kiss her hands. She had prayed so fervently to Heaven for this man who was now at her feet that she believed she was listening to his passionate speech by a miracle of resurrection.

Martín was about to continue when they heard voices and banging at the door.

"Leonor!" called Don Dámaso from the other side.

Leonor hastened to the door, peered through the keyhole and beheld her father, accompanied by Ricardo Castaños and some soldiers who were standing behind them.

"You're lost if you don't flee," she said, running back to Martín. "There is an officer with soldiers out there."

"Leonor!" Don Dámaso shouted, knocking upon the door.

"Run, Martín," the girl warned, opening another door. "You know your way around. You can cut though Papa's study to the street, while they search this chamber."

"And others will follow me there," answered Rivas.

The pounding redoubled and Ricardo Castaños threatened to break the door down.

"If you love me, run, for God's sake!"

"If I make it through this alive, I will return," said Rivas, "but if it weren't for your reputation, I would prefer to dispute my liberty right here."

Leonor pushed him out of the door and fell into the sofa, nearly faint. Her father's voice awoke her from this harried trance, and she proceeded to the door and took her time opening it.

"Señorita," Ricardo said to her, "a regretful duty obliges me to request permission to search this chamber."

"Go ahead and search," said Leonor imperiously, before adding ironically, "A victor does not sully his glory by lending himself to what you call a *regretful duty.*"

"Girl!" Don Dámaso muttered under his breath and then declared, "It's only right that the defenders of Order apprehend these dissidents. You see, Captain, you are a witness that I have opposed no resistance. You won't find me hiding any demagogues because when it comes to revolution, the people who have something to lose are the people who lose!"

The soldiers searched every compartment of Leonor's suite, and Don Dámaso resumed his anti-Liberal dissertation while his daughter trembled for the fate of Martín, who found his way to the patio through Don Dámaso's study. At this moment Leonor left her quarters (which the soldiers continued to search) and went to see if Martín had left the house.

Martín had made his way to the street door, which was bolted and guarded by two armed policemen, who drew their swords and lunged at him. Seeing that it was impossible to retreat or hide, Rivas turned his back to the wall, drew his weapon, and clashed swords with the policemen, who called for assistance. Just when Rivas warded one of them off with a furious blow, Leonor arrived at the patio and saw the young man attacking the other guard. The officers inside were alerted by the shouting and rushed out to surround the young provincial, who continued to defend himself dauntlessly

"Save him, Papa!" Leonor screamed. "They're going to kill him!"

Added to the shouts of the police were the cries of Doña Engracia and her lady friends who dropped their rosaries to see what was happening on the patio. They arrived at the same time as the soldiers who came to the aid of Martín's assailants.

Trembling, Don Dámaso stepped forward, saying, "Resistance is useless, Martín. Surrender yourself."

"If he doesn't surrender, shoot him," shouted Ricardo Castaños, who not only regarded the provincial as a political enemy, but as a personal rival and the cause of his unhappiness.

Leonor screamed when she heard this order and ran to the entrance when she saw two soldiers loading their guns.

"Surrender yourself! They're going to kill you," she cried out to Martín, who instantly obeyed her voice like a command.

Four soldiers seized and disarmed him.

"I hope that you will treat this young man with kindness and consideration," said Don Dámaso to Ricardo. "As a member of the administration," he added emphatically, "I will intercede on his behalf with the President."

The order was given to arrest Martín Rivas. Surrounded by his captors, he was taken away after he locked eyes with Leonor, who, paler than a corpse, seemed to want to send her soul in this silent yet eloquent adieu.

LX

Following the counsel of prudence, Amador Molina waited outside the Encina manor after leading the police to Martín Rivas. When they emerged from the house with their prisoner, Amador accompanied the police (now that he saw no risk) to the station where Rivas was to be incarcerated.

Don Dámaso's household was in an uproar, with everyone offering his own theory as to how Rivas appeared out of nowhere when the street door had been securely barred since dawn. So swiftly did the news of the arrest spread from house to house and from street to street that within the hour Don Dámaso's salon was filled with inquisitive neighbors who came to talk about the remarkable episode.

Don Dámaso remained in the antechamber surrounded by his gentlemen friends, and Doña Engracia in the salon, surrounded by her lady friends.

We shall hear some of the more quotable conversations that characterize the excitable, fertile imaginations of the ladies in one room, and the zealous, reactionary opinions of the gentlemen in the other.

"We are lucky to be alive," Don Dámaso was saying to those who had called themselves Liberals the day before, as did he. "What would we have done if the riffraff had triumphed!"

"The Government ought to shoot a few dozen rebels dead on the spot," argued a man who had locked himself away in his water-closet the whole morning, praying to all the saints in Heaven to save his cowardly hide.

At the same time, a lady friend of Doña Engracia asked, "Is it true that the vicious fiend murdered three policemen in cold blood, right here on the patio?"

"Oh, dear!" exclaimed another. "What would I have done with a monster like that in my house? I think I would have been frightened to death! How on earth did he enter when the door was barred?"

"By the roof," commented another, "for those Liberals have no respect."

"Or through the sewer, for they'll stop at nothing."

"We ought to put bars on the drains."

Doña Engracia cuddled Diamela while her lady friends chattered away.

In the antechamber, one of the gentlemen was saying, "Now is the time for true patriots to stand with the Government and show those demagogues that the public is outraged."

"That's just what I was thinking," said Don Dámaso. "Good citizens should present themselves before the Government. Shall we all go to the Palace?"

"Right, right," all the gentlemen agreed.

They took their hats and proceeded to La Moneda with airs of victors to demand the death penalty for those who had struck the fear of God in them early that morning.

Leonor, meanwhile, had withdrawn to her bedchamber, where she wept in despair over Martín's fate. She clung to her memories of their last conversation, of his loving words that sounded like celestial music to her soul, and of the dauntless strength with which he had defended himself against so many adversaries at once. Where there was love in her heart, there was also pride, and she vowed to devote her life to this brave and worthy young man. The sudden thought that Martín was facing new perils awoke Leonor to action. She realized that instead of lamenting by herself she should be defending his life at all costs. She dashed to Agustín's quarters, where she found her brother drinking a steady flow of kirch in order to settle his nerves since the morning's revolt.

"Oh, little sister, what a traumatic day! I must confess that I can sympathize with the ladies and the fainthearted gents because I can imagine how frightened they must have been."

"What we should be thinking about right now is how to save Martín."

"Why us? What are we supposed to do?" said the dandy, downing another glass of liquor.

"Papa must appeal to the Ministers, the President, anyone in power."

"Slow down, *ma belle,* today's a windy day to walk the rope, especially since Martín had the unfortunate idea of hiding here. They might think we had some part in the revolution if we speak up for him."

"You're afraid to stand up for someone who saved your neck! Agustín, I knew you were flippant, but not ungrateful," said Leonor, glaring at her brother with scorn.

"No, I'm not ungrateful, dear. But in Politics, the safest bet is always the best bet. Oh, what the devil! Let's see what we can do for poor Martín. I can't deny that I'm greatly indebted to him, though I don't see why we must go full steam ahead."

"There's no time to waste thinking about it. We have to take action. If you're unwilling, then I'll speak to Papa, and if he takes this as coldly as you do, then I'll go by myself and intercede for Martín with friends who won't let me down."

"Gracious, little sister, you're all riled up! One would think he was more than a family friend . . . "

"A lover, is that what you're implying? I don't care what you think," she added, storming out of the room.

"Caramba! She's acting like she was *my* older brother," Agustín said to himself as he watched her dramatic exit.

Leonor retired to her suite after asking her maidservant to alert her when Don Dámaso arrived. An hour later, he joined his wife in the sitting room. Agustín, who had seen him cross the patio, entered shortly thereafter.

"The Palace was full of people," said Don Dámaso, removing his hat. "There was a complete consensus to condemn the revolutionaries. The most emphatic civic valor reigned there, and I think that if it were necessary we all would have marched into battle, singing, right then and there."

No sooner had he spoken these words, which showed no trace of the Liberal who was preaching the cause of the people earlier that day, when Leonor walked into the room, holding her head up high with a determined look.

"How did it go, Papa?" she asked, sitting beside him.

"Perfectly, my sweet. The President thanked me for my adherence to the cause of Order," he gloated.

"I'm not asking about that," replied Leonor. "What happened to Martín?"

"Oh, Martín? They must have taken him prisoner. Poor boy!"

"And you did nothing for him?"

"It wasn't a good time, my sweet," replied Don Dámaso. "Emotions were running too high. It is better to wait."

"Wait? Martín has never waited to help us!"

"No one denies that Martín would be an accomplished young man if he had not gotten himself mixed up in all that Liberal madness."

"It's not for us to judge him," said Leonor. "We must use our influence to get him out of prison."

"We will use our influence. Don't you fret about that. I'm in very good standing with the Government now."

"Yes, but meanwhile time is passing, and Martín may be sentenced," exclaimed the girl with notable frustration.

"That is inevitable," answered Don Dámaso calmly, to the exasperation of Leonor, who stood up indignant, declaring, "Papa, you must go and speak to the Minister of Interior at once!"

"That might compromise my position because Martín was arrested in my home. We ought to let a few days pass."

"Then I will go and see the Minister's wife myself," exclaimed Leonor, rankled by her father's insensibility.

"What a lively concern you have for Martín!" the gentlemen said in an accusatory tone.

"More than a lively concern," replied Leonor, filled with emotion. "I love him."

These words were no less shocking to Don Dámaso, Agustín, and Doña Engracia than the explosions from the morning's battle. Don Dámaso jumped to his feet, Agustín withered, and Doña Engracia scooped up her napping Diamela and gave her a frightful squeeze.

As the startled pooch growled, Don Dámaso exclaimed, "Child, what are you saying!"

"I am saying that I love Martín," replied Leonor, with a proud and secure demeanor.

"Martín?" repeated Doñ Dámaso, incredulous.

Leonor did not deign to answer; instead, she sat down majestically. Don Dámaso instantly recognized his daughter's ascendancy over him. Although he was prepared to arm himself with severity, he faltered before her serene, defiant determination. He lowered his eyes and said, "You shouldn't say things like that."

"And why not? Martín is poor, but he is noble and intelligent, and that is all I need to say. Would you prefer that I hide my feelings? Isn't it natural that I should confide in all of you?"

Leonor stated her position in a manner that invited no response from her captive audience of three, all of whom lacked the nerve to contradict her. Doña Engracia soothed herself by petting Diamela, Agustín muttered some words to himself, half in Spanish, half in French, and Doñ Dámaso began to pace around in an attempt to hide his lack of character.

Leonor continued. "Papa, you know very well that Martín is a young man of great promise; you've often said so yourself. And he is from a good family. All that he lacks is money, but given his aptitudes, he won't be poor for long. What wrong is there in loving him? He is far superior to all the other young men who are courting me, and so it's only natural that I prefer him. Maybe it was out of sheer desperation that he took part in that uprising. Now that he is in grave danger, we must repay him for all that he has done for us. After all, he saved Agustín from that shameful intrigue, which would have made us the laughingstock of Society, and furthermore, he managed all the family business with an expertise that you used to praise every day."

"As to that, it's the pure truth, and I would be lying if I denied that a good deal of my earnings this year were owed to Martín," conceded Don Dámaso, relieved to find an excuse not to impose the parental authority that he obviously lacked.

The girl continued to urge her father to intercede on Martín's behalf. It was not long before Don Dámaso, a spineless creature, complied with his daughter's demands. He set out to use his influence to help the young provincial, reasoning, "I'll see that he is exiled because once he is out of the country Leonor will forget about him and marry someone else."

LXI

Martín was brought to the police headquarters and imprisoned in a narrow cell with an armed guard standing by the door. He had nothing to look at but four dingy white walls, a ceiling made of bulky poplar boards, and a barred window without shutters. Without a single piece of furniture, the prisoner sat on the brick floor, rested his back against the wall, and crossed his arms over his chest. He hung his head, as if the weight of his thoughts were keeping him from holding it upright. The most recent events of the day were foremost in his mind. Leonor's beauty, her loving words, her tender concern, and the profound sorrow of her parting look brightened the barren cell with a light from within his enamored soul.

To see Martín's passionate expression and drifting gaze, one would have thought that this desolate prisoner was dreaming of conquering an empire. Soon, however, unhappy memories surfaced and his expression fell bleak. He heaved heavy sighs of grief, stood up, and went to the window.

"Poor Rafael!"

Martín's grievous sighs became heartbroken sobs.

"So noble and valiant! Poor Rafael!"

Martín wept until his tears were spent and his eyes burned red. Then he remembered the stoic resignation of his friend's courage and the serene acceptance with which he had sacrificed his life.

"Perhaps he was better off than I am," Martín said to himself. "I'd rather die fighting than be shot in captivity."

He did not flinch or wince at the thought of death. Gifted with a rare, tranquil valor that needs neither witness nor admirer, Rivas calmly faced death, defying the proverb that says "no one can look into the face of the sun or the eyes of death."

However, when night had fallen (after he had mulled over all the scenes of the day, as well as his life) and when the last ray of sunshine crossed the floor diagonally and faded into a point before vanishing completely, Martín felt the pangs of bitter regret. "If I hadn't been so proud," he chastised himself, "I would've known sooner how Leonor felt about me and I wouldn't be where I am right now. I would be at her side."

Within a few hours Rivas contemplated all of the possible scenarios that he might face. Physically and mentally depleted, he sat down in the same spot against the wall and tried to find forgetfulness in sleep. Just when he began to drift into a slumber, the door creaked open and startled him. A soldier entered carrying a tray of food. Behind him entered another man carrying a cot, which he set in a corner. The soldier placed the tray on the windowsill and whispered to Martín, "Read this and write back." Then a tightly folded piece of paper fell to the ground and the soldier turned his back to arrange the bed so that Martín could read the following note:

Papa has arranged for us to send you food daily. You'll find paper and a pencil inside the pillow so that you can write to me. Agustín will bribe the guard to bring you food. Take heart, for I'm watching over you. I've thought of a way to visit you, but if it doesn't work, don't think for a moment that you've ceased to reign in the heart of

Leonor Encina

Martín, whose breath was taken away by what he had just read, answered the following:

If love can repay your sacrifices, you know that my heart belongs to you. This morning when I faced death, your sweet voice opened the gates of paradise for me. And now your voice fills these gloomy prison walls with magical pictures. Oh Leonor, my head is spinning from all of this! Amidst the chaos, your love is a light of peace shining over me.

You must have received word of Rafael's death. He died a hero. His noble heart was ravaged by the gales of misfortune. My profound bliss inspired by your love, I am sorry to say, is not enough to dry my tears for him. Forgive me, Leonor, for saying this, but if the happiest of lovers cannot forget a friend, you may judge by this how much he meant to me . . .

"Com'on, hurry up," the soldier said to him. "I haven't got all day."

Martín designated the place where he had left his friend's body, beseeching Leonor to convey this information to the family of San Luis. He gave the soldier the letter and what little money he had. Barely touching the food, Martín watched the cell door slam shut and the key turn in the lock. With Leonor's letter against his heart, he despised the wrath of his enemies, but felt as though he could almost pardon them. This little piece of paper helped Martín to endure his isolation until the break of day, when the same soldier brought him another letter from Leonor, who declared in tender, simple words a profound love that far exceeded his wildest expectations. After two more days of correspondence, he began to feel that his prison term was the happiest time of his life.

Meanwhile, the case against Martín Rivas was rapidly building because political trials in Chile were rushed through the justice system as quickly then as they are today. Since this notorious convict had not only confessed to his participation in the insurrection on April 20th, but also to the liberal principals which he professed, the prosecution wrapped up their case in four days and condemned Martín Rivas to death.

Leonor received news of the death penalty shortly after her father had shown her a letter that granted Don Dámaso and his family permission to visit Martín from six o'clock to half-past six that evening. It was already too late; they would have to wait until the following evening. Leonor found it torturous to think about the verdict and to have to wait so long to see him, especially at night when no one was there to promise her that the penalty would not be carried through. Her passion, under such duress, grew to gigantic proportions, and she could not think for a moment about Rivas's death without thinking of her own.

After a night of weeping, Leonor shook her brother out of a deep sleep.

"What are you doing up so early!" he exclaimed, seeing Leonor standing over him at the crack of dawn. "It looks like you haven't slept a wink."

"Well I haven't. How could I sleep with that horrible sentence?"

"Calm down! It won't be carried out."

"Who can assure me of that?" asked Leonor, whose eyes filled with tears.

"Everybody says so."

"That's not enough. I need you to help me."

"I'm all yours, *ma belle.* Your wish is my command."

"You must come with me to see Martín."

"How are we supposed to do that?"

"Ask Papa for the letter of permission. Tell him you're going to see Martín, and we'll go together."

"As I said, I'm all yours."

As six o'clock, Leonor and Agustín presented the authorization and were brought to Martín's cell.

Martín was standing at the windowsill, reading one of her letters when the door opened. Leonor saw him straighten up and hide the letters. When he recognized her, Rivas ran to the door and held out his hands.

"Damn!" exclaimed Agustín, looking around. "It couldn't be less warm-n-cozy in here. My poor chap," he added, embracing Rivas, "it's abominable."

Martín smiled wistfully and forgot his troubles the moment he looked into Leonor's teary eyes.

"It's the only seat I have," he said, pointing to the cot.

The girl sat down and turned her face away to dry her tears.

"Come on, little sister," Agustín said to her, softening. "Keep your chin up. The power of reason must overcome emotion."

Martín laughed at this pithy maxim spoken so ruefully by Agustín, and Leonor looked at her lover brimming with pride.

"We must handle things as they come," said Rivas, wanting to resist the disconsolation of his visitors.

"But this sentence!" cried Leonor.

"I've expected it from the start, and I'm not upset," said the prisoner modestly. "What I never expected," he whispered to Leonor, "was your letters."

Through the tears on her lashes, her eyes sparkled as she heard these words. Agustín, intentionally or coincidentally, stepped in front of the cell door and blocked the view of the guard who was passing by. Martín took Leonor's hand at this moment as they gazed into each other's eyes.

"If I weren't so happy about your love," he said to her, "then maybe I would have room in my heart for fear. But," he added lightheartedly, "I have a strange feeling that I am not going to die."

"Nevertheless," replied Leonor, "we must give serious thought to your escape."

"That seems very difficult to me."

"But not impossible. Here is the plan I've come up with: I'll come back with Agustín at this time tomorrow, wearing one dress over another. You take one and leave with Agustín in my place."

"And what about you?" asked Rivas.

"I'll stay here," she answered. "What can they do to me when they find out?"

Martín wanted to drop to his knees and worship her like a goddess for acting as though it were perfectly natural to sacrifice herself to spare his life.

"Do you think I would consent to saving my life at the cost of your honor?" he said, kissing her hand.

"All that matters is to get you out of here alive," replied Leonor, distraught. "Martín, you mustn't be delusional. The Government wants blood from anyone who took part in the revolution. How can you be sure that you'll be pardoned? And, even if they do, what penalty will substitute for the death penalty? Nobody knows and that makes me tremble."

"Caramba," said Agustín, who moved closer toward them. "Leonor is right. This is a dungeon of gloom and doom. You must try to escape."

"If you're brave enough to stay here, Martín can leave with me right now," Leonor said to her brother, who turned as pale as his shirt collar and broke into a cold sweat at the thought of risking his neck for anyone.

"But they'll recognize him as he leaves, little sister," he said, cowering, "and then, how will I ever escape?"

"They would have to set you free," replied Leonor.

"Agustín is right," said Rivas, "they'll recognize me on the way out."

"Of course, that's completely ludicrous!" observed the dandy, calming down a bit and checking his watch as though he were eager for the appointment to end.

"If Agustín brings me a file and two revolvers tomorrow, I'll make an attempt," said Martín.

"Agreed. There is nothing more to say," exclaimed Agustín, looking at his watch again, afraid that his sister would propose another plan of escape that would involve him.

At this moment the jailer announced that it was time to leave. Leonor and Agustín said goodnight to Martín, promising to do everything possible to break him out of jail the next day.

LXII

The judicial proceedings proceeded more swiftly than expected, thereby foiling their plan of escape.

When Leonor and Agustín asked to see Rivas, showing their letter of permission, they received this snide reply: "No can do."

"Why?" asked Leonor apprehensively.

"Because he is condemned to death."

Leonor clutched Agustín's arm to keep herself from collapsing. Weak in the knees himself, Agustín assisted his sister to the street where the carriage awaited them. She collapsed in the back seat, melting in tears.

"Home," Agustín said to the driver.

The carriage began to move. Leonor lifted her head moments later, and one might have said that from her teary eyes glistened a ray of hope.

"It's not over yet!" she exclaimed, throwing herself into her brother's arms.

"Of course not, little sister, *ne te fais pas de soucis.*"

Leonor, trusting in his air of confidence, asked him with delirious elation, "Have you thought of a way to save Martín?"

"Who me? Nothing strikes me at the moment," the dandy replied, hoping that Leonor would not coerce him into some sort of sacrifice.

"Well, I've thought of something."

"Let's hear it."

"Take me to Edelmira Molina's house."

"What for?"

"You'll find out when we get there."

"But little sister, it seems inappropriate that you . . ."

Leonor did not allow Agustín to finish his phrase. She lowered the front window and said to the driver, "Stop." Then, looking at her brother, she demanded, "Show him the way."

Agustín obeyed without a murmur, and the driver followed his directions.

"We must talk to Edelmira," said Leonor after a few moments of silence.

"But going to her mother's house isn't the smartest way to handle this," answered Agustín.

"Why not?"

"Because they cordially detest me, after . . . well . . . you-know-what happened with you-know-who."

"You're right," said Leonor, pressing her hands to her feverish forehead, "but it is absolutely essential that I see Edelmira today. Let's see," she added frantically, "well, hurry up and think of something. My head is burning. I can't concentrate."

She covered her face and let her head fall back on the seat of the carriage. Her sobs were rising and falling like stormy waves.

"I'll think of something," said the dandy, "but let's not go to Doña Bernarda's house because we'll lose everything."

"Home!" called Leonor to the driver.

Then she turned to her brother with her eyes aflame and her brows furrowed, forewarning the force that she was capable of displaying. She said, "We'll go home, but I'm warning you that you have two hours to arrange a meeting with Edelmira."

"But, little sister, how do you expect me to get her out of the house?"

"I don't know, but I will speak to her today, and if you can't manage that, I'll go see her myself."

"I don't recommend it."

"Nothing is going to stop me! Don't you see that Martín is condemned to death? Don't you understand that to kill him is to kill me?"

Agustín voiced no objection to this outcry from the depths of her afflicted soul, and he was convinced that to prevent her from taking any desperate action he would also have to stop at nothing to fulfill her wishes. Suddenly recalling Amador's unquenchable greed, he said, "There is a way you can speak with Edelmira."

"How?"

"If we pay her brother to bring the girl over to the house," he said, as the carriage pulled into Don Dámaso's driveway.

"I'll give you the money," said Leonor, when they stepped out of the carriage. "Meet me in your chamber."

Leonor returned a few moments later with 30 ounces of gold that she handed to her brother, saying, "Take this. I trust you. You don't want to see me weeping for the rest of my life, do you?"

"Caramba! You're loaded, little sister. Where did you get that stash?"

"Papa just gave it to me. I explained my plan."

"Yet you keep me in the dark."

"You'll find out soon enough."

Agustín left the house and Leonor fell to her knees, imploring divine protection for the success of her mission. Then she went to Agustín's desk and began to write a letter to Rivas, in which she revealed her plans, flagrantly professing the love that had slowly ripened within her heart into a delicious, irresistible passion.

Agustín had since arrived at the Molina residence. As he crossed the threshold, his stomach turned with dread at the memory of being bullied into a bogus marriage. But, for his sister's sake, he found the presence of mind to go forward.

Amador was wary of his unexpected caller who said, "I wish to speak with you in private."

"We're alone here," replied Amador, ushering him in and closing the door behind him.

"I'm going to be perfectly candid," said Agustín, without sitting down.

"That's the way I like it. There ain't nothing like candor," remarked Amador.

"How would you like to earn 500 pesos?"

"Five hundred pesos! Are you kidding! Who wouldn't like it? Smoke?" he said, offering a freshly rolled cigarette.

"No thank you. The service I ask of you is very simple."

"Don't worry, I'll do it."

"My sister wants to speak with Edelmira."

"About what?"

"I don't know, but I suspect she may be able to negotiate Martín's release. He is condemned to death."

"Poor Martín. I'm to blame for his capture, and I feel horrible about it. Look here, I'll bring Edelmira over, but I ain't doing it for the money, though I could really use it. I'm doing it because I want to help Martín."

"Magnificent! The minute you bring Edelmira to the house, the money is yours."

"Just for the record, I'm as poor a goat, but I ain't doing it for the money."

"*Je le crois bien,* but it never hurts to have more."

"That's the way I see it. It only hurts to have less."

They bade farewell, Amador promising that he would bring Edelmira in half an hour, and sure enough, Amador and Edelmira arrived soon after Agustín had informed his sister of the results of the interview.

Leonor brought Edelmira to her chamber, leaving her brother alone with Amador. When the two girls found themselves behind closed doors, they scrutinized each other and were surprised at what they beheld. Edelmira found, instead of the haughty expression that she had formerly seen in Doñ Dámaso's beautiful daughter, a sweetness that aroused immediate sympathy. Leonor noticed that the rosy blush of Edelmira's cheeks had been replaced by the pallor of sorrow and her natural vivacity by discernible melancholy. By these signs, Leonor knew, with the sagacity of a woman in love, that Edelmira was still enamored of Martín. This idea, which would have perturbed her on any other occasion, seemed on the contrary to enliven her spirits.

"Do you know what happened to Martín?" Leonor said, making Edelmira sit beside her.

"I knew that he was arrested, but now," she added in a shaky voice, "my brother tells me that Martín is condemned to death."

Both girls looked at each other with tears in their eyes, and Leonor flung herself into Edelmira's arms, crying, "You're my only hope! You must save him!"

Edelmira's heart ached at the sound of this woeful plea, which she understood as a confession of love.

Leonor rambled on frantically, with tears streaming down her face. "I did everything I could, and I thought Martín would be pardoned by now, but it seems they fear him too much for they refuse to pardon him, and I've run out of ways to try and set him free, and I'm willing to sacrifice my life for him, but nothing has come through, and when I heard the fatal news this morning that he was condemned to death, I don't know why, but I thought of you in my despair. Please tell me it was a blessed inspiration. You told me the last time you were here that you wished to repay Martín, and now is your chance. You know how noble and valiant he is, and they want to murder him!"

Edelmira was moved by the sight of Leonor's affliction. Oddly, Leonor's remarkable beauty amidst such arduous despair, far from causing jealousy (which the beauty of a rival often stirs in the heart of a woman), appeared to fascinate Edelmira.

"Señorita," she said, "I'm willing to do what I can to save Martín."

"For God's sake, I can't think anymore," cried Leonor, covering her face with both hands. "My ideas escape me the minute I think of them . . . Let's see . . . What made me think you could save Martín? Oh, didn't you say a police officer wanted to marry you?"

"That's true."

"He is young, isn't he?"

"Yes."

"Then he still loves you. You're too beautiful for him to have stopped loving you just because you slighted him. I'm sure he still loves you. Martín is a prisoner in his district and you can persuade him to facilitate his escape. Offer him anything he wants. Money, advancement, my father will deny him nothing. I'm begging you. Please, please save him."

"Señorita," said Edelmira, "I'll do whatever I can. If you can arrange for Amador to accompany me to see Ricardo, perhaps we can save Martín."

Leonor threw her arms around Edelmira, thanking with her tender caresses. "Let's go see your brother," she said. "We have no time to lose."

They left Leonor's chambers and entered Agustín's, where they found Amador drinking his tenth shot of liquor and smoking an enormous Havana cigar with the solemn air of a magnate who presumes to be of great importance.

Leonor announced her new plan in a few words, and after urging Amador to accompany Edelmira, she approached Agustín and asked him for the money she had given him. The dandy quietly placed 30 ounces of gold in Amador's hand, whose face beamed with unspeakable joy.

"To save my buddy Martín," Amador said, "I'll do what you ask, Señorita."

"Go with them," Leonor told Agustín, calling him aside, "and don't waste any time. If the policeman gives you any trouble, tell him that Papa will pave his future. I'll take care of that."

Then she gave Edelmira a sisterly embrace and mustered enough courage to offer her hand to Amador, who reeked of burnt tobacco.

"Send me word of the results with Agustín," she said to Edelmira, crossing the patio. "You're my only hope."

"Don't fret, little sister," said Agustín, "I'll take care of everything. May lightning strike me dead if we don't break Martín out of prison."

They said goodbye at the threshold, and Leonor returned to her bedchamber, where she collapsed upon a sofa, overcome by emotion and anxiety.

LXIII

Ricardo Castaños was the sort of lover, as we have witnessed through the course of this story, who could bear the scorn of his beloved with the resignation that philosophers advise in the face of life's adversities. Even though Edelmira had jilted him, his feelings for her had not changed. Thus, when he saw the unexpected threesome enter his unit at police headquarters, his jaw dropped open and his cheeks turned bright red. At a loss for words, the young Captain offered chairs to Edelmira and her two chaperons.

Edelmira broke the silence that ensued Ricardo's courteous gesture with this self-possessed assertion, "We've come here to discuss a very important matter."

"Señorita, I am at your service," he answered, reddening even further.

"Although these gentlemen," continued Edelmira, acknowledging Agustín and Amador, "know my reason for coming, I would prefer to speak with you in private because I would be at greater ease to explain myself."

"There ain't no clerk here," chuckled Amador, "so there ain't no threat of perjury if you say the wrong thing."

"The lady is right," replied Agustín. "I'm in favor of a tête-à-tête and, besides, wouldn't you rather smoke a cigar?"

"Come, then," said Amador, "let's go have ourselves a hardy puff."

The two young men stepped out to wander the hallway outside

the Captain's station, while Ricardo remained standing, struggling to find some way to begin the conversation. Edelmira saved him from the embarrassment, by telling him, "You find it strange to see me here."

"Not strange, Señorita, I'm just surprised to see you," replied Ricardo.

"I know that I've been unkind to you, and I'm sorry for that."

"You are most kind, Señorita, and I thank you for it."

"Do you still love me?" asked Edelmira, gazing deeply into his eyes.

"Do I still love you? I swear that I walk past your house every day just to look at it."

"There is only one way you could convince me."

"Simply name it, and you'll see that I'm telling the truth."

"I want you to save Martín Rivas."

Ricardo shuddered, enraged. He said, "I wouldn't even if I could."

"Well, if you want to prove you love me, you must save him."

"Oh, wouldn't that be charming, indeed! To keep your lover alive! I'd rather see him dead."

He uttered these words with such deep resentment that Edelmira was convinced that he was still wildly in love with her. Rising from her seat, she said, "Well, if they execute him, you will never see me again."

"Prove you're not in love with him, and then we'll start talking."

"Only if you save him."

"How will you prove it?"

"By marrying you, if the offer stands."

These words made the officer stagger. After a pause, he inquired, "So why are you so concerned with him?"

"Can you keep a secret?" asked Edelmira.

"Of course."

"Then I will tell you. I want to save him because I promised Agustín's sister. He only came with me to bring her news of your decision."

"Is she in love with Martín?"

"Yes."

"And you're not?"

"No."

"And how am I supposed to save him?"

"Can't you oversee his watch tomorrow?"

"It's not my shift."

"Can't you switch with someone?"

"Yes, I can."

"If you're on duty, you can pay the guard to sneak him out."

"That's fine, except for one problem: I have no money."

"Agustín will provide that."

"And how do I know you'll keep your promise once Martín is free?"

"I'll swear before witnesses, if you like, in the presence of my mother, who hasn't stopped talking about you."

"You know, Edelmira," said Ricardo, after some reflection, "I've always been wild about you. What more would I want than to marry you? But you're asking an awful lot. If I let Martín escape, they can fire me."

"Oh, if you think more of your career than of me . . ."

"That's not what I meant to say, but I'll be out in the street if I lose my salary, and I love you too much to drag you into the dirt with me."

"If that's the extent of your worries, then trust me that you have nothing to fear."

"How so?"

"Supposing a rich man, grateful to you for enabling Martín's escape, were to promise to secure your future. Would you still find yourself compromised to do what I ask of you?"

"No, I wouldn't, but I already said I would do it for you."

Edelmira called Agustín, who was standing outside the door with Amador.

"Will you kindly tell this gentleman everything that Leonor has entrusted us to do before we left the house."

"Everything? Good gracious, that's no simple task! My sister talks like a parrot and my memory is like a sieve," answered the dandy.

"You must recall the part about Ricardo's job," prompted Edelmira, "and what would happen in the event that he were to lose it."

"Oh, that part! She says that Papa will be wholly responsible for your future, and Leonor can make a promise like that because she has Papa wrapped around her little finger."

"Now you see that I'm not deceiving you," Edelmira said softly to Ricardo, whose face brightened when she, who had always scorned him, suddenly adopted this intimate tone with him.

"I didn't say you were deceiving me about that," he said. "But tell me you'll keep your promise and marry me, and you won't complain if I end up penniless."

"If Martín is free tomorrow night," answered Edelmira, making inaudible efforts to hide her emotion, "I will marry you any day you please."

"On my honor, he will be free," said the Captain, taking Edelmira's hand and sealing his oath with an ardent kiss.

The girl insisted upon repeated reassurances from the Captain, and Agustín promised to bring enough money to bribe the watchman.

Edelmira, Amador, and Agustín returned to Don Dámaso's home, where Leonor awaited them with feverish anxiety.

When Edelmira told her that Martín would be saved, Leonor wept tears of joy and wrapped her arms around the girl, showering her with kisses.

"And how did you manage this?" asked Leonor without noticing that Edelmira, wallowing in the depths of despair, had hidden her face so as not to show the tears streaming down it.

"I promised I would marry him," replied the girl, whose words were choked by sobs as she seemed to abandon the courage and resignation that she had mastered during her interview with Ricardo. Leonor looked at Edelmira with an indefinable expression, somewhere between admiration and jealousy (which lurks in the depths of all true love), and said to herself, "She loves him as much as I do. Poor girl, she has a heart of an angel!"

After this flash of involuntary speculation, Leonor cried, "God alone can reward such generosity, but if my eternal gratitude means anything, please accept my friendship, Edelmira."

These words, spoken from the heart, eased Edelmira's woe and returned her repose.

Leonor professed her appreciation profusely with words of tenderness that poured forth from her heart and made Edelmira forget the social distinction between them.

The next day Ricardo and Amador met with Leonor and Agustín at the Encina mansion to plan the breakout that they would attempt later that evening.

LXIV

Martín was bidding a sad adieu to life and to love with heroic serenity. The idea of being separated from Leonor brought him more sorrow than the realization that he would be put to death in the prime of his life. He tended to his last testament with peace of mind. Material concerns did not rob him of any precious time, for he had no worldly goods to bequeath. What he did possess was a priceless treasure of love to which he wanted to consecrate his soul during these solemn final moments.

He wrote a long, emotional letter to his mother and sister. Each sentence endeavored to brace them for the terrible grief that awaited them.

Death is not an evil under the present circumstances. If I were to live, I would have to overcome all but insurmountable obstacles to find the happiness which Leonor has allowed me to aspire to, and the struggle to overcome them would bring insufferable humiliation. My faith in God fills me with courage and your prayers will pave the road that I must travel to Heaven's gate.

When he had closed this letter, he felt at liberty to devote himself entirely to Leonor. To speak to her of his immeasurable passion, he would have to write a classic love story with its ideal aspirations and its bitter pain, which he had already forgotten in the last few days of happiness. The tragic ending awaiting the protagonist was the only dark shadow over this bright and rosy picture of youth and love. Martín was adding the finishing touches with the care of an artist for his masterpiece, when the cell door quietly opened.

It was evening and Martín did not recognize the visitor until the man removed his hat and approached the table where Martín was writing by candlelight.

"What brings you here, Señor Don Ricardo?"

"Read this note," replied the captain, handing Rivas the following message:

Your escape is arranged. Ricardo Castaños will bribe the guard to lead you out. Act fast and be wise. Remember that the success of this plan not only determines your life, but also that of your loving
Leonor Encina.

"Hurry up and burn it," said the officer.

"Why?" asked Martín, who kept all of Leonor's letters as though they were treasures.

"Because if they catch you, that letter would be the end of me."

"You're right," Martín said, burning the paper.

"Good," said Ricardo. "I'm leaving you now, and all you have to do is walk out that door. The guard will lead you to a safe route."

"One word," said Martín, approaching Ricardo. "I never would have expected anyone to do this for me, especially you, who have considered me an enemy."

"That isn't true. I pursued and arrested you because it was my duty."

"Nothing more than duty? Be honest with me. You always thought of me as your rival, didn't you?"

"That's true."

"But you were seriously mistaken. There was never a romantic word between us."

"Really?" asked Ricardo, sounding relieved.

"Yes, really. I give you my word of honor. If you love this girl," added Martín, "I pray that you won't harbor any prejudice against her. I have no other means of showing my gratitude than telling you the truth and entreating you to accept my friendship."

"I thank you," replied Ricardo earnestly, shaking Martín's hand.

The officer walked out, leaving the cell door open, after advising his prisoner to blow out the candle before following him.

Martín's flight paled in comparison to the nerve-racking, hair-breadth escapes which novelists exploit to titillate the imagination of their readers. The guard simply abandoned his post and led Martín through desolate paths until they arrived at a similarly desolate courtyard, where they climbed a staircase to the roof and lowered themselves into an alley.

"Goodbye," said the guard, who wandered down the street thinking of the gold coins jingling in his pockets. The money was given to Ricardo Castaños by the fair and delicate hands of Leonor.

Rivas went directly to a carriage that was parked in the alley. A man rose to receive him and a familiar voice said, "*Tu es sauvé,* Martín. Let me give you a hug!"

Agustín Encina embraced him like a brother, then added, pointing to the carriage, "My sister is waiting for you inside."

Just then, Leonor stepped out and said to Martín, as he took her hand, "The waiting was mortal dread. I was expecting to hear the alarms at every moment."

"Get inside so we can get going," said Agustín. "We're too close to the prison to count victory."

Leonor took the back seat of the carriage, Martín sat beside her, and Agustín sat opposite them.

"Not far from here," he said to Martín, "we've got a horse waiting for you so that you can make your way through the backwoods in case the authorities come after you."

"How will I ever pay you back for what you've done for me!" said Martín.

"It wasn't selfless, was it? Saving you meant saving my own happiness," Leonor murmured in his ear.

"Pay us back? Rubbish!" said Agustín at the same time. "We're the ones who are paying you back for all you've done for us. Would you say it was a small favor to rescue me from that money-grubbing brother-in-law, Amador? You know what they the French always say, *Un bienfait n'est jamais perdu!* And that's the unvarnished truth."

Agustín continued prattling along the ride, while Leonor and

Martín, paying little heed to him, whispered suspended, adoring phrases that spoke a thousand times more clearly than the most brilliantly composed discourse.

They arrived at a narrow, remote street in the suburbs, near Calle San Pablo, off the road to Valparaíso, and the coach stopped at Agustín's command. The threesome stepped out of the carriage, and Agustín walked toward a rider on horseback who was holding another horse by the reins.

"We must separate here," said Leonor to Rivas. "Write me whenever you can. Should I swear that I will think of you every moment?"

"No, but tell me once more, Leonor, that what has happened to me in these last few days is real, for at times I feel that I'm dreaming. And what about our love, which I've only dreamed of in the solitude of my heart?"

"Martín, our love is as true as all the rest."

"And will it last forever? Tell me it will," pleaded the young man, holding dearly to her hands.

"It will last throughout my life," she said, "and you mustn't think I'm saying this out of a passing affection. You are the only man I've ever loved. And who would have thought that I was going to fall for you when you first arrived at our doorstep?"

"And I," said Rivas, "who saw you as a goddess! Oh, Leonor, how small I felt when you received me with that haughty look of yours."

"And how could I imagine," she said with childish giddiness, "that beneath the exterior of a poor provincial beat the heart that would enrapture mine." Then she said, with sudden melancholy, "Martín, the punishment for my pride is that I'm madly in love with you."

"Are you sorry that you've made me happy?"

"I'm sorry that I didn't let you know sooner."

"What does all that matter now," said Martín, "when those words alone make me forget the past."

"But now we must part, and I'm only letting you go because I know that your life depends on it."

"And I'm only willing to go because I know that my thoughts of you will help me overcome any evil fate that may await me, and because I know that my perseverance will be rewarded when I return to your side and hear you say the kind of things that you've just told me."

"We must wait for our happiness until then," she said, sighing at the thought that she would soon cease to hear his voice.

"And the day will come soon. Tell me it will!" said Martín, who was suddenly reminded by her sigh of the fact that they would be separated.

"Soon, yes, very soon, because I won't rest until you're granted a pardon. Nothing will stop me. I don't care what my parents or the neighbors say! Oh, I have the strength to take on the whole world. Martín, do you realize that you're the only one who has ever overpowered my will? It's nearly a miracle. I don't understand it myself, but from now on your will is my command, and I'll only disobey if you tell me to stop loving you."

Rivas was transported to Heaven by these words, but was promptly brought back to earth when Agustín warned, "Hurry up, Martín. Say goodbye and get on this horse."

Before interrupting them, the dandy had smoked half a cigar as he chatted with the rider, not far from the carriage, and muttered to himself from time to time, "I should be a good sport and let them enjoy their last few moments. After all, the poor boy has suffered enough and deserves a little amusement."

By the grace of twilight, Martín kissed Leonor and walked away from the carriage. She covered her face with her hands and yielded to the flood of tears that she had been fighting back throughout their conversation. Then Rivas warmly embraced Agustín and mounted his horse.

"We'll fight for you from this end, my dear chap," Agustín assured him. "Be careful that they don't catch you before you leave Valparaíso. Your guide has some luggage packed with some clothing and letters of recommendation to certain merchants in Lima, friends of Papa, and you'll also find some money to help you get by until you're settled in Lima. The rest is set forth in the letters I mentioned. Well, this is *adieu,* my dear chap. *En route!*"

The two young men shook hands, and Martín set his horse into a gallop after looking back one last time at Leonor, who remained in the carriage with her hands covering her beautiful face, bathed in tears.

LXV

Santiago, October 15, 1851
Dear Mercedes,

Five months of separation, my dear sister, has only made my heart grow fonder. I found Leonor more beautiful and loving than ever. The proud girl, who disdainfully greeted a poor provincial who sought her family's patronage, now bestows upon your brother a treasure of love that brings him to his knees in adoration. The very eyes that used to daunt me with their contempt, now shine with an angelic grace that sends my soul into the farthest region of pure passion. She bows her majestic head in poetic surrender, and her rosy lips now smile at me with words of love. She is the same lofty Leonor, transformed by the mysterious influences of love.

From Lima I wrote to you all about my life in Santiago since the day of my arrival. I selfishly told you all about the past in order to forget the present sorrow, but at least I've acquainted you with all the people whose lives have crossed mine. Now let me tell you what has happened to them since.

Agustín, as dashing as always and busy Frenchifying everything, married his cousin Matilda a few days ago. He told me that they're 'as happy as angels in heaven.'

I went to Alameda my second day back, which was Sunday. I was walking arm in arm with Leonor (you can imagine my pride) when we came upon a couple coming toward us from the opposite direction. I recognized it was Ricardo Castaños, who with a triumphant air, offered his arm to Edelmira. We spoke with them for a while. Later I asked my-

self whether this poor girl, born into a social class inferior to her noble sentiments, was happy. I really couldn't say because the serenity and joy of her words seemed to contradict the melancholic expression in her eyes. Perhaps, I say to myself now, Edelmira has made a good man happy by marrying him, a man like me, who recognizes the nobility of her soul—that is the answer nearest the truth.

As for the rest of her family, I learned from Agustín that Adelaida is married to a German man who works for a carriage factory, and Amador is hiding from his creditors who want to see him imprisoned. Doña Bernarda is living next to Edelmira and gambling and drinking more than ever.

One of the first visits I paid was to the home of Rafael's aunt. The poor lady told me with tears in her eyes what her brother had to go through to recover the body of my unfortunate friend. My heart sank after I visited Rafael's room, which his aunt left untouched since the night of April 19th. This is the only cloud overshadowing my felicity. Rafael's vigorous character and his noble, manly heart will live forever in my memory. It grieves me to think of his loss. His noble instincts were mightier than his sorrows. In the heart of this despairing lover, the call of liberty gave rise to another world of love, where the melancholia of the first faded away like distant shadows. You will understand how much he meant to me when I tell you, dear sister, that I speak with Leonor as much of him as our future together.

You know enough about Leonor from my letters to understand how she was able to persuade her entire family to consent to our marriage. She wished for it, and they granted it. Don Dámaso, after obtaining my pardon through powerful channels, admitted to his daughter that his situation was not much better than mine when he was first married.

Doña Engracia has shown herself to be as docile as ever before her daughter's will. Agustín treats me like a brother, and the extended family follows his example. What more could I desire? Words can't describe my happiness. Leonor appears to have reserved for me alone a treasure of sweetness and submission, which no one thought her capable of. She said that she wants to make me forget the haughty way she used to treat me. Speaking to me of Edelmira's sacrifice, she told me last night, 'I can only admire her because I realize that I wouldn't have had her generosity. You, who have taught me the meaning of love, have also taught me the meaning of selfishness.'

I would continue, my dear Mercedes, but if I told you every blessed sign of her womanly affection, this letter would never end, and the post leaves today.

Give Mother a tender embrace from your loving brother,

Martín

Fifteen days after sending this letter, Rivas sent his sister a brief message, announcing his engagement to Leonor.

I would have wanted to bring you this news in person, but you know Leonor! 'You're not going anywhere without me!' she said. So, you and Mother must come quickly. All that I'm missing for complete happiness is the both of you at my side.

Don Dámaso Encina turned all of his business affairs over to Martín Rivas in order to devote himself more freely to the political fluctuations which he hoped would one day land him in the House of Senate. Don Dámaso was one of many master-weavers who disguised his lack of conviction by acting in the name of Moderation.